French Riviera

ONE TOO MANY BROTHERS

A COLOMBE BASTARO MYSTERY
BOOK ONE

NINO S. THEVENY

SÉBASTIEN THEVENY

TRANSLATED BY
JACQUIE BRIDONNEAU

SELF-PUBLISHED

Sébastien Theveny

FRENCH RIVIERA
One Too Many Brothers

A Colombe Bastaro Mystery

Translated from French to English by
Jacquie Bridonneau

Original Title: *Un frère de trop*

First self-published in France, 2017

All rights reserved. No part of this publication may be reproduced, stored in a retrieval system, or transmitted, in any form or by any means, electronic, mechanical, photocopying, recording or otherwise, without the prior permission of the publisher.

This book is sold subject to the condition that it shall not, by way of trade or otherwise, be lent, re-sold, hired out or otherwise circulated without the publisher's prior consent in any form of binding or cover other than that in which it is published and without a similar condition including this condition being imposed on the subsequent purchaser.

❀ Created with Vellum

*For my little sister, Paloma,
Who was once tempted by journalism.
She'll understand.*

Prologue

LITTLE LILIE GRABBED *her Playmobil toy: this was her favorite activity now, one of the only ones she paid attention to. It wasn't too hard and she always seemed to be having fun.*

She could spend hours on end playing with her Playmobil figures and their tiny brightly colored accessories: she invented stories, enjoying them in her own little world.

That symbolic game allowed her to make up for the fact that she was seriously lagging behind in speaking skills...

"Kiki? Kiki?" asked one of the plastic characters, sitting next to a bright yellow table.

"Yes! Nice little kiki!" invariably answered the other character, in this infantile scenario.

And Lilie smiled, Lilie smiled...

Innocent little Lilie.

PART One

WIND IN THE SAILS

CHAPTER 1
Nothing's set in stone yet

THE MEDITERRANEAN, *July 15, 1986*

LYING ON THE TEAK DECK, the three siblings were enjoying the end of the hot afternoon. Their dad's sailboat was gently rocking on the little waves that hit its light wooden hull; the sails were lowered, except for the mainsail, which had been sheeted. Ever since Edouard passed his sailing course at Glénans Sailing School, imitating Pierre-Hugues, his older brother, they'd been going out more and more often in summer. As so many people flocked to the French Riviera this time of year, the two brothers just wanted to get away from the tourist-filled beaches and relax a few miles offshore. Pierre-Hugues had just celebrated his twenty-sixth birthday, two years older than his brother, while Marie-Caroline, their younger sister who had just turned twenty-one, was sailing with them for the first time.

She'd been wanting to go out with them for a few years now, but their father had always refused to let them sail alone. At the Lacassagne's everyone respected their father's authority, even their mother didn't have a say if she disagreed with her husband. Charles Lacassagne, a rich self-made-man, through judicious property development with a fortune estimated at several millions of euros, was someone everyone respected, whether it was in a board meeting, in his family, at the bank, at a charitable event; no one dared to oppose him. Anyway, his decisions were quite often wise recommendations and those who followed them often made good deals.

This sailing trip was a first for them. The two young men promised to take good care of their little sister.

Their father accompanied them to the front porch of their huge mansion in the little town of Gorbio.

"Be careful now!" he shouted to them. "Accidents happen all too quickly. And make sure you don't take any risks and if the weather gets bad, go back into the port. I'm counting on you, especially you Pierre-Hugues. You're the oldest one here and it's up to you to make sure your brother and sister aren't in any danger. Godspeed to you all!"

Then Dominique, the family's chauffeur, started the limousine to drive them to Saint-Jean-Cap-Ferrat's port, where their boat slip was located. Little Lilie insisted on coming with them to the seaside and stayed while they weighed the anchor.

Marie-Caroline had even begun to take sailing courses at Glénans. Her whole family loved the sea. Once the sailboat was out of the port and marina, Pierre-Hugues let her take the helm for a few minutes while he put his swimming trunks on in the cabin.

They sailed west, with the coast on the starboard side. Once they'd cleared Antibes, they turned straight south and headed out. When they'd gone a few miles past Lérins Islands, they lowered the sails, dropped the anchor and dove into the sea, that *Mare Nostrum* who had watched them grow up, after they were all born at Princess Grace Hospital in Monaco, those children who had all taken their first steps on the beach, on a boat or on a landing dock.

After swimming and horsing around in the water, they all climbed back onto the sailboat.

"Caro, can you make us some lemonade?" asked Pierre-Hugues, his face hidden beneath a large straw hat.

"Hey, I'm not your maid! When at sea, the old saying 'no captain, only sailors!' goes."

"Gotcha," chuckled Edouard. "But now that I'm thinking of it, I think it's time for a drink, don't you?"

"Doudou," added Pierre-Hugues speaking to Edouard, "those are some very wise words! I'm going in once more and after that, let's crack out the drinks. Our old man isn't here to chaperone us!"

Turning talk into action, he walked starboard, stood up straight like an I, raised his two hands above his head and plunged right into the calm waters without splashing.

Marie-Caroline also got up, smiled wryly at Edouard and went down into the center of the boat to get the drinks ready. She shouted out to her brother,

"Doudou? What do you want?"

"A glass of Bordeaux, *s'il te plaît*!"

"What about Pierrot?"

"He'll probably want his whisky, as usual. You know he does love pure malt."

"Everyone knows that!" Marie-Caroline replied. "Especially our old man, as they always share a glass of it Sunday at noon. Daddy and his dear oldest son, both ensconced in their leather armchairs, sitting next to the little table in the library, with their crystal glasses. The patriarch and his successor…"

"Quit your bitching," Edouard replied, sticking his head into the galley. "When it's time to take over, we'll see if he's capable of doing it. Plus, nothing's done yet anyway."

"Yeah, all that because he was the firstborn and he's a guy. A little old fashioned, isn't it? Salic Law was rescinded centuries ago, in my humble opinion!"

"Caro! We said that we'd make the most of this outing to patch things up. So, quit bickering and have fun. We're here, all three of us, and you can't really say that we've got a lot to complain about, can you? We've got this sailboat just for ourselves, the beautiful French Riviera where we live, the sun, our father's empire holding its arms out to us, there are loads of people unhappier than us!"

"I'm not contradicting you. Just regretting that he's the only one he ever talks about. Pierre-Hugues here, Pierre-Hugues there. And Mr. Prefect, I'd like to introduce my son to you. Have you met Pierre-Hugues, Mr. Senator?"

"Ha, ha, very funny! I love it when you lower your voice to imitate Dad! You're good at it, little sister! Did you ever think of a career in show business?"

"Good idea! Maybe I could be a dancer at the Crazy Horse cabaret. I can already see Charles Lacassagne's face when he sees his daughter in magazines, topless and with a feather up her butt! Can you get the bottles, and I'll grab the glasses and ice cubes."

"Bring some peanuts up while you're at it," added Edouard from the deck.

While they were getting everything out, Pierre-Hugues climbed up the ladder at the end of the sailboat, his black hair slicked back, a tanned and muscular body showing that he had plenty of time to take care of himself and work out in the family's private gym. Young, good-looking, with a Mediterranean style that he inherited from his mother, Lucie, without mentioning his potential fortune, it was sure that the oldest Lacassagne son would be a good catch. But he wasn't looking at the moment. He often seduced, regularly conquered, but this was something that never seemed to last, much to the dismay of his father who was hoping he'd marry a rich heiress, so their assets would be doubled! He often set up events with other rich businessmen, foreign princes or political leaders who had a daughter they wanted to marry off, but Pierre-Hugues loved his freedom too much to be interested in wearing a ring on his finger.

As for Edouard, well, let's say that he was physically... less advantaged. Though intellectually well endowed, perhaps proportionally to his extreme myopia, his Coke bottle glasses went well with his curly blond hair and pale skin he'd inherited from his father. For the past two years he'd been going out with Julie Schneider, a nice-looking young lady from a middle-class family he'd met at Nice Business School, in classes they attended together. They hadn't yet spoken about getting married, they were making the most of their youth, but his father did seem to like her, even though she wasn't rich. After all, Edouard was the youngest son, no big deal! And no big expectations, so...

Marie-Caroline, the youngest (not counting Emilie with her differences, poor kid...), her mom's little doll, was a beautiful freckle-faced redhead. Ever since she was fifteen, she'd attracted men like honey attracts bears. But when they insisted too much, she always took off. Marie-Caroline loved her freedom, her books and going to movies, especially films by Jacques Rivette, Francois Truffaut and Eric Rohmer, that New Wave that's no longer new, but does know how to make movies about women and love. Marie-Caroline wanted to marry her Prince Charming, if her old man approved!

"Where's that little Scotch?" asked Pierre-Hugues when he climbed onto the wooden deck.

"Ready to be decanted, Your Highness," replied Edouard ironically with an exaggerated bow.

Dripping wet Pierre-Hugues ran up to him and vigorously rubbed his younger brother's hair.

"Quit monkeying around, little brother."

Just like kittens, the two young men were having fun, running after each other, horsing around, observed by Marie-Caroline's half fun filled, half blasé eyes. Things had been quite tense between them for the past couple of months and ever since they'd decided to bury the hatchet, they'd become more like young, innocent children. Leaving internal strife and sterile jealousy behind them. Together for the better? To avoid the worst?

"Hey, you two, you're going to make us capsize with your nonsense!" she joked, covering the sounds of the waves lapping intermittently against the sailboat's hull.

The sea, calm up until now, was beginning to have little waves. The sky, immaculate during the afternoon, was becoming a bit overcast as the sun was setting. Perhaps the night would be a bit bumpier than planned.

The three of them sat down at the coffee table with its three glasses that were waiting to be filled. Edouard grabbed the bottle of Bordeaux, filled his glass as well as Marie-Caroline's. Then he opened the bottle of whisky to pour his brother a glass of his favorite beverage.

When the bottle touched the edge of the glass, Pierre-Hugues suddenly interrupted him.

"Wait a sec! To celebrate our reconciliation and seal our secret pact, I'll raise a glass of Bordeaux, just like you."

Edouard smiled, delighted by that conciliant and symbolic gesture. He closed the bottle of whiskey and served him a glass of Saint-Emilion instead.

"This is the good life," said Pierre-Hugues, looking at his glass of wine in the last rays of sunlight. "Don't you feel you're privileged?"

"Sure, like 'the world's your oyster,'" replied Edouard. "But don't forget that without our old man's fortune, we wouldn't have a sailboat, we wouldn't be spending the night here at sea."

"And just think, what about if we had to pay for our schooling?" continued Marie-Caroline. "We'd have to work all summer and each weekend instead of lazing here at sea with drinks in our hands!"

"To Dad!" they said, raising their glasses.

An hour later, the bottle was nearly empty, and the atmosphere had ratcheted up. They'd been discussing their futures in the Lacassagne empire. Fueled by alcohol, they imagined the upcoming family-owned empire, when the patriarch would retire, or even pass away. But that wouldn't happen for ages!

When would they head the company? And who would direct it? Who would be the next magnate of the French Riviera's real estate and profitable offshore investments? Whose first name would be on the Lacassagne's patrimony and on its bank accounts domiciliated in Luxembourg, the Cayman Islands or in Zurich?

Nothing was yet set in stone, but their father wanted his firstborn, Pierre-Hugues Lacassagne, to take over from him.

Up until now, the two younger siblings never seemed to be jealous, but now that they were adults, both had a few questions about how all that accumulated wealth would be divvied up when the time came. Just assumptions, but legitimate ones and as years went by, ones that were becoming more and more present.

"Call me Captain!" shouted out Pierre-Hugues, raising his glass as if it were a scepter.

"In your dreams!" answered Edouard. "There's no hierarchy here! All equal!"

"All equal egos!" continued Marie-Caroline, without missing a beat.

"Bravo!" Pierre-Hugues said, laughing. "Your future is laid out for you: the next game show host!"

"You think you're big shots, don't you?" said the young lady after downing her Bordeaux. "The only thing that's important is numbers, right?"

"Yes, Madam!" Edouard said loudly. "Especially those with lots of zeros!"

"Before the decimal point!" added Pierre-Hugues, laughing.

"Okay, we've got stuff to do," Marie-Caroline said, putting an end to that line of thought. "We're drinking, but it's time to eat something else than just peanuts."

"Into the galley, lady!" shouted out Pierre-Hugues. and "Go cook us up a chicken, stat!"

She just sighed, disdainfully raised her shoulders, but did go down to get something that would soak up all that alcohol. She came up a few minutes later, with a nice loaf of bread, and a few tins of sardines and mackerels in tomato sauce on a tray.

"That's your feast?" asked Edouard. "We're not going to be stuffed, that's for sure!"

"My dear sir," said Marie-Caroline. "Did no one ever teach you that you should eat breakfast like a king, lunch like a prince and dinner like a beggar?"

"No beggars here on this boat!" said Pierre-Hugues maliciously. "Well, we'll just have to make the best of things and enjoy this modest but succulent meal!"

He opened a tin of sardines, cut off a thick slice of bread and spread the oily substance on it. It was delicious though for the amateur skippers.

Clouds were coming in and the wind was picking up. The forty-five-foot-long sailboat began to rock gently in the waves. Between the wine and the meal though, no one was paying attention to the weather. They should have, as in just a few hours their beautiful luxury boat would be tossed from port side to starboard. Had they been wiser, they would have hoisted their sails now and headed off to their home port. But those with at least six or seven glasses of alcohol are rarely wise.

Marie-Caroline even absurdly and without him realizing it, served Pierre-Hugues another glass of Saint-Emilion: the second bottle was nearly empty now. Her older brother's eyes were heavy. He didn't seem to notice what was going on around him.

When night fell, the tins of sardines were just as empty as the bottles. Only a few crumbs of bread were left, and the wind quickly blew them away into the sea.

An hour later, the three sailors who had dozed off were suddenly awakened by a gust of wind that must have been stronger than the others. The sailboat was pitching and dangerously leaning to the port side, pulling on the chain that anchored it to the bottom. The salt spray made the deck slippery and hard to hold onto. Marie-Caroline and Edouard were the first ones awake, and Pierre-Hugues was finding it hard to emerge. Two bottles of Bordeaux after a hot and sunny day must not have been the right recipe to fight off seasickness!

"What's going on?" he mumbled to his brother and sister.

"The weather surprised us," explained Edouard, going to the mast. "If we don't get out of here, we're going to be shaken up something crazy. Caro, go down into the cabin and make sure everything's attached."

"Yes, captain."

"Pierrot, you okay? You think you can help me hoist the sails? We have to get back to a port, tough luck for our night at sea."

A flash of lightning lit up the sky, as if it were putting an end to the sibling's outing.

"Fuck," groaned Pierre-Hugues, rubbing his face. "It feels like I'm wearing a lead helmet, and my head is on backwards. That Saint-Emilion was a bitch! I should have stayed with my whisky. I guess I'm more used to it."

"Come on, shake a leg there! You man the windlass to raise the anchor while I unfasten the sails. Think you'll manage?"

"Hey! Lower your tone when you talk to me. Who the hell do you think you are? I'm not an idiot, and I think I've been sailing longer than you."

"Oh Mr. Bragger is back... Mr. Better Than You!" replied Edouard suddenly going towards his brother.

"Shut up, Doudou, we've got other things to do!

But Doudou didn't want to shut up, as if his repressed bitterness had just surfaced. The alcohol must have disinhibited him, and the panic of the moment freed him.

"I can't stand your superiority! For years now everything has been about you and you only!" yelled Edouard, violently pushing his older brother away.

"What are you talking about? You had too much to drink, Edouard."

"You're Dad's favorite, the only one of us that's

important for him. Don't tell me you never noticed? If he only knew!"

"What are you talking about? Quit making things up!"

At that very second a wave that was stronger than the others flowed over the sailboat's rail and hit Pierre-Hugues right in the face. He fell over onto the soaking wet deck.

"Wow! That was a big one," he grumbled, getting up. "Caro, make sure the hatches are closed!"

A clicking sound confirmed that she had heard him.

"Okay now," said the big brother to Edouard. "Let's calm down and make sure this boat stays afloat. We'll settle everything else later."

"For sure," muttered Edouard glaring at his brother.

That salty wave that had hit him seemed to have been a wake-up call and Pierre-Hugues was finally able to weigh the anchor, so they'd be able to sail into the port.

Now the boat was freed though simply blown around in the wind, as the sail had not yet been raised. Only then would the skipper be able to control it. That was what Edouard was trying to do. The rope holding the sail in had been unrolled and he'd successfully raised it. The triangle of cloth was formed, all that was left was to control the boom, that horizontal bar that allowed you to head where you wanted depending on the wind and course.

The boat suddenly veered, and the boom unfortunately slipped out of Edouard's hands. It made a huge semi-circle, sort of like a baseball bat, and in its curved trajectory, brutally slammed into Pierre-Hugues' chest as he was walking across the deck to the helm.

The violence of the shock laid him flat once again, cutting off his breathing. But the deck was wet and the sailboat leaning towards the port side: Pierre-Hugues inexorably slid towards the sea without being able to hold onto anything. Edouard watched him, paralyzed by what was happening, before shouting to his brother.

"Pierrot! Hold on!"

He ran to his older brother, who was still sliding. His legs were already outside of the sailboat, the waves up to his thighs. At the very last moment, Edouard grabbed Pierre-Hugues while holding on to the side rail.

"Don't let me go Doudou!" screamed Pierre-Hugues.

Edouard didn't say anything, he may not even have heard him with the sound of the wind. He looked straight into his brother's eyes while their fingers locked together tensed up in the effort to hold on to Pierre-Hugues and prevent him from sliding into the raging waters.

The boat was drifting, sails throbbing, the mast swaying. The noise of the elements joined mechanical ones: waves breaking on the hull, the bow of the sailboat suddenly plunging into the troughs, the wind howling in the starless night.

Edouard shouted to his sister.

"Caro, help!"

In the cabin, she wasn't aware of what was happening on the deck and didn't hear her brother cry out to her, busy putting everything away that could be dangerous in the storm. A few seconds went by before she saw shadows through one of the portholes that were moving about and made her think they were legs kicking. She immediately ran up to the deck.

In the storm she made out two men, one lying on his stomach on the slippery deck, the other one hanging over the side of the boat, holding on to a hand. She rushed over to grab Pierre-Hugues' other hand.

She never made it though, because at that very instant, Pierre-Hugues' fingers, as if in slow motion, escaped from Edouard's hand.

With a scream smothered by the wind, Pierre-Hugues Lacassagne, Charles Lacassagne's eldest son, the one who was to inherit his real-estate fortune on the French Riviera, disappeared into the dark waters of the Mediterranean Sea.

Stupefied, Edouard and Marie-Caroline remained immobile, lying on the deck, their hands dangling over the side of the deck, looking into the deep sea that had just swallowed their brother.

CHAPTER 2
In a state of shock

THE PHONE on the bedside table rang in the middle of the night. Emerging from a deep sleep, Charles Lacassagne picked it up.

"Hello."

"Is this Mr. Charles Lacassagne?"

"Yes, who's calling at this time of day?"

"*Gendarmerie nationale*, Théoule-sur-Mer Squad."

"What's wrong?"

"Are you Pierre-Hugues Lacassagne's father?"

"Yes, why?"

"Your son had an accident."

"What do you mean, an accident?"

"Mr. Lacassagne. I can't tell you anymore about this on the phone. Your son Edouard and Marie-Caroline are here at the station, they're both in a state of shock. It would be better to talk about that here. Do you have a car?"

"Of course, I'll be right there."

Charles Lacassagne jumped out of bed, nearly tripping in the sheets. He threw on some clothes and Lucie, his wife, who slept in the bedroom next to his, walked in.

"Charles? What's happening?" she asked, worried.

"I have to go to Théoule. Pierre-Hugues had an accident."

Lucie gasped, putting her hand on her face.

"Good Lord, is it serious?"

"I don't know yet. Edouard and Marie-Caroline are already there, at the gendarmerie, apparently they're both in a state of shock."

"But what happened though? Why doesn't anyone ever listen to me here? I was afraid about this outing. Our children, all alone."

"Be quiet! They're no longer children, they're three adults now! Stop feeling sorry for yourself! I have to go now."

"Wait till I get dressed."

"Lucie, it would be better if you stayed here. For you and for Lilie. Who will babysit her?"

"I can call Brigitte, I'm sure she'd accept."

Charles stopped his wife right there, taking her firmly by the wrist.

"Stay here! Police stations, especially at night, are not places where women like you should be. I'll take care of things."

Knowing that he wouldn't give in, Lucie gave up and went into little Emilie's room. The six-year-old was sleeping peacefully, not disturbed by all that agitation.

Charles woke his chauffeur up and they immediately set off from the little village of Gorbio to the Théoule-sur-Mer gendarmerie.

An hour later, they arrived. A gendarme greeted them.

"Mr. Lacassagne, Sergeant Petrucci is waiting for you. Please follow me."

When he walked into the office, Charles immediately saw Marie-Caroline and she ran up to him.

"Oh! Dad! It's horrible!"

She burst into tears, hugging him. Gently running his fingers through her red hair, Charles gently rocked her.

"Okay, I'm here now, it's finished."

He looked over towards Edouard, who was slumped over in his chair, facing the chief of police.

"Edouard? Are you okay?"

"Father... I tried... I did everything I could, I'm so sorry..."

"What are you talking about?"

Right then, Mr. Petrucci walked in.

"Mr. Lacassagne. Sit down please. I'll explain what we already know. Your son and daughter showed up here, completely panicked. They told us that Pierre-Hugues, their brother, fell overboard and despite their attempts to recover him, they were unable to. Because of the stormy weather at night, it would have been nearly impossible. Edouard told us where to look and we sent out several patrol boats to cover the area where he fell into the water. As for now, we still haven't found him. I'm sorry, but each minute counts and I'm afraid that hope is dwindling to recover your son alive."

Charles stoically listened to him. He was clutching Marie-Caroline's frail shoulders while she continued to sob.

"Young man," said Petrucci. "What time did the accident happen?"

Edouard emerged from his torpidity.

"I'd say around midnight: it had been dark for about two hours I think."

"What did you do next? Did you dive in, or throw out a lifeline?"

Edouard hesitated.

"Yes I did, but without knowing where. I couldn't even see five feet in front of me. I couldn't find my brother. I thought of course of diving in, but with those waves, I was afraid that I'd drown too."

"I understand," said Petrucci, nodding. "A wise decision: the sea is filled with dead heroes."

"You know, I couldn't think straight. What was I supposed to do? Dive in to try to help my brother or leave my little sister who doesn't know how to sail all alone on the boat during a storm?"

"Did you send out any distress signals?"

"I think so."

"You think so?"

"I don't know anymore, sir. I'm so upset, I'm exhausted."

Sergeant Petrucci nodded, thinking. Marie-Caroline interrupted them.

"I sent out a distress signal."

"Was it a parachute flare, a handheld one, or a smoke signal?"

"A parachute flare."

"Right. After that, you turned on the Argos beacon? Your sailboat must have one."

"It does," said Charles, who had just found enough strength to speak. "We were one of the first ones to get one."

"Interesting," sighed Petrucci. "It took us nearly an hour to get the signal and send the rescue teams out in the sea, and we were the closest. Mr. Lacassagne, were your children used to sailing alone?"

"It wasn't the first time they went out alone. My two sons have been sailing for years now. But they'd never taken their sister with them."

While he was speaking, he continued to coddle Marie-Caroline.

"She was so happy to accompany them. Weren't you, sweetie?"

"That's right. Things had started off so well. We were having a good time, the weather was perfect, and they even let me take the helm for a few minutes."

"My daughter already sails well."

The gendarme kept writing everything down.

"Then the weather got bad, and everything suddenly was out of control," added Edouard.

Petrucci spoke up then.

"Plus, your reflexes weren't as good then."

"What do you mean by that?" asked Charles.

"I'm not the one saying this. It's the results of the alcohol breath tests that just came in… You had been drinking onboard, hadn't you?"

Marie-Caroline and Edouard looked at each other, panicked, as if they were wondering what the other person would answer to this.

"A few bottles," admitted the young man, ashamed.

"Enough to give you a buzz and weaken your alertness."

"How much?" their father asked. "I'd forbidden alcoholic beverages abord the sailboat."

"Not enough to be condemnable," Petrucci said, seeming to regret it.

"Now what?" asked Charles.

Petrucci got up from his armchair and joined the Lacassagne family on the other side of his deck.

"The best thing would be for you all to rest. The patrol boats will keep on looking for your brother. We'll also be questioning all the fishermen or boaters that could have been in sea not too far from you. But with this bad weather that surprised everyone, I don't think we'll have much here to tell the truth. Your sailboat was taken to Théoule Marina. For the moment, you won't be able to access it: we have to fulfil all the legal obligations. For tonight, you just have a few papers to sign, and you can go back home."

It was already light out when they reached the family's villa in Gorbio.

The Lacassagne family now had one fewer member.

CHAPTER 3
One foot in front of the other

DAYS WENT BY, sad and painful ones for the Lacassagne's, who rarely went out of their villa in the hinterlands of Nice, as if they were fleeing the fatal attraction of the Mediterranean Sea, that traitor who had stolen Pierre-Hugues from them.

Edouard and Marie-Caroline wandered around the silent rooms of their family's huge cut stone house. Both of them had to go to the gendarmerie a couple of times for paperwork, both felt heartbroken and guilty.

Charles remained dignified despite his affliction and continued to assume his professional obligations, going to the head office of his company in the historic center of Nice. Business is business, as his American colleagues always said.

Lucie was inconsolable for the loss of her first child, the one who looked so much like her, the one who shared her interests, who had inherited her Italian features, her smile, that up till now, had been beautiful.

From dawn until dusk her eyes were now red and tearful, her eyelids drooping from lost sleep, as she never stopped hoping for some good news that never came.

As for poor little Lilie, what did she understand? Six years old, as if she had lost her best friend…

Days turned into weeks.

Hope turned into hopelessness.

Doubts turned into certitude… it was finished.

Five weeks had gone by, and no one was able to give them any hope, not a single body had washed up on the shore, so they finally decided to organize a ceremony for those who had disappeared at sea.

The Lacassagne's, fervent Catholics who rarely missed Sunday mass, wanted to pay a last homage to their son who would now only be present in their thoughts and prayers. They believed that Pierre-Hugues was now in heaven, and that he probably was aware of their pain and how much he was missed. With that specific ceremony, they hoped to communicate with his soul, as his body was still missing.

Archbishop Poirier, the bishop of Nice, was a friend of the family and had accepted to celebrate that mass.

Usually this type of celebration pays tribute to a group of sailors, soldiers, or athletes who lost their lives at sea during their jobs, their functions, or because they were passionate about boating.

But Lacassagne's generosity and social standing with the Church allowed him to conduct a private celebration.

The entire Lacassagne family, including Charles and Lucie as well as their children, Edouard, Marie-Caroline and even little Emilie, boarded the Chéron dispatch sloop and left the Toulon Port.

They were accompanied by Nice's Vice Mayor, as well as a flag bearer, a trumpetist, and a young man playing the drums, plus a cohort of movers and shakers in the region, most of whom had declared they were friends of the millionaire. There were politicians, businessmen, a few show-biz celebrities: all in all nearly fifty people were sailing off in the direction of the zone where Pierre-Hugues Lacassagne had drowned.

When they cut the motors, the group came to the bow of the boat where the flag bearer had erected his mast. The trumpet and drum played "Day is Done." Some of the attendees were looking off into the horizon while others were looking down into the sea, their eyes glazed over, with the crazy hope of seeing their dearly departed come back up.

They were silent as Archbishop Poirier advanced, holding a Missal, to say a prayer. The smooth sea made gentle noises against the metallic hull of the dispatch sloop, the only sound they heard outside of people clearing their throats or sobbing.

His prayer was both for Pierre-Hugues and the members of his family, without forgetting all of those who had lost their lives at sea. He pronounced words like prudence, danger, fate, fatality, memory and contemplation. Then he blessed the flowers that two deacons threw overboard. The flowered wreath floated.

In a couple of days it would join Pierre-Hughes deep down in the sea.

Lucie was heartbroken when she had to leave the place where her oldest son had drowned: she suddenly realized that never again would she see her little Pierre-Hugues, that his body might never be washed ashore so that she could begin to mourn. She knew that often people who drowned at sea were permanently lost for their families, either washed ashore on some isolated coast somewhere far away or stuck at the bottom of the sea in the rocks or eaten by marine wildlife.

What a horrible vision for a mother.

Marie-Caroline, feeling how hard this was for her, took her arm to help her debark.

Little Emilie, who had observed the ceremony like a lost ghost, took her father Charles' hand.

Edouard was walking behind them, hands crossed behind his back, stern features, as if he had forgotten that to walk all you need to do is put one foot in front of the other and then do the same thing over and over again.

Lilie

The Playmobil toys were on the side of the tub. She often got new characters, new decors, new vehicles. Her family knew that she expressed herself best with them.

Lilie had asked for a boat, and this was what she was playing with, that afternoon, in her bath.

On the little red and white boat, she'd put three figurines: two boys and one girl with yellow hair.

The plastic ship rocked up and down in the turmoil of the water that she had made with her legs.

"Plouf! Pehu fall in!"

The little Playmobil with black hair fell over the rail and sunk immediately, falling to the bottom of the bathtub, disappearing under the foam of her bubble bath...

CHAPTER 4
A long exposure in water

IN THE FALL OF 1986, a guy who was walking along the rocky Cassis coastline looking for delicious sea urchins, made a macabre discovery...

The coastguards were alerted and at the bottom of a little creek nearly inaccessible by land, recovered a body in a state of very advanced decomposition. They broadcast that information to all the police stations and gendarmeries in the south-east of France.

When Sergeant Petrucci read the note, he quickly drove to Marseille where they'd transported the body. Something told him he'd maybe be able to close one of his cold cases here.

He relied a lot on his gut feelings, his instinct. Bodies were not washed up in a day and it was quite possible that this one could have traveled from Lérins Island to Cassis, in the three months it had been missing.

The name Lacassagne lit up in his head. He

hopped into his car, a blue Renault 11, and rushed off to Marseille to have a look at the stiff.

The coroner greeted him with a professional and relaxed manner. This wasn't the first time that Petrucci had been in a morgue, and he wasn't nervous. Nonetheless, this time it wouldn't be pretty, and he appreciated the fact that Doctor El Brahmi spontaneously warned him.

"I just want you to know, Sarge, it's quite disgusting."

"Thanks for the heads up, Doc! I've already seen quite a few cadavers being dissected."

"Anyone who'd drowned?"

Petrucci shook his head.

They neared the table where you could imagine a body enclosed in a white casing with Marseille Hospital written on it. El Brahmi added:

"Make sure you wear this mask. People who have drowned have gas and that's something you don't want to breathe in."

The gendarme obediently put it on.

When the doctor unzipped the casing, Petrucci, in spite of himself, stepped back and puckered up his nose in disgust.

"This is how we found the body," El Brahmi said.

"That skin color is normal?"

"Yup, in our jargon we call this a "chocolate covered marshmallow," but it's not as attractive as when you buy one in a store," the doctor said, joking.

The cadaver's face was blackened, swollen, tumefied and nearly bald.

"The mid-scalp baldness that you see here is typical of a man who drowned," explained Dr. El Brahmi. "In the first step of a drowning, the body falls to the bottom. Men are in a ventral position then, bent over, with their buttocks sticking up. That explains the lesions that you can see on the knees, the back of the hands, toes and on the top of the skull."

"That's interesting," said the gendarme, effectively noting those lesions on the body. "And women?"

Dr. El Brahmi seemed to be delighted that the subject interested him.

"The opposite: women are in a decubitus dorsal position."

"What?"

"Oh sorry, I mean, on their backs, sorry for the technical jargon. That means that lesions are on their heels, elbows, on the back of their skull and on their buttocks. Which confirms that this is a man here."

"That's true, a man, even though it is hard to recognize. Anything else you can tell me, doctor? I want to tell you something: as soon as I had the info about this body that washed up, I thought about one of my unsolved cases. The oldest Lacassagne son, who accidentally drowned this summer not too far from Lérins Islands."

"Yeah. I remember that. There was a lot of news coverage on it: he was the son of the millionaire from Nice, the real estate magnate, wasn't he?"

"That's right. Do you think this could be his son?"

"It's technically not impossible. If you consider the number of weeks since the accident took place, added to other parameters like the distance, undersea currents, storms that happened and that could have accelerated the movement of the body... In that case, it is possible. Anyway, from a medical point of view, the body does have signs of having been in the water for a long time."

"Could it have been three months? Can you date the moment of death?"

"Not precisely, no. But what I can tell you is that this guy didn't drown just a week ago!"

"How do you know that?"

"Let me explain. When they're under water, cadavers have two ways of moving, horizontally and vertically, and we can break these down into three steps. The first one: it sinks progressively to the bottom, because the density of a dead body, meaning that the lungs don't have any air in them, is slightly more than the density of water. At the same time, it can also move horizontally with the tide, courants or ships passing."

"Gotcha. And then what?"

"The second stage: it remains at the bottom for a while, before progressively going back up to the surface."

"That's the third stage then?"

"Exactly. That's when bacteria begin to denature the cadaver."

"Bacteria? Which ones?"

"Just those that were already present inside the body, in the intestinal flora. That's putrefaction, or rotting, in other words. That leads gas to be formed and gives the body a specific density allowing it to float and slowly go back up to the surface."

"How long does that take?"

"Generally, in seawater with a lot of salt in it, it goes back up in three to seven days, compared with twenty to thirty days in freshwater. After that, it will float with the currents, wash ashore, be caught in a fishing net, or be ripped apart from a ship's propeller."

Just thinking of that Petrucci quivered.

"Luckily, that's not the case here."

"Right, excepting the usual deformation of the abdomen, the blackish color of the skin and the lesions we mentioned, nothing was really harmed here."

"So in conclusion, it could be the Lacassagne heir?"

"Potentially yes, nothing prevents us from thinking that. Now, to identify him formally, we'll have to do other analyses. For example, study his teeth to determine his age."

"Precisely?"

"Almost. Forensic odontology isn't something new, and it allows us to estimate how old cadavers are, give or take a few years. For me, the body has all the anthropomorphic signs of a young man, I'd say twenty-five to thirty at the max."

Petrucci went to the other side of the table, looking carefully at the body, paying attention to the clothing.

"His clothes seem to have resisted quite well.

The man fell in, wearing a pair of shorts and a polo with the brand on his chest: a well-known crocodile."

"Textiles seem to resist better than skin then."

Petrucci suddenly picked up a plastic bag with a watch in it.

"It was on the cadaver's right hand. It stopped at one fifteen."

"You think maybe that that was when he drowned?"

"Could be. This is a luxury watch. Look: it's a Longines, a popular brand for people who sail or ride. It must be waterproof. Let's see, sometimes they say so on the back."

Dr. El Brahmi took the watch out of the plastic bag and examined it under the neon lamp above the dissection table.

"I don't know if it's waterproof, however, what's engraved on it will interest you."

He handed it to Petrucci. His eyes lit up when he saw it.

"Doctor, may I use your phone?"

CHAPTER 5
A pure formality

I'M REALLY sorry to have to inflict this one you, Mr. Lacassagne," said Petrucci respectfully when the businessman walked into the Marseille Forensics Medicine Institute.

"You were right to call me," answered Charles, who seemed to be exhausted. "In a way, I'm relieved that this is over. The last few months have been terrible."

"I believe you."

"If it's alright with you, I'd prefer to be alone," continued the millionaire. "If, like you said, it's frightening, I prefer to spare my children and my wife."

"Just one person in the family is enough to identify a body. Plus, as you'll see by yourself, it's a pure formality."

They went into the cool room where they joined Dr. El Brahmi next to the dissection table.

They all shook hands.

"Doctor, could you please raise the sheet so that Mr. Lacassagne can identify the body?"

The coroner raised it, and Charles gasped. What he saw was terrible, nearly unbearable.

"It's hard to say. The face is so distorted you can hardly make out the features. Though the height and weight do seem to correspond to my son's."

"Do you recognize any clothing?"

"I think I saw him wearing this pair of shorts and this top. Lacoste was one of his favorite brands."

Petrucci was taking notes.

"Mr. Lacassagne, was your son a lefthander?"

"No, why?"

"Like I said on the phone, and that's why I wanted you to come, we also found a watch that he was wearing on his right hand, which is why I thought he was a lefty."

"Strange you noticed that. Pierre-Hugues was a righthander but he always put his watch on his right wrist, which most people don't do. One of his little habits. Can I see it?"

"Of course, here."

Charles took the watch and turned it over.

"P.H.L. 1980. It's his watch. I gave him this watch for his twentieth birthday."

CHAPTER 6
Die mad, die twice

THEY FINALLY GOT his body back and could begin to grieve. Pierre-Hugues Lacassagne's mortal remains were transported to the cemetery in the little village of Gorbio, where his father's ancestors were also buried. This was a little cemetery on the hillside, with high white walls and groves of cypress trees. Typically Mediterranean.

All of Nice's movers and shakers were there to support that influential family, or just to say they were there, as this was an event that couldn't be missed. People would still speak of it years to come in high society. They'd say, "I was there," with both a compassionate and proud expression. This was sure to make front page in the local papers: a tragic accident in a rich and famous family.

Of course, there was no open casket viewing: this would have been much too horrible! The body had travelled from the Forensics Medicine Institute in

Marseille to Gorbio cemetery in a coffin that the gendarmerie had sealed.

Now four undertakers were carefully lowering the coffin into its final resting place, closely observed by the grieving family, next to the hole.

This was very difficult for little Emilie, but Charles had wanted her to be there, despite her young age and condition, so that one day she'd perhaps remember the ceremony, if not now, maybe in a few years. So that she could understand that her big brother, the one she was closest to, would never again be there to play with her.

Tears filled her slanted eyes, her nose was running and she noisily snorted, holding Brigitte, her babysitter's hand, who was also holding her son Simon's hand. They were both about the same age.

Lucie, her mother, was sobbing, at her left. She was burying her oldest son. This was even worse for her when she thought back on the last few weeks they'd spent together. Those weeks she'd like so much to change now... She was so terribly sorry that she'd been upset with Pierre-Hugues, that she hadn't tried to understand. You should never leave anyone when you're angry. But death never makes an appointment: it knocks whenever it wants, steals loved ones from us, without caring if we had had the time or willingness to bury the hatchet.

Die mad, die twice... Lucie teetered under the weight of remorse and affliction.

Charles realized that and hugged his wife, putting his protective arm around her thin shoulders. His little wife who seemed twice as small as he was, the one he jokingly called "the half of my half," or "my quarter." But it was true that he hadn't called her that for a while now. Ever since they'd decided to sleep in separate bedrooms. It wasn't because they didn't love each other anymore, it was just easier that way. Plus that way Lucie was closer to Lilie, who often had trouble sleeping.

Charles zoned out for a moment, trying to remember the last time he'd called her "my quarter." One thing led to another, and he surprised himself by thinking of when they'd first met each other. They'd ironically met not too far from the little Gorbio cemetery, in the village square. He remembered the date perfectly; it was in May of 1958 when General De Gaulle returned to power in France.

~

Gorbio, May 28, 1958

Young Charles Lacassagne, who had just turned twenty, a tall and slim young man, but one who was athletic, said he'd give a helping hand to the Sganarelli Circus that had just pulled in, to help them put up their big top. Back in the day, travelling Italian circuses went all around the south of France, with their jugglers, clowns, trapeze artists, dog and goat trainers, and ... a trick rider.

The sun was already beating down on the dry hillside at this time of year. Mother Nature was thirsty as were the men assembling the metallic bars and canvas in the big top. People were crying out:

"La stanchezza comincia a farsi sentire...

"E anche la sete!"

Charles worked like a dog, sweat running down his forehead and glistening on his back, on his strong muscles.

"You should really have something to drink" whispered a little singsong voice behind him. "And put a hat on too, otherwise you'll get sunstroke."

He dropped the bar that he was assembling, turned around and came face to face with a svelte little brunette only about five feet tall, who must not even have been eighteen.

"Thanks," he said, with a wide grin.

He took a long drink from the gourd she'd handed to him, nice cold water, wiped his lips with his wrist, and said,

"That's really nice of you."

The young lady smiled back at him and asked,

"What's your name? Do you live here?"

"Charles. And yes, I live in this village. That's where my ancestors came from. What about you?"

"Me? No, I'm not from here," she joked.

She timidly laughed and continued.

"My name is Lucie... Lucia actually, I was born in Italy."

"That's a pretty name."

"Thanks. It means 'light.'"

"So that's why you have such luminous eyes?"

Lucie turned her head, embarrassed, looking away with her dark brown eyes.

"Oh... you shouldn't say things like that. I'll let you get back to work, thanks for helping."

Then she turned around, the gourd flopping against her hip.

"Wait!" Charles shouted out to her, surprised to see her walking away. "I didn't want... I mean, like I was awkward and..."

Lucie laughed.

"That's not what I said."

"Will we see each other again?"

"Maybe."

"When?"

"Very soon!"

A few hours later, Charles was seated in the first row of seats that he'd helped install earlier that afternoon. In 1958, circuses were really popular, and the show was sold out. Everyone who'd helped got in for free. Charles loved circuses and wouldn't have missed this one for anything, despite the fact that his father had said they were for the lower classes.

The show had started a while ago. All the kids laughed at the clowns, they admired the little goats dancing about and held their breath when the trapeze artist flew through the air without a safety net.

Charles suddenly gasped: a superb bay horse accompanied by music trotted into the circus ring, with a little five-foot tall lady with long dark hair and a superb smile standing on its back. He couldn't keep his eyes off her for the entire performance, his heart nearly stopping at each acrobatic move. When she discreetly waved at him upon leaving, he thought he was imagining things.

∼

THE NEXT DAY THOUGH, he'd invited her to share a glass of lemonade at the village café, Charles thought back, tightening his grip around Lucie's trembling shoulders, at the edge of the tomb where his oldest son was being buried.

That was the beginning of a long love story.

Twenty-eight years ago, in the spring. It was already hot outside. People were sweating and sweltering happily.

Now it was fall, the wind was blowing, people were shivering.

A quarter of a mile and nearly three decades separated those two events. But an abyss had opened and wouldn't close quickly.

The coffin was lowered to the bottom of the tomb, the priest said the liturgy, people expressed their deepest sympathy, before going back to their everyday activities. Just as the Lacassagne family did, going back to their huge villa, where they'd never hear one of its family members again.

Lilie

Lilie was playing with Simon in the garden, with Brigitte who was sitting in a chair on the patio, looking after both of them.

The little girl wanted to take some of her Playmobil toys out. She'd chosen seven of them: big ones and little ones, girls and boys.

She'd also taken a large matchbox, having emptied out the bracelets and rings that she usually kept there.

When she got to the edge of the property, she dug a little hole with her fingers in the ground that was still moist from a recent storm. Simon helped her, without saying a word.

She opened the matchbox.
Put one of the Playmobil figures in.
Closed it.
Put it into the hole.
Covered it with earth and leaves, and said,

"Bye bye, Pehu."

When they went back in, there were six Playmobil figures.

CHAPTER 7
I had high expectations

IN 1986, right before Christmas, Charles Lacassagne decided to hold a family meeting to prepare for the future. Sitting around the dining room table were Lucie, Edouard and Marie-Caroline. Emilie was playing with her inseparable plastic figures on the floor next to them.

Like each Sunday, they'd gone to mass and had piously prayed for Pierre-Hugues, that his soul would rest in peace. Lucie was the one who was the most impacted: she was still grieving. Logically children don't die before their parents.

As for Charles, he was working harder than ever, seemingly with more energy than before. He said that it helped him, as when he was working, he wasn't thinking.

Edouard was in his last year of doctoral studies in economy and already working part-time in his father's company. His father was coaching him and that helped him forget some of the pain. He was a very studious young man and already an efficient employee.

Marie-Caroline also had a foot in the corporate door, or perhaps a toe would be more accurate, and she sometimes accompanied her father when he was meeting clients or suppliers, while continuing her linguistic studies.

After they had said grace, Charles stood up.

"Children, Lucie... I'd like to talk about the future of our household and our business. I thought a lot about the tragic accident our family had this summer and its consequences and possible implications. I'm sure it's no secret for you that I had high expectations about my three children for my succession."

"Charles, do you think this is the right time to talk about this?" asked Lucie.

"Yes, I do, dear. What good is it to lament each and every day? Our grief is understandable, but it shouldn't prevent us from moving forward. On the contrary, we have to pick ourselves up and think about the future. So, as I was saying, I had high expectations for my three children. Unfortunately, it must have been the day for our dear Pierre-Hugues to join the Good Lord. And what will tomorrow bring? You know, I was hoping that he'd quickly begin to manage the holding. Of course, you two children would have helped him."

"The holding! That's the only thing you can say!" scoffed Lucie, wiping her nose. "That's all our family is for you, a holding?"

"Lucie!" shouted Charles.

Emilie turned around, suddenly surprised by her father's tone, as he rarely raised his voice. He calmed down immediately though.

"Please, let me finish. As Pierre-Hugues is no longer with us, I've decided to remain at the head of our company until my body and brain tell me it's time to let go. I the meanwhile, I'd like you to assist me."

"Of course, father, you can count me in," said Edouard, nodding.

"I'll be there too," continued Marie-Caroline.

"Edouard, when graduate, logically this summer, I'd like you to be our full-time accounting and financial head of the holding."

"I'd be honored."

"As for you, Marie, I'll be creating a job as public relations and community manager for you, I'm sure that will fit you perfectly!"

"Oh! Well, I sure wasn't expecting that. I don't know if I'll be capable of that. What does that consist of exactly?"

"You're beautiful. You'll be the best showcase possible for our company. Your role will consist of meeting all the important people in our region as often as possible, you know the ones that could give us a helping hand when we need it."

"Who are you thinking of?"

"All our dear elected delegates, local ones but also our deputies, senators, or other bigwigs who might be in the region. Sort of like a representation and lobbying job. You'll be the feminine and attractive star of the Lacassagne holding. Something I've never been able to do, that goes without saying! But besides that, you'll be in charge of communication."

"That's a little scary. I don't know if I'm capable of doing that."

"A Lacassagne is always capable of anything! I'm counting on you Marie, in the upcoming years."

"I'll do my best."

"The world is changing," Charles continued. Everything is picking up speed. Competition is ferocious. But there's still so much money to be made here in the French Riviera! And I don't want to be lagging behind. Quite the opposite: we have to stay in the limelight, whatever it takes. New technologies are going to revolutionize the way we work twenty years from now. I've got the feeling that pretty soon everything will be about communication, relationships, networks. Of course, you have to master know-how, but also and above all, make everything known. The cards our business has are going to be reshuffled... same thing for the cards our holding has."

Lucie suddenly got up.

"You're disgusting me. Like we're merely pawns on a chessboard. The king and his knights. Come on Lilie, let's go play with your Playmobiles in your bedroom, okay?"

"Yes, Mommy."

And they left, hand in hand.

"Your mother can't understand. Neither can poor

little Emile. On a chessboard, rooks always progress sideways. But us three, we understand each other!"

"That we do," answered both Marie-Caroline and Edouard, with a smile full of complicity.

"We have to respect your mother's anger; she's got the right to be angry. We all don't confront death with the same arms. Now, let's pray... for a better future."

That is how the cards that were to become in the following two decades, the Lacassagne empire, were dealt. The 1980s and 1990s were booming years, bringing wealth to the family and especially to the holding.

But then the day came, right before he was to turn eighty, when Charles finally made the decision to let go of the reins, to give up his keys: it was time to transfer his assets.

And that was when everything went pear-shaped.

For better or for worse…

That was in Nice, in the summer of 2016…

PART Two

HEADWINDS (30 YEARS LATER...)

CHAPTER 8
The Grim Reaper's breath

NICE, *summer of 2016*

When I arrived in the French Riviera, at the beginning of the summer of 2016, I was far from imagining to what point my career and personal life would both be overturned. Up till then, I had been a modest journalist employed by *"New Business in France"* magazine, writing a few, not very interesting articles on the lives and success stories of France's industrial leaders and most important businessmen. I made a pretty good living out of it, but to supplement my income, I sometimes rented myself out to rich people wanting to tout their success and let the general public know about it and was commissioned to write and edit their biographies. I'd thus jointly signed three or four "autobiographies" that frankly didn't sell very well but had satisfied the egos of the businessmen who had commissioned them from me.

My little reputation had gone from the north to the south of France and had arrived in Charles Lacassagne's ears. He was pushing eighty and probably felt the Grim Reaper's breath on his neck, making him decide to write his memoires and have them published. Like any self-made man worth his salt, he'd started with next to nothing had was now at the head of what the world called the Lacassagne empire and wanted to leave a trace of his success. Tell the whole world, for posterity, about his financial acumen and his humanism, before kicking the bucket.

"Jerome, this is an opportunity for you and for our magazine!" said Gerard Laclos, my editor-in-chief. "You can't turn down an invitation from one of Europe's largest fortunes. In addition to his autobiography, I'll give you the central pages for the September edition!"

"Um... I don't know... you know, going to the French Riviera in summer."

"No, seriously? A financial wizard is giving you a golden bridge to listen to him, write and embellish what he tells you in a book that you're sure is going to be published and you're hesitating? Plus getting out of Paris will do you good!"

Gerard wasn't mistaken. I was going through a dry patch, full of doubts and disillusion. After two years of ups and downs with a certain Cynthia, more downs maybe than ups, I was feeling that our relationship had bottomed out. That both relieved me and saddened me. Cynthia could be adorable... when she wasn't possessive and so terribly jealous! An exhausting relationship, one that distance and a summer in the south of France could put an end to without too much pain. Gerard, whom I'd spoken to about my sentimental life, urged me to get away from the capital and that tigress.

"There you go!" he'd concluded. "You got it made! You'll be leaving for Nice next week! And I'll be paying for your travel expenses. As for accommodations, I think that this dear Mr. Lacassagne took care of that."

"Yes, he reserved a room for me at the Negresco, perhaps with a balcony overlooking the *Promenade des Anglais*. I must admit it could be worse."

That's how I accepted Charles Lacassagne's proposal.

The Paris-Nice bullet train was speeding along. Concentrated on my laptop where I'd started to make notes, I glanced at the scenery out of the corner of my eye, without making out any details. Just a succession of shadows, light and flashes. I didn't know it then, but that's what the next weeks would be like too.

Had I known the can of worms I was about to open, I perhaps would have gotten off in Avignon and turned around, going back to my comfortable Parisian apartment, my little articles in *New Business in France*, and Cynthia's tender but sharp claws.

Or not!

The day before I'd gone to her place, to break up

with her gently, without fighting, without screaming, without a scandal.

"How can you do that to me!" she'd shouted out, going around the leather couch. "I don't understand! What's the problem?"

"Calm down," I'd said. "You know, we already talked about this more than once: you're too possessive. I can't do anything without you feeling I've betrayed you, without you sticking your nose into my business trips, without you looking through my contacts to see anyone who could take your place. You're jealous of all my colleagues, you suspect me of going out with all the ladies I interview. I can't stand it anymore, I swear!"

"Jerome, that's crazy, I never looked into your professional phone if that's what's worrying you," she confessed.

"Not that one! It's password protected. As for my personal phone, my email account, my mail, my agenda, well you've been in them all."

"You're paranoid, sweetie."

"No, I'm a good observer."

Then Cynthia started begging.

"I promise I'll change. Jerome, I love you. I promise, you can believe me."

"Cynthia, we already had this conversation loads of times, in the same order and nearly the same terms. You change for a couple of days and then you're even more jealous. I can't do this anymore."

"Don't say that, Jerome. I hate it when you say things like that."

And she'd tried to butter me up with kisses and caresses in the right places. And it did work, I'm almost ashamed to say.

"Here's what we'll do. I accepted a job that will keep me busy this summer, in the south of France. I'll probably be there two months, depending on how quickly the project goes."

"Two months? That's too long," Cynthia moaned.

"I don't actually have a deadline. I'll be interviewing a businessman who wants to dictate his memoires to me. I'll be meeting him, his family, his professional contacts and who knows who else. Then I'll have the book to write. Plus a couple of pages for *New Business* that Gerard's already ordered. So you see, I'm going to be busy."

"Don't tell me you won't have any free time? Maybe I could come and join you for a weekend or two? It would be so romantic."

"Cynthia, you don't understand. A weekend or two in Nice won't change you. We've already spent weekends in fantastic places, of course they were wonderful. But as soon as we returned to Paris, you became that green-eyed monster once again. The problem is that you're only comfortable when I'm only with you or you're in charge of what I do all day. That's not how I see a balanced couple. Cynthia, I'm sorry, but it's over."

Tears and begging had succeeded the kisses and caresses.

"Please Jerome, I can't live without you."

I was finally swayed once again, and we decided to split the difference.

"Okay then, here's what I propose," I said. "We'll say then that this will be a break for us, give us time to think things over and we'll see what happens in September then."

After hashing this out for over an hour, she finally accepted that compromise. I didn't stay over at her place though.

∼

By the time I'd reached Lyon, using the Wi-Fi connection on the train, I'd read through Charles Lacassagne's biography. He'd gotten married to an Italian whose family had come to France to escape Mussolini's regime. The couple had four children: two boys and two girls. They were a traditional family, one that was very generous to the Catholic Church: in 1987, Charles Lacassagne had donated a million francs to charity. Last summer, their oldest son drowned in a boating accident in the Mediterranean. I immediately thought that this tragic accident could perhaps bring a bit of humanity to the real-estate magnate's autobiography. Could his fortune replace his son? A question that should be addressed. Perhaps though not in those terms.

My phone vibrated, cutting off that line of thought. There was a new email from someone named Colombe Deschamps. A nice name, but not one I'd ever heard before, even though it was rare enough that I would have. Plus, in the subject zone, it was written: "Following our phone conversation."

It had completely slipped my mind. I quickly opened the message.

From: Colombe Deschamps
To: Jerome Bastaro/NBF

Object: Following our phone conversation

Dear Mr. Bastaro,

With this email, I'd like to follow up our quick phone call of last week where I said that I'd like to interview you.

My name is Colombe Deschamps. Perhaps you remember that I'm in my last year of my master's degree in journalism and to prepare my final dissertation (next September), I'm required to shadow a professional journalist for at least a week.

I tried to phone you several times, but you didn't answer. So I contacted New Business in France, and they said that you'd be in Nice this summer. They advised me to send you an email.

I actually am a student in Nice and that seemed to be a sign to me: you are the person I should shadow, if of course, you agree! I've read some of your papers and appreciated them, as well as the two biographies that you jointly wrote.

I'd be delighted to shadow you.

If of course that isn't possible, please let me know asap so that I can try to find someone else.

I look forward to hearing from you.
Best regards,
Colombe Deschamps

Now I DID REMEMBER that quick phone call. As I was busy, I'd asked her to call me back later. As for the other messages, I didn't get them. They must have been on my private phone, the one that Cynthia regularly put her hands on. Now I understood how the messages from a girl named Colombe, asking to meet me, had disappeared from my voicemail, magically...

As I was sorry to have left this young student

without a response for so long, I immediately wrote back.

From: `Jerome Bastaro/NBF`
`To: Colombe Deschamps`

Object: `Re: Following our phone conversation`

Dear Miss Deschamps,
`Thank you for your reminder. I didn't forget you, I just had a few problems with my voicemail.`
`Please don't hesitate to contact me on 06.24...`
`Best regards,`
`Jerome Bastaro`

This time I'd given her my professional number, the one that the green-eyed tigress couldn't access.

I dozed off until we reached Marseille. After that I looked at the Mediterranean scenery rushing by through the train's safety glass. Charles Lacassagne's secretary, a lady named Marie-Therese, had told me that someone would be picking me up at the station to drive me to the Negresco Hotel. I would be meeting

Mr. Lacassagne the next day at the holding's head office, in Nice.

The chauffeur was there, holding a little sign with my name on it. He insisted on carrying my suitcase, though I protested, and we walked to a limousine parked in front of the station.

Inside that sumptuous vehicle, I was given a bottle of mineral water, a flask of whisky, as well as all the local and national papers. In just an instant, I realized how wealthy Mr. Lacassagne must be.

He dropped me off in front of the Negresco, where a porter grabbed my bag even before I saw him open the trunk to get it and the chauffeur reminded me that he'd be picking me up tomorrow afternoon at three, so I could meet his boss. Another porter opened the hotel's door and amazed, I discovered its mythical lobby, modestly called the "*Salon Royal*", the one I'd already seen in over twenty French or Hollywood films.

When I went into the room that the Lacassagne holding had booked for me, I said to myself that I'd made the right decision in accepting that "summer job," that had lots of advantages! I was in the "Napoleon Suite." What a privilege! I didn't believe my eyes.

It must have been over 500 square feet. And it overlooked the sea and the *Promenade des Anglais*.

Napoleon, Masséna, for someone who loved the First Empire, it was perfect! I didn't really care though for the golden yellow decoration with imperial bees in the background, nor the portrait of Bonaparte that was right above my head when I laid down on the huge bed with its bordeaux colored sheets.

Enjoying the tranquility and well-being after having traveled for half a day, I zoned out and flopped down on the bed, hypnotized by the soft purring of the AC unit, something that was needed here at the beginning of the summer. I soon fell asleep.

My cell phone woke me up with a jolt. I hadn't got undressed before hopping onto the bed and it was vibrating in my pocket. I took it out and saw the tigress's name on the screen.

Already! I had the feeling that it would be hard to get rid of her. I didn't answer and left Cynthia's exhausting logorrhea on my voicemail. I threw my phone on the bed, ran into the huge bathroom, got undressed and took a long shower, as if cleaning myself of those bittersweet memories of my new ex-girlfriend.

Fifteen minutes later I came back out, refreshed, shaved and wanted to go out and discover the city of Nice, one I'd never been to before. The patios of the cafés were starting to fill up and people were out and about for happy hour.

I picked up a pair of jeans and a T-shirt and put my phone back in my pocket after having discovered one more text message from the tigress:

Cynthia: Why no answer? U with someone?

I felt like answering: "Hopeless!" but I decided not to say anything. I didn't want to exhaust myself with useless texting and even deleted her voice message before I got to the end. The first sentences were enough for me.

I gave the concierge my key, he thanked me as if I had just saved his life, and then allowed the porter wearing an improbable hat with a red feather in it to open the double doors for me. I really was pumped to make the most of this opportunity in Nice to forget the Parisian morosity, and while I was at it, boost my modest journalist career.

While I was wandering around in the Old City, my phone rang again. I sighed, thinking: "Not her again!" but discovered "Unknown caller" on the screen. Was the tigress trying to play a trick on me to make sure I'd pick up? She certainly was capable of something like that. On the other hand, it could have been my future employer here in Nice, or someone who worked for him, so I decided to pick up. When I said "Hello," a gentle feminine voice responded.

"Mr. Bastaro?"

"Speaking," I murmured, still fearing that this would be Cynthia.

"This is Colombe Deschamps, you gave me your number in the email this afternoon."

"That's right. Hello. Nice to meet you, Miss Deschamps. How are you?"

"Fine, thanks, and you?"

"Great. It's almost happy hour, so it could be worse. So, tell me everything."

"Like I explained earlier, I have to shadow and observe a journalist doing his work on a daily basis, and as I really appreciate the way you write, I would like to do this with you."

"That's nice of you. Any dates?"

"As I just finished my school year, I've got all summer. Meaning I could start tomorrow if that's all right for you!"

I was a bit taken aback by her ease in organization.

"Um, well, to put it bluntly I'm not actually working on a typical task here. I mean that I'm not reporting right now."

"Ah! I see. That's too bad then. Can I ask what you're working on now? Why did you come to our beautiful city of Nice? Does it have anything to do with the last elections?"

"Not at all! I never deal with politics: too devious!"

There was a lull in the conversation and at the other end of the line, I could feel her disappointment. I tried to fill in the gap.

"I don't really know if I'll be able to help you. The job I'm working on now isn't exactly what you need for your thesis."

"Could you explain what you're doing then?"

I quickly thought things over, trying to analyze whether the fact of having an "intern" would be beneficial or not. I decided to trust my intuition though.

"Okay Miss Deschamps, here's what I can offer you: let's meet up tomorrow, same time, and we'll talk about all of this over a drink. And then both of us can have an informed opinion about whether to continue. It that okay with you?"

"Perfect!" she said, enthusiastically. "In the worst-case scenario, I'll at least be able to finish the "Interview with a Professional" part for my report!

"Great, let's say seven then at..."

I quickly looked at the name of the bar where I was sitting.

"The Master Home, Rue ... wait a sec... Rue de la Préfecture, you know where it is?"

"I do. See you tomorrow then. And thanks so much, Mr. Bastaro, have a nice evening."

"See you tomorrow."

Two hours later I went back to my room at the Negresco, after a couple of glasses of pastis and a traditional Niçoise salad: not too original for my first meal here, but it was delicious.

As I fell asleep, I was thinking that the next day I'd be successively meeting one of the richest men in France for whom I'd be working, and then a young student in journalism with a joyful lilting voice who wanted to see me at work.

I was far from imagining that those two meetings would turn my life upside down.

CHAPTER 9
Did they dream of jewels and gold?

THE NEXT DAY, I left the hotel and met Charles Lacassagne's chauffeur who was right on time, with a gloved hand ready to open the back door of the black limousine.

I got in, just like a diplomat, smiling, musing over what those who saw me must have been thinking. I also wondered what the very rich, for whom this was an everyday occurrence, must think. Did they still notice the little people who envied them? Did they still know what middle-class French people did every day? Did they only dream of jewels and gold, like Uncle Scrooge, swimming in his golden coins?

I began to speak to the chauffeur because I was uncomfortable, alone in the back seat, like some sort of oligarch that I certainly wasn't. He said his name was Dominique and that he'd left Corsica where he was born to become "Monsieur's" chauffeur forty years ago.

"Exactly forty years this year," he added proudly. "I began serving him in 1975, when I'd just turned twenty. And I've never left."

"A credit to you," I agreed, admirative.

"I can tell you that I know Nice at the tips of my fingers, as well as the outskirts, the coast, from Italy to Marseille."

"You must have driven a lot then for him.

Perhaps the key to success?" I asked, without conviction. What the heck did I know about success? Next to nothing.

"Are you familiar with the region, Mr. Bastaro?"

"Not much. I'm counting on my mission here and your immense local knowledge to discover it."

"My pleasure! But of course, Monsieur will have to decide."

"Of course."

We remained silent for a few minutes. Dominique, paying attention to his driving in the long sedan with its tinted windows, and me, looking at the sea and the splendid *Promenade des Anglais* while driving towards the airport.

In a few minutes we were there, in a district that must have been the business district, if all the banks that were there meant anything.

"Here we are," confirmed Dominique.

He opened the door and escorted me into the building, where after having taken the elevator for a few seconds, we entered the head office where a lady, about fifty or so, was at the front desk.

"Marie-Therese, could you please tell Monsieur his guest has arrived? Mr. Bastaro, I'll be in front of the building when you're finished."

Then he disappeared while the secretary pressed the interphone button.

"Your guest is here, sir."

She listened to the answer, got up, and invited me to follow her to a hall on her right. A door was ajar at the end of the hall. We went into a vast office with modern comfort. An elegantly dressed elderly man with white hair was sitting behind the desk, with luminous eyes and a friendly smile on his lips. Charles Lacassagne!

"Mr. Bastaro! I've been expecting you. I'm delighted that you accepted my job offer!"

He winced as he got up and held his hand out to me, one that was both firm and gentle, the hand of an old person who had known how to take good care of himself.

"Pleased to meet you, Mr. Lacassagne," I answered sincerely.

"Sit down, please. "Oh! Marie-Therese, could you please bring the contract we prepared? Would you like a cup of coffee, young man?"

"Yes, please."

"Marie-Therese, one coffee and my infusion then."

"Of course."

And she quietly stepped out. Charles Lacassagne went back to his desk.

"Do your accommodations suit you?"

"Really, Sir! I wasn't expecting... I mean... the Negresco! It's certainly not necessary to spend so much money just for a hotel. An ordinary hotel is fine for me."

"I wanted you to be at ease, in a quiet place, one where you've got room enough to move around and comfortable for when you'll be working on transcribing our discussions."

"Thank you very much, I certainly appreciate the value of your gesture."

"That's an important word. During my life, I quickly understood that there's a huge difference between the cost and the value of things."

"I agree with that," I said politely.

"You'll see, the theme of money will be dealt with often in our discussions, as money was an integral part of my life. I earned a lot of it, with perseverance, craftiness, and sometimes good opportunities, but I've always respected its value. I'm a man with many values: I was raised with Christian and republican values, respecting people. But we'll talk more about that later on."

"Of course. Speaking of which, how would you like to work? Have you already thought of that?" I asked, coming back to the practical aspects of the job.

"To be honest with you, I've got a general idea of what I'd like to see in this testimonial: I'd like to explain to any eventual readers that money is nothing if it hasn't been earned honestly and it doesn't contribute to personnel and domestic happiness."

I'd started taking a few notes.

"I see. You'd like people to understand that even though you've built a huge financial empire, you are still a man, a father, a husband? Is that right?"

"Absolutely!" said Lacassagne, enthusiastically. "I can already tell I made the right decision when choosing you. You understand quickly and I'm sure that you're better than I am at writing things. During my life, I've written more contracts than novels!"

"Everyone should stick to what they know."

Then we heard two gentle knocks on the door.

"Come in. Marie-Therese, thank you. We were just talking about contracts, here's the one that I've prepared. This one is for you, I'll let you read it."

I took the two sheets of paper that were simply a typical public writer contract between Charles Lacassagne, who would be talking about his life, and Jerome Bastaro, who would be writing what he said. Outside of the process, which included: discussions with note-taking, recording, writing, planning the book, a first draft, corrections, rewriting, and the final proof, the contract spelled out my compensation, guarantees and commitments of each of the two parties. Then I saw something I didn't like.

"Excuse me, Mr. Lacassagne, but I'd understood that my name would be on the book, as the joint author with you. It doesn't seem to be the case here."

Charles Lacassagne swallowed his mouthful of tisane before answering.

"That's true, I changed my mind. With this

contract though, you'll have an advantage. Let me explain. With a joint signature, of course, we share the copyright, but just imagine that the book doesn't sell. Who cares about the life of an eighty-year-old guy who became a millionaire? With my network, I'd sell probably a couple of thousand books. Would a proportional compensation be enough to pay you for your time listening to me rattle on, writing everything down and putting it into a readable book?"

"Well, that depends on the percentage you'd grant me."

"Of course. Nonetheless, in this case we're betting on sales, without any guarantees. And you're worth much more than that, I'm sure."

"That's nice," I said ironically.

"No, what I'm offering you is much more: I'll sign the book, alone and be the sole owner of it, you'll be in the background writing an interesting story, with style and literary content. In consideration of this, you'll be paid a flat fee."

I mentally thought about the idea of working as a "ghostwriter," because that was what he was talking about. I'd be anonymous, wouldn't see my name on the cover of the book, but on the other hand I'd quickly be paid for this which would help me butter my bread. Then "the" question.

"So how much would this flat fee be then? I see here nothing's written down."

"I thought I'd let you fill it in. How much would seem fair to you?"

I had no answer to his question. Figures were dancing in my head. I couldn't give him an answer that would seem to be ridiculous or on the contrary, indecent. I was a writer, not a financial wizard: figures were Greek to me. Finally, Lacassagne continued.

"How much time do you think you'll need to draft the final version?"

"It's hard to say now, but as a ballpark figure, I'd say about two months."

"And how much do you make a month, Mr. Bastaro?"

"A little more than two thousand euros."

"So, if you think you'll be working on this project for two months then, that would be roughly four thousand euros, if you work full-time."

"I'm following you up to now."

"And would that be enough?"

I laughed at his unabashed candor with monetary negotiations.

"You like to play, Mr. Lacassagne!"

"Ha ha! A privilege of my age. And my professional experience. So Jerome, may I call you Jerome? Let's not dilly-dally. You could be my grandson!"

"Of course."

"So, Jerome, like I said: let's not dilly-dally. Take this pen and write: fifty thousand euros."

"What?" I gulped out.

"Fifty thousand: a five with four zeros after it! Plus of course room and board at the Negresco, you just have to give your expenses to Marie-Therese."

"But... why me?"

"Let's just say that it's what a crazy old man wants. A last whim at the end of his life."

"You mean..."

"I just mean that no one lives forever! I've already had a good life. Lots of people never reach my age. Sometimes life just isn't fair. To make a long story short, I know that my spool doesn't have a lot of thread left on it. That's why I made this double decision: firstly to let go of the reins of the Lacassagne holding and then to leave a written testimonial of my professional success. And that's where you come in."

"Thank you for trusting me. But why so much money?"

"You don't want it?" he said, cutting me off.

"That's not what I said."

"So, a done deal! With fifty thousand euros I'll be purchasing your complete involvement for two months or more if required. Wait for me here, I'll be back in a minute. When I walk back in, I want to see your signature at the bottom of the contract. If not, I'll rip it up and look for someone else."

With that, he got up from his imposing armchair and went out of the office, slowly, but majestically.

I had just enough time to ask myself a host of questions, to imagine different scenarios in which I saw myself with all that money that represented nearly two years of my current income. What did I have to lose? Spending the summer in the French Riviera, listening to the souvenirs of an old stick-in-the-mud millionaire and putting them all down in a book that wouldn't be mine, but would be paid fifty thousand euros.

I'd already made my decision when I heard my new boss walking back, with his soft footsteps accompanied by others, who were more assertive.

"Mr. Bastaro," said Charles Lacassagne, "I'd like to introduce my son Edouard to you."

I saw a tall man, with greying blond hair, whose blue eyes could be seen behind a pair of round glasses. Though twenty-five or thirty years younger than his father, you could see he'd look just like him.

"So. You must be the journalist and author then?" he asked, holding out his hand to me.

I thought I detected a bit of contempt or suspicion in his snappy voice.

"That seems to be my role," I replied, handing his father the two pages of contract that I'd signed.

Charles Lacassagne smiled and turned to his son.

"Edouard, please make yourself available to Mr. Bastaro each time he needs to talk with you. I'm sure he'll have questions that he wants to ask you about our family's history, as you're one of the most important members."

"Of course, father. Right now though, I've got an appointment with Mr. Roetger, our notary, so if you'll excuse me."

"Of course, son. Don't be late."

"I'll see you soon, Mr. Bastaro."

I felt like that was just a polite formula for him.

Charles Lacassagne sat back down in his armchair. He signed the contract and was writing out a check.

"Here you go Jerome, the upfront payment in accordance with our contract, fifteen thousand euros. I'll give you the same amount when you give me the first draft and then the remainder when the book is ready to be published. Do you agree?"

"I certainly do," I nodded, putting that highly symbolic piece of paper in my wallet.

When I joined Dominique at the car, he was speaking with Edouard Lacassagne. When Edouard saw me, he squinted at me behind his round glasses and walked away, without a word, with a nasty looking smile on his lips.

CHAPTER 10
The dark waves of the Mediterranean

AT ABOUT HALF A MILE FROM the Lacassagne holding's head office, that same evening, a very stout man was walking towards the line of taxis waiting in front of the Nice Airport. He was pulling a large suitcase behind him.

Upon smelling the sweet sea breeze, he took a deep breath. The fragrance of Nice by night seemed to please him. He pushed a lock of his greying hair out of his eyes and went into the first cab.

"To the Coq Hardi Inn, please," he said, with a bit of an accent in his excellent French.

"Right away, sir. Would you like to drive along the magnificent Promenade des Anglais?"

"Thank you, yes," he answered sinking into the comfortable leather seat of the Mercedes.

He'd just spent long hours squeezed into the seats in tourist class: sometimes his overly abundant waistline was a handicap. He'd had to stop over in Paris, as there weren't any direct flights to Nice.

He stretched his legs and back and began to enjoy the scenery of the dark waves on the Mediterranean Sea.

CHAPTER 11
A singsong voice from Nice

"MR. BASTARO?"

I looked up in the direction of that voice I'd already heard on my phone. I saw a short black skirt and two tanned thighs. Then I raised my head, looked at a face with a big smile on it and twinkling eyes and a head of long brown hair falling down to her shoulders. She put her hand out to me, and I naturally shook it.

"I would imagine that you're Colombe?"

"Such insight!" the young lady answered, laughing. "You're right. Pleased to meet you!"

"Likewise," I answered, still shaking her hand with its long gentil fingers. "Have a seat."

I quickly moved my stuff over on the little bistro table, awkwardly piling up several sheets of paper where I'd started to plan how to carry out my upcoming interviews with Charles Lacassagne.

"Thank you so much for your time," said Colombe, with her sweet singsong voice from Nice.

"No problem, I'm happy to help students in journalism. I was once one myself you know. What would you like to drink? Sorry, I've already started with a cocktail. It's hot outside here. But another pastis would be welcome."

"I'll try their mojito."

I ordered for us.

"Well? How could I help you?" I asked.

"So, like I said, for my final dissertation, I have to shadow a journalist for a few days, ideally a week or two actually in 'immersion,' as they call it."

"What's the subject of your dissertation?"

"The art of asking THE disturbing question... without confrontation."

I see, the importance of diplomacy during interviews."

"Something like that, yes."

I thought things over before continuing.

"And what I'm doing in Nice could be a part of this? Of course, I'll be interviewing someone, meaning I'll be asking him questions about his ideas, projects and all that stuff to publish the content. The hic is that what I'll be doing isn't really journalistic work as it won't be published in a newspaper. And I don't think there will be any 'disturbing' questions."

"There won't?"

The server came with our drinks. I raised my glass of pastis in a toast.

"Cheers!"

I enjoyed a sip of that nice cool aniseed flavored

drink while Colombe sipped her mojito through a straw. I continued.

"It's more of a task for a public writer. To tell you everything, today I was hired by Charles Lacassagne, the real estate magnate, ever heard of him?"

"The developer?"

"Yup. The guy who founded the empire that made him a millionaire. Now he's eighty and he wants to leave a trace of his life. I'm in charge of gathering his oral memoires to turn them into an autobiography."

"That means that you won't be signing the book, otherwise it would be a biography."

"Exactly: I'll be the ghostwriter and he'll be signing my book. What do you think? Interesting enough to shadow me for a week or two?"

I could see that Colombe Deschamps was thinking this over while sipping her mojito. The pros and the cons. She'd finally decided.

"That could actually be really interesting for me. I mean, interviewing someone like that who everyone knows, a benchmark in the south of France, money coming out of his ears. Everyone can't say they've done something like that. I'd love to."

"I understand, when you consider it under that angle."

"But there's more."

"Like what?"

"Well, I imagine that outside of your discussions, you'll need some documentation? Stuff to flesh out your story? Make it more alive, realistic, rooted in its environment and times."

"Keep going."

"For that, you'll have to do research, go through archives, consult official documents. Something that takes time - time you won't have to write."

"I see where you're going with that. I think that could be interesting for me. Convince me. Just one sentence."

Colombe thought it over and summed it up.

"I'll be your assistant for this job. The ghostwriter's ghostwriter! The writer's shadow!"

I burst out laughing.

"Good arguments, Miss Deschamps. I like them. I feel like I did ten years ago when I started out."

"Plus, icing on the cake, it won't cost you a penny! It's volunteer work because it's homework!"

I finished my pastis before continuing.

"Fine with me. But I still have to run this by Mr. Lacassagne, we've signed a contract, make sure you can be there during our discussions, taking notes, for instance."

"That's understandable. Okay! I hope he'll accept! That would be a chance of a lifetime for me! I can't wait!"

Colombe Deschamps did seem to be excited about shadowing me in this adventure.

As for me, being accompanied by such a nice and cute student also delighted me. Her twenty-three years of age, compared to Charles Lacassagne's eighty would be refreshing.

These next two months in Nice were going to be very pleasant ones.

She left a few minutes later after I'd promised to contact her once I'd received approval from the millionaire.

Smiling, she held out her hand.

"Hope to see you very soon then."

CHAPTER 12
His last hurrah

THE DOOR OPENED, revealing the silhouette of a stocky man wearing glasses and a cowboy hat. He walked up to the front desk and Marie-Therese tactfully greeted him.

"Sir? How can I help?"

The man took off his hat, putting the beige-colored Stetson on the counter. When he began to speak, she could tell he had a slight accent.

"Hello Ma'am, I'd like to speak to Mr. Lacassagne. This is the head office, isn't it?"

"That's right. Who would you like to speak to? Mr. Charles or Mr. Edouard?"

Then man paused, thought that over.

"I'd like to speak with Mr. Charles Lacassagne. He's the boss here, isn't he?"

"Yes, he is. I'm sorry though, Mr. Charles is out of the office today. Can I leave a message for you?"

"I'd rather see him in person. Could you phone him and tell him I'll meet him here?"

"He's not here today. I can't bother him, I'm sorry."

"It's really important."

"May I have your name please?"

"It's even urgent you could say."

"Your name, please?"

"Angel Sharpers."

Marie-Therese picked up a pen to note his name on the visitor's registry.

"How was that again? 'Ann-gel Sharpei'"?

The man smirked.

"Hand-gel Char-peur" if you prefer. Really though Ma'am, I'd appreciate it if you could try to reach him. Like I said, it's quite important, and rather urgent. I'm sure he'll want to meet me as soon as possible."

Marie-Therese sighed, visibly irritated by the sudden intrusion of this unknown person with an… American… accent?

"What's this about?"

"Please tell him that I'd like to speak about the transfer of the Lacassagne business."

"Transfer?"

"Yes, I believe that Mr. Lacassagne is about to, let's say, let go of the reins?"

"You seem to be well informed."

"It's common knowledge. You'd have to live on the other side of the world or on a desert island not to know that. Mr. Lacassagne is well-known in the media.

I have to meet him as soon as possible about this. Please."

"I'll see what I can do," the secretary conceded.

She picked up her phone and pressed button one:

"Sir? I'm terribly sorry to bother you, I know you're with the Parelli brothers, but I've got a man right in front of me who says he absolutely has to speak with you."

...

"Someone named 'Ann-Jill Charmeur...'"

...

"It's about the transfer of your company, Sir."

...

"Perfect, I'll tell him."

And she hung up.

"You're lucky, unless it was your name that made him decide. Mr. Lacassagne will be back in half an hour or so. Could you come back?"

"I'll just wait here, if that's alright with you."

"In that case, we've got a waiting room. Just follow me."

Marie-Therese led Sharpers to a small, windowed room that had three large leather armchairs surrounding a coffee table with several magazines on it. There was something for everyone: finance, sports, local papers, foreign papers, all organized by theme.

"Can I get you anything to drink? A soda, perhaps?"

"A glass of water would be fine, thank you."

Charles Lacassagne closed his cell phone and turned to the Parelli brothers.

"I'm sorry gentlemen, I've got to deal with something urgent at the office. Let's finish our visit and meet for lunch later this week to talk things over. Of course, you'll be my guests. I'll ask Marie-Therese to set things up."

Charles and the Parelli brothers were overlooking the city of Nice from the high hills, walking through a lot that the two brothers had finally decided to sell, for a price and conditions that had not yet been decided. Charles had arguments and years of experience in that. He had been wanting to purchase that huge piece of scrubland for years now, but the Parelli brothers had never wanted to sell. That would be his last challenge, his last triumph, his most ambitious project. He was dreaming of building a gigantic complex of medicalized senior residences there. At that altitude, the air was pure, the view overlooked the immensity of the Mediterranean, amid the fragrances of Provence. This would be a very profitable project, one more manna for the holding. Charles and his architect had drawn up the plans. He'd carefully prepared things, chosen contractors he could trust, with whom he'd already worked, and he'd even selected the doctors who would be heading this residence, one that he'd named: "Hellebores", the name of that flower that symbolizes a resistance to time. In a nutshell, everything was ready for that to become another cash cow for him!

It would also be his last hurrah, the last project he'd be heading himself, before giving the reins to his children, Edouard and Marie-Caroline, and to retire, going back to the home he was born in: Villa Gorbio, just a few miles away as the crow flies.

~

Angel Sharpers, comfortably seated in one of the leather armchairs, was reading the New York Times, to see what was going on back in the States. He'd already been waiting for roughly an hour now. Marie-Therese had already come back twice to apologize for Charles being late, offering him another glass of water, that he'd refused politely.

Raising his eyes from the paper, he saw a man wearing round glasses with greying curly hair walk by. He looked both serious and upset and was wearing a strict grey suit with a black and grey tie.

That must be the son, Sharpers mused. Edouard Lacassagne.

The American smiled wryly before going back to reading his paper.

~

"Oh, it's you. Your visitor is waiting for you," said

Marie-Therese, relieved, to her boss. "A curious person," she added.

"Thank you, Marie-Therese."

Charles quickly went to the waiting room.

When Angel Sharpers saw him, he jumped up, the New York Times falling off his lap. He bent down awkwardly and tried to reorganize the double pages of the paper, hampered by his huge pendulous abdomen.

"Don't worry," Charles Lacassagne said with a smile. "So, who are you?" he added, holding out a well-manicured hand.

"Angel Sharpers," he responded, shaking it.

"I've been told you're impatient to meet me?"

"Thanks for fitting me in. I indeed do have a very interesting proposal for you."

"Please follow me, Mr. Sharpers."

The boss walked in front of him to his office, invited him to sit down in an armchair in front of the acajou desk, and then sat down in his own luxurious seat.

"I'm listening. I don't have a lot of time, so please cut to the chase."

Sharpers cleared his throat.

"Time is money. Everyone in the States always repeats this. So, it's about the sale of your company."

"Well, who told you I wanted to sell?"

"No one. On the other hand, what if I told you I'd like to buy?"

"Interesting. I'm not sure however that you'd be able to acquire a company like ours."

"Mr. Lacassagne, what do you know about my financial means?"

"Nothing. I don't even know a thing about you! I'd like to know more about your 'pedigree,' Mr. Sharpers, that's it, isn't it?"

"As for myself, nothing interesting. I'd just like you to know that I'm American."

"And you're completely fluent in French. How did you learn to speak it so well? Were your parents French?"

"My mother was."

"And why the heck are you interested in my company in particular? Why would an American be interested in a small French investment holding?"

"You said small? Mr. Lacassagne, you're being modest here! Your reputation has already gone beyond France, and you know it. You're one of this country's richest persons."

Charles burst out laughing.

"Flattery will get you nowhere, but good try. So you want to acquire shares in one of France's largest fortunes then? Meaning that yours is even larger?"

"Don't worry about that. Like you say here, I've got a good backbone."

The two men glared at each other: it was like two cowboys ready to have a shootout. After a long pause, Charles continued.

"Specifically, how do you hope to do this?"

"Quite simply. Legally. With a takeover bid. Your

company is listed on the stock exchange, so it's easy to make an offer."

"That I could refuse."

"Only once, you know that."

"I recognize your American methods there, Mr. Sharpers."

"Mr. Lacassagne, believe me that I would have preferred for us to agree here. But if things don't work out, nothing prevents me from initiating a public takeover bid."

Charles wasn't shocked: you could tell he was used to negotiating. For nearly fifty years now, he'd been heading profitable businesses that led him to become one of France's wealthiest persons.

"I must admit that up to now, I hadn't considered this. But if it's so important to you... And in my opinion if you came all the way from the States to our beautiful city of Nice just to speak to me, you must be serious. I'll have to think about this. You know Mr. Sharpers, I'm at the head of a 'family-owned company,' so I'm sure you know that I'm not the only decision-maker here. I'll have to talk with my wife and children, who are also stakeholders in the company."

"That's legitimate," conceded the American.

Lacassagne got up, a sign that this meeting was over.

"You can give me two days?"

"Of course. But only two. Whatever your decision is after those two days, I'll be putting in my takeover bid before going back to New York."

"I'll show you out," concluded Charles, holding out his hand to Angel Sharpers.

∽

When Sharpers left Lacassagne's head office, Charles asked his son Edouard to join him. They spoke for over an hour, and after that Dominique drove the father back to Villa Gorbio and the son returned to his apartment in Vieux-Nice, the historic and most beautiful part of the city.

CHAPTER 13
Touting what's false to find out what's true

TOUTING what's false to find out what's true

Edouard closed the heavy wooden door of his apartment, where Malabar, his elderly cat, was waiting for him. The poor pussy would have liked to leap into its master's arms, as it did just a few months ago, but couldn't jump anymore because of its rheumatism, so all it did was rub its little nose against the bottom of his slacks and mew softly, a pure formality.

"My little Malabar, lucky I have you," said Edouard, running his hand through his fur on his backbone.

Edouard, now over the age of fifty, lived alone in a luxurious apartment of over 1,300 square feet located right in the historic district of Nice. This was just one of the many properties that the holding had acquired over the past few decades. Since his separation with Julie Schneider, he'd decided he was better off alone. In spite of that, he continued to go out, meet new people, and have fun at parties that were sometimes a bit on the wild side. In a nutshell, his life now consisted of three things: working in his family's holding, spending money without counting, and taking care of his old Malabar. Edouard's Holy Trinity: in the name of the Father, the Cat and the Holy Party.

Edouard emptied a tin of cat food into Malabar's Hello Kitty bowl, flopped down in the couch, and mechanically turned on the TV to listen to his favorite channel: BFM Business. He muted the sound, just reading the news banners on the bottom of the screen, took his cell phone and clicked on one of his favorite contacts. On the other end of the line, a masculine voice answered.

"Hey Philippe, how's it going?"

"Hey, Edouard! Not bad, what about you?"

"I have to talk to Caro. Is she there?"

"Caro! It's your brother. She's coming. Are you okay? You seem tired, Edouard."

"The routine, Philippe, the routine. Don't worry, but thanks for asking."

"Okay. Here she is. See you soon? Why don't you come have lunch with us one of these days? The girls love seeing their uncle, you know."

"I know, I've got so much work. I'll see what I can do. Bye Philippe, and thanks."

"Ciao."

After a moment of silence, Marie-Caroline picked up the phone.

"Hi, Doudou. Why are you calling so late?"

"Caro, there's stuff going on lately that I don't like."

"What are you talking about? Do you have a problem? You're not sick, are you?"

"No, it's the holding... It's Dad."

"What, Dad? He's okay, isn't he?"

"Yeah, he's fine. You haven't heard of his latest whim?"

"Which one? He's had several. Another fantastic deal? He could have told me. At the end of the day, I'm the one who has to smooth things out and take care of the mayor and his cohorts."

"No, actually nothing directly related to the business. So he must not have told you yet. He's decided to write his memoires."

"Really? He didn't tell me. After all, why not? There's nothing bad about that. It's legitimate at his age after a successful life and career, what's bothering you?"

"Like you say, nothing. It does seem to be legitimate. But still, I don't want a journalist, because he's hired a journalist to do this, to stick his nose into our business."

"Hey Doudou, it isn't our business, it's our dad's, it's his life, his career, that's what he'd like to put into words I'd imagine."

"I'm not so sure about that Caro. I'm sure you'll

find out soon. Dad will certainly ask you, like he asked me, to make yourself available to Jerome Bastaro, his ghostwriter."

"Sure, Edouard. Where's the problem? If that can help. You know, that's sort of what I do every day at the holding: speaking, meeting, telling stories, embellishing them. I feel flattered that he wants to include us in his autobiography, that means he trusts us, he counts on us, that we're a... a loving family."

"Well I don't want a journalist to be hanging around under our feet. I don't like people like that: they snoop, dig through garbage, and tell lies to find out the truth."

"What are you afraid of?"

"Dad wants his memoires to include a part of humanity. He wants to show people that beyond his thriving business, he's the head of a family, he's a loving person, that he was able to overcome tragic events, junk like that. You get it?"

"Seems laudable to me."

"Jesus, you don't understand!" shouted Edouard, pushing away Malabar who was purring next to him on the couch.

"Understand what, Doudou?"

"Understand that he'll be stirring up shit! Taking our skeletons out of the closet!"

"Doudou..." Marie-Caroline sighed. "All that is ancient history, and you know that as well as I do. Of course, Pierre-Hugues will be a part of this. We know it! But those wounds are healed now. That was thirty years ago. There's nothing to be afraid of, Doudou. Plus I'm here, don't worry. You can always count on me, okay?"

"Okay, okay... I trust you. But still, bringing all of that back, it gives me a knot in my stomach."

"It'll be okay. I'm there, bro."

"That's not all," continued Edouard, massaging his temples.

"Tell me."

"A strange guy came into the holding this afternoon. He wanted to meet dad. An American. He wants to launch a takeover bid for our company."

"Really? And what did dad say?"

"He wants to talk to us about it. Everyone's invited to Gorbio tomorrow, even mom. A 'family council'! But I wanted to warn you about that before."

"That's nice Doudou. So, try to calm down. It would have been worse had you panicked. I have to go, haven't finished eating dinner yet. See you soon, take care."

"You too. Say hi to the twins for me. Tell them I love them."

Marie-Caroline hung up, closed her eyes for a while, took a deep breath and went back into the kitchen where Philippe and their thirteen-year-old twins, Lauriane and Leana, were finishing their dessert.

"You okay, hun?" asked Philippe. "Something seems to be bothering you."

"I'm fine. Work, difficult situations... Hope you left me a piece of pie!"

Marie-Caroline had married Philippe Micoud, an insurance agent she'd met through work. At that time she was already thirty-five and he was two years older. They'd gone out for several months before deciding to live together in Philippe's apartment in Nice. Then, just like in a fairy tale, they quickly got engaged, got married, and the twins arrived. They'd built a splendid designer home in Saint-Laurent-du-Var, one with a sea view.

Marie-Caroline liked her calm everyday life: a little cocoon where she felt loved, protected and calm.

That night though, in spite of all her efforts to appear relaxed for her family, she had trouble smiling. The phone call she'd had with her brother kept running through her head.

That night she didn't sleep much.

CHAPTER 14
Mum's the word

THE DAY after I met with Charles Lacassagne, serious talking began. We agreed that he'd pick me up at nine at the Negresco. Right on time, the limousine Dominique was driving pulled up in front of the palace. The chauffeur got out and opened the back door for me. And inside was the big boss, a large smile on his face!

"Welcome to my mobile office, Mr. Bastaro!"

I shook his hand, greeting him, and sat down in the fantastically comfortable seat of his sedan. Charles continued.

"You know, I must have spent as much time in my car as in my office. Right, Dominique?"

"It is. Monsieur is telling the truth here. We've driven a long way together. All in all, it would be interesting to see how many times we've gone around the world."

"You could say that I've spent more time with you

than with my own wife," the big boss joked. "Business has married us."

"You're flattering me here, Monsieur," concluded Dominique, carefully driving and looking back into the rear-view mirror.

"Dominique has been my chauffeur ever since the holding began. Did I already tell you that Jerome?"

I mentally noted that he was using my first name again, as he said he would during our first meeting.

"Since when?" I asked.

"Since 1975!" the chauffeur proudly replied.

"What a memory, Dominique," continued Lacassagne. "Jerome, I'm sure that this man should have an important place in the book about my life. You'll have to remember him when you're writing it. Without him, I wouldn't have the possibility to move around like I do for my business. The same is true for the safe way he drives, and the certitude I have of his discretion, allowing me to work when we're on the road. I've often negotiated with people by phone, here in the car, or even with my partners who were sitting in your seat. And I know that Dominique has never said a single word about all those transactions. He knows nearly as much as I do about the holding. That's right, isn't it, dear friend?"

"Mum's the word," Dominique answered. "The conspiracy of silence: I'm from Corsica, and we're the ones who invented the *omerta*!"

"Ha ha! Spoken like a true gangster! Seriously though Dominique, please allow Jerome to interview you, maybe tonight. Would that be okay for both of you?"

"Fine with me!"

We both answered at the same time.

While speaking, we'd already driven a few miles along the *Promenade des Anglais*, a road I'd soon know well. I could see the hot sun through the tinted windows. A notebook and pen in my hand, I lost track of time for a moment looking at the calm Mediterranean Sea. Charles's soft voice brought me back to reality.

"Here's today's program, Jerome. Rather than giving you facts and figures, I thought it might be interesting for you to see what *Immobilière Lacassagne*, as that was its name when I took over my father's business, has accomplished. We'll take advantage of this beautiful weather, almost as if we were tourists, to visit the projects, successes and complexes that I've built in the past decades."

"What a great idea!" I said, enthusiastic about discovering my employer's empire.

We traveled about the entire morning, both in Nice and in some surrounding cities and villages. Dominique did seem to know the region at the tip of his fingers, easily driving us from one part of the county to another, following the instructions of his boss. Charles Lacassagne was inexhaustible when speaking about his buildings. He was even emotive sometimes.

"This is the very first villa I built back in 1975.

Here's its name: *Les Jardins de Lucie* [Lucie's Gardens]. I'm sure you understand."

I understood his emotions. The tribute he'd paid to his wife seemed to be a strong symbol, if not of love, at least of recognition of the part his wife had played in his successful life. I thought I'd put that someplace in the biography to make him more loveable.

We kept on like this, point to point, he was telling me things and I was writing them down, sometimes with a few drawings and recording everything on my Dictaphone. We stopped several times to stretch our legs, allowing me to take photos that I was thinking of including in a colored insert in the book.

"This private hospital here was also signed Lacassagne... This modern hotel complex, one of our holding's most recent investments... See that glass building over there - it's the home to fifty offices... This whole business district, it was yours truly who build it!"

He was as proud as a little kid!

We slowly left Nice and drove towards Saint-Jean-Cap-Ferrat, the peninsula with some of the highest property prices in all of France.

"We'll stop for lunch here," said Charles.

Dominique dropped us off in front of the port and began to look for a parking place while we went to the restaurant where he'd reserved a table for three on the patio.

"I love it here," said Charles. "Perhaps nostalgia, probably linked to events that took place a long time ago, nearly thirty years now... But I've never forgotten them."

I saw a glint in his eye right then, that might have actually been a tear, if such a person could show his emotions and weaknesses in public.

"Let's eat! A redfish would hit the spot right now. When we're finished, we'll go see the boats."

Dominique joined us and each of us ordered a refreshing cocktail called a *mauresque*, made with pastis and barley cordial water, something that I'd heard of but never tried.

It was warm out, the sun reflecting off the calm waves, lapping beneath the metallic pontoons.

A very convivial, and instructive lunch, one that gave me lots of ideas for my project. Charles was inexhaustible about his professional life. He told me about all the history of the Lacassagne empire, starting back when he took over his father's little company, up until now when he was getting ready to hand over the reins to his children, at least the two of them who had the capacity: Edouard and Marie-Caroline. I was eager to meet them, to complete the portrait of their father by the prism of their own lives.

Dominique didn't take part in our conversation, except when Charles asked him something, and in that case, he replied rather laconically. He ate inattentively, contemplating the landing dock. He even got up once or twice to have a cigarette.

When we were having coffee, a group of well-dressed businessmen walked up to us. One of them shook Lacassagne's hand.

"Hello! Charles, I haven't seen you here for ages!"

"Christian! What a pleasure!"

He turned to me.

"Jerome, I'd like to introduce you to an old friend, the mayor of Nice, Mr. Christian Estrosi."

"Vice-Mayor, Charles," he corrected him with a smile. "For a couple of days now."

"That's right, I forgot about the result of the elections. But everything comes to an end sometimes. Look at me, I've finally decided to step down. I think I'm old enough, don't you?"

"You certainly deserve to rest, Charles. Nice and the south of France have both benefitted from your vitality, your initiatives and your business sense. We'll miss you, you know. I have to go now. Call me for dinner, we'll have something simple."

"Of course! I'll ask Marie-Therese to call your office."

The President of the *Provence-Alpes Côte d'Azur* Region walked away as quickly as he'd come, escorted by his suited and booted cronies, who followed him like puppies.

"Jerome, you have to get on well with politicians. And never ever give your own opinion! And never join or support a party! You have to remain free, far from the mess they call politics. Today it's him, tomorrow it'll be someone else. One day it's the right, then next day the left. It's just like musical chairs, but you, if you're above everything, you'll stay in place. Then they'll come to you, and you'll be able to make them eat out of your hand, especially when you've got power and money. You can believe me, Jerome."

I nodded. I was already aware of the strong links between politics and business. They were both interdependent. I'd had the living illustration giving me the key to better understanding the success of the Lacassagne family: influence, power, ruse and experience.

Charles paid the bill and got up.

"Let's go see the boat!"

∼

Mr. Lacassagne had let Dominique go for the afternoon and he quickly disappeared into the old part of town while we headed towards the pontoons.

The Saint-Jean-Cap-Ferrat Marina had an undeniable charm, and I was immediately attracted to it. Full of bustling cafés, restaurants and shops, it was the home to many small yachts and splendid two-masters, some extremely modern and others that seemed to date a bit, though they were all carefully taken care of. Farther away we could see the larger and more luxurious yachts moored in the sea.

Charles guided me easily around the pontoons. He explained:

"You know, Saint-Jean-Cap-Ferrat isn't just for tourists. People from the south of France all take their vacations here."

"I think I've heard of some really huge mansions here."

"Perhaps Nellcote Villa, whose price increased tenfold in not even ten years. Everyone talked about that. In 1999 it was purchased for eight million euros, and in 2007 it sold for 83 million!"

"Exceptional! Had they done a lot of work in it?"

"They may have put in an extra pool, but it boiled down to offer and demand. Speculation! You might want to know that our 'real estate' subsidiary knows what's going on here."

"Lots of good deals?" I wanted to know.

"That's true. Round about 2000 I had an inkling of what was about to come. With a new rich population, especially the Russians. Like Roman Abramovitch, that billionaire who bought the Chelsea soccer club and just loves it here. A large part of our success is due to Saint-Jean-Cap-Ferrat."

While talking, we reached a sailboat in its slip that gently was rocking with the tiny waves, its buoys delicately tapping against the port walls.

"This is it," said Charles Lacassagne suddenly.

I was surprised at the change in conversation.

"What do you mean, sir?"

"The boat on which my oldest son died, about thirty years ago."

That brutal and dry sentence was nonetheless full of emotion, as if time had not erased anything. I said to myself that a tragedy like that must have marked him for life. I didn't know what to respond to that.

"That was back in 1986, wasn't it?"

"Yes, a dark and terrible year for our family. A turning point, maybe. A year that you'll often hear about from all of us, family, friends, employees, and I want it to play a key role in your tale, Jerome."

"Of course, sir," I answered, simply, while checking that my recording device had recorded this informal conversation.

"Help me pull out the gangway."

When it was installed, I helped him step onto it, and we set foot on that infamous sailboat. I had a question.

"Excuse me for asking, Mr. Lacassagne. But if this sailboat was where the tragedy took place, why did you keep it?"

"Hmm. You know, Jerome, I asked myself the same question hundreds of times, especially at the beginning. Why torture myself by keeping this permanent reference of the drama? I nearly sold it once or twice. But then I admitted that this boat would be a tangible proof of Pierre-Hugues when he was young. This sailboat, it's him, it's me, it's the whole Lacassagne clan. Pierre-Hugues loved sailing. He loved it when we set out, hoisted the sails and drifted with the courants, he always stood up on the rail and dove in, headfirst, into the sea."

"I understand."

"He was one with the water, like a fish, he loved swimming, diving, he was good at it, a true athlete. I can still see him doing somersaults when he was diving in. He was so graceful!"

"Something everyone can't do, I agree. Did you often go sailing like that?"

"Once or twice per month, in the summer. My wife was the only one who didn't come with us, she always got seasick."

"So, this boat doesn't have the same symbolic meaning for her then?"

"Honestly? She hates it. She urged me to sell it, right after the accident. And then she finally ended up understanding that it was a symbol for us: her husband and her other children. Including Emilie, she also loved sailing, she would stand at the bow, wind blowing through her hair, and she'd never stop smiling!"

We were walking around on the sailboat's teak deck while speaking. Charles ran the palm of his wrinkled hand across the rail, where he undoubtedly thought of his son when he was diving in.

"Come and see the cabins," he said, taking his keys out. "In sailor's language, we call this the berth," he added.

"I've heard that word before, though I must confess that I have quite a few deficiencies in the nautical world."

"Believe me, it's a specific one. It's a bit of land right in the middle of the ocean, sort of like a home away from home on a capricious sea. Some people think that a sailboat like this one is just a big toy for rich people. It is an investment, but for me, as I was born right next to the Mediterranean, I always knew that one day I'd have one."

"So how much does a big toy like this cost?"

"About a hundred and fifty thousand euros. Then you have to add maintenance and a permanent slip in this quite selective home port. But for me, each time I go sailing, I love it, and it calms me down. Moments beyond the limits of time, where I forget the hustle and bustle of business. I need these hours stolen from my company where all I hear is the wind in the sails and the sound of the hull as it hits the waves... what a pleasure! Would you like to join us next time, Jerome?"

I wasn't expecting that. But to tell the truth, I was dying to go, ever since I first set foot on the deck.

"I'd love to, Mr. Lacassagne. That'll allow me to understand your passion and thus describe it in your biography, as I'll understand how much this boat and the sea are important for you and your family."

Now we were in the cabin, a luxurious space made from different types of wood and leather. As Charles touched the various elements, he continued with his souvenirs of the ship.

"After 1986, it remained docked for several years. None of us wanted to go sailing again. But life goes on. You lift your head back up. You face your fears and their ghosts. Without forgetting, nonetheless. Never forgetting."

I checked that my device was still on as I didn't want to miss any of that improvised confession Pierre-Hugues's father was giving me, that millionaire impacted by fate. But he quickly cut this line of thought off.

"Let's go back, I'm getting tired."

We walked back to the port where Dominique, leaning up against the limousine and having another cigarette, was waiting for us. Charles told him he'd like to go back to Villa Gorbio and asked him again to let me interview him when he'd driven me back to Negresco. The chauffeur nodded.

"With pleasure, we'll talk for a moment on the patio, overlooking the Promenade."

I took advantage of the fact that Charles was a bit less loquacious to bring up the subject of Colombe.

"Mr. Lacassagne, I've got something to ask you, if I may."

"Certainly, Jerome."

"I hope this won't bother you. To make a long story short, a few days ago a young student in journalism contacted me. She's from Nice and for her final dissertation, she needs to shadow a professional journalist in his work."

"And she chose you?" Charles asked.

"That's right, as I was in the region. I explained what I'd be doing here with you and that it wasn't really what you would call journalism. But she insisted, saying that she'd of course heard of your family and that she'd be overjoyed to meet you during her internship. Do you see any drawbacks in her joining me to speak with you and your family?"

Lacassagne smiled.

"Well, considering my extensive experience, I'd say that it's a good idea to help the younger generations, especially as they often have good ideas."

"That's a 'yes' then?"

"In principle. But I don't know if she'll actually learn anything."

"A new experience, I suppose. Plus I have to add that having an assistant for my interviews, but above all for research and documentation for the book, could help make it more factual, help situate it in its geographical, social, historical context and all that. Or even help with writing out what I've recorded and editing the biography. She'll have her work cut out for her. But we'll be more efficient. So, if you accept, I'd like to introduce her to you as soon as possible, even if it's just to put a face on her name."

"Well, have her come tomorrow evening to the villa to meet Lucie and Emilie, who you also don't yet know."

"Perfect! That's very nice of you sir, and very generous too. But I wouldn't like to let that stop you from speaking to me freely when she's there. If so..."

"Don't worry about that," Charles said, cutting me off. "After all, we're working on a confession - true story here. I can guarantee you we don't have anything to hide."

I don't know if I believed that though and even after the car had dropped Charles off at his villa in Gorbio, that sentence was still running through my mind.

CHAPTER 15

Back in prehistoric times

COLOMBE DESCHAMPS still lived with her parents in a little house built back in the 80s in Villeneuve-Loubet.

She sat on the couch and opened her laptop, landing directly on the streaming platform where she could watch her favorite series, 'Once Upon a Time.' When it started, she reduced the window and locked it into the lower left-hand corner of her screen so she could surf the internet while watching. There was so much she wanted to find out.

Ever since she'd met Jerome, she couldn't sit still, anxious to accompany, shadow and help him. She'd never been this motivated about an internship or a paper. Nothing was lacking to please her: summer on the Coast, getting to know Lacassagne, but also, though she wouldn't admit it, shadowing this Parisian journalist who miraculously was in Nice. Like fate was smiling down on her. And she had to fight the fact that he was also candy for the eyes. Plus he was older: thirty at least! Though she wasn't immature, she was only twenty-three.

Anyway. She mentally shook her head to try to focus on her personal task. Exploring the worldwide web.

She googled "Charles Lacassagne Nice" and had a myriad of results, from many different sources. In the couples of lines in the summaries, she had info about the business side of the holding as well as family events. Other sources quoted politics, and many well-known names popped up in the results.

Just like any normal internet user, she immediately went to Wikipedia where she was able to consult his bibliography, his business activities and acumen. She learned that Forbes magazine estimated his wealth to be roughly two and a half billion euros, a sum that included both the holding's equity and the old man's own assets. That made him one of France's ten wealthiest persons, though he was far behind Bettencourt, Arnault, Dassault or Pinault. Colombe Deschamps suddenly regretted that her last name wasn't Dessault, so it would rhyme with the last three billionaires. A hell of a lot of money, she mused. She quickly ran through the post, because to tell the truth, she found it boring, all that talk about money and finance she didn't understand at all. What she loved was the family history, blood ties, and sagas. So, still watching her series with Regina and Emma Swan's intrigues, she paid closer attention to the biography section in Charles Lacassagne's article. She learned that he was married to an Italian woman named Lucie and that the couple had four children: Pierre-Hugues, Edouard, Marie-Caroline and Emilie. Looking at their birthdays, Emilie was much younger than the other three, perhaps a symbol of rejuvenation.

There was a whole paragraph on the oldest son, Pierre-Hugues, who had perished in a tragic accident while out at sea in his family's sailboat.

Colombe clicked on the Google 'images' tab to try to put a face to each name. She was familiar with Charles' eighty-year-old face, as she'd often seen him in the papers or on television but had no idea of what the other members of the family looked like. Especially Pierre-Hugues, who died much too early, even before Colombe was born, like prehistoric times!

She linked the names to the photos and found that there was a family resemblance. Edouard and Marie-Caroline both looked like their father whereas Pierre-Hugues had his mother's features. As for Emilie, it was hard to say who she looked like.

Colombe was lost in her work.

She didn't hear the soft metallic sound.

Plus she was still paying attention to her series.

She suddenly jumped.

Someone was trying to open the door.

Her heart leaped when she understood someone was fiddling with the lock.

She tried to look out of the living room window, but because of the angle, she couldn't see what was going on at the front door. She did though manage to make out two men's moccasins before someone began knocking on the door.

"Colombe, are you there?"

Her father's voice!

She ran to open the door. She had left the key in the lock, as usual.

"Perfect, sweetie! With a technique like that, all the burglars would be scared off!"

"Hi Dad. Hi Mom. How was your trip?"

"Fantastic!" her mother replied. "I'm glad you advised us to go to Barcelona: Park Güell is enchanting. And the Sagrada Familia…"

"I knew you'd love it. Are you thirsty? Something cool? A tea?"

"Sure, a cup of green tea would hit the spot. How are things with you?"

"Fine," Colombe said joyfully, turning the kettle on.

"When are you starting already at the Palais?"

Colombe had landed a summer job as a hostess at the *Palais de la Méditerranée*.

"Normally, July 1st."

"Normally?"

The young lady bit her lip.

"Well, maybe I found something else. A little more matched to my career projects, you could say."

She poured the simmering water into the cups with the teabags in them.

"Tell us more," her father said.

"Well, I met someone and..."

"You're going on vacation?' asked her mom, cutting her off.

Colombe burst out laughing.

"Not at all! It's not a boyfriend, it's a professional opportunity! Remember, for my final dissertation, I have to shadow a professional journalist? And I found one through pure luck. Plus he's here in Nice this summer!"

"Someone well known?"

"No. But that's no big deal. But he does rub shoulders with celebrities!"

"Who with?" asked her mom. "People from showbiz? VIPs? That's what you say, don't you?"

"Yup. You're doing great! Let me explain: do you know the Lacassagne family?"

"Everyone here does," replied her father.

"So, hold on tight: maybe, and I mean 'maybe', because I'm waiting for the confirmation, I'll be shadowing the journalist who will be writing the memoires of old man Lacassagne."

"Watch your language there!"

"Oops, sorry, I mean Charles Lacassagne. Any better?"

"And does that interest you?"

Colombe swallowed a mouthful of her tea before continuing.

"Do you realize it? Maybe I'll be able to go to their house, and all that. I'm sure it must be a mansion! You know there's a private chauffeur who drives the old man around?"

"Colombe!"

"I mean, the patriarch."

The two parents looked at each other, smiling above their cups of hot tea. Nearly together, they continued.

"And this journalist, maybe he's got a name?"

Right at the same time, Colombe's mobile began to vibrate. She nearly fell off her bar stool to pick up. And on the screen: 'Jerome Bastaro.'

CHAPTER 16
If only I knew how to write

"COLOMBE? It's Jerome Bastaro. How are you? Am I bothering you?"

I could tell by the tone of her voice that she was either out of breath or intimidated.

"Hi, yes, speaking. Funny, I was just talking about you to my parents."

"They want me to come over for lunch on Sunday?" I joked.

"If you only knew..."

"Knew what?"

"Nothing. So how are things going with Mr. Lacassagne?"

"Fine, thanks. Actually that's why I'm calling."

I paused; she waited a few nanoseconds before giving in.

"Come on, don't keep me waiting!"

"So, like we said, I told him about you."

Another pause.

"And? And? Please Jerome, don't torture me."

I admitted I'd played enough with her nerves.

"Mr. Lacassagne agrees!"

I let her manifest her happiness and when she calmed down, I continued.

"Charles Lacassagne specifically asked you and I to go to Villa Gorbio tomorrow at the end of the afternoon. Are you free?"

"Of course! I would even hop there if I had to!"

'You won't have to; we'll go together in his limousine."

We agreed on where to meet and I hung up, enjoying the comfort of the limousine. We'd dropped Charles off at his villa and Dominique and I went to Nice, to have a drink and talk about the Lacassagne family.

~

Dominique took me to a little discreet bar, though it was near the Promenade.

"You could say this is my local," he joked, with a hint of his delicious southern accent from his birthplace in Corsica. We people-watched on the shady patio, looking at passersby that the heat of June had partially undressed. Mini-skirts or shorts; baseball hats or straw ones; people passing by on foot, on their bikes or on their skateboards: you could tell that summer and its long vacations were beginning.

"Thanks for showing me this place," I said to

Dominique, after the server had brought us each a glass of Perrier with a slice of lemon.

"I've been coming her for years. I've got quite a few friends from Corsica here."

"You must know the city pretty well by now. You've actually spent your whole career serving the same employer! Something that's rare nowadays."

"It's because Monsieur Charles is a good boss, almost like a father to me. He's fair and he's good. Lots of his rich counterparts don't have the same humility as he does. Especially all those 'nouveaux riches' like those from Qatar or Russia who've moved to the Coast."

"A family company then?"

"That's right. The Lacassagne family! The clan."

From the tone of his voice I was wondering if he admired them or was jealous of them.

"You must know all the family members then?" I asked, hoping to complete my information from a different point of view, one outside of the family.

"If I know them! Of course! I've driven all of them, right and left, day and night, in France and even abroad."

"So your role doesn't stop with driving the boss then?"

Dominique had another sip before answering.

"No, I'm the chauffeur for the holding and the chauffeur for the family."

"Always on call, then?"

"Twenty-four-seven, except during my vacation!" he said with a laugh.

"A true vocation! You must live near them then?"

"Couldn't be truer nor any closer. I live at Gorbio itself. An outbuilding in the villa, so I'm available quickly."

"If I understand correctly, you could have written Lacassagne's memoires by yourself?" I joked. "*Memoires of an Executive's Chauffeur* - not bad for a title, huh?"

"You're right, I could have. If only I knew how to write, like you journalists or authors. But I don't. I only know how to drive and get around: did I tell you I never use any navigation devices? I know Nice and the region by heart."

"Like the taxi drivers in Paris who have to memorize trips and roads for their test."

"Come on," he said, cutting me off. "That's an urban legend, it's been finished for years now. Now they all use Satnav devices, even on their phones! As for me, it's all right here!" he added, tapping on his forehead with a knotty index finger.

Dominique would soon retire. He must have been about sixty-five, sporting white hair that made a nice contrast with his well-ironed black shirts. Slim, he was only about five feet five. A typical Corsican specimen, to tell the truth.

"Outside of Charles," I asked maliciously, "which members of the family to you prefer to drive around?"

"That's a strange question, Mr. Bastaro. Like when you ask kids: 'who do you like better, your mom or your dad?' Can you imagine a kid having to answer that? Okay, it's not exactly the same thing for me... But I'll try to give you an answer. To tell you the truth, nowadays I mostly drive Charles and Lucie around: Charles for work, of course, and Lucie because she doesn't have a driving license. And of course little Lilie. Well, I say 'little' because we've always called her 'little Lilie,' even though she's thirty-six now. I take her to the center on Monday mornings and pick her up on Friday afternoon."

"What center?"

"The ESAT. You know, the center for disabled people."

"Emilie is disabled?"

There was a moment of silence before Dominique spoke again.

"You could say that. It's true though, you don't know her. She'll be there tomorrow at the villa."

I didn't want to insist on that subject that was delicate, so I began asking about the other members of the family.

"What about the others? Edouard, Marie-Caroline, do you drive them around too?"

"Ah, those kids... not too much anymore. They have their own cars. Sometimes I have their father and the two children together, for some work-related meeting or a business dinner. But I've driven them since they were little. You know, I've known them as children or teens.

When I began working for Monsieur, in 1975, Pierre-Hugues must have been fifteen, yeah, that's right, he was born in 1960, and he was nearly a young man then: very handsome, dark hair, and always a smile on his face, always in a good mood. Not at all like his little brother, Edouard, both physically and for his personality. Edouard was a more taciturn and silent child, he rarely laughed. In 1975 he must have been twelve and was already serious: like a little adult in a child's body. Blond curly hair and his Coke-bottle glasses."

"Looks like you're describing an intellectual there, Dominique," I joked, checking that my recording device was on.

He'd told me I could record our conversation.

"Spot on. Edouard is serious, a hard worker, someone who's thorough."

"And Marie-Caroline? I haven't seen her either. What was she like when she was little?"

"She was just a kid when I started. A cute little girl with long red hair and pale skin. Always smiling, a daydreamer too. I really liked that little girl. I drove all of them to school and to their activities. Pierre-Hugues was quite the athlete, Edouard played chess in a club and Marie-Caroline took dancing and horseback-riding lessons."

I continued, feeling that maybe we'd exhausted the theme of nostalgia.

"Are you married, Dominique?"

"No. I wouldn't have had the time to take care of a

wife," he said, laughing. "I did have some lady friends though."

"Your whole life dedicated to the Lacassagne family, then?"

"Right, like a vocation you could say."

I was quite pensive for a moment, wondering how a man could devote his entire life to his job and forget about having fun, forget about having a family. This was something I could not fathom. But Dominique was an old-school man, one born back when serving others still made sense.

I thought that maybe as a young man from Corsica, he had considered himself to be a part of their family, after having spent forty years with them. I also thought he must have been affected by the loss of their oldest son. I decided to ask.

"Tell me, Dominique, can I ask you a question that's ... that's sort of sensitive?"

"Go ahead."

"How was Pierre-Hugues' death for you? You knew him well, ever since he was a teenager."

Dominique seemed troubled by that question. He finished his drink, looking out into the Mediterranean, that immensity that had swallowed then spit back up the cadaver of the family's oldest son, the family he served with so much dedication.

"Hmm. Pierre-Hugues. It's not a secret that I loved that child. To tell you the truth, he was my favorite. I suffered a lot that summer, not like a father of course, but let's say, like an uncle. You know, I'll never forget that July 15th - it's printed indelibly in my mind, as it is I'd imagine like in all the other members of the Lacassagne family. I remember that morning I drove Pierre-Hugues, Edouard and Marie-Caroline to the port of Saint-Jean-Cap-Ferrat..."

∽

Tuesday, July 15, 1986

Dominique took the picnic basket that Brigitte, the housekeeper who was standing at the top of the steps at Villa Gorbio, had handed to him. She'd prepared a few tins of sardines, a big loaf of fresh bread, and two bottles of Bordeaux wine. Charles had told his children, actually no longer children at that age, that they could take a bottle of wine with them to toast their first outing in the sea between siblings.

"Let's go," said the chauffeur, opening the doors to the Lacassagne heirs. Pierre-Hugues sat in the front, as usual, whereas Marie-Caroline and Edouard sat on either side of Lilie, their little sister. She'd insisted on coming with them to the port. But she was sad that she couldn't sail with them. That was only the case when Charles was at the helm.

The three eldest children didn't want a little kid, especially someone like her, hanging out with them. The limousine started up, squealing on the white gravel in the main driveway, while Lucie, Charles,

Brigitte then Simon all waved at the group of young sailors.

"You'll have a great day sailing!" said Dominique as he left the wrought iron gate of the property.

"It's so exciting to be just the three of us for the first time," added Marie-Caroline.

"Be careful then," recommended the chauffeur, paternalistically.

"I'll watch out for the kids," Pierre-Hugues said with a laugh.

"Sure old man!" replied Edouard. "We don't need taking care of."

"Come on guys," said Marie-Caroline.

" Cummon," little Lilie babbled awkwardly.

Marie-Caroline ran her fingers through her hair and gave her a noisy kiss on her plump little cheek.

"Love you, Lilie,"

"Wuv, Caho," replied the child.

It was already hot out at ten in the morning. In three quarters of an hour, Dominique, driving carefully, drove from Gorbio to Saint-Jean-Cap-Ferrat. He didn't want to dent that beautiful limousine, nor endanger all the Lacassagne heirs. Accidents happen all too quickly on the little roads in the mountains behind Nice. Especially in the first part of the trip, between Gorbio, Pinella and Roquebrune-Cap-Martin, with its shoe-laced roads. But Dominique was a good driver. He'd now been working for the Lacassagne's for the past ten years, driving them all over the country. Charles totally trusted him, blindly you could even say, which allowed him to concentrate on his work when Dominique was driving him someplace.

Many boaters and yachtsmen were getting ready to sail when they arrived at the port. Tourists were walking up and down, going into the shops or already sitting down at the many cafes, either for a last cup of coffee or the first pastis of the day.

Dominique unloaded the trunk: the picnic basket and little backpacks for all of them, with swimsuits, Pjs and fresh clothing for the next day. He brought everything down to the galley, and Edouard began to prepare the sailboat.

Little Emilie was happy to be on the deck, though she knew she wouldn't be going with them.

It was finally time to leave. The brothers and sister all waved to Emilie, who was holding Dominique's hand, on the dock. Pierre-Hugues was at the helm and the boat was already at the mouth of the port, then at sea.

Emilie refused to leave before the sailboat had disappeared behind one of the hills, sailing towards Nice, and Lérins Islands.

She and Dominique started off back.

"Lilie, scare."

"Lilie, why are you scared?"

"Boat, Pehu."

Later on, about two in the morning, his boss brutally woke him up to drive him to the Théoule-sur-Mer gendarmerie.

The coastal squad had been called in for the Lacassagne sailboat.

No one said a word driving to Théoule. Both were lost in their thoughts.

On the way back, the boss was despondent.

"It's a nightmare, Dominique. A catastrophe for our holding and a terrible event for our family."

The chauffeur couldn't find any words to ease his boss's mind.

⁓

"It was terrible for Monsieur Charles," summed up Dominique.

We were still sitting outside facing the Promenade des Anglais.

"Awful," I responded. "I don't know how a father, a mother, a brother or a sister can get over something like this. I would imagine that this event impacted their entire lives."

"I'm sure it did. After that, no one was the same. Even now, we don't talk about it."

"Do you think I should ask them about this? The whole family?"

"You can always try. After all, it's up to them to answer or not."

CHAPTER 17
The harrowing whistle of the broken line

CHARLES LACASSAGNE, hunkered down in his imposing armchair, let the phone ring. It was an outside call, one that Marie-Therese at the front desk had transferred to him. He ran a hand through his white hair, sighed deeply, and decided to pick up.

"Hello."

"Mr. Lacassagne? Angel Sharpers here, remember me?"

"How could I forget you?"

"The two days are over Mr. Lacassagne. Were you able to discuss my business proposal with your family?"

"I talked about it with my children and my wife, and my financial advisor was also there. I'm sorry, but I won't be accepting your offer, Mr. Sharpers."

"In that case then, I have no other choice than launching a hostile takeover."

Lacassagne's head was bobbing, both pensive and resigned.

"You do know that I could counter-attack?"

"You could try to find a white knight of course. But the sum involved is quite high."

"Mr. Sharpers. Can I ask you what your motivations are? Why you're interested in my business? Why attack me? Right when I'm about to retire? Why wreck my departure?"

Sharpers was silent for an instant. He heard Charles's respiration on the phone, heavier and heavier. He finally answered.

"I've got my reasons, Mr. Lacassagne. Good reasons. I didn't simply stumble upon you. You'll understand soon. Good-bye, Mr. Lacassagne."

And he hung up.

The phone still against his left ear, his eyes lost in emptiness and his forehead wrinkled by questions he had no answer to, Charles continued listening to the harrowing whistle of the broken line.

CHAPTER 18
The yellow felt ball

"HERE COMES THE LIMOUSINE," I said to Colombe.

We were in front of the Negresco where we'd decided to meet. She came wearing a very nice black dress that looked just perfect on her. High class, a bit sexy even. Perfect to impress old Lacassagne.

She seemed more cheerful than ever: meeting the richest family in Nice, except for the Russians and Qataris.

Dominique was alone. Once I'd introduced them to each other, Colombe sat down in the back seat, and I joined her.

She quickly got along well with him and during our ride there, she marveled at how comfortable the limo was, while looking out at the city that both knew so well. They talked about their favorite districts, which weren't the same, as Colombe preferred Fabron and Dominique, Carabacel. They exchanged a few good addresses of bars, restaurants and shops.

I listened to them babel on, looking out over the landscapes, from the peaceful sea up to the wild and multicolored hills and mountains.

In no time at all we'd reached the villa, where Charles Lacassagne was waiting for us on the bottom of the large hand cut stone stairs.

"Welcome to my ancestors' home," he said loudly.

"Mr. Lacassagne, this is Colombe Deschamps, who'll be working with me this summer."

"Pleased to meet you Miss," he replied, kissing her hand.

She blushed bright red right up to the roots of her hair and replied shyly, something I wouldn't have believed possible for her, as she'd been so spontaneous and lively up to now.

"This is a true honor for me, Sir."

Two people appeared at the top of the steps. A tiny lady with white hair attached in a chignon who must have been Lucie, his wife, followed be another, whose age was difficult to determine, but you could see she was no longer young, and could tell by her features that she was disabled.

"This is Lucie, my wife. And my daughter Emilie."

"So nice to meet you," said Lucie gently, shaking our hands. I immediately thought about Suzanne Flon, the actress, remembering her voice in the movies I'd seen.

Emilie mumbled a greeting without looking at us nor proffering her hand.

The two-storied building was constructed with beautiful ocher-colored stones and each window was framed with splendidly cut white stones. The roof made from orangish tiles was typically Mediterranean.

Charles showed us into the lobby. I could see from the corner of my eye how astonished Colombe was looking at the pictures on the walls and the Etruscan pottery. I personally was less surprised as I'd already visited apartments in Paris in the 16th and 17th districts with similar luxury. I chucked *in petto* to myself.

Charles led us to the back of the house where there was a huge tree-filled park, so big that it was hard to tell where it stopped from the patio where we sat down to have something to drink.

The afternoon was drawing to an end, the sun was still shining high, the air was full of summer Provencal fragrances: lavender and rosemary.

Conversation flowed easily between us. Lucie told us how nice it was to live out in the country here, whereas Charles spoke about the history of the village and the village of Gorbio, then about his genealogy. How the Lacassagne family came to this region to become a family everyone knew, recognized and thought well of. You could tell how proud he was of his patrimony, how much he loved this region and how he respected his ancestors: three key themes for that traditional man.

Emilie was walking around in the park, on the carefully tended lawns, beneath the fruit trees with their carefully trimmed branches.

"She's always loved this soothing park," said Lucie, looking at her.

No one knew what to say here. We watched the young lady wander around from flowerbed to flowerbed, smelling roses or picking flowers. All you had to do was look at her to understand.

Charles got up.

"Jerome, I've got something I want to show you."

Then he turned to his wife.

"Lucie, why don't you show the rose garden to Miss Colombe? Lilie will love that."

"A good idea, Charles. Colombe, you'll see, it's just magnificent."

The ladies joined Emilie and went behind a flowered laurel hedge.

I followed Charles to the other side of the park, where there was a clay tennis court that had seen better days, behind a row of trees. The net was sagging on the ground, the poles were rusted, the lines could barely be seen, and weeds were growing here and there in the ocher court.

"A long time ago, these weeds never would have had the time to grow."

"You played tennis?"

"I did what I could," he answered with a smile. "Though I must say my sliced backhand made them tremble, Pierre-Hugues complained enough about it!"

"I play tennis too, and to have my own tennis court would be a dream come true... But I do live in an apartment," I regretted. It was easy to see that no one had played here for ages.

"I'm nearly eighty, Jerome. My legs and lungs aren't the same as they were thirty or forty years ago. Except for Rod Laver, who is about as old as I am, it's hard for an eighty-year-old to run after a yellow ball. No one's played here for at least ten years. We used it several times when we were having family reunions or charity events. Some guests or relatives used it then. But personally, I haven't set foot on it since 1986."

And right then he put his white leather shoe right onto the clay court. Just like he did thirty years ago, in the past he could never forget, that was omnipresent for him.

"Don't Edouard and Marie-Caroline play?"

"Hmm. Edouard doesn't like sports. He's an intellectual. And Marie-Caroline has never liked racket sports. I nonetheless would have imagined her with a little white skirt, as elegant as Gabriela Sabatini. But no, for her it was riding and dance lessons. I only played with Pierre-Hugues, that's why I quit."

Thirty years later, his oldest son was still on Charles' mind, still alive in his heart: there was a before and after summer of 1986. The year when everything was overturned.

"When he was only fifteen he was already a formidable player!" continued Charles, walking up to the greenish and moldy net. "A fast service and an instinctive volley, so decisive! Why did he abandon us? He'd have known what to do now to get us out of this situation."

I wondered what he was talking about. What situation? But I didn't dare ask, I could see that his eyes were squinting, as if looking back to the past to unravel the present that seemed to bog him down.

Charles, a hand on the white top of the net, was lost in his thoughts.

Back in 1986, in spring. He was thinking of the fragrances of the season: rosemary, lavender, thyme, the sap from the parasol pine trees surrounding the tennis court. And how the clay court smelled after it had been watered a few minutes before.

∽

Pierre-Hugues, that handsome young man, athletic and formidable, his twenty-five-year-old son he was so proud of and who he was counting on, was on the other side of the net.

This son was facing him, ready to serve the match point. He was leading 6-2, 5-1, 40-0 and once again, he was going to clobber his dad, just like he had been doing for the past ten years.

The men both appreciated those moments of complicity around the yellow ball. Charles was the first one to put a racket between his hands. He'd given him private lessons, right there in the villa, with a coach from the French Tennis Federation. Nothing was too good for his oldest son, or for him.

With his left hand, Pierre-Hugues bounced the ball once, twice, three times, while raising his racket with his right hand.

Charles imagined the future of his son right next to him. But what he'd just discovered quelled his certitudes and reshuffled his cards.

Pierre-Hugues threw the ball into the air while bending his legs. His ball was very high.

Very high: that was the position that Charles would give his son in his holding.

Before understanding everything.

The racket whipped through the air and slammed into the yellow felt ball, sending it off far away.

Very far, with an ambitious outlook, a modern touch for a family-owned business, a renaissance, a breath of youthfulness.

That was before he knew who his son really was.

The ball hit the corner of the service square, too far for Charles to reach it.

It was an ace, a decisive serve: his son had won the match.

Charles had lost.

The two adversaries walked up to the net to exchange the traditional handshake.

"Congratulations son!" said Charles.

But his heart wasn't in it. I could hear bitterness in his voice.

Charles took his son's hand then raised his eyes to his face.

And was petrified.

The young man whose hand he'd just shook wasn't the one he'd been mentally playing against.

It was the cadaver with its dark brown color and swollen features, that "Negro's head" that his drowned son now had at the Forensics Medicine Institute in Marseille.

Charles wanted to scream and drop those swollen fingers holding his.

Nothing came out.

He was like a statue.

Breathing was impossible.

∽

I WAS WORRIED ABOUT CHARLES' distant look in his eyes. He suddenly raised a hand to his heart, his mouth dropped open, his eyes rolled.

And he fell over.

∽

COLOMBE WAS HOLDING Lucie Lacassagne's arm and Emilie was walking in front.

"Faster, faster," she laughed, turning around.

They'd been walking for a while now down the paths of the elegant and well-kept-up rose garden.

"Lilie," Lucie said, "you know I can't walk that fast

now. Little Lilie, always so cheerful, poor kid. She hasn't changed that much over time you know. I imagine you recognized her disability?"

"Down's syndrome?" asked Colombe.

"That's one of the risks linked to a late pregnancy. But we assumed it, it was God's will."

"It must not have been easy," the young lady said.

"No, it wasn't. But Charles and I handled it. You could say like all those who admire General De Gaulle, we accepted our fate just like he did with his daughter, Anne. We love Emilie. And without counting, we spent our time and money, so she'd have the best care possible."

"Care? Is she ill?"

"Perhaps you know that Down's syndrome, outside of the visible part of it, the facial features, speaking, and morphology, also leads to a series of troubles and malformations. People suffering from this genetic disease also have trouble hearing, seeing and often have heart problems and have to be operated on at an early age."

"Was that the case for Emilie?"

"It was. When she was just five, she had open-heart surgery. We were afraid she wouldn't make it. But God protects his innocent children, even the weakest."

"Mrs. Lacassagne, I imagine that raising a disabled child must take a lot of effort and time. Were you working too?"

Lucie sighed and didn't answer Colombe's question right away. Emilie joined them and took Colombe's arm, with a huge smile on her face.

"Nice, flowers, Colombe?"

"Yes, it's a beautiful rose garden. Beautiful colors! And they smell so nice!"

Emilie pretended to sniff the air, showing her acquiescence.

They'd arrived at a small stone bench, next to a bed of forsythias.

"Let's sit down a moment," Lucie said.

The three of them sat down, with Colombe in the middle.

Lucie continued.

"I've never worked," she said, as if speaking to herself. "Or at least I never got paid for it. Charles' business took off quickly, so I took care of our children's education, then housekeeping in the villa, which is not a doll's house, as you've seen."

"A full-time job, I imagine."

"Totally. Luckily I didn't have to maintain the grounds, we had a gardener for that. Sometimes Dominique helped out too, when there wasn't any work for him in the holding. Then things got more complicated when Emilie was born. Even a bit before. I was nearly forty when I got pregnant with her. I had to stay in bed quite early on in my pregnancy. So I couldn't manage the house alone. We hired someone to help. Her name was Brigitte, a courageous young lady. Charles hired her. She was a poor single mother, who had just had a baby too, and his father had passed away.

Her little Simon was just a few months older than our little Emilie."

"Simon, Simon," said Emilie, her eyes twinkling, affectionately squeezing Colombe's arm. "Where, Simon?

Lucie ignored her daughter's question.

"Brigitte worked a couple of hours per day. Then when Emilie was born and she was diagnosed, we hired her full-time. She and her cute little son lived with us. Both of them were raised together, like brother and sister, and that put some laughter in the house and also they weren't only children then, as our three others were nearly adults."

"So you had some company plus some help here. Tell me, while I'm thinking of it, does this Brigitte still live around here? Do you think I'd be able to meet her? It would be interesting to get her point of view: if I understand correctly, both she and her son were almost members of your family."

"That's right. At that time she lived in the village, but now I think she lives in Nice. I don't know her exact address, but I imagine it's in the Yellow Pages, under the name Brigitte Garibaldi. You could try to contact her. And do say hi to her if you see her."

Right then, Colombe heard someone shouting. A powerful masculine voice shouting "Help! Help!"

The three ladies jumped up. Colombe and Emilie ran towards the voice, up to the old tennis court.

I was shouting for help as loud as I could.

Charles Lacassagne had collapsed and was having a hard time breathing. I just got there in time to grab his head so it wouldn't hit the concrete slab below the clay tennis court.

His eyes seemed to be glassy, and his mouth was twisted into a mocking sort of rictus, making me suspect he'd just had a heart attack or maybe a stroke.

"Sir, Sir, can you hear me?" I shouted, taking him by the wrist to see if there was a pulse.

Just a few seconds later, Colombe, Emilie and Dominique ran up to me, outdistancing Lucie, from the rose garden and villa.

Lilie's mouth dropped open, petrified by the sight of her father lying on the clay tennis court.

"Call the rescue squad!" I shouted out to them. "I think he had a heart attack!"

Colombe dialed 112 on her phone while I continued to try to track my employer's vital signs.

CHAPTER 19
A certain kind of solitude

THE RESCUE SQUAD CAME QUICKLY.

Charles hadn't totally lost consciousness. They took him in for observation to the hospital in Nice. Lucie was able to accompany him.

As for Colombe and I, Dominique took us back to Negresco Hotel, with Emilie, who seemed to have fallen in love with my young assistant! Then he drove her to the hospital too.

"Jerome, that's awful," said Colombe when we walked into the hotel lobby. "Now what's going to happen?"

"It's hard to say," I answered both for her and for myself.

Charles' attack and his hospitalization had quashed our plans.

"Do you think he'll want to continue?"

"What I do know is that we can't influence the events. All we can do is hope that Charles recovers quickly in the best possible conditions. After that, if he's capable and still wants to, we can continue with our interviews. For now though, I'm going to continue as if none of this took place and start writing what we've already learned. Is that okay with you?"

"If you want."

"Colombe, you don't have to think of me as your boss."

The young lady blushed. That made me smile internally.

"Umm, okay, that's fine with me."

"What about a drink? We can order at the bar and room service will bring it up to my room, pretty classy, isn't it? That way we can debrief. What would you like?"

"If they make them, I'd like a mojito."

I ordered a mojito and a *mauresque* and we walked to the elevators.

When the door closed, I felt that this proximity was making her blush once again. She seemed quite emotive, which was refreshing in my opinion.

We sat down in my suite, and I turned on the TV, a bit mechanically, but also to have some background noise.

"Take a load off," I said, pointing to a beige leather couch with a glass table in front of it.

I sat down in the armchair that was next to it, putting my notebooks, my Dictaphone and a few pens on the table.

There was a soap that I had never seen in my life on

Channel 1. I picked up the remote and flipped to BFM, a continuous news channel that you could turn down or up when you saw a picture or some info on the banner at the bottom that interested you.

Colombe, sitting down like a well-bred and educated little girl, seemed a bit uncomfortable, rubbing her knees with the palms of her hand and looking around my suite.

"So?" I asked. "What did you think of the Lacassagne villa? Was it what you had been expecting?"

"Wow! Even better! So classy. Plus the tennis court, the rose garden, the gardener, the chauffeur, the babysitter…"

"What babysitter?

"The ex-babysitter or rather the lady, sort of like a maid, that they hired when Emilie was born, after they learned she had Down's."

Colombe told me about what she'd learned about that Brigitte lady, whom I'd never heard of.

"I think we should meet her," she continued.

"You're right. You can take care of that?"

"Sure, if that's alright with you."

"Totally! You're my right hand now. Plus that will give me more time to write what I've already gathered."

I heard a knock on the door, and a server entered with our drinks. He put the tray down on the pedestal table next to the door, bowed respectfully and disappeared, after having closed the door.

"Like we're in a James Bond movie!" Colombe said rhapsodically when he disappeared.

"Um, yeah, but I'm not a secret agent."

"But you are on a special mission!"

"Right. Anyway, as long as no hitmen are after me, I'll wear Sean Connery's hat if you want," I joked, toasting her. "Cheers! And to the success of our impromptu association."

"Cheers! And thanks so much for letting me shadow you."

We both sipped on our drinks, and I decided to try to structure our work.

"So, I don't want to make it long here. This is how I see things. For you, the next step will be to find that Brigitte lady, and hope she'll tell us how her life was with the Lacassagne family. In a biography, it's always interesting to have opinions of secondary characters, if I could call them that. Those who work for the powerful, on an everyday basis, but who see, hear and feel the atmosphere, what's going on with the family. For example, I really appreciated my interview with Dominique, the chauffeur, who's known the Lacassagne family for ages now, who saw their kids grow up, the boss get old, the business prosper and expand, all that."

"Lucie said her name was Brigitte Garibaldi. And that she lived in Nice."

"Okay. Try to track her down. And find her! So I'll try to set something up with Edouard, someone I barely saw till now. He seems strange to me though."

"How come?"

"I don't know, just an impression that I had the

first time I ran across him in the holding. Like he was really high-class, or patronizing, I couldn't put my finger on it. He didn't seem to appreciate the fact that his father hired me. We'll see though."

"I'd imagine it all hinges on Charles' health, doesn't it?" Colombe added.

I sighed.

"I do hope he'll be fine. Because here, if he kicks the bucket, no more contract, no more work!"

There was a silence. The situation didn't seem too clear to us anymore.

"What about Lucie? What did you think about her? From a feminine point of view. For me, she's the spitting image of a housewife who does everything it takes for her rich husband and her children. I'm actually quite moved by her."

"Me too. And paradoxically she's both fragile and strong. At the same time, I see someone who has a strong character and convictions. Without knowing why, I also can feel a type of loneliness in her. In her eyes, and sometimes the way she speaks. The way she looks at that poor Emilie. Talks about Pierre-Hugues. You can tell that that tragic accident and her daughter's disability really impacted her and made her stronger, while isolating her in a world of regrets."

I listened to Colombe with admiration. This student seemed to have a keen eye, one that was very perceptive and mature in the way she judged people.

"You're a good psychologist, Colombe! You already saw all of that?"

"I think so. Anyway, I'd like to find out more. See her alone, I'm sure that she has a lot to say and that she's quite at ease with me."

"Fine with me! I'll let you take care of…"

And I stopped right there: the BFM journalist had said something that struck me:

"… *the holding that Charles Lacassagne created. This is Steve Gabard, live from the Paris stock exchange. Steve, this news surprised the whole corporate world.*"

"*Indeed, Marc. We just learned that there's a takeover bid for the Lacassagne holding, though the director just announced a couple of weeks ago that he'd be handing over his shares to his heirs, who are also his associates.*"

"*Do we know who made this takeover bid?*"

"*Of course. Angel Sharpers, an American citizen, made it. We don't yet know if this offer concerns a pension fund or his personal fortune.*"

"*When will we find out?*"

"*All takeover bids are examined by the AMF, the French Market Authority, who must adjudicate on the conformity of the bid. Or to put it simply: they examine the buyer's file. There's a legal delay of twenty-five to thirty-five days to give the AMF time to study the validity of the bid, the financial capacity of the buyer, things like that.*"

"*What do we know about Sharpers?*"

"*Just that he's a rich investor who made his money when Silicone Valley was starting up, back in the 1980s…*"

. . .

"Did you hear that?" I asked Colombe. "They're talking about 'our' Charles Lacassagne. Good Lord, that is crazy!"

"What a coincidence."

"I wonder if Charles already knew."

"What do you mean?"

"I don't know. Just that we get this info right after his attack. Like a public takeover bid is something big. They want to acquire the company. That must shake you up. And when you're eighty years old, something like that can cause problems."

"Like heart problems?"

"I would say so. Well, maybe it's not linked, but it's possible."

"That is crazy," Colombe continued. "And he didn't say anything about that? Like it's so important for his company."

"No. Not a word. But with hindsight, I think he must have been preoccupied, serious, like he was lost in his thoughts, when we were at the villa earlier on. I'd imagine he couldn't get it out of his head. Then he came back to when his son died. All that was like a Molotov cocktail."

When I said 'cocktail,' I was suddenly thirsty and finished off my *mauresque*.

"So, Colombe," I continued. "Let's call it a day. A long day filled with emotions."

"For sure."

"Anyway, right now we can't do anything else. Tomorrow I'll try to find out if this project is still on the books. If so, we've both got work to do. If not, well, I'll take a few days off here in the Riviera before going back up to gray old Paris. Could I ask you to show me around?"

"My pleasure," said the young lady, once again blushing. "I know lots of cool places."

I got up. So did she.

"I'll show you out."

We left the suite and took this tiny elevator once again.

I told her I'd call her the next day.

At night, I ordered a frugal dinner that I ate inattentively with the TV on, while I went through my notes and recordings.

CHAPTER 20
Whatever happens happens

THAT SAME NIGHT, a few miles from the luxurious Negresco, but in a frugal room, Angel Sharpers was also watching TV on a continuous news channel.

Slouched in an artificial leather armchair, his cowboy hat at his feet, his potbelly hanging over his white T-shirt that had seen better and cleaner days, he smiled wryly when he heard Steve Gabard's speech live from the Paris stock exchange.

He grabbed his cell phone, his large greasy fingers trying to type on the alphanumeric keys and wrote a short text message.

"Countdown has started... Whatever happens happens!"

His smile turned into a toothy grin, and he soon began to laugh out loud, alone in his rented room. A pithy laugh from a fat man, making his jowls, chest and huge flaccid stomach all jiggle.

This laugh, one that shook his enormous body, exhausted him. He felt for a fleeting moment that he would suffocate.

His phone suddenly vibrated in his large chubby hand.

He looked at the text message in response to his.

"About time! We're in a hurry."

He quit smiling.

He closed his eyes, put his head back and fell asleep in the armchair squashed beneath his mass.

CHAPTER 21
Closed like a prison door

THE FOLLOWING MORNING, my phone next to the bed put an end to my restless night.

I checked on the time on it. Ten! As I'd had trouble falling asleep, I'd slept in late, in the silky sheets of my king-sized bed, with the benediction of the Emperor, whose portrait was hanging on the wall above it.

I mentally shook myself awake before answering.

"Mr. Bastaro? Edouard Lacassagne here."

This name woke me as well as a large coffee would have.

My boss's youngest son was calling me to give me some news about his father. Charles wanted me to know that he was still expecting me to finish our project. He would be released from the hospital in a couple of days to rest at home. I was to meet him there. In the meanwhile, Edouard was expecting me at the holding to fulfill the chore of answering my questions.

He'd agreed to grant me half an hour of his precious time.

I had a copious breakfast of an omelet, sausages and bacon so I wouldn't have to eat again until that evening. As I had two hours, I decided to walk there. All I had to do was head west, following the coastline.

I went down to the Promenade des Anglais, crossing the boulevard in front of the hotel and decided to go down to the beach. Since I'd arrived in Nice, a few days ago - which already seemed like an eternity to me! - I still hadn't even dipped the tips of my toes into the sea. I wasn't all that keen on beaches and swimming, but still: when you're in Nice in July, right across from the sea and you never even go there, it's a sacrilege.

As I was walking through the water up to my ankles and holding my shoes, my phone rang.

Well! I'd totally forgotten her. The tigress. Cynthia. I didn't feel like picking up. This was too pleasant a moment to spoil.

I clicked on "Answer with a text message" and chose the sentence: "In a meeting, I'll get back to you as soon as possible. Thank you."

And sent it.

I was hoping she'd understand my laconic answer and give me some breathing room, at least until I got back.

I left a message on Colombe's voicemail to tell her how Charles was doing.

I sincerely hoped the Lacassagne patriarch would

recover quickly. Though he was eighty, he'd seemed solid as a rock to me. I was eager to see how he was getting on.

After having left the beach, I was in the business district and soon at the foot of the holding.

It would be a lie to say that Edouard Lacassagne gave me a warm welcome. On the contrary, he was as closed as a prison door, quite unpleasant at first though he later became a bit more cooperative.

I was surprised that the meeting took place in his father's office.

When I was shown in, he was sitting in the same armchair as

Charles was when I arrived in Nice. He didn't get up to greet me, and just pointed at the seat on the other side of the desk.

"Have a seat, Mr. Bastaro," he said coldly.

"Thank you for granting me a bit of your time, especially in these conditions, I mean with your father, who..."

"Let's get down to business," he said, cutting me off. "I don't have time to beat around the bush. I only agreed because I respect my father, a crazy old man who wants to be the hero of a novel. In spite of what happened, he wants to continue with this ridiculous project. Anyway. What do you want to know?"

Not a great introduction to motivate me here, but I decided to try to make the best of things and conduct a traditional interview, without putting my heart into it, just getting the facts.

"Mr. Lacassagne, I'd like to speak to you about two of three things related to your father and the rest of your family and of course this empire that you contributed to building. Could you tell me what job you have in the company?"

"I'm an associate, just like Marie-Caroline, my sister. We have a third of the holding's shares and our father has the other two-thirds. I'm in charge of the financial and accounting departments of the company, my sister takes care of communication, and our father is in charge of strategy, investments and of course, directing the company."

"How long have you worked together?"

"Since forever! Our father conveyed the company's corporate values to us ever since we were little. Personally, I always knew I'd be working in his holding. And as the company grew in size, my father always made it clear he wanted it to remain a 'family' business. I like working with figures, so that's what I studied. At the beginning of the 80s, I did internships here and as soon as I graduated, I began working here full-time."

"All mapped out then?"

"For me yes, I knew I'd be working with my father."

"It must not always be easy to work with your family?"

"Of course, there are ups and downs. But one of the advantages when you have father-son-daughter associates is that when you have to make decisions or solve problems, it's always easy to get together with your family. By definition."

"I understand. Relations are more direct than between bosses, employees and unions. No one's going to sue you. But it's easier to quit your job than leave your family. Easy to find a new one, hard to change fathers or sisters. Or brothers."

He frowned. I could tell my last remark troubled him. I'd used that word on purpose to shift the conversation to another subject I wanted to know more about.

"Speaking of which," I quickly continued, "I know that you underwent a family tragedy in 1986 when Pierre-Hugues, your oldest brother, passed away."

"Indeed. But all of that is water under the bridge now, nearly thirty years later, and I'd prefer not to talk about that. Let's stick to business, Mr. Bastaro."

He'd finished his sentence, and I felt he was challenging me to continue. I decided to put my question differently.

"I understand. And this must have been difficult for the holding? The other day your father told me how much he'd been counting on Pierre-Hugues, and you of course, to assist him in his company."

"Of course, outside of the loss for our family, it was a huge loss for the company. My father considered Pierre-Hugues as the future cornerstone of the holding. He kept praising him."

I wanted to ask him if his brother was the favorite, but I didn't want him to clam up. I let him continue.

"Of course, he had the qualities required to head a business like this one. But that's not all you need. You have to manage, communicate."

"Team-work, you could say."

"In a company as large as ours, you have to have several types of talents. When my brother drowned, it nearly messed everything up."

"Yet the holding survived."

"And is thriving!"

When Edouard said that he sat up in his father's armchair, as if proving his legitimacy. Then I got down to the nitty-gritty.

"Will you be the one heading the company then in the future, Mr. Lacassagne?"

His face lit up with a smile.

"I don't think I have the choice now. I spent my whole life helping my father. Now he's stepping down, and I'm fifty years old. That's all I know how to do."

I could tell he was proud and relieved to finally be where he'd always wanted to be his whole life. Now I dared ask another question as he seemed to be ready to tell me some secrets.

"Did you and your brother get along well? You were never competing with each other?"

"Competing? Good Lord, no. I don't think so. We each had our place: the oldest brother, the youngest brother, our sister and our dear little Emilie. Of course, we were young and like with all siblings, sometimes it was like cats and dogs. Sometimes partners-in-crime sometimes in competition for our parents' appreciation."

"Were you jealous of one another?"

∽

Gorbio, March 1986

Edouard stretched out in his bed. It was ten in the morning, a Sunday like so many others where the sun was shining, and spring had sprung in the countryside around Nice. He'd opened his window because he loved hearing all the little noises during the night in the park around his parents' villa. He loved falling asleep listening to the cicadas, crickets and toads who all lived in noisy harmony in the little pond behind the rose garden.

He'd come back late last night. He'd been out with some friends and Julie, his fiancée, with whom he still didn't live because in his family two people only lived together once they'd tied the knot officially. What a bunch of bull! he thought, squinting at the brightly lit room.

Outside he heard another typical Sunday morning noise here: the noise the tennis ball made when Charles and Pierre-Hugues were playing on the property's clay court.

He'd never liked sports but would have liked to spend time like his brother did with their father.

Moments just for them, instants of complicity playing a virile sport. A virtual combat but one that brings people closer together.

The only time Edouard spent with his father was when they were talking about the company. They were only close when discussing business, turnover or accounts receivable.

That was why Edouard worked so hard for the holding. To keep in touch, to not break the only link he had with his father.

So he'd count on him, just like he counted on Pierre-Hugues.

He heard them counting the points. 40 - 15. Advantage. Game. Tie. One set to zero. Second serve. He'd never understood the rules nor how they counted the points. And he'd never been able to hit the ball twice in a row either. He hated holding a racket in his hand. What he liked was holding a calculator.

He got up and walked to the window. His puny body and white skin were exposed to the sunbeams coming in. He put both hands on the windowsill and could see both of them playing.

Those two sure looked alike. The same svelte and athletic bodies, the same moves on the court wearing the same white shorts and T-shirts.

Pierre-Hugues had a hairband on to keep his long brown hair out of his eyes. He kind of looked like that American tennis man, what was his name, that guy who was always mad about something. He couldn't remember. An Irish or Scottish name: Mac something or other.

Anyway, he didn't care!

He watched Pierre-Hugues serve. Pierre-Hugues who hit the ball from the back of the court. Pierre-Hugues who ran up to the net. Pierre-Hugues who smashed. Pierre-Hugues who won another point. Pierre-Hugues who knew how to do everything easily and graciously.

Pierre-Hugues who was perfect!

Edouard was fuming in the background. His skin was burning, his gut was searing.

He felt like jumping out the window and running up to the tennis court, ripping the racket from his brother's hands and breaking it into two on his knee. Or on his head.

He felt like screaming out to his father:

"Look at me Dad! I exist! Even if I don't know how to hold a tennis racket! Even if I look like the teacher's pet, an intellectual who can't see a thing without his glasses!"

But he didn't do a thing. He never did anything.

Too timid.

Too mousy.

∾

"Me, jealous? No, not at all," replied Edouard, putting his elbows on his father's desk.

"Listen Mr. Bastaro. Let's call it a day. I've got a phone conference in a couple of minutes."

He got up and nearly pushed me out.

"Talk to my father when he's feeling better. He's the one who's got stuff to tell you. It's his life, his story, his idea. Thanks."

When I left the building, I stopped, pensive, right on the square in the middle of the business district. That was a funny reaction, I said to myself. A U-turn in his thoughts.

I felt he was troubled and then suddenly absent when I'd asked him if he was jealous of his brother. I was far from imagining that he'd react like that.

I concluded that I'd have to dig deeper into that subject.

Relations between family members were always interesting.

Especially when there was unexpected drama.

CHAPTER 22
Other fish to fry

I WALKED BACK to the Negresco slowly, thinking about that strange interview I'd had.

I called Colombe to tell her about it. And in return she told me that she'd found the former employee, Brigitte Garibaldi, and that they'd arranged to meet later on in the afternoon.

I thought back on this takeover bid deal which came at the worst possible time for the Lacassagne family, right now when they certainly had other fish to fry. As soon as I got back to my suite, I opened my laptop, logged into the hotel's Wi-Fi connection and started to look for info: I wanted to know more about how public takeover bids took place but also more about this enigmatic Angel Sharpers, that American with his pockets full of money who wanted to acquire the Lacassagne empire.

But I didn't find much information that interested me. Most of it was quite technical, from finance, stock exchange or new technologies sites. On a more mundane level though, like most internet users, I quickly read through his Wikipedia page:

"A<small>NGELICU</small> S<small>EGEAU</small> S<small>HARPERS</small>, *an American businessman, was born on April 24, 1959 in Monte-Carlo. He is the son of the American diplomate, Stuart Sharpers III and a French mother.*

(...) In the middle of the 1980s, Sharpers moved to the United States where he founded several start-up companies in San Jose, California, in the heart of the famous Silicon Valley, a leading place for information technology.

(...) In 1992, his first companies were listed in the New York Stock Exchange on Wall Street.

At the beginning of 2000, his fortune and assets were estimated to be 800 million dollars.

Private life.

On June 12, 1993, Angel Sharpers married Sylvia Bellavista, a model of Venezuelan origin. They have two children, Katheline, born in 1995 and Victoria born in 1997."

T<small>HERE WAS MORE</small>, but that didn't interest me.

However, I was intrigued by some of the info. Especially where he was born.

Monte-Carlo was right next to Nice and for a journalist like me, that was an interesting coincidence.

Don't you often say it's a small world?

Curiosity was getting the better of me. I wanted to contact this guy. Understand who he was. What he was doing here and now. What his motivations were.

Why he came to Nice, of course a beautiful city, to launch a hostile takeover bid on a French company when there must have been loads of profitable businesses in the US that would have been easier for him to acquire.

I sent Colombe an email with a link to Sharpers' Wikipedia page to see what she thought of it.

That night, I felt like going out to eat. I spent about half an hour in the shower, thinking, got dressed and got into the elevator.

When I gave the concierge my large brass key, he called out to me.

"Good evening, Mr. Bastaro. I've got some mail for you."

He turned towards the key boxes behind him and handed me a white envelope.

"Here you are."

The envelope just had my name on it. So it didn't go through the mail.

"Jerome Bastaro / Negresco."

When I saw it, I was afraid that my tigress had come down from Paris to surprise me and invite me out to eat.

Not something I would have appreciated!

"Who gave this to you?" I asked.

"A little kid."

I didn't know what to say.

Curious to see what was inside this envelope, I ripped it open while walking in the lobby and took out a simple white piece of paper.

The few words written on it left me speechless.

CHAPTER 23
Plenty of choices here

"STOP DIGGING UP THE DIRT."

A short sentence, but one that made its point. But who sent it?

Who knew I was at the Negresco? Only a few people, to my knowledge.

I mechanically turned it over, looking for who knows what, who knows who, maybe the kid? Or who wrote this warning?

I walked up to the front desk.

"When did you get this?"

"About half an hour ago, Mr. Bastaro."

"What did the kid look like? Did you know him?"

"No, not at all. You know, one of those kids you find here on the streets. Someone asked him to bring the envelope here for a few euros. I'd say he was about ten. Black hair, tanned, like lots of kids here in Nice. I'm so sorry but I can't help you much here."

"Thanks anyway," I mumbled.

I was annoyed when I left the hotel, but I wasn't going to let anyone intimidate me. I'd signed a contract and would do my job, whatever the cost.

I wanted to share this strange event with Colombe and called her. As she had just left Brigitte Garibaldi's house, I invited her to have dinner with me, so we were both up to speed concerning our recent progress... or lack of it!

We decided to meet at the port where she knew of a restaurant that didn't look like much, but where the food was original. The Gousto proposed a menu mixing Mediterranean and Peruvian cuisine.

Sitting across from one another in the restaurant, Colombe and I had a good time, analyzing our days but also forgetting them from time to time. We talked about this, that and the other, and as we'd had quite a bit to drink, also often burst out laughing. It was nice to work together, and I was happy to have accepted her as my assistant. When you share your doubts and fears, you've already eliminated half of them!

"I wonder who would find it funny to send me this type of warning," I said after the server had brought our food.

I'd chosen the *lomo saltado* and Colombe had decided on an octopus ceviche.

"Do you think it could have been Edouard?" she asked. "Seeing how he doesn't seem to appreciate you for his father's project."

"I can't see him as the author of a poison-pen letter, but nothing astonishes me anymore. But no one threatened to kill me, so I'm not going to get worried, I'll keep on digging. I'll probably see Charles at home tomorrow or the day after, I think they'll release him."

"Are you going to tell him about this?"

"I don't think so."

"How come?"

"I don't want to distort our relationship. Plus, he doesn't need any more emotions right now."

"True."

"So tell me about your visit. Interesting? Did you record it?"

The day before, I'd lent her my Dictaphone before she left my hotel.

"I did, and she's a charming lady. She must be about sixty, not bad looking at all, and really sweet. Like your grandma who bakes cakes just for you. And she made one just for me, to go with our tea."

"How sweet!" I laughed. "So where does she live?"

"Not far from here. And this is surprising to tell the truth. I wasn't expecting her around here."

"What do you mean?"

"She lives in an apartment that's not bad at all, in the Mont Boron district."

"Doesn't ring a bell, but like I said, I don't know the city very well."

"I know. Well, let's just say for a former maid, server, cleaning lady and someone who only worked in odd jobs, she's in a pretty nice part of town."

"A high-class part? Like the 16th district in Paris?"

"Let's just say a district where more doctors and

executives live than cleaning ladies. Except when they work there of course."

"Maybe she inherited the apartment."

"Could be," replied Colombe. "Must be, as she hasn't worked now for nearly twenty-five years, if I understood correctly. Ever since she quit working for the Lacassagne's.

"An heiress and an annuitant?"

"Good annuities then. Especially as she raised her son Simon alone, because his father passed before he was born."

"I remember. That's why she began working for them when Emilie was born. Simon, who was raised with Emilie."

"He himself."

"He must be around Emilie's age now: thirty-six."

"Right."

"Did Brigitte talk about her son? What does he do? Where does he live?"

"She told me he's a painter. Someone who paints pictures I mean. I think he lives in Paris."

"Probably in Montmartre, if he's the Bohemian type."

The server interrupted this conversation with our desserts. There were so many choices that it was a hard one to make, but finally we both chose the "Tiramigousto", which was the Gousto restaurant's bespoke tiramisu. A feast!

As the restaurant also had a wine bar, we'd chosen

a bottle of Chateau Sainte-Marguerite 2010, a delicious Côtes-de-Provence.

We'd polished off the bottle and the cozy atmosphere and delicious meal had loosened us up and we were having a great time. The more I saw Colombe, the more I appreciated her, and I could tell that it was reciprocal.

While we were speaking, she innocently slipped in the question asking me if I had a girlfriend waiting for me back in Paris. "Absolutely not!" That was only half-true, but she liked the answer.

We made toasts to the sun, to her vacation, to our mission, to the unknown author of the message and to finding Peru here in Nice!

Between dessert and when I walked her back to her car, we talked about the Lacassagne family, their holding and employees, both past and current ones. Or in a nutshell, everything that gravitated around that patriarch and that we'd have to understand in order to well describe him in that "portrait" he'd ordered from me. I said to myself that we'd not yet seen Marie-Caroline and I needed to meet her. But for the moment, she was a bit discreet.

Colombe jumped as we were saying goodbye.

"Oh! I almost forgot. Here's your Dictaphone if you want to listen to what Brigitte had to say. If you have trouble falling asleep, she'll do the trick with her soft voice."

"Thanks. Did you have time to glance at Sharpers' Wiki page?"

"Not yet, I'll look at it when I get back."

My face neared hers.

I could see a small twinkle in her eyes, like a question, in the light from the streetlight. And I kissed her on both cheeks.

"Good night, Colombe. Have a safe trip back home."

"Here, it's three kisses," she said before getting into her Fiat Punto.

"You sure you're okay? You did have a bit to drink. I can call a cab for you."

Thanks, that's nice of you, but I'm fine. Bye!"

"Be careful driving," I said as she left.

I looked at her taillights as they disappeared in the first intersection saying to myself that this summer would be a scorching one.

CHAPTER 24
The kids loved it

I STILL HAD a bit of energy left that night, despite the high level of alcohol running through my veins. So comfortably sitting up in my bed leaning against the wooden headboard and with a pillow behind my back, I uploaded Brigitte Garibaldi's recording on my laptop.

I felt like hearing the voice of this person I hadn't met yet. It was important for me to hear each person speak.

I clicked on the audio file.

It was the beginning of a nice one-hour conversation between Brigitte and Colombe, one that gave me a good idea of what things were like at Villa Gorbio in the beginning of the 1980s.

That conversation immediately sparked an unexpected and moving image in my head. One of an ideal Christian family who took in a single mother and her orphaned child. Quite a touching one.

Too good to be true?

I was interested in a long passage that Brigitte's peaceful and gentle voice told Colombe.

"I loved the years I spent working for the Lacassagne family. These are people with a heart of gold. A God-fearing and charitable family. Just look at how they took me in. And I can tell you that it wasn't because they pitied the single mother that I was.

When they learned about Emilie's disability, poor Lucie didn't feel that she could cope with this alone. Charles immediately asked me to move into the villa full-time. He knew that I was alone with my little Simon. It was 'win-win' as you say. I worked for them in exchange for a decent salary, a nice place to live, and that allowed me to raise my son in the best conditions. Had I had to raise him in my tiny apartment with what I earned as a waitress, things would have been different.

It was so lucky the Lacassagne family and I found each other. I really felt like I was a part of their family. I didn't feel like I was an employee, if you see what I mean. Neither the parents nor the children tried to boss me around. As if I were an auntie or a second cousin you could say.

Plus they didn't treat Emilie and Simon differently. Just as if my little boy were the poor Emilie's twin, a twin who was normal...

I especially remember Sunday mornings when we all went to mass together, as the Lacassagne family members were all very devout, as I said. Lilie and Simon must have been about five. We all came together and sat down side by side right up in front, so we were near the altar. And then, you can see how sweet it was, and it just goes to show that there wasn't any difference between them, when the kids got tired, Charles put them on his knees, Lilie on one side and Simon on the other. Very protective. Believe me the kids loved it. And I loved the fact that we were accepted for what we were, us just normal working people in this well-known and opulent family."

I turned the audio file off on that vision of Sunday bliss.

It really was a beautiful image and Brigitte described it with emotion! By the sound of her voice, I could feel the respect and admiration she had for all the Lacassagne family members, and of course Charles.

Nonetheless, something seemed wrong though. Two opposing images in my head. One, Brigitte sort of like Cosette, in *Les Misérables*, taken in by a devout Christian family. The other, Brigitte as an annuitant, someone now seemingly well-off, who lived in a luxurious apartment in the upper-class part of Nice, if Colombe had described this correctly.

Not too bad, I thought to myself.

Did living with rich people rub off on her? And how was she able to afford all that? I couldn't wait to meet her.

With Colombe's help of course, and while I was falling asleep, I thought of her beautiful smiling face. And I think I even dreamed about her.

CHAPTER 25
The smallness of men faced with an all-powerful sea

I GOT UP PRETTY EARLY the next day, eager to explore and dive into all the new info about the Lacassagne family.

We met in the Masséna gardens, right next to the Negresco, where we admired the lush and bucolic greenery.

"Colombe, we've got work to do! Tonight Charles is coming back home. He asked me to meet him there. In the meanwhile, we have to try to contact Marie-Caroline and this strange Angel Sharpers."

"I had a glance at his Wiki page last night. I wonder what a rich American like him is doing here: probably something linked to the region as he said he was born in Monaco."

"Maybe he knew the Lacassagne family in the past?" I wondered to myself. "We'll have to dig into that."

We were sitting on a bench in the shade of a huge

umbrella pine tree. Colombe was wearing a light and airy skirt. And just looking at her perfectly shaped legs was starting to make me dizzy. I think she even noticed.

What was going on between us? Any more intimacy would surely complicate things, wouldn't it?

I preferred to ignore that question for now and get back to our investigation, which had fallen by the wayside a bit.

"I also want to know more about what happened to Pierre-Hugues. Though he's absent, this guy sure takes up a lot of room in everyone's souvenirs and memories. His tragic death seems to have upset a lot of people too and changed the way the cards had been dealt.

"Of course, he's here but he's not here."

"Can you take care of doing the research on this accident back in 1986? I'm sure that we could learn a lot if we read everything that was written then."

"No problem, I'll look on the web and see what I can find in the local papers, the municipal archives and all that. They call me the librarian's helper!"

"Get going then!"

I personally thought that working would not be in harmony with the scenery and atmosphere. I was in the "here and now", thinking only of my charming assistant and berating myself for having forced her to hit the library and look for old information. The heat of the Mediterranean summer made me want to laze around and perhaps flirt.

But I didn't dare.

As if that young lady, much younger than I was, intimidated me.

"Ok!" she said. "I'm on it."

And she whipped out her cell phone and started surfing the web.

I forgot my vague desire to flirt and took out my laptop to start imagining a plan and table of contents for the book.

I was thinking of a three-part, traditional construction. One: the business; two: the man; three: the family. I started trying to lay out sequences and chapters.

We worked side by side, in the shade, in silence. Suddenly Colombe jumped up.

"It's open! Want to go?"

"Um... sure, but where?"

"The municipal archives. They're open now. I want to take a look at the microfilms from 1986," she said enthusiastically, getting up. "We'll be able to find all the local articles, and even some national ones. That way you'll be able to relive those weeks, as if you were there."

I obediently followed her.

Of course she was right and had a great idea. We were able to consult the data base with keywords such as "Lacassagne," "1986," "Pierre-Hugues," plus combinations of all three.

The results gave us several microfilms of papers like *Le Provençal*, *Le Méridional*, and *Nice-Matin*.

We thus were able to consult a good dozen articles

on the viewer and even directly make JPEG copies that we transferred to my computer to read them later.

All these articles plunged us back into the summer of 1986.

"I wasn't even born yet," said Colombe. "But I feel like I'm there."

Starting out with a few lines in the local news, then Pierre-Hugues Lacassagne's disappearance at sea was covered more and more as the days went by. Journalists, including a certain Helene Fenocchio often wrote articles with testimonials from people who knew Pierre-Hugues when he was a child, or knew his parents or brother and sisters. Quite flattering testimonials about the whole family, with people saying how they knew them and what they thought of them. With each time people expressing their sympathy for that Christian family, one that had done so much good for the city of Nice. But there were a lot of words that didn't say too much. Like water slid off the Lacassagne family's backs.

Like.

We paid close attention to one article: the reproduction of the minutes written by the Théoule-sur-Mer gendarmerie, signed by Sergeant Petrucci, who was the first person who had spoken to Charles as well as Marie-Caroline and Edouard, the two who'd made it back on that night of July 1986.

We learned that for a while the sailboat had been shut down and sealed in Théoule, while they took care of the standard observations and investigations when someone drowned at sea.

The following articles continued with how much anxiety resulted from a corpse that still had not been returned from the sea.

And finally, there were headlines in the local papers when the cadaver finally reappeared and was given back to its family.

Helene Fenocchio published a very moving double page in *Nice-Matin*. She wrote about fate, wealth, money, the lives rich people led, and the smallness of men faced with an all-powerful sea.

There was one last article on the ceremony paying tribute to those who'd lost their lives at sea, the one the family had organized when his body had not yet been found.

Little by little, the interest journalists had for Pierre-Hugues's death slowly waned away. Just a few short paragraphs here and there, often on the anniversary date. And then nothing.

Now the name of the Lacassagne family was only in the business section.

Pierre-Hugues was dead and buried.

The holding was still alive and kicking.

"That's how the wheel of news turns," I said ironically. "See, Colombe, one day you're on the first page and the next day you've got two lines on the obituary page."

We'd spent nearly two hours in the database

reading the articles and my stomach was now starting to beg for less spiritual nourishment.

"How about a Niçoise salad?" I proposed, totally lacking in originality.

I closed my laptop with its copied files, and we went outside. Librarian's helper: not my thing.

"Maybe we can try to get through to that journalist, Helene Fenocchio, who covered the event?" suggested Colombe.

"Could be a good idea if she's still working. Plus the gendarme who took their statements. What was his name already?"

"Petrucci", replied Colombe without missing a beat. "Like the pianist, but probably taller."

" Petrucciani, the pianist, Michel Petrucciani, you almost got it right."

Then my phone started vibrating. Unknown caller. I picked up.

I was light years away from imagining who I'd be talking to.

CHAPTER 26
Feeling like the hunted hunter

"HELLO, MR. BASTARO," I heard.

A masculine voice.

"Who's calling?" I asked, as I didn't recognize the caller.

My eyes popped wide open when he answered.

"Angel Sharpers, I think you probably know my name, don't you?"

"Mr. Sharpers?" I articulated carefully for Colombe. "How did you get my number?"

"I've got relations. But don't worry about that. I'd imagine that you'd like to meet me. Am I wrong?"

"No, I'm just surprised that you were quicker than I was. I was hoping to reach you this afternoon. You're making things easy for me, thanks."

"It's only normal. I believe that we share the same acquaintances and centers of interest."

"It's flagrant if you believe the medias."

"So let's not waste any time with civilities."

He gave me an address in the center of the old city.

"Mr. Sharpers, I won't be alone. I'll have a young intern with me, Miss Deschamps. Would that be…"

"Of course! I appreciate the company of women. Come as soon as possible!"

"We'll be there in half an hour."

The person that we met that day was a typical American. He looked like he owned a ranch in Texas, with sunglasses that he never took off during the whole interview and a huge and overflowing gut hanging out over his belt. Morbid obesity would have been a better term for it as it was all over: his neck, his arms, his stomach, his fingers… Like the cartoon character, Obelix wearing a cowboy hat!

He didn't get up to greet us. Probably too difficult for his knees. On the other hand, he never stopped ogling Colombe from head to toe and that immediately made me want to hate him or sock him in the middle of his enormous jowls.

Despite the air conditioning, he was sweating like a pig, regularly wiping his forehead and neck off with an old handkerchief. I still wonder if he was actually sweating or if he was exuding a surplus of body fat.

But I had to admit that after my initial impression of repulsion, the way he spoke excellent French with a tad of Texan accent, was both friendly and pleasant.

I was also stupefied that he was able to get my professional phone number so easily. I was feeling like a hunted hunter.

"What can I do for you?" I asked, sitting down.

"You are the Mr. Sharpers who put in the takeover bid for the Lacassagne holding?"

"In flesh and blood," he laughed. "Mostly flesh though."

He burst out laughing, with this pun he'd keep on repeating. I wondered why the takeover bid was so funny. There was something I wanted to know and began questioning him.

"Why did you choose the Lacassagne company? Like aren't there any good companies to take over in the States, the country of unabashed capitalism?"

"I'm sure there are. But let's just say I like it here. I like this region, this climate, French people."

"You were born near here, is that right?"

"In Monte-Carlo, yes." My father was a diplomat, but I'm sure you've already got this info. So we can skip all these biographical details."

"If you want. Would you like to lead the interview?"

Colombe was paying attention silently.

"Of course. Without going into the details, could I ask you what brought you to Nice, Mr. Bastaro, to interview Charles Lacassagne?"

"It's quite confidential, Mr. Sharpers. Why should I tell you, an unknown person about that?"

"Listen," the American said. "Do you want to beat around the bush or get right to the facts?"

"I prefer to get right to the facts," I admitted.

"Good, me too. If I said that we're sharing a few interests, what would you say?"

"That you haven't said enough."

"And if I added that things are not what they appear to be? Plus you shouldn't always believe everything people tell you?"

"I'd say that your French is pretty good for a foreigner."

"You're funny, Bastaro, I like that. Okay, enough joking around. I know that Charles Lacassagne hired you to write, as a ghostwriter, his beautiful biography."

I was dumbfounded. Who could have told him that?

"How did you find that out?"

"You find things out quickly when you've got connections. Who cares who told me, what's important is that I know this. Oh, by the way, what about something to drink?"

We each ordered a cool bubbly drink that must have reminded him of his country.

"So, I was saying," the businessman began again. "This Charles wants you to write about his life. His version of course, the one that praises him."

"I'm also a journalist. I always check my sources. Professional deformation, probably."

"Of course! But can you always know what's true?"

"What are you talking about? Why? What's it to you?"

"You'll find out soon enough. I'm telling you this because I know things. Especially that behind beautiful walls, you sometimes will find mold. And behind opulence, there's often a frightening lack of humanity as well as emotional poverty."

"You lost me there. Can you be a little clearer?"

Sharpers took off his cowboy hat, put it on the table and sighed noisily.

"I unfortunately cannot support what I'm saying by any certitudes. And that's how our interests converge."

"You don't have any certitudes, but you've got assumptions? Theories? Suspicions? About what or who?"

"About the people we're both interested in. But not for the same reasons."

Jesus! What was he trying to say here? This was getting curiouser and curiouser.

"And why are you interested, Mr. Sharpers? Money? Are you saying that you're going to reveal some things about the Lacassagne family that could facilitate your takeover bid?"

I suddenly felt like I knew what he was up to. Sharpers wanted to reveal some dirt on the Lacassagne holding. From there, the market would go crazy, the value of shares would crash, and he'd be able to scoop it up for next to nothing... Brilliant.

These revelations though would have to be exact and very compromising.

"I'm not motivated by money, Mr. Bastaro, you can believe me. Or not just. I'm concerned about the truth."

"What truth? Who are you, Mr. Sharpers? Where are you from? What do you want?"

"You'll soon understand."

CHAPTER 27
This dear country where I was born

SHARPERS SAT up in his seat. We would be dumbfounded by what he was going to say.

"I knew the Lacassagne family well when my father was a diplomat in this area. I was one of Pierre-Hugues' good friends."

Good Lord! We were getting closer here! Colombe and I looked at each other. We couldn't wait to hear what Angel Sharpers was going to say next.

"Pierre-Hugues and I met when we were both about twenty. I think he was about a year older than me. We met at the swimming club where we went at least once a week. He was the good-looking one, you know: tan, athletic, easy on the eyes."

The American sighed.

"The world was his oyster. The girls loved him. And then, fate: he died so young. All his hopes vanished, a whole life destroyed, one that would have been perfect."

"But it was an accident," said Colombe, speaking for the first time here.

"An unfortunate and terrible navigation accident. At least that's the official version."

"Of course," I said. "We were able to read the synthetic report that the gendarmerie wrote."

"Petrucci?" asked Sharpers.

"You're right," Colombe said. "How did you know that?"

"I read French papers, I like to keep up to date about what's going on in this dear country where I was born."

"You don't believe that, do you?" I asked.

"Let's just say I've got my doubts. It probably was an accident. But maybe not."

"Meaning?"

"Well, like you never know what really happens when you're on a boat, all alone in the ocean, at night. No witnesses, no cameras, no one to rescue you for miles and miles."

"Mr. Sharpers, what you're saying is serious."

"Oh, I'm not affirming anything, just exploring hypotheses, building possible scenarios."

"Based on what?"

"Based on how well I know some of the Lacassagne family members."

"Which ones?"

"I already told you: I was one of Pierre-Hugues' best friends and I often ran across his brother Edouard and his sister Marie-Caroline. At parties they had as students, for example."

"And I suppose you want to tell me all about that," I asked.

"All the years that have gone by didn't erase the memory I have of a party in June of 1986, in one of our friends' houses, in Saint-Paul-de-Vence. There must have been about fifty people hanging around the infinity pool, in the house and in the bedrooms too. Anyway, a great party, with girls, alcohol, and lots of other surprises. I was there with Pierre-Hugues, Edouard and Julie, his girlfriend..."

CHAPTER 28
It all depends on the last lap

JUNE 21, *1986, Saint-Paul-de-Vence*

"Hey, you're here too?" shouted out Pierre-Hugues when he saw Angel walking into the party that the son of a rich olive grove owner whose pool was nearly as large as the villa itself, was having.

"Hey, Pierrot!" he answered. "Did you come with your brother and sister? You actually got Doudou to move? And where's that beautiful Caro?"

"She couldn't come, she has to study for her midterms. But Julie's here, I think she's in the pool. It's going to be a scorching summer, my friend! Gotta drink, quench your thirst. Follow me, I'll show you where the bar is!"

The two friends walked into the garden where there were several tables set up with munchies and a large variety of brightly colored cocktails which all were way too easy to down, especially in a heatwave like that.

The music was loud, blasting through huge speakers set up around the pool, in the garden and inside the villa. That evening, like every June 21st since 1982, with the nationwide music festival on the longest day of the year, you could play music as loud as you wanted and legally disturb your neighbors.

The teens were drinking, swimming, kissing or groping to the music of Niagara, Queen, Elton John, Cock Robin, Gold, or even Stephanie de Monaco, their near neighbor who was now a popstar.

Right now, Samantha Fox was proposing that people should "Touch" her... perhaps foreshadowing the debauchery that the heat and alcohol would spark in a few hours for all of them.

Pierre-Hugues had chosen a cocktail made with curaçao and Angel had chosen some strange-looking orange beverage.

"Cheers! And here's to a good time!" Sharpers said. "Lots of choice tonight. Just look at all this superb livestock, these splendid specimens with water running down their suntan lotion... Doesn't that give you any ideas?"

"Just as many as you have, you pork," said Pierre-Hugues, toasting his glass against his friend's. "Wanna bet? Which one of us will get the first broad?"

"Your dice are loaded! You know you're irresistible! You know I won't be winning here."

"You play to win, not to lose Angelicu. Just say to

yourself that after a few drinks and in the dark, one of them will give in."

"You're a real SOB, you know that?" laughed Sharpers, poking his shoulder. "How about a swim?"

They immediately put down their empty glasses, took off their tops and shorts, and dove in together in a magnificent nearly synchronized dive, just wearing their swimsuits.

Those in the pool moved away from them and began to whistle encouragements, yell out bravos, and urge them to race on four lengths of that 70-foot pool.

"Come on guys..."

"I'll show my tits to the winner!" shouted out a non-prudish blond.

"Everyone's seen your tits!" replied a masculine voice from the other side of the pool, making everyone laugh and whistle.

The two friends hoisted themselves out of the water, and took place on one side of the pool, which had now been deserted. All the other attentive spectators were watching from the sides.

Their hands on the edge, heads bowed and legs ready to push them off into the water, Pierre-Hugues and Angel were immobile like two antique statues.

Suddenly someone whistled with his fingers in his mouth, a shrill signal giving them the green light.

The two adversaries dove in and swam under the water for several yards. Sharpers came up first, as he wasn't a good swimmer under water. Pierre-Hugues came up just in front, and both swimmers, side by side, swam with their powerful arms and legs in a beautiful crawl. They made waves, splashed, but sprinted well.

The spectators encouraged them by clapping, whistling, while continuing to laugh and drink, as if that could help them.

And they swam well! You could tell that they were used to doing laps in the swimming club's pool. Sharpers came in first in the first length and then in the second. For the third, they were head-to-head. It would all depend on the last lap.

And as usual, Pierre-Hugues was the first one to touch the edge.

Once again Angel lost and wouldn't have the opportunity to admire the view of the tits promised to the winner.

Indeed, just a few minutes later, Pierre-Hugues took the blond into the villa: a promise made is a debt unpaid, like the old saying goes.

Sharpers, now alone, began looking for Edouard Lacassagne. As he couldn't find him in the crowd of people, he finally walked up to Julie who was sitting in the shade, having a Coke.

"That's a drink for good girls," he said, coming up to her. "Looks like you're not having a lot of fun. I was looking for Edouard, but I can't find him. Do you know where he is?"

"No idea, he can be wherever he wants, you know. And right, I am bored. Can you stay with me a while?"

"My pleasure."

Sharpers sat down next to her. They talked about

this, that, and the other thing: the great party, alcoholic beverages flowing like a river, Pierre-Hugues and his success with the fairer sex, and Edouard with his seemingly serious character.

"Sometimes I worry about Doudou," admitted Julie Schneider. "Generally, he's really sweet, but sometimes I don't even recognize him. He's strange or he retreats into his own world or sudden gets all upset."

"What about you guys?"

"We're fine. Sometimes he's really distant with me. And I sometimes think he's not interested in me anymore. I've even wondered if he had someone else."

"You mean he's cheating on you?"

"I don't know. You know we're engaged, Angel? We'll get married when he gets his job in his father's company."

"That'll come pretty soon, don't worry. Come on, let's go have some fun. Come and dance with me."

They joined a group of partygoers who were dancing to the tune of *Venus* by Bananarama.

Pierre-Hugues didn't spend much time with the blond. He flitted from group to group, at ease, telling jokes, attractive and charming almost in spite of himself. Like a magnet attracting people to him. To love, a lover, a magnet, to magnetize. A good-looking young man.

He wandered towards the pool, to the buffet, in the living room, on the dance floor where he often found himself in the center, the boys looking at him enviously and the girls, eagerly.

Later on that night, while walking next to one of the rooms with its door ajar, he heard snickers, laughter, and exclamations. All coming from masculine voices.

"Wow! What a broad, look at her curves!"

"Awesome! She's streamlined like a Porsche. No way I'd go down the small of her back in a kayak, too risky!"

"Too slippery you mean! Too many rapids."

Pierre-Hugues was attracted by that type of sexist comments, so he walked in.

There were two guys lying on a bed ogling a trucker's calendar, perhaps Pirelli, with incredible dolls sporting breathtaking plastic.

"How about sharing, guys?" he said when he walked in.

"Have a look, you won't regret having come. We found the calendar under a pillow. Have a look at this little lady - Manu's got good taste!"

Manu was this party's host, the son of the olive grove magnate.

Pierre-Hugues looked at the calendar. And it was true that Manu did have very entertaining reading! Though he personally preferred the pictures. And what pictures!

"Let's start back at the beginning, I missed the first ones."

"Sure. And you missed some good ones!"

The models he discovered on glossy paper were better than good: they were beautiful and desirable, with their suggestive positions and their playful and flirty eyes, eyes that didn't leave you indifferent. He felt heat throbbing through his entire body.

Young blonds, brunettes, tall, short, thin or plump, he liked all the girls.

Suddenly though, he looked at a page and his heart jumped.

He didn't believe his eyes.

Was it a dream?

Or rather a nightmare?

There was no doubt here. Unless it was an extraordinary resemblance.

Pierre-Hugues shouted out:

"Put that away!"

"Hey, what's bugging you? You got tachycardia or what?"

"She's a real looker this one!"

He was suddenly ashamed and felt like clocking those two guys.

He grabbed the calendar from their hands. He stared at the photo of a young redhaired lady with cute freckles on her face.

That completely nude girl showing her stuff to the vicious gluttony of thousands of men, who, all over France, were drooling over that page.

He ripped it out and put it in his pocket, ignoring the protests of the two others.

Rolled into a ball, the photo of this flaming redhead, was easily recognizable.

His sister, Marie-Caroline Lacassagne.

CHAPTER 29
The soul of a minstrel and a joker

"MARIE-CAROLINE POSED NUDE IN A CALENDAR?" Colombe asked as Angelicu Sharpers told her what he knew of what happened that night in 1986 in Saint-Paul-de-Vence.

"That's right. And not just once. When Pierre-Hugues discovered that, he went right up to his sister. He couldn't keep that to himself, for him that was something totally unacceptable. He initially didn't know what to do about this. He asked me for advice, as he trusted me. I told him to talk about this frankly to Marie-Caroline, to clear the air."

They spoke the next day.

June 22, 1986, Villa Gorbio

"What the hell is this?" asked Pierre-Hugues to his sister, taking out the wrinkled piece of glossy paper that had been in his pocket since the night before.

Marie-Caroline was listening to Sting.

"I can't hear you!" she shouted back.

"Caro, turn that fucking music down. And explain this to me."

He showed her the photo and Marie-Caroline, already fair-skinned, turned instantly bright red.

"Don't tell Dad!" she begged him, as she couldn't deny the evidence. "Please, Pierrot."

"Are you crazy or what? You know there's thousands of people, maybe even millions, I have no idea, who can see you nude in this disgusting magazine?"

"They don't know me."

"They could. Can you imagine the scandal it would cause for our family? Lacassagne's daughter poses in the buff for truckers."

"But Pierrot, it's art."

"Art, my ass! You know what guys who buy calendars like this do? Truckdrivers, teenagers?"

"Um, they hang it up on a wall in their bedroom or in the cab of their truck, that distracts them and makes their life easier. I'm there for them."

"Don't be so naive, Caro! Those guys, they're not looking for art. You're just a good-looking girl posing nude for them and without meaning to offend you, they jerk off to your photos! If you get what I'm saying."

Marie-Caroline started to cry.

"Stop it, Pierrot, stop it. I'm not like that, what do you think? There's nothing wrong with that. I like my body, I love to pose, I'd like to be a model, or even better, an actress."

"Are you nuts? You are nuts. You're not going to become an actress by showing off your ass. Anyway you know that dad would never allow you to be an actress and even less a model: those jobs aren't serious enough for him."

"But that's what I like doing! He couldn't prevent me, could he?"

Pierre-Hugues sighed.

"Honestly, are you completely crazy, my poor sister? How are you going to make a living? Forget that, keep on going to school and calm down, you know your future is with the holding."

"Well screw you Pierrot, on your high and mighty! I can do whatever I want. If I want to show people my ass, I'll do it!"

"No, you won't" threatened Pierre-Hugues waving the photo over his head. "I'll show this all to dad and we'll see what he thinks."

And he began to walk out. Marie-Caroline ran up to him.

"Don't do that, Pierrot! You could regret it."

"Yeah, sure. And how?"

"It's not complicated at all. I could tell dad stuff too if I wanted."

"What stuff? What are you talking about?"

"That's right, Pierrot. You're not exactly perfect you know. And our father would be bowled over if he discovered some things about you."

"Really? Like what?"

"You know very well what I'm talking about Pierrot."

"No, I don't. What do you know?"

"Let's just say that if our father learned that his favorite little boy was taking advantage of him and making fun of him, I'm not so sure that he'd appreciate it."

*

"Well, well, sure sounds like blackmail to me," said Colombe Deschamps to Sharpers. "You know what she was talking about?"

Angel Sharpers sat back up in his armchair, groaning at the effort.

"I can't really remember. But I'm sure that it must have been sufficiently dissuasive because their father never knew about Marie-Caroline's so-called 'artistic' photos. Or at least I don't think he ever found out. And her career as an actress was over before it started."

It was really crazy what that curious snitch from the States was telling us: the dark side of a respectable family where every member had something shameful to hide. I couldn't wait to ask Marie-Caroline some questions, but I didn't know where to start. Now that Sharpers had put those images in my head, she'd become quite different from the person I'd imagined.

"You and Pierre-Hugues must have been really close then?" I asked.

"Really close, that's undeniable," Sharpers answered, laughing. "Not like two brothers though. Well, that's not actually a good example because sometimes two brothers aren't as close as two friends are."

"Are you insinuating that Pierre-Hugues and Edouard didn't get along?"

"Listen, I'd say they were like any two brothers. Like cats and dogs, as the old saying goes."

"That's true that you love French expressions! Did you know Edouard well?"

"Much less than Pierre-Hugues, of course. All I can say is that all the Lacassagne children were very different. Pierrot had the soul of a minstrel and a joker, at ease everywhere, always in a good mood. Edouard, on the contrary, was always too serious, very introverted, sometimes as if he was absent, or indifferent. Marie-Caroline, she was a dreamer, romantic, but at ease in high society. As for little Lilie, um, I suppose you've heard about her?"

We both nodded.

"So Lilie is... Sweet little innocent Lilie," the American continued. "All in all, four very different siblings with different desires and hopes, even though they were all controlled by their father, this Charles, who you now know. As for their mother, Lucie if I recall, she was always in the background, a homemaker. So, anyway, all these people apparently got along well, living under the same roof in a villa in Gorbio, on the outskirts of Nice. They lived well and never lacked anything. Today I wonder: when you never lack anything, do you still always want more? And when you've got everything, can something simple still move you?"

I didn't know if that question was also an introspection. But I didn't want to interrupt him.

"However," continued Sharpers, "in the summer of 1986, I could feel that there was something between them."

"Did you hear them arguing?" asked Colombe.

"Not really. But I heard, knew, and understood lots of things. Today I'm persuaded that this tension increased during the spring and beginning of summer until it culminated the day that boating accident took place in July. That curious accident that happened at just the right time."

"What do you mean?" I jumped in.

"I've got the impression that it wasn't just a coincidence."

"A coincidence?" asked Colombe.

"It wasn't just fate. An accident that wasn't completely accidental."

"I can't wait to hear more, Mr. Sharpers," I insisted. "Can I offer you another round while you're explaining it to us?"

"I'll have a whisky then."

Sharpers continued after the waiter came with his drink.

"I'll tell you everything I know. After that, Mr. Bastaro, you'll have two options."

"Which ones?"

"Two possibilities. The first one: you keep on writing the eulogy that Charles Lacassagne ordered, the one that praises him, or the second: you'll tell the whole truth and nothing but the truth of sordid family revenge in the rich Lacassagne family. So? Which one?"

"Tell me more. I'll decide then."

"So, here's what I remember, it was back in May of 1986..."

PART Three

BOTTOM SURGE

CHAPTER 30
The sweet scent of violets

GORBIO, *May 1986*

DOMINIQUE DROPPED his boss Lucie off, as well as Emilie, in front of Villa Gorbio, after a busy afternoon. Window shopping, the old part of Nice, a snack while they were there, followed by the traditional ice-cream at Fenocchio's.

Lilie's favorite was the sweet scent of violets with their petals picked in Tourrettes-sur-Loup, on the outskirts of the city.

"Hello, Madame," Brigitte said from the top of the steps. "Hello, Lilie, was your ice-cream good?"

"Too good, Bizitte," the little girl said, pretending to still be licking on her ice-cream cone.

"I was just preparing you a blueberry pie for dinner. I hope there will still be room for it in your little tummy?"

"Yum, yum!" answered Lilie before running to the garden where Simon was playing with a child-sized wheelbarrow, picking up some freshly mowed grass.

Dominique went back to Nice to pick Charles up from the holding earlier than usual. His boss had called him on the phone in his car, a Radiocom 2000, an innovation that few people in France owned. A little gadget that had come out just a few weeks ago and that Charles was really proud of!

Lilie was playing on the lawn with her almost-twin, Simon. They got along fine, and it was a joy for Brigitte, who felt like she was a part of their family and not merely an employee. It was a beautiful spring. A harbinger of a hot summer?

"Brigitte, how about having some lemonade on the patio?" said Lucie. "Take your apron off and sit down with me."

Lucie was such a thoughtful lady. She knew how to obtain favors without annoying people or exaggerating: a perfect housewife, a millionaire's wife, no whims, easy to work and live with.

She put her purse down in the entrance and went out to the patio where there was a small wrought iron table with a glass top, big enough for three or four people to have a cold drink in the shade.

∽

At the holding, Charles was finishing up one last file before calling it a day. He was happy that he'd succeeded in concluding a fantastic real estate deal for a hotel complex in Villeneuve-Loubet. Seaside tourism was booming in the middle classes and that town had decided to invest to attract more of them. Charles, recognizing a good business opportunity and pulling a few strings from his political acquaintances, was now harvesting the fruit: his holding would expand once again!

He consequently allowed himself to leave the office earlier than usual. As soon as he heard Dominique, he closed the file, put it in a drawer and grabbed his jacket from the coat rack next to the door.

"Ah. Dominique, could you take me back to the villa so I can spend some time with my wife and my little Lilie. With this nice weather, it's a sin not to be at home with your family."

Then he turned to his employee.

"Marie-Therese don't stay late tonight. I'm letting you off early: out with you!"

The boss was really in a good mood today, the secretary thought.

⁓

LUCIE AND BRIGITTE were having their lemonade on the patio, looking at their respective children out of the corner of their eyes. They were the same age but didn't go to the same school. The little boy was ready to go to first grade whereas Emilie attended a center for disabled children. That was a relief for Lucie.

"Brigitte, now that Simon will be in first grade and Lilie's at the center more and more, we can perhaps free you a bit more."

"You mean, let me go? "Oh! Madame."

"Don't be offended by this please, it's not easy for me, you can believe me. If you want, you can still take care of housekeeping. Once or twice a week, for example. For everything else, I can take care of it now. I need to feel useful again, do you understand?"

"That's understandable, Madame. But still, it's going to be hard for me, I'm used to living here, used to you, the children and to Monsieur too, even though we don't see him very much."

"Simon can still come and play with Lilie whenever he wants. And I'm sure she'll ask for him! They get along so well."

"Look how much fun they're having together," said Brigitte, pointing at the children running on the lawn that despite a dry spring, was still green.

"Such a good gardener. Maybe he's got English blood in his veins!"

"I think Simon understands her better than anyone, our little Lilie. Even though she's different, he accepts and protects her."

The two ladies remained silent for a moment, thinking about their children and the nearly fusional relationship they had. Brigitte interrupted this silence.

"I'll have to find a place to live. Here I didn't pay for lodging."

Lucie affectionately tapped the back of her hand.

"Don't worry about that, Brigitte. I'll speak to Charles about that, and I'm sure he'll find a solution for you."

"Thank you, Madame. Now excuse me, I have to check on my pies."

∽

From the inside of the limousine, Charles could see his wife on the patio. Dominique opened the door for him, and he walked up.

"Hello, my dear wife," he said, kissing her on the forehead. "Well? How was your trip to Nice? Am I ruined?"

"Come on, Charles! A day in the shops isn't enough to empty your coffers. Even had I done my shopping in Monaco!"

"That's true. By the way, I just signed the contract we were talking about, the Villeneuve-Loubet one."

"Congratulations. I'm very happy for you."

"For us, you mean. I work for all of us. For our well-being as a family."

"Of course, I didn't forget."

"And where is my dear little daughter?" shouted Charles out to the garden.

"Daddy!" replied Emilie joyfully.

The little girl ran up to him, her head bobbing. She jumped into her father's arms, not realizing that she was the only one who did this. He'd never been a touchy-feely father, but with that child, who was like an afterthought, he was freer than with his other children.

Simon ran up behind her.

"Hello, Mr. Charles," he said politely.

"Hello yourself," replied Charles, running a hand through his hair. "What were you playing?"

"Running!" replied Lilie. "Play, Daddy?"

"Alright, but you have to run fast or else I'll catch you and gobble you up!"

He put her down and began to run after them, still wearing his suit that he rarely took off.

∽

Lucie, exhausted by her outing in Nice, decided to give herself a break, just for her, while Brigitte made dinner and Charles played with the children. She was going to relax in a nice bubble bath, turn the lights down and put a cassette of *The Four Seasons* by Vivaldi on.

∽

Charles felt happy but tired, so he decided to sit on the patio too.

"Brigitte, could you bring me a nice cold beer?"

The employee knew what that meant: she had to take a glass out of the freezer and fill it with a nice, amber-colored pilsner. One of Charles's rare pleasures on days he was feeling happy. Brigitte brought it and asked the question she'd been fearing.

"Charles, is it true what Madame said to me? For my job?"

"Brigitte, I already told you not to call me Charles here."

"Excuse me, Monsieur."

"And yes, it's true. We can manage here at home now that Emilie's bigger. But we'll talk about this later, let me enjoy my beer. Thank you, by the way, it's nice and cool."

Brigitte went back into the kitchen, Charles sipped his beverage, and the children played together in the yard.

It's so nice here, Charles thought. It was rare that he could take time off, with all the work he had at the holding. That said, it was worth it: just look at the Villeneuve contract. He nonetheless couldn't wait until his three children joined him.

Lilie came up to the patio.

"Too hot," she said.

And she ran to the shade, in the entrance, next to the place where Lucie had put her purse when she'd come in a bit earlier.

∽

LUCIE WAS HUMMING in her bath, covered with a huge layer of white bubbles. The only thing that emerged was her head so her ears could enjoy the notes written by Vivaldi. *The Four Seasons* always transported her, sometimes into melancholy, but often into peaceful calm.

～

Lilie was rummaging around in her mother's purse. She knew she shouldn't do that, that it was not nice. But as everyone seemed busy inside and out, she thought no one would catch her at it.

She loved her mommy's purse, with all that adult stuff in it, mommy's things, things that she didn't even know what they were. Plus, there were also coins, so shiny and pretty, plus bills with monuments and bearded men drawn on them.

Lilie rummaged around.

～

Charles wiped his mouth off with the back of his hand. He suddenly heard Lilie.

"Oh! Pehu, Pehu, too cute!"

Then she ran out onto the patio, right to her father, proud to show him what she'd found.

She held up a photo.

"Daddy, look! Pehu! Pehu and mommy."

Charles Lacassagne stared at the photo. He squinted. Something funny was going on.

"Yes, honey," he finally said. "It's mommy. She was beautiful back then…"

Lucie got out of her bath and put on a terry bathrobe. Now she wanted to extend her pleasure by doing her nails, something she didn't do often enough. But should. After all, at the age of forty-six, it's still time to take care of yourself, to please yourself and others.

~

Charles had taken the photo from Emilie, who'd left to play again. Frowning, he looked at each detail in the sepia-colored print.

Lilie was right, this was Lucie in that photo.

Lilie was nearly right; it could have been Pierre-Hugues in the photo.

But it wasn't.

~

Lucie whistled softly to herself on carefully applying her bright red nail polish on her toes that were separated by little cotton balls.

Antonio Vivaldi had just begun his fourth season; it was nearly time to eat. She could smell what was cooking.

~

Charles was sure of himself. That wasn't his son that was in the photo in his wife's purse. Yet, the resemblance was striking, you could even say evident. No way could he have been mistaken. The man with his arm around Lucie was the spitting image of Pierre-Hugues.

A carbon copy of his son, about the same age.

Except in the photo, Lucie wasn't more than twenty years old.

～

Lucie went downstairs, first going to the kitchen to see if she could help Brigitte with anything. Marie-Caroline and Edouard were planning on coming. Pierre-Hugues was in his apartment in Nice.

The table would be set for five people, as Brigitte, Simon, and Dominique all ate in the kitchen.

～

Charles's head was spinning. Was it the beer or the photo?

Who was that man on the picture that must have dated back to the end of the fifties or beginning of the sixties?

He put the photo in his pocket.

～

Summer of 2008, southern France

THERE WEREN'T TOO many people in the village square. Perhaps they were all having a siesta. Nonetheless, the young cashier could see two silhouettes coming towards each other.

She saw the elegantly dressed lady first. Then a more ordinary man. They were both looking at each other, and neither of them moved.

From where she was sitting, the cashier couldn't hear them. Anyway, they didn't seem to be talking. They were simply looking at each other, judging each other. Then smiling.

They both looked around, making sure they were alone, far from any prying eyes. Then they hugged, first timidly, now passionately.

And kissed, forgetting everything else.

"Two tickets," they asked a few minutes later.

What a lovely couple, the cashier thought to herself.

CHAPTER 31
A new organized disorder

THAT NIGHT, at dinner, the joyful atmosphere had fallen just like a soufflé that wasn't cooked right. Charles had lost the good mood he'd had after his real estate success in Villeneuve-Loubet. Lucie and Emilie were exhausted after having spent the day shopping. As for Edouard and Marie-Caroline, their good moods dwindled during the meal, with their parents who didn't say a word or answered simply 'yes' or 'no.'

Edouard tried to bring the conversation over to Villeneuve-Loubet, but his father's answers were succinct, dispassionate. Lucie noticed the change in his mood. Just a few hours ago her husband was running around on the lawn chasing his daughter.

"Is everything alright, Charles?" she asked. "Are you feeling okay?"

Charles had barely eaten anything. A distant gaze, his mind full of questions and doubts, he answered inattentively.

"Fatigue, decompression, I guess. I'm going upstairs."

He wiped off his lips, put the napkin down next to his plate, got up awkwardly pushing his chair, and left the dining room without saying a word.

Emilie got up and ran after him.

"Daddy, kissy."

Charles let his daughter grab his trousers and hug him, then he crouched to pick her up.

The little girl saw something on her father's face, something she'd never seen before. Never.

There was a tear running down Charles's cheek.

When she was finishing her blueberry pie, Lucie wondered about the sudden U-turn in her husband's mood. He had been so happy when he'd returned. It was so rare to see him come home early and play with Lilie in the yard. Perhaps too much relaxation, or too much sun, she thought. Charles wasn't used to not being serious!

∼

It was finally time to put Lilie to bed. Lucie had her brush her teeth and went to her bedroom with her to read her a book. Lilie adored stories about beautiful princesses who were in love with a prince charming. She loved their pink frilly costumes.

Once she was ready to fall asleep, Lucie went back downstairs. When she walked in front of her husband's room, she saw a ray of light. Charles was probably sitting at his desk, with a small lamp on, writing a letter or reading one of Victor Hugo's books that he always had available on the mantel of the fireplace. Forty volumes bound in purple leather, classified chronologically. Charles loved poetry and Hugo was one of the best, so he often read a bit before going to bed.

～

CHARLES WASN'T READING, Charles wasn't writing. He was looking at the picture that little Lilie had found in Lucie's bag. Once again, he peered at the details, examining the faces in the hopes of finding something that would spark his memory, that would allow him to say that things weren't as he thought, that this was an optical illusion or a doctored photo. This young man who looked so much like Pierre-Hugues couldn't be the one he was thinking of.

Yet.

Charles remembered.

～

GORBIO, 1958

Charles had just met a beautiful Italian who was only about five feet tall. That little lady was a part of a traveling circus who had come to the region for a couple of shows. A young lady, who had given him something to drink from her own gourd when he was helping them put the big top up. He had a drink of cool water and was mesmerized by her eyes.

Now, the young lady, an elegant and skilled trick rider, was in the center of the ring, standing on a beautiful bay horse. Charles only had eyes for her. Or almost.

Because, at the back of the ring, nearly hidden behind the red curtain, there was a brown-haired man also looking at the young artist, a nearly jealous look. Perhaps he was in love with her? Or just there to help, should she fall?

In 1958, Charles didn't really see that man there in Gorbio. Only the subconscious part of his brain recorded it. And over twenty-five years later, reminded him of it.

∽

Charles found him in that photo, his arm around the waist of the person he would marry a few months later.

The photo, beneath the yellowish light of the lamp on his desk, highlighted the image of this man, who was employed by the traveling circus back in 1958, a member of Lucie's troop, the spitting image of Pierre-Hugues today.

Charles suddenly realized why his children were so different: both Edouard and Marie-Caroline had inherited his features, whereas Pierre-Hugues looked Italian, dark hair and tanned skin. Just like Lucie, he'd always believed. Yes, like Lucie. Or rather, like that Italian acrobat on that despicable photo he wanted to tear into a thousand pieces.

~

Lucie picked up her purse that she'd put down in the entrance. She was surprised that it was wide open and that inside nothing was in its place, as if a mole had tried to dig a tunnel through it.

A mole named Emilie, she thought smiling to herself.

She went upstairs and tried to put things back in their place. And how do ladies always put things back into their purses? They simply dump everything out on their beds, take advantage of the occasion to sort things out, eliminate at least a third of them, change their minds and put that third back in, then stuff all that's left back in a new organized disorder, till the next time, till the next season!

When she picked up her wallet, she noticed that her little daughter had also been in it. The zipper of her coin purse was open, and her ID papers were stuffed here and there in the various compartments.

The photo!

Where was the photo?

The photo that she kept there, nice and warm, near her heart when she was carrying her purse.

That dear picture that was over twenty-five years old.

Lucie dumped everything on her bed once again and rummaged around frenetically in the papers and eclectic items on the bedspread. She couldn't find that souvenir.

She left everything on the bed and ran to Emilie's room.

∽

LUCIE CHEATED ON ME, fooled me and lied to me all these years, Charles seethed, his fingers clutching the photo he wanted to rip apart, separating the two bodies.

He thought about running into his wife's room to ask her what the hell this was, shake her, maybe even beat her!

He didn't.

He trembled.

Little by little he calmed down. He thought about this. After all, maybe this was just fair? Didn't he also have things he wasn't proud of? Had he always been faithful to his wife? Didn't he have his own secrets? Let him who has not sinned cast the first stone, thought Charles, a faithful Christian and avid Bible-reader.

∽

LUCIE WALKED into Lilie's room. She was still awake, the covers pulled up and only her little laughing head could be seen.

Her mother sat down on the bed and ran her fingers through her hair.

"Sweetheart, you played with mommy's purse, didn't you?"

"No, mommy, no play…"

"Lilie, don't lie. You know Jesus is always watching you and he doesn't like it when you lie. My purse is a mess like each time you play with it."

The little girl looked down, caught in her own trap.

"Did you find a picture in it?"

"Yes," admitted Emilie, who didn't want to have any problems with Jesus next Sunday at church. "Picture you and Pehu! Nice picture!"

Lucie winced.

"Yes, that photo, sweetheart. Pierre-Hugues and mommy. Do you still have it?"

"No, mommy."

"Where is it then?"

"Give it Daddy."

Lucie closed her eyes.

∼

CHARLES DIDN'T KNOW what to do with the picture. Show it to Lucie and ask her what it was? Or put it away and pretend nothing had ever happened? What would be the best solution? Here and now?

And Pierre-Hugues in all that? Did he know? Should he know?

Charles was heartbroken, he had had so many hopes for his oldest son, he was the one who would be replacing him at the head of the Lacassagne holding, his charism and initiatives would even make him Edouard and Marie-Caroline's boss.

But what if his son was not his son?

Could the ties of the heart be stronger than ties of blood? Education more powerful than genes?

After changing his mind several times, Charles put the photo in a drawer in his desk, locking it with a tiny key that he hid in one of the volumes of Hugo's works, *Les Contemplations*.

∽

NOW HE KNOWS, Lucie thought. And that thought paralyzed her.

She'd been hiding that secret from him for twenty-seven years now, too ashamed to have violated their marriage so early. It was a spur of the moment thing.

But Antonio, handsome Antonio, who she went out with before meeting Charles, what they had was so powerful. And their attraction was inevitable when they saw each other again, just a few months after she'd gotten married. The acrobat came back to the region with the whole circus troop and of course Lucie wanted to see them again. After all, those people had been like her family, in good times and bad.

And when she went into the big top that afternoon and saw Antonio practicing on the trapeze, her heart also made a double flip.

~

Pinella, Alpes-Maritimes, 1959
After his last Salto jump, Antonio let go of the trapeze and let himself fall into the enormous net that covered most of the circus ring. He bounced a couple of times and then fell on his back, his hands stretched and out of breath.

Lucie looked at him tenderly and with a bit of nostalgia, thinking back on this world she'd left for another lifestyle: marrying Charles, becoming a housewife. She had a twinge of sorrow when looking at her former lover: yes, she knew she'd have a better life with Charles, but she wondered if she hadn't lost what was most important. Passion!

Antonio glided to the edge of the net and when he was on the ground, looked out at the bleachers. There was a wide smile on his face, showing off his white teeth. He ran up to her.

"Lucia! Bellissima Lucia! What are you doing here?"

He climbed up the ten or so wooden bleachers separating him from Lucie and hugged her. A good sport, Antonio! Just as happy as a little puppy when its mistress comes back.

The acrobat was tacky and sweaty, but Lucie

hugged him back. And his odor, Good Lord! This perfume of an athletic, powerful and muscular male. That odor that took her back a few months when she was still a part of the troop and was in a secret relationship with Antonio. They had tried to hide it, but everyone knew they were seeing each other. An open secret.

"Antonio, you're smothering me!

"Oh! Sorry, sorry. I'm so happy to see you again. How are you? What's new? Are you coming back?

"Oh Antonio... No, I won't be coming back with you. But when I found out that you were here, I jumped onto my scooter to say hi."

Antonio took her hand.

"Come on then. Everyone will be so happy to see you."

They went from trailer to trailer so she could greet all her old friends: Maria, Guiseppe, Pippo, Monica and *tutti quanti*. They laughed, cried, and hugged each other. They drank, ate and spoke loudly with arm movements and shouting: a true Italian reunion!

Then the sun began to set, and Lucie said she had to go. Antonio accompanied her to the end of the village where she'd left her scooter. They cut through the lavender fields, and the intoxicating odor of the purple flowers made them lose control. They were holding hands, pretending not to look at one another, then with shy and embarrassed smiles, and suddenly, Lucie, as if driven by a primal instinct, gave in. She kissed him, caressed his muscular and nude torso, bit his neck.

And they made love there, in the middle of the lavender fields...

∼

Summer of 2010, southern France

This little village on the outskirts of Nice was the meeting place for this couple who seemed to be clandestine.

There was something special, as if the man and woman both were branded with guilt, thought the waiter who was bringing them a glass of lemonade.

He saw lots of couples coming and going with his little summer job that enabled him to pay for his schooling in Paris. In the summer, back down south where he was born, he judged human nature at the café where he served pastis and lemonade. No need to have studied psychology, he was able to recognize young couples, old lovers, couples having problems or illegitimate ones.

He didn't really know where these two should be classified, he found them to be sort of embarrassed, which was touching for him.

"It's so nice to be here, just the two of us," the lady murmured.

"It's our little secret," replied the man.

The waiter, shamelessly eavesdropping, smiled and went back to wiping off his lemonade and beer glasses, with a better idea of who this strange couple was.

CHAPTER 32
Lightning, gusts of wind, rain and hail

NICE, *May 1986*

DAYS AND WEEKS WENT BY, gloomy and strained for most of the Lacassagne family members.

Lucie was despondent and didn't know what to do. She was nearly sure that Charles had discovered her little secret and understood that when they were first married, she'd cheated on him. There was no way he could not have seen the resemblance between Antonio and Pierre-Hugues.

Several times during those sad days she hesitated to tell her husband everything, then changed her mind. Why bother? she thought. Such a long time after. What would that change? What was done was done, nothing could be changed nor amended. It's easier to forgive someone if they admit what they did, isn't it? Could something like this be forgiven?

Plus, Charles wasn't a person who liked to talk things over, unless he had been the one who had initiated the discussion. Since he'd discovered the old photo, he'd barely said a word out loud. In the Lacassagne family, the husband was someone who was feared, nearly like God in the chain of command.

So, Lucie didn't say anything and hoped that Charles would forgive her. He, after all, had raised Pierre-Hugues as his son.

But Charles's attitude had changed. In regard to his wife, who he now ignored. He seemed to be coming back from work later and later. He came back when it was dark and left early. He even traveled more and more abroad, this time taking Edouard with him.

He'd eat dinner silently, just concentrated on what was on his plate. When a family member started to talk about something, he didn't take part in the conversation, or just to add a sentence that no one could object to: Charles knew how to be unequivocal!

Of course, during those weeks, the door between their rooms remained closed. He'd even locked it. The message was clear: the little intimacy that they'd shared up till now had suddenly dried up. It was difficult for them to be a couple, with the ghost of the other person between them. A ghost with the same face as their oldest son.

Pierre-Hugues also was impacted by this. Much to his dismay, his father was paying much less attention to him. Their traditional Sunday morning tennis match was cancelled, as Charles either said he was too tired or had too much work. Some Sunday mornings he even had Dominique drive him to the holding in Nice.

Their just as traditional glass of whisky together in the library was also scrapped. Charles said he had stomach pains and that allowed him to beg off that moment he spent with his son without arousing any undue attention. Without having to talk about that terrible photo.

Edouard and Marie-Caroline both realized something was going on, but that was fine with them. If their father could pay more attention to them, that certainly didn't bother them, far from it. For years they'd felt they'd been excluded.

Charles only stayed the same with Lilie. His dear little daughter still made him smile and run around in the yard. Lilie loved to run and play with Simon and Charles. She loved it so much that her father even sometimes had to force her to rest, so her little heart wouldn't be under too much strain.

Poor little Lilie was a bit sad as she knew she wouldn't be seeing Simon as much, now that Brigitte would be moving away. As planned, the Lacassagne's decided to cut back on her work schedule. The employee and her son would move to Nice where Simon was already registered in his new school. He'd make new friends quickly. Brigitte would be coming just twice a week to clean and help with meals, if needed.

So, as summer was beginning on the French

Riviera, tension was rising in Gorbio, beating to the same tempo as the stifling heat.

CHAPTER 33
As eccentric as a tribe of Papuans

THE DEAFENING PUNK music was blasting into the ears of those kids with their pink or blue hair, and pierced ears, noses or eyebrows. Beneath leather jackets, badges were swaying to the irregular tempo of the Sex Pistols, and thick Dr. Martens boots were hammering the rhythm on the nightclub floor.

Everyone though wasn't wearing a punk uniform. There was a young man sitting on one of the benches near the dance floor, having a cocktail and closely observing the hip-swaying dancers. Chains and straps hanging from their pants were bouncing up and down in rhythm with the next song, interpreted by The Ramones.

This young man didn't have a mohawk cut nor a safety pin stuck in an earlobe, though he was sporting a leather jacket with studs in the back and tight leather pants. People who knew him would certainly be quite surprised to find him there in an outfit that was in total contradiction with his usual clothing. Indeed, they'd have trouble recognizing him. People usually saw him wearing a checkered sweater, a linen shirt and flannel slacks, with teacher's pet glasses and slicked down hair.

Sometimes though Edouard Lacassagne took a trip to the wild side, to the Blue Boy, the place to be in Nice for punk music lovers. He needed to evacuate all the tension inside, all the impulses, all the fears he'd been storing deep inside, as when day broke, he had to be squeaky clean, polite, a perfect son and employee.

Once night fell, at the Blue Boy he could embrace the dark side of his personality. Edouard was never a rebel, just someone with two distinct sides to him. People thought he was smooth, he was multiple. People thought he was docile; he knew how to rebel.

When he went to the Blue Boy, Julie, his fiancée, never came with him. She didn't like that atmosphere, but knew how important it was to him.

Edouard emptied his glass and jumped onto the dance floor.

～

HALF A MILE AWAY, another atmosphere, another decor, other fauna, more refined. Soft background music was being played in this lounge on the Promenade des Anglais where Pierre-Hugues was sipping a piña colada with his friends, both male and female. One of them, a little blond with green eyes answering to the nice name of Vanya, was devouring him with her eyes. Pierre-Hugues was aware of that and was having fun ignoring her. He'd already noticed that nothing beat pretending to be indifferent to attract women ready to swoon at his feet. Upping the tension, raising desire, before quashing it in a spray of pleasure, that was the technique of that Don Juan who was aware of his charms.

Most of the people in this group were from upper-class families in Nice. Sons or daughters of. Future leaders, decision-makers, movers and shakers of the decades to come.

Young people without a worry in the world, who had time to have fun, with their careers already traced out for them.

Pierre-Hugues was probably the one who'd have the most comfortable career, because of his father's fortune. These were sons or daughters of politicians or industrials, whereas others, such as that Vanya, had Russian origins. Their parents were little by little gouging the coast with their millions, buying up land, villas, businesses and could be seen in their beautiful cars and just as beautiful bright white yachts docked on the coast.

At the table people were speaking French, Russian, English and Italian. A "Three B" night as they called them: Luxury Broads, Open Bar, and end of the evening Bonking.

When Vanya got up to have a cigarette outside, overlooking the sea, Pierre-Hugues was right behind her. Phase two of his seduction plan.

∽

Red and green mohawks were mingling on the Blue Boy's dance floor.

People dancing with a bottle of beer in their hands, or smoking, or even both, at the same time.

Decibels were filling the dancers' eardrums and if that were not enough, shrill or guttural shouting accompanied the music. Dancers were shoving each other playfully, laughing without really knowing why and rubbing up against each other.

Edouard was shoulder to shoulder with them. Leathers making noises when they touched, straps and metallic chains clanging when they swayed and strobe lights reflecting on badges with messages to overturn the system.

At that instant he had completely forgotten his fiancée, at home with her parents and probably already sleeping, or perhaps still studying, as Julie was very conscientious.

The DJ changed records, and the atmosphere ratcheted up once again with *Antisocial* by Trust, triggering hysteria amongst the excited group.

"Edouard Lacassagne, you're losing your cool!"

∽

"The Mediterranean is so beautiful at night," whispered Vanya blowing the smoke from her menthol cigarette nearly into Pierre-Hugues' face.

He knew how to recognize signs of desire in women.

"Of course, the lights on the coast. And the boats at sea. That's why I like this bar, the view is so nice. Speaking of views, we don't see you here very often."

"You're right. My father doesn't stay in one place for more than a couple of weeks and I go with him. We'll be here another two weeks and then we're going to Andalusia. See those lights over there, in the direction of Cagnes? On the water?"

"Yeah," said Pierre-Hugues, squinting.

"That's his yacht."

"Nice one by the number of lights it has. Thirty meters?"

"Round about I guess. I don't know too much about boats. For me it's just a way of getting from here to there. As long as it's comfortable, it's okay for me. My dad made me a nice room. Wanna go see it?"

He burst out laughing.

"You know I've already seen lots of yachts. But I'm sure this one must be special if it resembles you. Elegant, sophisticated, a fast trip. Lots of power in its body."

"Such a poet you are," said Vanya, putting out her cigarette. "Pierre-Hugues, have you ever made love on a yacht?"

"Well, you're not a bad poet either Vanya!"

"I don't beat around the bush. And I know what I want. But maybe it's because I don't speak French very well?" she asked, exaggerating her accent.

"Or you just speak your mind?"

"Always!" she replied, kissing the young man on his mouth.

And he didn't protest.

∼

Edouard, all sweaty, went back to the bench where he'd been sitting before Trust had flung him into ethereal heights, increasing his thirst. He ordered a bottle of champagne to share with his shady table of friends. They all knew that Edouard was loaded and took advantage of it. They rang him dry and in exchange supplied him with a few products he had taken a taste to.

When he came to the Blue Boy, Edouard always had a wad of cash with him. But when he left, his pockets were always empty, though his head would be spinning and sometimes his veins were a bit swollen.

That night he was tempted by a new substance. He'd like to taste some of those little pills with pretty drawings on them that you slip under your tongue. He'd never yet tried them and per chance, Warren, the young English punk sitting next to him, his official supplier, had some in his pockets.

Content of their pockets changed hands. Cash for that substance that makes you high and that the Beatles had hidden in one of the titles of their songs: *Lucy in the Sky with Diamonds.*

Warren took the money, and Edouard slipped the

pill under the tip of his tongue, without having taken a gulp of champagne before.

Tonight, Edouard would be flying high!

∼

Pierre-Hugues and Vanya joined the group in the bar right when everyone had just gotten up to go take a walk on the Promenade.

"Hey, you lovebirds," shouted out one of members of the group, "let's go for a walk, breathe in some salt spray."

Pierre-Hugues paid for the drinks. He liked inviting people. So much easier when you're using your father's money!

There were about ten young men and women walking during that nice night. Couples were forming or starting to. Men were lending their jackets to the little ladies. They laughed, looked out at sea, admired the lights on the coastline, the Nice-Côte d'Azur Airport in the distance, as if it were set in the water. And of course, they were fascinated by the city lights. The facades of the luxury hotels, including the splendid Negresco, subjugated them too, though they were used to only the best. Weren't they all born with silver spoons in their mouths?

From time to time, someone burst out laughing, then one would start running after someone else, just like kids at recess, running into other passersby who were also enjoying that delicious night.

Then they sat down on the benches on the Promenade and listened to the waves lapping against the pebbles on the beach in front of them, then the sound of the cars on the avenue behind them: two different types of music, complementary ones in an urban coastline.

One of them suddenly spoke up.

"Hey guys, wanna have some fun? There's a really original nightclub near here. Follow me!"

He described the clientele of that discotheque, and it piqued their curiosity. They followed their intrepid guide who was going to show them around a country and its tribes they hadn't even known existed.

Time for adventure!

∽

EDOUARD'S MOUTH WAS DRY. He didn't know if he should have some water or a glass of champagne... He decided on the champagne. At the same time, he began to sweat profusely. He thought it must be his leather jacket, so he took it off. He was only wearing a white T-shirt that reflected the purple light in the discotheque. He felt like he was sparkling and liked that feeling.

Warren whispered something in his ear, but he couldn't understand his English. That just made him laugh and he tapped him on his thigh. Edouard didn't say anything, finding the man's hand on his thigh both tender, strong and sure, a pleasant feeling.

Slouched on the bench, he stared with his dilated pupils at the dance floor. The dancers seemed bizarre to him. Not like they usually were, more brightly colored, more brilliant, nearly phosphorescent, he thought. And their heads had blown up, like mushrooms.

"Warren! Look at those mushrooms dancing!"

"Yeah, dude!" the Englishman said, laughing, moving closer to Edouard on the red leather bench.

∼

THE DISCOTHEQUE LOOKED PRETTY shoddy from the outside, but Pierre-Hugues still wanted to see what went on behind the door. The bouncer, when he looked at their clothing, didn't want to let them in. Then the Lacassagne name plus a banknote discreetly slipped into his hand relieved his professional dedication. He let them in, with a little frown just in case anyone was looking.

Once inside, their ears were deafened by the music, as they were all used to discreet music in lounges. Heavy guitars, electric riffs mixed with loud singers.

The small group walked up to the bar, followed closely by the local fauna's eyes, though they were not hostile.

"This is... exotic," Vanya said to Pierre-Hugues. "Exciting too."

He smiled, thinking that yes, a group of crazy punks must seem as exotic as a tribe of Papuans from

New Guinea to the daughter of a Russian billionaire touring France.

∽

Edouard and Warren were dancing. The young Lacassagne was jumping up and down like a young goat. The Englishman stayed right next to him: as he'd supplied him with his drugs, he felt like he was responsible for him.

"Warren! Look at her!" shouted Edouard, pointing at one of the dancers with his chin. "Don't you think she looks like a pantrich?

"What?" "Pan-trich? What is it? You mean, an ostrich?"

"No, a pantrich. You never saw a pantrich in your whole life? Gotta get out more! They grow in trees but watch out! Only once per year, right at midnight on December 31st!"

"My goodness," Warren thought. "Edouard is completely nuts".

∽

"Pierrot? Isn't that your brother there, on the dance floor? The guy hopping up and down?"

Pierre-Hugues turned around and stupefied, discovered his brother. That last person he could have imagined in a place like that. He put his glass down on the counter. Edouard wearing tight leather pants!

Edouard jumping up and down like a spring on the dance floor, in front of everyone! Edouard having fun!

"Doudou? What are you doing here?"

Edouard turned around and was face to face with his older brother. His dilated eyes seemed to open even more.

"Pierrot? And you, what the hell?"

What an answer! His breath stunk of alcohol, his elocution was heavy, and his eyes, Good Lord! Where was he?

"Have you been drinking? Smoking? And what did you take?" asked Pierre-Hugues, worried.

"So what?" Edouard immediately answered. "What the fuck is it to you? You came to spy on me?"

"Okay, calm down Doudou, you're not normal. I better take you back home."

Pierre-Hugues tried to take his arm, but his brother brutally pulled away.

"Just leave me alone, will you? I can do whatever I want, I'm a big boy now. Don't tell me what to do. So just go back to your group of daddy's sons like you and leave me alone. Get it?"

Unrecognizable Edouard, thought Pierre-Hugues, hesitating between forcing him to come back home or finally letting him there, having fun like he wanted to.

"A problem?" asked Warren, with his large, tattooed biceps and his proud red mohawk.

"No, it's okay," Edouard stopped him. "This is my brother. But he was just leaving. Right, Pierrot?"

"Yeah. Have a nice time. After all, you're right, it's your life, do what you want."

Pierre-Hugues went back to his group of friends saying that he had neither the power nor the legitimacy to decide things for his brother.

∽

Both groups though, both universes, shifted towards each other as time went by. The punks accepted the group of rich kids and finally the rich kids didn't find the punks so strange after all. In a nightclub, like everywhere else in the world, all you need is tolerance.

Good-looking Pierre-Hugues, with his wad of cash and infectious smile, always knew how to be accepted anyplace. He didn't need to prove anything; he was there and that was it! All he had to do was open his mouth to win the hearts and minds of an audience. Such as Vanya, who was swaying up against him on the dance floor, in the middle of a group of yellow and black mohawks. Pierre-Hugues moved his body with elegance and virility. So well that young punk girls were attracted by his overflowing charism, but quickly pushed away by Vanya, who had visibly decided that tonight Pierre-Hugues was hers. During one of the dances, she reminded him of her idea to finish the night on her father's yacht.

An idea that he immediately accepted.

He tried to see what his brother was up to a couple of times, but finally decided he didn't have to worry. After all, had fate not brought him here that evening, Edouard would have managed without him.

He might as well take advantage of the atmosphere, endless alcohol and Vanya, who he was kissing, caressing, on a bench seat they'd found hidden from indiscreet eyes, in the back of the discotheque. That little Russian polyglot pleased and excited him enormously. Nonetheless, nature was calling and Pierre-Hugues's bladder made him pull away from her.

"Excuse me my sweet little Czarina, but I have to take care of a physiological need that is more important than…"

"You know how to talk to women," laughed Vanya. "But that's fine, I have to pee too! We can go together."

They took off with their arms around each other to the basement where the restrooms were. In front of the ladies, Pierre-Hugues was tempted to go in with Vanya. She sweetly got him to change his mind.

"Come on lover boy, this isn't very romantic. See you later!"

Pierre-Hugues went into the men's room alone.

But in the discotheque's restrooms he was about to receive a huge shock.

You could still hear the music down here, but at a volume that didn't prevent you from hearing conversations. Or little moans.

As he was doing his business in a urinal, Pierre-Hugues heard the voice of a man with a British accent in one of the stalls behind him.

"Oh yes, yeah, more, it's good, so good!"

Pierre-Hugues laughed, still holding his sex.

All of a sudden he quit laughing.

"Yeah, keep on, like that Doudou. You're pumping me like a fucking god, Doudou!"

Pierre-Hugues dropped his limp sex, not believing his ears. That couldn't be him. Jesus, not his Doudou.

Then he heard a moan. A moan of relief, one he perfectly identified.

Behind him the door of the stall opened, but he didn't want to turn around, he didn't want to see. He didn't want to know. But the mirror in front of him couldn't have cared less and he saw his brother coming out of the stall after Warren.

CHAPTER 34
Vanitas vanitatum et omnia vanitas

THE SUN WAS ALREADY SHINING high in the bright blue sky when Pierre-Hugues got up after a restless and nightmare filled sleep. He even wondered if the whole evening was a part of one of his dreams: the lounge, the Blue Boy, the punks, his brother wearing tight leather pants and the more than embarrassing situation to top it all off.

But when he turned his head, he saw Vanya's calm face, smiling in her sleep. So, it all was real. Looking around, he was sure he'd never been here before. The bright slightly curved walls made him think he was in the hull of a ship; he could feel it rocking gently. His brain was now awake, and he remembered a sentence he'd heard the little Russian say. "Pierre-Hugues, have you ever made love on a yacht?"

Now he had, he was nearly sure of that: he never slept with a new partner before having made love to her two or three times. Or once, on nights when he was too tired or had had too much to drink. But last night, he didn't have that much!

Pierre-Hugues made sure he didn't wake up the pretty Russian when he got out of bed, put his boxers on, which he found on the bearskin rug that was at least two inches thick, and went to the door. He felt like breathing in some sea air.

Vanya's room was right on the starboard gangway. Leaning on the rail, the young man admired a magnificent panorama of the Nice coastline. The diurnal rhythm had started up again in Nice he could tell by all the vehicles on the Promenade. A plane was landing not too far, and two others were circling the airport waiting for their turn. It was the beginning of summer, the rush of tourists and probably people coming back from the Cannes Film Festival where Michel Blanc had won an award for his role in *Tenue de Soirée*. The actor interpreted the role of a transvestite who Gérard Depardieu forced into having sexual relations: One of Bertrand Blier's crazy movies, whose subtitle is "*Putain de film.*"

Pierre-Hugues wondered why he was thinking of that. Funny how thoughts have their own logic. But when you start thinking about them and compare your first thoughts with the last, often there's no coherency at all.

The image of homosexual Michel Blanc however brought his thoughts back to the vision of Edouard in the Blue Boy's restrooms, leaving one of the stalls on the heels of that English Warren, with his tattooed biceps and safety pins stuck in his earlobes.

Edouard, a homosexual!

Edouard, who was engaged to Julie Schneider, a nice girl, one Pierre-Hugues really appreciated. Did she know that? Did she accept it?

Pierre-Hugues felt cold anger rising in him. Last night he had been incapable of reacting when he saw his brother in the restrooms. Shocked, perhaps. All he did was go back upstairs, haggard, ordering another cocktail. He'd toasted Vanya and then they both went back to the isolated seats. All the rest was vague.

But now, standing in his boxers on the deck of the Russian's yacht, images came back to him, triggering primitive anger. Someone like him who loved women so much, how could he ever understand his brother's behavior? Had he been in front of him, he would have shaken some sense into him. Asked him if it was true, how long he'd been playing everyone, and if it was just an experiment or if he really preferred men. And how could he have cheated on Julie like that. As well as his family: himself, his sisters, his parents.

He wondered if Marie-Caroline knew. Those two were so close that he could have told her, and it would have been their own little secret, one that didn't include him.

And what if people found out? If Charles heard of it? If a photographer or paparazzi happened to be there? That wouldn't be the first time a Lacassagne was on page one, but this time it wouldn't be in a business daily.

Pierre-Hugues was suddenly surprised to feel a hand on his nude stomach, one that was gently caressing him, even going lower, beneath his boxer shorts. A hand accompanied by sweet kisses on his back.

"Hello, my little candy cane," Vanya said. "Getting some fresh air?

Pierre-Hugues turned around and looked into her magical green eyes.

"Morning, Vanyouchka."

She was just wearing a mini baby-doll whose transparency allowed him to admire her firm little breasts.

The two kissed, the yacht swayed, and a seagull squawked above them. It could have been idyllic had Pierre-Hugues not been tortured by so many questions.

"You're up early," continued Vanya.

"I didn't want to wake you up."

"You should have. I love to make love bright and early in the morning."

"I missed something then."

"You'll never know!"

They both stopped talking and looked at the coast, sunlit with beams reflecting down from the glass towers in the Arenas district.

"See those buildings over there, behind the airport?" the young man asked.

"Yeah. Where it's all shiny?"

"Right. That's the new business district for Nice. It was inaugurated just a couple of months ago. And see the tallest one in the middle, the black one? That's the head office for our holding. That's where I'll be working one day, in an office overlooking the sea, and maybe I'll even see your yacht sailing off somewhere."

"You sound pretty sad. Isn't it fantastic to dominate the city and the economic world? Don't you dream about that?"

"I don't know," replied Pierre-Hugues wearily. "I don't know anymore."

Looking at the black building that reflected the sun's light, his thoughts were elsewhere. He thought of the vanity of all that: power, business, wealth. Was that really what he wanted? On the other hand, he certainly took advantage of it: he had whatever he wanted, went wherever he wanted, and did what he wanted whenever he could. So many people would like to do that but can't, whereas he could do anything. But was that really what he was hoping for?

He thought of the lyrics of one of Johnny Halliday's in his new album, Gang, that was on the radio now.

"On m'a tant donné bien avant l'envie [They gave me so much before I even wanted it]

J'ai oublié les rêves et les mercis [I forgot my dreams and thank yous]

Toutes ces choses qui avaient un prix [All these things came with a price]
Qui font l'envie de vivre et le désir [That make the will to live and want]
Et le plaisir aussi [And pleasure too]
Qu'on me donne l'envie! [Make me want!]
L'envie d'avoir envie! [Want to want something]
Qu'on allume ma vie! [To light up my life!]"

"Something wrong my little Frenchie?" Vanya asked, seeing as he was out of it. "You hungry? I'm starving! Come on."

And they went to get dressed and then up onto the deck where a fat, bald man was already sitting down for a huge continental breakfast.

"Dad? This is Pierre-Hugues Lacassagne."

And she kissed her father on the lips, Russian style. Pierre-Hugues shook his hand.

"Ah. What an honor it is for me to have a Lacassagne on my boat! A real personality in Nice, people say."

"Thank you for having me, Sir," replied the young man, sitting down at the table where there were all sorts of Danish pastries, fruit juice, different kinds of bread, fresh fruit and cold cuts. Like breakfast in a five-star hotel.

"My daughter's friends are always welcome here! Would you like a coffee?"

Pierre-Hugues nodded, letting Vanya serve him

with a wink meaning that her father seemed to appreciate him.

"Young man," asked the father. "Have you ever tried caviar for breakfast?"

"Well I must say that I've already had caviar, but not on toast next to my cup of coffee."

"That's a pity! It's just delicious when your taste buds are still sleeping! Try this one," said the Russian pointing at a small golden dish filled with brilliant black balls that were so tiny you couldn't ever confuse them with vulgar lumpfish roe caviar. "This is beluga caviar, and it comes from sturgeon in the Caspian Sea, the best in the world probably."

"Better than Iranian?" asked Pierre-Hugues maliciously.

"Not a doute! Try some on this blini, you'll be convinced."

The young man did and was. You have to know how to live dangerously when you're a billionaire!

"So you're Charles Lacassagne's son then?"

"One of his sons," corrected Pierre-Hugues with a scratchy voice.

"Such a small world! You father and I did business together a couple of years ago."

"I didn't know that."

"He advised me to acquire a constructable lot in Saint-Jean-Cap-Ferrat. Something that's going to increase in value as years go by."

"That's what they say, yes. You can always trust my father. He has these feelings in his bones."

"In his bones?"

"Just an expression. It means that he's good at finding profitable affairs. The key to his success."

"I understand. Do you work with him then, Pierre-Hugues?"

"Not completely yet. I'm still finishing school. Anyway, you have a beautiful boat," continued the young man, wanting to change subjects. "Can you go around the world with it?"

"I already have. A fantastic experience. We're lucky, young man, to be able to take advantage of our money and our free time, aren't we? We certainly can't complain."

Pierre-Hugues answered evasively. He was back in his thoughts again. Luxury, wealth, power: what was their finality? Was that really what he wanted? And what about Edouard, he suddenly thought. Perhaps he was afraid of the future that his father had already planned out for him too? Money, a wife, children one day too perhaps, all those projects that would be finished without wanting them. No more needs, no more dreams. Maybe that was one of the reasons why his brother was losing touch, trying to find out who he really was, hiding things, pretending to be happy without daring to say he was suffering? Isn't it written in Ecclesiastics: "*Vanitas vanitatum et omnia vanitas?*" Vanity of vanities. All is vanity! Illusions and deceptions.

Pierre-Hugues finally began to understand his brother and suddenly felt more indulgent about his behavior. After all, who was he hurting - no one, or perhaps just himself. The only sticking point in that story of drugs and homosexuality was the risk of a scandal breaking out if people found out about it.

Yet... would it be that terrible? For whom? And with what consequences?

Pierre-Hugues decided he'd just have to have a little discussion with his brother, asking him to be more careful. Everything else, who he fucked, he couldn't care less!

Plus, was he the Lacassagne child totally above reproach? He knew he also had things he was hiding.

CHAPTER 35
Like a Swiss cuckoo clock

NICE HOSPITAL, *June 15, 1986*

EMILIE WAS CRYING her heart out in the arms of Lucie, her protective mommy. Emilie was crying because Emilie was scared. Scared because tomorrow she'd be having a serious heart operation. Her Down's syndrome also led to a host of physical and functional disorders, including that heart defect that the surgeons would try to correct. The operation itself wasn't too complicated, but as with any surgical procedure, there were risks of complications.

Despite her disability, Emilie understood that she might be in danger tomorrow. So, she cried because she was afraid, despite the caresses and tender words of her mother and big sister, Marie-Caroline, who was also trying to calm her.

But Emilie was also crying because she was sad. Her

big brother, her Pehu she adored, wasn't there. Pierre-Hugues had promised to bring her a magical stuffed animal and he'd forgotten. She was counting on him to help her with the doctors, so she could fall asleep and then wake up again after, when her little heart would be all better and it would work like a Swiss cuckoo clock.

Lilie was six years old. She was crying in her hospital bed, much too big for her, though she was in the pediatric ward.

"Want Pehu! Want my magical teddy!"

Marie-Caroline took her hand, but it didn't help.

"Don't cry, Lilie," she whispered, "I'll go get you one downstairs, okay? Will that make you feel better?"

"No, want Pehu animal," sobbed Lilie.

A nurse who had heard her popped in.

"Sweetie, what's the matter?"

The nurse had rosy, pink cheeks and that usually was enough to make any kid smile, even ones that were not feeling well. But Lilie was different.

"Want Pehu!"

She was becoming more agitated, nearly hysterical now.

"Maybe I should get a doctor, Ma'am," the nurse said. "He could prescribe a light sedative for her."

"No, please wait!"

She turned to her daughter.

"Listen Lilie, mommy's going to call Pierrot. He'll come and bring you your magical teddy. Okay? Okay, honey?"

As luck would have it, that week Charles and Edouard were both in Germany for business. Lucie was thus alone for her daughter's delicate operation, with Marie-Caroline, but without Pierre-Hugues who had his mid-term exams.

"Marie? Can you try to get through to your brother at school? Emilie will feel better with him here."

Marie-Caroline nodded and went to the lobby where there was a phone booth with an Alpes-Maritimes phone directory.

"See Lilie? We'll get Pierrot for you."

Little Emilie seemed calmer already. Her big brother was coming.

When Marie-Caroline came back, about a quarter of an hour later, her sister had finally fallen asleep without needing any medication, her plump little hand tightly squeezing Lucie's fingers.

Lucie could tell something was up though, just looking at Marie-Caroline.

"I couldn't get through to Pierre-Hugues."

"What do you mean? You did get through to the school?"

"Yes, I phoned the switchboard, then they put me through to an academic secretary, then to student services, then to the professor's break room, then to the student union."

"And?"

"And no one can find Pierre-Hugues."

~

Pierre-Hugues wasn't that far... as the crow flies! He was in the old city and more precisely on Halle-aux-Herbes Rue. On the last floor, without an elevator, beneath the roof, in an attic room that was nearly as charming as the young lady who lived there, and who, at that very moment, was lying on the bed, drunk with pleasure, on the wrinkled sheets next to her lover.

Pierre-Hugues stretched, a large smile of pure bliss on his face. He almost felt like falling asleep too, he was so relaxed, so hot too. It was nearly summer and beneath the rafters, the sun was blazing, especially after all their excitement, even at the end of the afternoon.

Mireille, his playgirl of the moment, snuggled up to him.

"Once more, honey."

Pierre-Hugues smiled and glanced at the clock. Then he jumped up.

"Shit, I hadn't realized what time it was. Sorry Mimi, I gotta go."

He kissed her on the forehead and threw on his clothes.

"See you tomorrow," he said as he rushed out the door.

He ran down the steps four by four into the first toy shop on the way, buying the best, the biggest, the most expensive and the most fantastic of magical teddy bears that ever existed.

"What do you mean, they can't find him?" asked Lucie.

"Like I said. I had several departments, and no one could put their fingers on him. I think I would have been more successful if I'd asked to speak to the Pope."

"Don't make jokes like that please. Luckily your sister fell asleep. She's exhausted, poor kid. But still, there's something I don't understand. I just hope he won't forget about her operation tomorrow and that he'll be there when she wakes up."

At that instant the nice nurse with her big smile came back in.

"Ladies, I'm going to have to ask you to leave now. She's in good hands, don't worry. The team is fantastic, and Professor Siethbüller is an experienced surgeon, he'll make her heart brand new, one that runs better than a Renault Alpine! The operation will begin at seven, you can come right before noon, when she'll be waking up."

"Thank you so much," sighed Lucie, stroking Emilie's forehead tenderly. "I love you, honey."

In the parking lot for taxis, Dominique picked up Lucie and Marie-Caroline and drove them back to Villa Gorbio.

Pierre-Hugues ran down the hall of the pediatric ward, one that was nearly deserted at that time of day, outside of the nurse's aides picking up the meal trays.

"Excuse me," he asked one of them. "I'm looking for my little sister's room, her name is Emilie Lacassagne."

"Ah, little Lilie, room 19, on the right, the third one after the nurse's office. But she's sleeping now. Visits are over."

"I know, I'm so sorry. I just want to give her this," he said, holding up the stuffed animal, a huge beige doggy with nice deep black eyes, ones that made the nurse's aide give in instantly.

"Go ahead, but don't dilly dally," she said with a wink.

When he went into his sister's room, he noted that she was sleeping soundly, with her little face that always seemed to be smiling. Moved, Pierre-Hugues tiptoed into the room, up to the hospital bed. He put the stuffed animal on the bedside table, covering it completely.

"Your teddy bear will take care of you, Lilie. Everything's going to be alright. Sleep tight. Love you little one."

In the hall leading to the exit, Pierre-Hugues gave one of his famous winks to the nurse's aide.

She wasn't bad at all, he couldn't help but think.

∼

Back at Gorbio, Lucie and Marie-Caroline finished up some leftovers that Brigitte had prepared for them.

During Emilie's hospitalization, they'd given her several days off, with Simon of course.

"I can't understand Pierre-Hugues' absence," said Lucie. "How could he have forgotten his little sister? That's not like him."

"Maybe he came later?" suggested Marie-Caroline. "Do you want me to call the ward, see if they saw him?"

"No, that's fine. What bothers me is that he was supposed to be at school today. I'll take care of that later. In the meanwhile, I'll try to get some sleep, even if I'd prefer to be with our Lilie."

The two ladies went upstairs where all the bedrooms were. The villa seemed empty to them today. Their three men were absent, and little Lilie wasn't there to brighten up the atmosphere with her never-ending smile. That huge house in the middle of an enormous yard would almost seem harrowing had Dominique not been next to them, in his apartments.

∽

Pierre-Hugues wasn't sleeping. He was wandering down Promenade des Anglais with several other night owls, hopping from bar to bar looking for good music and refreshing cocktails. There were artists, students, and young workers. Everyone had to overcome that heat and get a bit drunk whether they'd passed or failed their exams.

Tonight he'd be sleeping, at least for a few hours, in the apartment his father had given him in the city center, so he'd have some independence. He was old enough. He'd sleep alone, or maybe with someone, depending on how his festive night ended.

THE NEXT MORNING while they were going to the hospital, Lucie asked Dominique to swing by the university. She'd called the dean's office for an emergency appointment. The Lacassagne name opened many a door and facilitated a lot of paperwork.

Sitting in Dean Blum's office, Marie-Caroline and Lucie didn't believe what they'd just heard, and the mother asked him to repeat it.

"Like I said, Mrs. Lacassagne, and here I'm sure of what I'm saying, your son Pierre-Hugues didn't take his final exams here. Have a look, he wasn't signed in."

"But, he is registered as a student, isn't he?"

"Yes, he's registered, but he never came."

"Since when?" asked Marie-Caroline.

"He hasn't come for the past two years."

WHEN EMILIE OPENED her eyes that morning in the hospital, the first thing she saw, right next to her head on the little white plastic table, was a huge beige doggie, with big black eyes that was looking right at her.

Finally, Pehu had come, as if in a dream. She had been sure he wouldn't forget her.

She grabbed her magical stuffed animal and knew that everything would be fine: her sick heart would now beat better than ever!

∽

"Not a word to your father about this," warned Lucie after they'd left the dean's office.

"But mom, this is crazy! It's not fair! Pierrot has been taking his money for two years and doing nothing."

"Listen, Marie. Please don't tell your father or Edouard. I've got a feeling that this could be catastrophic for your dad. I'll do it myself, after having talked this over with Pierre-Hugues. Am I clear?"

"Yes, mother."

∽

Emilie was still in the expert hands of Professor Siethbüller, that surgeon whose brother was also a bigwig in the medical world, in the field of obstetrics and genetics. The professor and his team were working on her little heart. It was both tense and calm: their solidarity and expertise made them a dream team.

In the hallway where she'd been walking up and down, Lucie pounced upon Pierre-Hugues as soon as he walked in.

"What is going on here?" she asked without an introduction. "You dropped out of school?"

This question was like an uppercut for Pierre-Hugues, destabilizing him right when he was going to kiss his mother. Knocked out.

" What are you talking about?" he stuttered.

Five-foot tall Lucie seemed to look down on her son.

"Don't treat me like an idiot, Pierrot. I just saw the dean and he told me everything. You can fool your father, your brother and sisters if you want, but not me. Why didn't you say anything? Two years, Pierrot, two years!"

Pierre-Hugues abdicated, nearly relieved that this was no longer his secret.

"Um, I didn't think," he started awkwardly. "I mean. It's no big deal, is it?"

"What do you mean, no big deal? You're kidding. For you, maybe. But just think of your father who gives you everything, who's preparing a future for you, all that on a silver platter and you... you... you're wrecking everything! Why?"

"Why? Because I'm tired of school, that's why. And I'm tired of being considered as the inevitable successor to my all-powerful father!" he exploded. "I'm young, I want to have fun, take advantage of life, you must understand that."

"And why should I understand that better than anyone?" asked Lucie.

"Your past, mom. Your origins in the circus, did you forget all that?"

Lucie sighed.

"No, I didn't forget a single thing. You can believe me. And each day that goes by brings me more reasons not to have forgotten this splendid era. But, contrary to you, my son, I left that environment that was so uncertain, for a more serious life, it's true, but a more comfortable one."

"But mom, I've got the impression that I was born for that, you know: to have fun, impress other people. Like artists do!"

"Well, you're the intelligent one here. So what do artists have to live on? Bread and water, that's it. Is that what you want? While you've got everything to be happy for your entire life? You won't lack for a thing, with a good job if you deign to finish school, you'll be working with your brother and sister. You don't want that?"

Pierre-Hugues sat down, holding his head between his hands.

"I'm lost, mother."

"What do you mean?"

"I feel like I'm torn between two things, two opposite desires. Father on one side, with what he's planning for me, and the other, what I think I want to do. It's a conflict. So yes, I did drop out of college. And I'm having fun, I don't regret it."

"Pierrot, I can understand that. But I can't approve of that attitude. I'm so disappointed in you. Wrecking everything like that!"

"Mother!"

"Shhh! Not another word. I'll cover for you this time, I've got my reasons, but I want to repeat: I'm so disappointed."

Right then a nurse walked in, relieved.

"Mrs. Lacassagne? The operation is finished. Your daughter is fine, she's in the recovery room. You'll be able to see her in about an hour."

∽

Lilie's little heart was repaired and doing well. That wasn't the case though of the relationships in the Lacassagne family, where for the past couple of weeks everything seemed to be falling apart, inexorably, as if the ties they had built for years were melting under the scorching heat of the summer of 1986 in Nice.

That heat that had just increased by a few degrees.

CHAPTER 36
A little bit of money to help out

GORBIO, *June 28, 1986*

ITE MISSA EST.

Mass had been said in the little church in Gorbio. As usual, no Lacassagne family member was missing when they left mass after everyone else, as they always sat in the front row, right across from the altar. Nearly every Sunday Charles stayed a bit to talk with Father Labuche and hand him a little bit of money to help with the upkeep of the church.

The family walked back home to their villa. Lucie and Charles were in front. Pierre-Hugues was next, holding Emilie's hand.

Marie-Caroline called out to her brother, Edouard. They were behind everyone else.

"Doudou, wait a sec, let them get ahead of us, I've got something important to tell you."

"What?"

They let the rest of the family distance them, and she continued.

"Did you know, for Pierrot?

"Know what?"

"About school."

"What about school? I don't know what you're talking about."

"I was sure you wouldn't know. Well, I'll tell you because it's you. But please, don't tell anyone, mother made me promise to keep this a secret, especially from dad."

"Quit beating around the bush. So? Something juicy?"

Marie-Caroline didn't really know where to start, so she went right to the point.

"He dropped out of college almost two years ago."

"What the...?"

"I swear I'm telling the truth."

"Who told you that? Are you sure?"

"No doubt about it - it was the dean himself. We saw him with mom the other day, when Lilie was in the hospital, and you were on that business trip."

"What the heck were you doing at the dean's office? Was she summoned?"

"No, not at all, let me explain."

When Marie-Caroline finished, Edouard stopped right in the middle of the sidewalk.

"That is crazy. How could someone not be caught for two whole years?"

"I have no idea, but that's what happened. No one knew it, he kept his cards close to his chest, Pierrot."

"But that's disgusting! Do you realize what this means? That S.O.B. has been taunting everyone for all that time. But our father most of all! We can't allow that Caro!"

"What are you thinking of?"

"Spilling the beans, of course."

Caroline turned around.

"Please, I'm begging you, don't do that. Mother doesn't want him to be worried about this. She said that he'd never recover from it."

"But Jesus Christ! Sorry for the blasphemy, Father Labuche's ears must be ringing. And you're accepting that? No! Pierrot is living the high life with our father's money. He believes so much in his dear Pierre-Hugues, he rolls out the red carpet for him, he's preparing a golden parachute for him to take over as the holding director. And little Pierrot, what does he do? Takes advantage of him behind his back. Whereas us, we're working our butts off for him, in exchange for what? Little crumbs of recognition from our old man."

"Don't say that Doudou. Our father doesn't treat us differently."

"He doesn't? Open your eyes Caro! He's got a favorite son, and you know it. Their strategic meetings, their tennis matches on Sunday mornings, their whiskies together in the library and all that. Those aren't differences?"

Marie-Caroline sighed.

"You're right. But haven't you noticed that for a while he's not been paying so much attention to Pierre-Hugues? As if he wanted some distance. Maybe he does suspect something."

"So! If he knows, why hide it? I frankly can't stand this, it's not fair."

"I understand completely, Doudou. But please, don't joke here. I wanted you to know too but keep it all for yourself."

"What's in it for us if we shut up?"

"I don't know. But maybe if we don't, we've got a lot to lose. We've all got our little secret gardens, don't we? You, him, me. You know what I'm talking about."

"Yeah, I know."

"I mean like it would be better for everyone just to shut up, to wait and see how things go. Even if he is our dad's favorite, we'll be getting our part of the pie, whatever happens."

"That's true," admitted Edouard. "Wait and see then."

"Let's shake!"

The brother and sister high-fived each other and they walked up to the villa.

"But if he tells, I tell!" Edouard concluded.

CHAPTER 37
Like a wolf among sheep

NICE, *July 11, 2016*

Colombe nearly jumped out of her seat.

"I don't believe it! Like a snake pit!"

"Isn't it?" replied Sharpers, wiping his forehead off with an old handkerchief.

"Just a question, Mr. Sharpers," I added. "How do you know all that?"

"Well, you could say that I was more or less directly a witness to some of these events. Plus I was able to put the different versions together. I can't guarantee that everything is true, because I couldn't check each detail myself. There are still a lot of unanswered questions today."

"Maybe questions that no one asked at that time?" asked Colombe.

"You could say that, yes. All that I can affirm is at

that time, you could tell there was a lot of tension between the Lacassagne family members. And I sincerely believe now that that antagonism could have caused the accident on the sailboat."

"The alleged accident, you could also say," I added.

"But one that would have been less innocent than an accident," added Colombe.

"Right."

We all looked at each other.

"How could we be sure of this, thirty years later?" she asked.

"*A priori* impossible," I answered. "The investigation was closed, perhaps botched too, but in any case, closed: accident, case closed! But after what you just told us, there are a hoard of questions with no answers."

"How exciting!" said Colombe enthusiastically.

"Very!" added Sharpers. "When you know that everyone had something to hide. Lucie and her lover plus their illegitimate son; Pierre-Hugues who wasted his father's money and dropped out of school; Edouard and his homosexuality; Marie-Caroline with her nude photos. Some people know, some don't. Some talk, others don't say a word. Plus, if one of them squeals, the whole Lacassagne card castle crumbles to the ground!"

When he said this, Sharpers mimed a pile of cards tumbling down.

"What are you trying to do, thirty years later?" I asked Sharpers.

"Find out the truth!"

"Yeah, but how? And how is launching a hostile takeover bid on the holding going to help?"

"It'll shake the coconut tree, Mr. Bastaro!"

"Nice image! But what about us in all this?" asked Colombe, now a de facto member of the team.

"You're the spearhead and the homing device. You're intimate with the family."

"Like a wolf among sheep?" I asked, joining Sharpers in his use of old sayings.

"That's right."

"But we still have to find out how to learn more about all this," Colombe added. "Because for now, all we have is what you said and the suspicions you have. With all due respect Mr. Sharpers, we don't have to believe you or trust you. You show up here with your takeover bid and your doubts on this 'Lacassagne affair.' What gives you the right to do this?"

I was both stupefied and proud of Colombe's spontaneity and temerity. Sharpers though landed right on his feet and answered with a smile.

"You are totally right, Miss Deschamps. So, maybe you could contact Gendarme Petrucci, the one who was in charge of this case from the very beginning. I'm sure he's got things to say, even thirty years later. Check in with the chauffeur, Dominique, again too."

"How come? I already interviewed him," I said.

"Yes, but you probably didn't ask him the right questions. He's one of the key characters in this family saga. He knows them all, he's lived with them, driven them around, listened to what they had to say. Or confessed? In my opinion he's an important and priceless witness. Drivers often overhear things."

I appreciated Sharpers' analysis and mentally noted to follow it. I was also excited about this investigation.

The American got up from his armchair.

"I'm sorry, but I'm really tired. Thank you for coming and I think you'll have plenty of things to talk about for your current mission with Charles Lacassagne. Do you agree?"

"All we can do is try," I concluded, shaking Angel Sharpers' pudgy hand.

A strange interview, as if we had just walked into an unknown world.

CHAPTER 38
This military song that represented our country

WHEN COLOMBE and I left the bar, there was a lot of commotion in the streets of Nice. Cars were beeping their horns, teens were walking on the Promenade waving little French flags, their faces or sometimes even their hair painted in blue, white and red. Others were wearing Portugal's national colors. I suddenly realized that France was currently focused on the Euro Soccer Championship, that was taking place here in France today, July 11th, and that it was the final between these two leading soccer nations.

I'd been so obsessed with the Lacassagne's that I'd forgotten the event. I wasn't too much of a soccer fan anyway, preferring tennis or basketball.

"It's the final tonight!" shouted Colombe, has if she'd read my thoughts. "Want to watch the match outside? They installed a fan zone in the Albert-Premier Gardens."

"You know, soccer…"

"Come on," she begged with a suddenly childish look. "Say yes! That'll give us a break. It's so hot plus it'll be a lot of fun. Say yes, come on..."

"Okay, but just for you."

After all, she was right: having a little bit of fun would allow us to forget about all this for a while. Plus spending more time with her was not unpleasant at all.

"Who are you for?" I asked.

"France, of course! I'll be rooting for that cute Griezmann... you won't?"

I was torn between my patriotic love for France and its great soccer stars on one hand, and my distant Portuguese origins on the other.

"Well, just to spice up the match, I'll be supporting Portugal then," I said with a friendly elbow nudge on her arm.

"You better watch it! Don't provoke me!"

As the afternoon was drawing to an end, we walked towards the group of supporters in front of the gigantic screen where we'd be watching the final. We both bought a pan-bagnat, a little round sandwich made from tuna, green beans, anchovies and black olives, one of Nice's staples, and something that would be easy to eat while watching the game outside.

It was about eight-thirty when we arrived. I took advantage of the half an hour we had before the kickoff to contact Gerard, my Parisian employer via WhatsApp and keep him in the loop concerning the latest developments in this case.

> "Hey Gerard. The Lacassagne file is getting complicated. Lots going on here. I have to investigate things more, but it's quite possible that the accident that happened to the oldest son back in 1986 wasn't that accidental after all..."

"I let my boss in Paris in on this," I said to Colombe, between two bites of pan-bagnat.

"Let him in on what, exactly?"

"That the accident maybe wasn't accidental... I get I'll get an answer in five minutes, unless he's watching TV."

I was wrong. He answered only three minutes later!

> "What are you talking about? You got something juicy? Serious? Concrete evidence? If it's news, I want to know."

"Right! Gerard smells a scoop here!"

"You're not afraid you're getting ahead of yourself?" asked Colombe. "All we've got is this guy's story, this Sharpers who turned up like a fly in the soup with his crazy theories."

"Not just, no. He just confirmed a couple of elements that I personally felt when we were interviewing the Lacassagne family and acquaintances."

"What did you feel?"

"Um, a general tension. The way everyone was

trying to flee the episode of the accident and Pierre-Hugues's death, while coming back to it each time."

"It's true that the date was a turning point in the family saga."

All around us the crowd was getting larger, foghorns were blowing away, groups of supporters were singing, and we could smell sausages being grilled.

I finished my pan-bagnat and got back to Gerard.

> "Still gotta cross-check things, but if all this is true, wow!"

> "Skeletons in the closet?"

> "Could be. I'm gonna try to find the gendarme who opened this file. I'll let you know!"

> "Okay, see ya soon, have a good match. Allez la France!"

> "Viva Portugal!"

> "Traitor!"

Then I turned to Colombe.

"Listen, tomorrow could you contact the Théoule-sur-Mer gendarmerie to try to find out where that retired guy Petrucci lives?"

"No problem, boss!" she answered, still chewing.

As if she'd swallowed a mouthful of consonants, as I could barely hear her vowels.

"Great. I'll ask Dominique the right questions this time."

Right then the giant screen lit up, generating an enthusiastic clamor from the crowd. It was nine o'clock and the players, side by side, were on the field awaiting their national anthems. When the Marseillaise started, the majority of spectators, including Colombe, rose as one, and began belting out that military song that represented our country. I also sang it as I was afraid that I'd be quite alone singing the Portuguese anthem. Which I incidentally didn't know a single word of.

Then the referee blew his whistle for kickoff. The crowd of spectators roared, hoping for a French victory. I could tell that Colombe, sitting tight up against me, was carefully following the actions of the players on the greens of the Stade de France in Saint-Denis. The French team begun well. At the tenth minute, good-looking Griezmann nearly beat the Portuguese goalkeeper who made a reflex save, much to the dismay of the French supporters, who were all up and persuaded that France would be scoring. A disappointed "Oh" spread when the goalkeeper caught the ball.

"What are you planning to do with Charles?" asked Colombe nearly shouting in my ear to make herself heard in the festive atmosphere.

"Good question, thanks for asking!"

Yes, what the heck would I do should the accident not be accidental? Could I decently continue to write Charles's autobiography?

"You're welcome! You're the one who told me the other day that a journalist's work consists in knowing how to ask the right questions."

"You're right. But I haven't asked myself that question yet. Let's dig into the hypothesis saying that it wasn't an accident. Should that be true, I'd act accordingly with Charles. I'll be seeing him tomorrow, I'll try to stay neutral."

"Meaning?"

"Well, he's paying me to write his truth, isn't he? That's what I've been doing up till now."

"And if there's another truth?"

"You mean 'the' truth?"

"Yeah."

"I'll have to weigh the pros and cons. Keep on writing his truth or quit. A question of journalistic ethics."

In the Stade de France, Moussa Sissoko kept on attacking the Portuguese defense. Here, in the fan zone, the crowd rose at regular intervals.

In the twenty-fifth minute the was a whiff of hope for the French team when the captain Christiano Ronaldo was forced to leave because of an injury. That talented player, who won the Golden Ball three times, seemed to have opened a gap where the French team could exploit an opening. The French supporters were already imagining a victory!

When he left however, there was a false rhythm up till halftime, as if the opportunity to win gave French players too much pressure.

I bought us two glasses of nice cold beer at halftime. We raised our glasses.

"Here's to the Lacassagne's!" I said.

"Here's to a French victory!" she answered with a wink.

She took a long sip of beer which left a small white mustache on the top of her lip. Sexy lady!

I couldn't stop myself.

I leaned to her and kissed the place where the foam was.

"What…?" she started to say, opening her eyes wide.

I interrupted her by kissing her even harder, and she finally responded with pleasure. We didn't care who won, here it was a tie. The ball was in the center.

"I'm sorry," I said when our mouths pulled away.

"Don't be. I've been wanting to do that too."

This time she was the one who leaned to me seeking my lips.

We only separated when the game started again.

In the second half, palpable pressure rose as no one had scored. Nothing was working, neither Giroud's nor Sissoko's playing could make a difference. Then luck ran out for the French team when Gignac hit the right post though the Portuguese goalkeeper was on the other side. Such a deception!

During the last minutes of the game, I sent

Dominique a text message. He'd given me his number so he would be available for me whenever possible, as that was what Charles Lacassagne had asked him to do.

"Hi Dominique. Would it be possible tomorrow to pick me up half an hour before we'd planned? I'd like to ask you a few more questions. Thanks. Have a nice day. Jerome Bastaro."

He answered just before the additional time.

"Hello. "No problem. Dominique."

Simple, but efficient.

We sat back down when the referee signaled that the additional time was about to begin, after having exchanged one more kiss. Colombe took my hand and held it until at the one hundred and ninth minute of his high-pressure game, Moutinho set up Lopes who kicked the ball into the back of Hugo Lloris's net, devastating France's hopes for victory.

All around us people were stupefied and the shocked silence continued to the end of the final whistle.

"Congratulations, Portugal won!" admitted Colombe, kissing me again.

To tell the truth I couldn't have cared less! Now what I was interested in was getting to the bottom of what I now was calling the Lacassagne Affair.

Especially as I felt like I'd been growing wings since my relationship with Colombe had risen to another level.

CHAPTER 39
Peasants at the Harvest Ball

NICE, *July 12, 2016*

COLOMBE and I had a hard time leaving each other the night before. And it wasn't because we'd been talking about the Lacassagne's. Nope. We'd taken advantage of that hot summer night to make out on a bench in the park. Because of additional time, the match only finished at about eleven thirty, in a morose but festive atmosphere. After all, French people love the Portuguese. Nearly cousins, seeing as how many Portuguese live in France. The square slowly emptied around us as other couples and partygoers were also taking advantage of the nice weather.

I only accompanied Colombe back to her car at about one in the morning: after all, we did have a big day planned for the next day.

That though didn't prevent us from sending an

incredible number of text messages back and forth till two. It's always impossible to leave when you're beginning to fall in love. Which, however, did remind me that Cynthia must have loosened her grip back in Paris because I wasn't receiving any more messages from her. She must have understood I needed some fresh air. That her air was polluting mine. She had taken my breath away. Now I understood this expression.

The air that I now wanted to sniff was Colombe's: fresh, lively and non-polluting! Like the air here at the seaside!

When I woke up our text messages started again, as if we were a couple of teens. It did me good to forget about money and grudges family members had.

I was though very well paid by Charles to write his biography. Meaning I had to get back to work. I was meeting Dominique right outside the Negresco at two. I used the time I had to look over my notes again and try to organize the novel about the Lacassagne empire, taking into account my latest interviews with Edouard, Lucie and Brigitte.

But the objectivity of my global overview was now compromised by what that Sharpers guy had told me about them. I no longer saw them the same way, they were now less monolithic, more ambiguous: more human actually!

That morning I didn't even write a single paragraph. I was bothered by that accident that took place in 1986 as well as my thoughts, which kept coming back to Colombe's lips, covered in a delicious white hops foam.

I had a sandwich sent up for lunch and at two, Dominique was parked right out in front. I got into the back seat.

"Hello, Dominique."

"Hello, Mr. Bastaro. How are you?"

"Fine thanks. And you?"

"As well as possible. Monsieur Charles gave us a huge fright. But he's already doing better. He told me this morning he's looking forward to seeing you. He wants you to get back to work on his project."

I jumped at this opportunity.

"So Dominique, like I was saying yesterday, I need your point of view on a few questions."

"I don't know if I'll be able to help you. I can't see anything I'd tell you that you don't already know."

"Let me try, anyway. As you've lived with the family for years now, you must know them all well."

"I'll do my best. But once again, I already told you everything. At least I think so. Where do you want to go for this discussion?"

"Well, how about having it here while driving? It's pleasant, comfortable and we've got air conditioning! Just drive wherever you want."

Right then Colombe sent me a text.

"Arrived in Théoule. I'll keep you in the loop. Kisses."

I thought things over a minute. I didn't want to

rush him with intrusive questions. I finally asked him my first one.

"Dominique, after having spoken to quite a few people, I understood that 1986 was full of all sorts of emotions. Do you share my impression?"

"Meaning?"

"I mean, did you feel that there was a sort of tension then? Do you remember how you felt at that time?"

I could see him frown from the rear-view mirror. He thought a few moments before answering.

"Mr. Bastaro, how would my feelings be important?"

"Everything's important for me. When you're writing about the atmosphere of a given period of time, everyone's point of view is interesting."

"I understand. But I don't know what to say."

"Let me help. What I'd like to know is that if you'd noted or even overheard any delicate conversations between siblings, Marie-Caroline, Edouard and Pierre-Hugues."

"Ah. That's what you want to talk about?"

"Yup. Did you feel there was a sort of tension between them?"

"You know, like all brothers and sisters, I suppose."

"Like cats and dogs then. But for them, I heard that it was a bit more than that."

"That's true," admitted Dominique, glancing at me in the rear-view mirror. "I must say that the months before Pierre-Hugues' accident were strange."

"What do you mean by strange?"

"Like there were two clans - Pierre-Hugues on one side and Marie-Caroline and Edouard on the other. And little Emilie wasn't in either of them, I'm sure you understand."

"Plus the three of them were already adults and Lilie was still a child. So, what did these two clans do?"

"Well, Edouard and Marie-Caroline were almost always together. They isolated Pierre-Hugues. I don't know why, but it was like they resented something he'd done. I sometimes overheard them talking."

"Do you remember anything they said?"

"The gist of it. They talked about betrayal, secrets, keeping silent and whistleblowing."

"You're sure they were talking about their brother and not, I don't know, about a movie or a book?"

Dominique thought this over.

"Hmm. Could have been a movie about revenge. But I'm pretty sure of myself: I often heard them say 'Pierrot' when they were talking about things like this."

"I see. And that didn't worry you?"

"Not then, you could say."

"What do you mean?"

"So like I said, for me it was just everyday bickering between brothers and sisters."

"Not then, you said. Are you insinuating that this was followed by moments that were even tenser?"

"I don't know why I'm telling you this Mr.

Bastaro. Maybe I'm relieved to talk about it. After all, no one can go to jail now."

"I'm listening."

"Well, one other time, I think it must have been end of June or beginning of July in 1986, I heard Edouard talking to Marie-Caroline. 'That's disgusting, if he continues, I swear I'm gonna kill him.'"

That confirmed my intuition!

"You're sure of that? Edouard said that talking about Pierre-Hugues?"

"I'm afraid so."

"What did you do about it? Did you speak to Charles? Or to Pierre-Hugues?"

"No. I thought those words were just lot of hot air, something he'd said because he was angry. I didn't want to worry Monsieur. Now I realize maybe that was a mistake."

"It's always easy to have 20/20 vision with hindsight," I reassured him, noting that his voice had trembled when he'd said that.

We were still driving around slowly. Dominique was driving almost mechanically on those roads he knew by heart now. We'd left the coast and were going inland. The road was narrow and shoe stringing. After a few minutes the chauffeur continued.

"Edouard had changed a lot. I had the impression he was no longer the same person, without understanding why."

I jumped at this opportunity to change subjects.

"At that time, he was engaged to a girl named Julie Schneider, wasn't he?"

"That's right. A nice polite girl, cute, from a good family."

"But they broke up?"

"Yes, the wedding everyone was hoping for never happened."

"Do you know why?"

"No, I don't, that was all private stuff. But at that time I also noticed that things weren't going well between Edouard and Julie. I often drove them to town or to parties at their friends' houses in the region. And I can tell you that in the car, it sure wasn't a party, far from it. I never even saw them kiss! Maybe too much prudishness, I can understand that. But they were always in the back seat, there where you are, and he was on one side, she was on the other. Edouard was scrunched up against the door, as if to put the most distance between Julie and him, as if he was fleeing. And several times when I looked in the rear-view mirror, I saw tears in Julie's eyes, and she was looking away."

"Like she wanted to escape?"

"Maybe."

"When did they break off the engagement?"

"Just a few months later. Beginning of 1987, I'd say, at the latest, as they'd already recovered poor Pierre-Hugues' body and buried him."

"And after that, did he have any other relationships?" I asked, thinking about Edouard's supposedly homosexual inclinations.

"Let's just say I never saw him with another woman. An old bachelor now."

"Speaking about bachelors. And excuse me if I'm shocking you with this question but do you think it's possible that Edouard could be a homosexual?"

Dominique took his time answering.

"Why are you asking me that?"

"Just an intuition," I lied. "Let's just say that without actually being effeminate and not going into any generalities, Edouard doesn't seem to be a very virile man either. His lifestyle, the absence of women in his private life. All of that sort of leads me to think that maybe... See where I'm going here?"

"Perhaps you're not wrong Mr. Bastaro," admitted the chauffeur.

But he didn't add anything. I hopped back in.

"Would you say that was one of those secrets between Marie-Caroline and him? And that Pierre-Hugues could have found out and threatened to spill the beans to his parents?"

"That could be possible. That or other secrets I suppose. But I don't think I'm wrong in saying that in every family there are secrets, big ones, little ones, unsaid ones, hidden ones. The Lacassagne family is like everyone else!"

"The Lacassagne family. Are you insinuating that other people had secrets too then?"

"Mr. Bastaro, everyone's got secrets! But I

remember they were having a family reunion, in the beginning of the summer of 1986 and there was a terrible atmosphere, everyone seemed to be judging the others, challenging them or avoiding them. And the discussion was pretty heated, I'd never seen anything like that before.

It was a Sunday at noon, at the villa. We were all having lunch outside, in the shade of the parasol pine trees in the back."

∽

Gorbio, July 6, 1986

Everyone was sitting around the table that first Sunday of vacation. Charles and Lucie, Pierre-Hugues, Edouard and Julie, Marie-Caroline and Emilie. Brigitte, Simon and Dominique were also invited to have lunch.

But the atmosphere was all but partylike.

Charles and Lucie were basically sad: no discussions, no compliments for anyone, sighs of exasperation.

Edouard was sitting between Julie and Marie-Caroline. More often than not, he was concentrating on his sister, having a secret conversation, staring at Pierre-Hugues, who was sitting on the left of his mother.

Pierre-Hugues looked exhausted and tortured. He

kept on glancing at his father, who was seated at the head of the table.

Dominique and Brigitte, the two powerless and silent employees, watched that non-verbal jousting match, that storm looming above the Lacassagne's.

As usual, the most cheerful, a privilege of their age, were Lilie and Simon who pecked at their dinner plates before playing, running around the table and on the beautifully cut lawn.

There were salads, cold cuts, chicken wings and cold fish on the table. Plus wine, red, rosé and white, as much as you could drink. Alcohol levels rose and tempers flared.

Tongues were loosened.

The men dared each other.

Edouard was the quickest to draw as alcoholic beverages always excited him. He insinuated, teasing his brother with hints about schooling, degrees and people who'd dropped out. Charles was listening closely, and Lucie was horrified. Pierre-Hugues fought back, albeit jokingly, humming *Antisocial* by Trust, talking about how punks have invaded France, and mentioning new drugs on the market and the havoc they could wreak from a neurological point of view. Then it was Marie-Caroline's turn to wince and look frantically at her parents. Voices rose and Lucie tried to calm everyone down.

Edouard had finished another glass of rosé and had lost all inhibitions. His allusions turned into direct attacks when he asked his brother with which one of his new hotties he was hanging out, when little Lilie was at the hospital.

Pierre-Hugues, who had just poured himself another whisky, counterattacked, mockingly, asking him why he wasn't wearing his black leather pants today.

Then Edouard exploded.

"Go to hell, Pierrot!"

And he rushed to his older brother, fists ready to fight, shouting unintelligible words. But Pierre-Hugues was so much stronger than he was.

There was total confusion: the women shouted, chairs were tossed aside, the children were crying and Dominique had to separate the two brothers.

Charles was angry.

"That is enough! Are you two crazy or what? That's not the way we behave in the Lacassagne family! We're not peasants at the Harvest Ball, after all! Calm down, you two."

Edouard was all red and out of breath whereas Pierre-Hugues seemed much more serene.

"Now pick everything up," Charles continued. "And sit down and don't say another word. We'll talk this over later, alone."

∼

"That was the first time I saw something like that take place at my employer's," concluded Dominique as he wound through the last curves leading to Gorbio where Charles was waiting for me. "Maybe that was the culmination of the summer of '86. After that, maybe they talked things over, as everyone seemed to have calmed down. Up until the accident!"

"Paying lip service to calming down?" I suggested.

"I think so. I was sure that something bad was going to happen. There was too much tension between them, too many secrets, too much money too. Believe me, Mr. Bastaro, money is the root of all evil."

We'd just turned into the driveway to the Lacassagne's villa. Dominique dropped me off at the stairs where Lucie greeted me. She took me to her husband who was waiting for me, sitting in his leather armchair in his library. It was a splendid room with sculpted wainscoting and the shelves were full of beautiful books. I thought to myself that many libraries would have been jealous of so many old books.

Charles said he was delighted to see me and continue with his story. I was finding it hard to ask the right questions. All I was thinking of was what Dominique as well as Angel Sharpers had just told me. Of course I didn't say a word about my meeting with the American. I was uncomfortable, like a soldier walking through a minefield. Or a double agent forced to get information from both sides.

I nonetheless spent nearly two hours with Charles before he said he was tired and asked Dominique to drive me back to Nice.

When I left the villa, I saw that Colombe had sent me a text message.

"Hello! Great news! Call me back. Kisses!"

My little assistant proudly told me that she'd succeeded in contacting ex-Sergeant Petrucci and that he was expecting us tomorrow. I congratulated her and said I was proud of her, that she'd be a good journalist. She wanted to know if we'd see each other tonight or if I had too much work. I told her I had work, but that I needed to see her.

At eight, we were sitting outside in a brasserie in the old part of town, the one where we met on the first day. Which seemed ages ago. We had shaken hands then, today we kissed each other enthusiastically.

She told me how she was able to get an appointment with the former gendarme from Théoule-sur-Mer. She'd introduced herself as someone who was writing a thesis on people who'd lost their lives by drowning and that the death of the Lacassagne son, in the 80s, would be a perfect example of this. She was hoping to meet and interview those who had witnessed this, like Petrucci. The gendarme she'd seen was one of his former colleagues. He'd given her his contact details. Petrucci, who was probably bored, immediately agreed to see her. Colombe had presented me as her professor.

No sooner said than done!

We ate while summing up everything we knew about the Lacassagne's family's past, including what I had just learned from Dominique.

The question we had, and that we hoped to get a response to tomorrow with the gendarme, was to understand how an accident could be requalified to premeditated murder.

Who would have a motive to shut Pierre-Hugues up for good?

"Edouard, his brother," suggested Colombe. "To hide his debauchery, the fact that he took drugs and was a homosexual. And then you add his jealousy when he learned that his brother, who his father seemed to prefer, had dropped out of school without telling him."

"Same thing for Marie-Caroline. Jealousy and her 'artistic' photos. And for both of them, a long-term hope to have a larger share of the fortune?"

"So, we've got: intimate secrets, plus jealousy, plus a bigger heritage. That sure gives us an explosive cocktail!"

"Exactly! Without taking into account what Dominique heard Edouard say. 'I'm going to kill him,' and all that."

"There is a difference between threatening someone and carrying it out."

"Of course, plus there are no tangible proofs, just what people told us. Who else would have profited from his death, and why?"

"Maybe Charles himself," proposed Charles, hesitating.

"Yeah. But why?"

"Because he knows that Pierre-Hugues isn't his legitimate son, just a child born when his wife had cheated on him with her former lover? And he no longer wants to turn his heritage and business over to a bastard?"

"Right. Colombe, do you think that these are valid motives for a premeditated murder?"

"Sure, the papers tell us every day that any motive even a small or a ridiculous one, is sufficient to off someone you don't want hanging around. Once I saw a guy who shot his teacher in high school because he'd failed an exam. Anything's possible, you know."

"And that's what's scary. Except here, we don't have any proof. I'm anxious to meet that Petrucci guy tomorrow. Maybe he'll help us put this all into order, with his point of view of being a cop."

Then we talked about other more cheerful things and finished the evening with a long walk along the Promenade, hand in hand, lips touching too.

~

Summer of 2012, southern France

How lucky they are to be sitting here on the patio of this luxury hotel bright and early in the morning, overlooking the village with its ocher-colored tiles and the blue Mediterranean Sea.

That's what the employee of the hotel was thinking of when she was clearing the table next to the couple who had been there for three days. She'd noticed their little habits. He always came down first, had a cup of espresso alone, and finally the lady joined him, already well dressed, well-groomed and subtlety made up.

That morning, she sat down across from the man and ordered a green tea with a bit of milk. Then she smiled at him, took his hand from across the table, and held it tenderly.

When the employee brought her the cup of hot tea, she overheard a few snippets of conversation.

"We shouldn't be doing this," the lady said.

"It's only fair. He cheated on you for years, almost right under your nose. He deserves to pay!"

Such a mysterious couple the young employee thought, picking up a tablecloth with coffee stains on it.

After all, it's their business though, she said to herself as she went back to the kitchens.

CHAPTER 40
Eight thousand jasmine flowers

SPERACEDES, *July 13, 2016*

The next morning, it wasn't Lacassagne's limousine waiting for me, but Colombe's Fiat Punto. Not as big of course, but much more lively, personal, full of its owner's communicative good mood: a little pink cat sitting in the corner of the dashboard and a vanilla perfumed fragrance diffuser made the inside of the car smell heavenly. Without of course considering the driver's own perfume and her smile that was just as large and bewitching as the Pacific itself.

She was driving us to former Sergeant Petrucci's house, a little house in the countryside in Speracedes, a village that wasn't too far from Grasse, the perfume capital of France and maybe of the whole world.

The former gendarme was waiting for us. I'd been expecting a fat guy with chubby cheeks and a moustache, the image I'd had of a retired gendarme. Instead of that, Petrucci was a slim freshly shaved man, smiling, with a friendly face. Maybe he was nostalgic of when he wore his kepi, as he was wearing a straw hat: gendarmes always had to wear hats!

"You must be Miss Deschamps," he said, holding his hand out to Colombe.

"That's right. Thank you so much for your time, Mr. Petrucci. And this is Jerome Bastaro, my professor."

We shook hands.

"Right this way."

He led us to the backyard, going around his house. He'd prepared a small table with three glasses, and a carafe of what seemed to be lemonade to me.

"Would you like a glass of violet water? It really hits the spot, you'll see."

He poured each of us a large glass.

"Well? How can a former gendarme help you, Miss?"

Colombe cleared her throat, looked at me and answered.

"Mr. Petrucci, my dissertation is about accidentology in the sea, and I'd hoped to get some information from you as a coastline gendarme, and in particular about that affair that took place here in the 80s, when the Lacassagne's oldest son drowned, a local tragedy. Your squad was the one who took care of the survivors?"

"Yes it was, and Good Lord, what a drama! Thirty years already. I'd nearly forgotten it."

I wondered how someone could forget the tragic death of the son of one of France's richest men, but I didn't want to interrupt him.

"You know, the sea is formidable, and no one is invincible, from the richest boaters and yachtsmen to the poorest fishermen. The sea is fair, just like God himself."

"Do you remember what happened?" asked Colombe, cutting off his lyricism. "Was it a stormy night?"

Petrucci looked to his left, as if he was recalling it.

"Yes, it was of course, otherwise I'd imagine that the accident could have been avoided. If I remember correctly, from what the two survivors told me, I think that the boom of the mast had hit the Lacassagne son, something like that. And that was what pushed him into the sea."

"That is what the official version says. We were able to read the synthetic report that you'd written back then," said Colombe. "The report also said that the passengers had consumed alcoholic beverages onboard. Do you think that could have been an aggravating factor?"

Petrucci sighed.

"Alcohol is dangerous Miss, on the sea like on the road. It certainly could have lessened their attention and vigilance. Stormy weather, alcoholic beverages, the heat, maybe even exhaustion."

"So, you're sure it was an unfortunate accident?"

"What do you mean?"

"I mean, your investigation concluded that it was an accident, is that right?"

Petrucci looked at us while finishing his violet water.

"To be precise, strictly speaking there wasn't an investigation."

"Really?" I said, astonished.

"Do you think that there's an investigation for each event that takes place? For an investigation Miss, someone has to file a complaint. And here, no one did. Against who? Against the storm? Against the boom? Against bad luck? Maybe against Neptune himself while we're at it! It was an accident. A tragic one, as someone lost his life, but what can you do? Accidents happen."

"So there wasn't a file opened on Pierre-Hugues Lacassagne's death?"

"Of course there was. But it was just a simple report that I wrote myself, as I was the one who had taken the statements of the two survivors, then Mr. Lacassagne's statement too."

"A report opened and then closed when the body was found?" I asked.

"That's about it. Just an administrative document."

"Mr. Petrucci, what exactly was in it?"

"Not much, if I remember well: the report I wrote, the coroner's report, plus the testimonial of the person who discovered the body in Cassis. About it."

"Nothing out of the ordinary then," I thought aloud.

Petrucci stared at me.

"Why should what happened not be ordinary, just because it happened to someone well-known?"

I felt cornered, I had to ask the question that we came to get an answer to.

"Mr. Petrucci. If someone today told you that this wasn't just an ordinary accident, could you open the file again?"

"Thirty years later? I don't see what you could add to open it again. Plus remember, this isn't a cold case, it's just an archived report. We're not on TV!"

"And if someone told you that it wasn't an accident?"

"What else could it be?"

"Murder, Mr. Petrucci. Premediated murder."

Petrucci didn't say a word and got up.

"Come with me."

We went to the back of his yard, and he turned around to see if we were following him. Which we were, a bit intrigued by that sudden change of pace. We went back about a hundred and fifty feet, until he stopped to pick a flower that he raised to his nose. He closed his eyes and smelled it, then handed it to Colombe.

"Smell this, Miss."

Colombe took the flower, a beautiful white rose.

"Hmm, what a powerful fragrance," she admitted.

We were surrounded by huge flowerbeds, of all sizes and colors, and they all gave off fantastic fragrances.

"This is my flower garden," the former gendarme said. "My passion ever since I retired. You've got violets, roses, orange blossoms, lavender, and tuberose. Heaven on earth that I take care of carefully every day. Did you know that it takes nearly eight thousand jasmine flowers to obtain one kilo?"

"That's impressive," I said - but to tell the truth, I didn't give a damn and was wondering what all this was about.

He kept walking through his flower beds.

"My dream would have been to be a 'nose'. You know, those people who work for perfumers, who can recognize odors of hundreds of vegetal, animal or synthetic fragrances and create unique associations for new perfumes. But it's not really a job, it's more of a talent. A gift I didn't get when I was born. So I became a gendarme!"

"That's a good job too," said Colombe. "A vocation, or a mission! But why are you telling us all this?"

"And why are you lying to me?"

I must say that this boomerang question knocked us out.

"Excuse me?" I said.

"Yeah, how come you're trying to pull my leg?"

I suddenly thought the old gendarme was nuts.

"I don't understand," stuttered Colombe.

"Don't pretend to be idiots with me. You can't teach an old dog new tricks. You didn't come here for some dissertation about drownings. So, what's your story? I don't think you're cops; I would have made you quicker. Private detectives working for someone either. You're journalists, aren't you?"

We were nailed. That former cop still had flair!

"I'm sorry. We are journalists and I'm sure that had we gone to Théoule, and introduced ourselves as such, you never would have contacted us, am I right?"

"That's true young lady. I don't really like journalists. But you both seem friendly and as you're both here, let's continue our conversation. And get straight to the point. Anyway, I quickly understood that you weren't interested by drownings in general, but by Lacassagne's death."

We resumed our conversation while walking through his flowers as well as his huge vegetable garden that he was equally proud of.

"Premediated murder, huh? That's pretty serious stuff. What makes you think that?"

"Not much really. However, and with all due respect, you didn't have any proof either that it was an accident."

"No, no proof that it was or wasn't. But as no one filed a complaint, we didn't open an investigation. Plus, the statutes of limitation are expired legally speaking. Meaning you can't file a complaint now for murder."

"But did you ever doubt that it was an accident?"

"I should have?"

"Let's just say that everyone talked about Pierre-Hugues as being an excellent swimmer. He was one of Nice Swimming Club's top swimmers."

"Now that you mention it, yes I do remember that it was a point that bothered me. But like I said, the weather was terrible that night and the sea was rough. You add a few grams of alcohol in your blood and then the shock of being hit with the boom. Even the best swimmers in the world wouldn't have survived."

"Did they attempt to recover him?"

"His brother threw out a buoy, but unsuccessfully."

Petrucci didn't say anymore and walked us to the front of his home.

"I really can't help you anymore," he said, holding out his hand.

"Thanks anyway," I answered. "And congratulations for your clairvoyance!"

"Oh, a gendarme's eye, that's all. And to conclude, I'd just like to tell you that it's too late now to file a complaint. You can still have fun writing about a hypothetical premeditated murder if you think you have enough evidence. But think twice. Charles Lacassagne is a big fish in a little pond and he's influential. Be careful! Just say a little birdie told you so!"

CHAPTER 41
Starving artists do exist

NICE, *July 14, 2016*

THE LADY WAS WAITING on track number three at the train station in Nice. She couldn't wait till the train came! They hardly ever saw each other, usually only once a year, in summer. He generally came down south. She didn't like to travel very much.

The train was twenty minutes late, stealing time from them and that made her sad. The Paris-Mediterranean trip was always late.

You just had to wait, which she did philosophically.

She finally saw the front of the TGV pulling into the station. Her heart began to beat faster.

The train stopped, its brakes screeching, and the first travelers got out, some running, others bitching, sweating, laughing, limping, or lugging baggage.

The lady stood on her tiptoes to try to see the head of the person she'd been waiting for.

Finally, he was there.

He ran up to her, a huge smile on his face. They hugged.

"Finally, you're here! You can't imagine how happy I am to see you. You could come more often you know," she scolded him.

"Love you too, Mom," he replied, teasing her.

"Kids! I love you, my little Simon," Brigitte said taking his hand like when he was little.

"Mom! I'm thirty-six years old now, I'm no longer your 'little' Simon."

"You'll always be my little Simon you know!"

They went through the lobby to the buses.

"We'll go home first so you can drop off your suitcase there. After that, we'll have lunch outside, okay my little honeybunch?"

"Fine with me, mom, but can you quit with all those ridiculous nicknames?" Simon said, laughing.

An hour later they were sitting in the old town outside in the shade.

"Well? How's life in Paris?" Brigitte wanted to know. "Tell me. Do you still live alone? No girlfriend? You can tell me everything, you know."

"Yes, I know. But no, no girlfriend. I'd tell you about her first, see what you think, you know.

"Oh! Quit making fun of me, you're a naughty boy sometimes. And your paintings? Do you sell any?"

Simon had lived in Paris for about fifteen years.

After having studied at the Paris School of Fine Arts, he moved to Montmartre, to be right in the heart of the historical part of Paris, where all the other painters lived, those who sold their paintings in the Place du Tertre. That's where he got his inspiration from, in the winding roads, sometimes even putting his easel down at the foot of the stairs in that district. Or sometimes he went down to the Seine River and worked at the end of Ile Saint-Louis, where he painted the waves, the riverbanks, people walking up and down the quays, and the bouquinistes who sat on their folding chairs, and even sometimes passersby or lovebirds kissing on the benches. But starving artists do exist, unfortunately.

"It's not easy, you know. I do sell some, but that doesn't earn me a lot of money. Last month, I had a show in a friend's art gallery. For the grand opening, a lot of people came and they liked my work. I even got an order from a Japanese collector who wanted to hang my pictures in his new Parisian apartment. That way I've got enough money for the next couple of months."

The waiter brought them two large seafood salads with whelks, king prawns and baby squid.

"If I could help you out more, I would," said Brigitte. "My pension is pretty small."

"Don't worry. You don't have to be sorry about anything, you already helped me a lot. Without your monthly check, life would be a lot more difficult. But I'm not complaining, I do what I love, and I make a living from my passion. Not a good living, but still. Everyone isn't as lucky as I am."

"But still, it's not fair."

"How come?"

Brigitte picked up a lettuce leaf before answering.

"Just because. I mean, with all your talent, you should make more money, a lot more. If you mother hadn't been a poor housekeeper, maybe you would have had another life."

"Stop that right now! That's ridiculous. It's not how you're born that dictates your life. It's your choices."

"If you're born on a straw mattress or in silk sheets, believe me, that does change a lot!"

"Could be," Simon admitted. "But don't feel that you're responsible for my life. I didn't lack anything until I left Nice. I'm the one who chose to be an artist, and I knew what it would entail. I knew it would be difficult, but it was my choice. A choice I totally assume. And who knows? Maybe one day I'll earn big bucks from it. Everyone's in the limelight sooner or later."

Brigitte took her son's hand.

"I hope I'll soon be able to help you more."

"You're gonna start playing the lottery again?" Simon joked. "Not too many people win millions you know! We could share it. And then take a plane and live in the Seychelles. I'd paint one lagoon per year, and you could work on your tan."

When they'd finished lunch, Simon wanted to take

a walk around the old part of Nice, remembering when he was little. He wanted to see his old primary school, his old middle school and high school.

When they'd left the Lacassagne family, a bit after their oldest son had passed away, Simon had to get used to new friends, new teachers, a new part of town, a new life. For a few years after they often went back to Gorbio where he was able to play with Lilie, who was like his sister. Then time went by they didn't see each other anymore. Simon hadn't forgotten her though.

"How's Lilie? Do you ever see her?"

"She's a big girl now. But I haven't run across her for a while."

"And everyone else?"

"Same thing. I haven't worked for them for twenty years now, we're no longer close. Everyone's got their own lives, their own problems. I heard that Charles is getting ready to step down and let Edouard and Marie-Caroline take over."

"Oh! That's true, but I also heard on the news that an American wants to buy them out?"

"Really? You know, money, money, money! *Pff*," Brigitte sighed. "How about an ice-cream cone at Fenocchio's? Like when you were little?"

"Ah. For once I'll be happy to be your little Simon again. Let's go, but I'm paying!"

They had a hard time choosing between the ninety-four different flavors the famous shop had. Brigitte opted for a traditional honey-pine scoop and violet and Simon dared a tomato-basil and zabaglione cream combo.

Enjoying their cones, they walked to the Promenade des Anglais where preparations for the 14th of July were beginning. Podiums were being assembled for concerts and crowds were on the beach. With this beautiful weather, the celebration would be a great one.

They walked a little over a mile along the coast, up to the Negresco and then decided to turn back. Simon wanted to dip his toes in the Mediterranean, less polluted than the Seine. The water was excellent.

They spent the whole afternoon wandering around and then had a light dinner while awaiting the festivities.

When it was finally dark, there was a huge crowd on the Promenade and neighboring streets, as well as on the beach. That's where Brigitte and Simon sat down to watch the fireworks, planned for ten p.m.

Beautiful! The rockets made multicolored rosette circles, filling the air with incredible noise. And the reflections of the fireworks in the sea increased the pleasure of watching them. Spectators were oohing and aahing, children were applauding, their eyes full of colorful stars. People came as couples, with friends, with family members. Every generation was present, people from Nice, vacationers, foreign tourists. Nearly thirty thousand people were watching the fireworks show from various places in the city. One of the best spots was right there at the seaside: on the Promenade des Anglais, in the heart of the equally famous Baie des Anges.

When it was over, Brigitte was tired.

"Sweetie, I'm not feeling too well. I don't know if it's because I'm tired, or if it's the heat, or something I ate, but I'd like to go home now. You can stay if you want."

"Come on, I'll go with you."

They caught a taxi that took them to Mont Boron, where Brigitte's apartment was. She swallowed a pill, and they sat outside on her balcony, in two sunbeds, to keep on taking advantage of this beautiful summer evening.

Below, they could see the sea and the Promenade, with its lights forming a twinkling rope.

Suddenly the sound of sirens ripped through the night.

CHAPTER 42

An unforgettable spectacle!

NICE, *July 14, 2016*

I woke up late the next day. The day before, after we'd left Petrucci, Colombe had dropped me off at the Negresco where Dominique was waiting for me. He drove me back to Gorbio where I spent I good hour with Charles. I was feeling more and more uncomfortable with him with all the doubts I now had about the alleged accident back in 1986. I tried not to show it though and listened to his official sales pitch: his successful life as a businessman. He spoke to me about his foreign exploits. Then I spent the evening trying to weave a story out of all the elements I had. It was tough, but I nonetheless worked until after midnight.

That's why I was sleeping in on that July 14th holiday. It was a day off, and Charles would leave me alone!

I texted Colombe.

"How about coming with me to see the fireworks tonight?"

"I'll meet you this afternoon, is that okay?"

"Fine!"

I KEPT busy while waiting to see her again.

We met at Place Rossetti and sat down at Fenocchio's for an ice-cream. It was hot, we were glad to see each other. Colombe turned around.

"Look, over there, at the counter, I think it's Brigitte."

"I never met her you know. I'll just have to believe you."

"Want me to introduce you two?"

"No, don't worry. It's a day off today! Plus I don't think she's alone, let's not bother her. How's your ice-cream? Can I taste it?"

She gave me a spoonful. And it was delicious, in more than one way!

"So, what are you planning on doing with the Lacassagne's?" she asked me.

She must have been reading my mind, that was exactly what was going through my head.

"I really don't know. I feel like I'm in an impasse. Stuck between my duty to finish the job I'm being paid for and between finding out what really happened to

Pierre-Hugues. But I'm afraid we're not going to make any more progress on that."

"You mean there's no way we'll find out the truth? Find out what really happened in 1986, and not just through hearsay?"

"Yup. But Sharpers put that story into my head and now I can't get rid of it. But I still think there's something to be discovered here, something that's not quite right. Like a worm in an apple that looks good on the outside but is rotten to the core. When you bite into it, it leaves you with a horrible taste in your mouth, one that lingers on."

"What do you think is the worm here?"

"I'd say money. Because whether you have too much or not enough, money always corrupts people and leads them to do terrible things."

"Enough with the Lacassagne family," said Colombe. "We're not going to let them wreck our day. Today is our day, our evening!"

"Our night?" I dared to ask.

"Who knows!"

We walked up and down the beach for hours, on the Promenade that was filling up with people and where the city had installed bleachers to listen to the mini concerts tonight for the 2016 Prom' Party. Five stages for five groups playing pop rock and blues, according to the posters. One of the podiums was just across from my hotel.

I'd planned a surprise for Colombe tonight. This morning, I'd reserved a table in the hotel's restaurant,

Le Chantecler, which is said to be one of the city's finest. Jean-Denis Rieubland, the Chef and *Meilleur Ouvrier de France* (Best Worker) in 2007, already had two Michelin stars! It would cost me, that was for sure, but with the advance that Charles had given me, I wasn't going to go broke.

Colombe and I walked to the Chantecler.

"No!" she exclaimed. "That's where we're going to eat? You are completely crazy, Jerome!"

Still, she kissed me gratefully. It was going to be a good evening.

All that I remember about this dinner is that we didn't mention the name of the Lacassagne's even once, which alone was quite nice. We spoke about our lives while enjoying crayfish with Espelette chili peppers accompanied by calf's head Cromesquis over a bed of rocket salad for me, and crab cannelloni with mango sauce served with citrus fruit marmalade, Prestige caviar and Kaffir Lime cream sauce for Colombe. Just thinking back on that meal I'm still licking my chops!

And I was also licking them while devouring Colombe with my eyes. Her beautiful first name, "Colombe" that means Dove, a symbol of liberty, perfectly matched what I was seeking at that time.

That evening an irrepressible desire mounted. I wanted her furiously and something told me that she shared my feelings. We had an aperitif and then a bottle of wine. The alcoholic beverages had finally disinhibited us.

When we'd polished off dessert, I couldn't resist taking her by the hand and asking a question, though my voice was trembling.

"Colombe, would you care to watch the fireworks from my suite?"

"That would be original. And you know what? I love originality!"

I quickly asked the server to put the dinner on my room tab, and we left the Chantecler, heading towards the elevator.

That elevator that a couple of days ago was much too narrow, was now just perfect for us! We kissed frenetically and impatiently before the door finally opened on my floor where a big bed was waiting for us.

When we got to my suite, I smothered her with kisses while we went through the living room and pushed her onto the bed. She kissed me back and quickly stripped herself of her clothing with nervous gestures that betrayed her own desire.

We were both quickly nude on my bed and we made love twice before our cravings were satiated.

It must have been about ten and we were both still lying on the king-sized bed when we heard the first explosions of the fireworks that had just begun.

"Come on, quick, the fireworks are starting!" said Colombe running to the window that overlooked the Promenade, without having stopped to get dressed.

"I think they just finished!" I replied with my two-bit sense of humor.

"Quit bragging!"

I stood behind her warm nude body at the window. We hadn't turned the lights on, so it was still dark in the room, and no one could see us.

How magical it was to appreciate fireworks without prudishness, in that heat, in one of the world's most famous palaces! I made the most of it. And Colombe, who I was holding tightly, could testify to this.

The fireworks lasted for about twenty minutes. Multi-shaped and multicolored sprays of light over the Mediterranean Sea, reflecting themselves in that aquatic mirror. Unforgettable!

When the show was over, we went back and made love once again. The thirst we had for each other wasn't yet quenched.

Suddenly there was chaos, inexplicable, incomprehensible horror. Beneath our windows, noise of a motor that was out of control, squeals of brakes, crumpled metal. Then the crowd began to scream, trying to flee, running blindly as fast as possible, pushing to escape a huge truck that seemed to be aiming for them. We could hear people shouting "Run, run!" and "Terrorist attack!"

Everyone remembers what happened next, no one will ever be able to forget it.

Too unreal to be understood.

Too murderous to be forgotten.

Many gunshots, maybe about fifty.

Sirens hurling.

Then silence.

Colombe and I were petrified, incapable of leaving the suite. We finally got dressed to go out though. We thought we might be of use to someone.

And right in the lobby of the Negresco we were able to. Injured people were pouring in. We stayed with them, and helped first-aid workers, nurses, volunteers of all types. Doctors who were guests in the hotel made themselves known.

And more and more victims kept on coming. Talking about a truck that was out of control. Crying. Moaning. Screaming.

Chaos like this in a venue that was usually so luxurious and calm was totally improbable.

All we could think about was what had happened.

We stayed until late at night, helping wherever we could.

When the last injured people had been evacuated to the neighboring hospitals, we were totally exhausted. I asked Colombe if she wanted to sleep at the hotel. She accepted, after having sent her parents a text message.

We hugged each other tightly for the rest of the night in that bed that was suddenly too big, without being able to sleep. Our minds were full of that horrible night that had bloodied our July 14th holiday, as well as our first instants of intimacy.

~

"Good Lord, mom! Turn on the TV," shouted Simon after having received at notification on his cell phone. "Put the news on."

There was live coverage. Brigitte shivered.

"Just think that we could have been there, if I hadn't been so tired. Honey, this is a sign."

"A sign of what? Yes, it's horrible."

"I don't know. I can't imagine what could have happened if you hadn't come with me and if you'd stayed on the Promenade a bit longer. But you're here. Come here."

They sat next to each other on the couch in the living room, their eyes glued to the TV screen where the same images were being shown in a loop, scenes that were taking place just a quarter of a mile or so from their apartment, at the foot of Mont Boron.

∽

Petrucci, in Speracedes, was also watching what had happened on his little TV. The small size of his TV did not erase the enormity of the images nor the Machiavellian approach that terrorist had who killed dozens of people, according to the journalists covering this tragedy.

The former gendarme had been watching the fireworks at the Eiffel Tower, live on TF1, when the programs were interrupted for breaking news. He'd switched to BFM to follow the story.

Tears were running down the face of the former

gendarme, someone who was there to defend people during his whole career and who had seen so many unimaginable things. He suddenly wanted to drown his wrath in alcohol. He grabbed an old bottle of rum that had been sitting in a kitchen cupboard for ages and that he'd forgotten ever since he decided to put an end to all that. When he'd traded his ethylic vapors for the more subtle fragrances of the flowers in his garden.

But the subtle perfume of violets or roses wouldn't be sufficient to forget the horror of the images: rum would do the trick here.

As testimonials, videos, portraits, reconstitutions, and synthetic images poured in, the level of Petrucci's bottle diminished and Petrucci fumed. Between anger, remorse and shame.

Shame for humanity, shame for himself. As the rum decreased, images and words he remembered increased.

He soon began to think about the visit the day before of the two snoop journalists wanting to know more about the drama that happened thirty years ago.

He hadn't said anything then.

But looking at the innocent bodies lying on the Promenade, who died for nothing, he said to himself that each life had a price.

And that a life taken was never forgotten just by saying nothing.

Speaking up to redeem his errors.

That whole night in bed Petrucci weighed the pros and cons.

When dawn broke, he made his decision. He picked up his phone and sent a message to the number Jerome Bastaro had given him, just in case he remembered something important.

∽

Brigitte didn't sleep a wink either that night. Unbearable images of the Promenade des Anglais where she and her son had strolled earlier kept running through her head.

But not just those. Older images too, ones older than thirty-five years and that now obsessed her.

Thinking that she could have lost her son last night, the son she'd raised alone, the son who never knew his father. And rightfully so.

Brigitte said to herself that it was time to tell him the truth. Now that he was thirty-six, it was time to confess and tell him who he was and where he came from. The shock would probably be brutal. But perhaps beneficial too. Yet she feared his reaction: it was so incredible after all.

She finally fell asleep thinking of this.

She'd tell Simon tomorrow.

∽

When I opened my eyes, I felt like I was suffering from a monumental hangover. All of Nice, all of France, must have felt the same way, I thought, remembering where I was: in my suite in the Negresco, right behind the Promenade des Anglais that the city employees were busy cleaning up.

Colombe was still sleeping. I got up trying not to make any noise.

I picked up my phone to read the latest information. But the battery was dead. I plugged it in. When the system rebooted, I saw loads of vocal and text messages.

Cynthia had tried to reach me the night before while watching the events on her television: I could hear the journalists speaking in the background. She wanted to know if I was alright, I found that touching. I quickly sent off a text message to reassure her. I then called my parents in Normandy who of course had tried to reach me too. My mother was grieving; my father was outraged.

One message left me speechless. It had come in about five in the morning. Petrucci, in a thick, slurred voice, asked me to call him back as soon as possible.

Which is what I did in the suite's living room.

"Come as quickly as you can, Mr. Bastaro," he said. "I didn't tell you everything yesterday."

"We'll be there by the end of the afternoon!"

We'd already agreed to join the Lacassagne family in Gorbio for their visit to Pierre-Hugues' grave, as was the case each year, on July 15th, the day he had drowned.

Today, July 15, 2016, that was exactly thirty years ago.

CHAPTER 43
A true male fantasy

GORBIO, *July 15, 2016*

WE DROVE DIRECTLY to the cemetery with its white walls, without going to the Lacassagne family's villa. We were a bit early.

At two, two cars drove in, including the limousine where Edouard, sitting in front, and then Lucie, Emilie and Charles in the back, got out. Charles was leaning on a white ivory cane. His recent attack seemed to have diminished him. I hadn't noticed it before, as each time I'd come to speak to him after he'd been released from the hospital, he was seated in his leather armchair in his library.

In the other car a family got out. It must have been Marie-Caroline, her husband and her two twin teenaged daughters. That fifty-year-old woman was still incredibly beautiful. A splendid redhead with pale skin and freckles. A true male fantasy, I couldn't help but thinking, remembering that she supposedly featured nude in a calendar. But as the place and time were not appropriate for thoughts like these, I mentally shook my head to rid myself of them.

We greeted each other and introduced ourselves to those we hadn't yet met. Charles thanked us for having come to pay tribute to their son on that sad anniversary date.

Counting Dominique, who remained respectfully behind our group, there were eleven of us around the tombstone. And I don't believe I was mistaken by thinking that everyone was not just thinking of Pierre-Hugues but also of the images of the unknown victims who had perished the night before on the Promenade. Both heartache and atrocity.

Emilie was sobbing, hugging Marie-Caroline. Edouard, Charles and Philippe, Marie-Caroline's husband, were all dignified. As for the twins, they weren't really concerned by that, as they had never even met their uncle, who died before they were born.

It was hard to make out what Lucie thought. Her eyes seemed to be elusive, not sad at all.

I held Colombe's hand, and she was both fragile and very attentive. Her eyes never left the marble tombstone.

PIERRE-HUGUES LACASSAGNE
1960 – 1986

. . .

Only twenty-six years old. Just a few years older than Colombe.

Charles said a prayer and invited us to the villa to raise a glass to toast Pierre-Hugues's life and memory.

On the patio, Emilie moved closer to Colombe and wouldn't let her away. I took advantage of that to speak to Marie-Caroline. I finally had that opportunity. Because of the circumstances, I didn't want to intrude and just asked her questions about her job in the holding, memories she had of her older brother, sailing and horseback riding, etc. A very civilized conversation!

We finally left, so they could be alone. And took her roaring Fiat Punto to drive to Speracedes and meet Petrucci once again.

Who had a monumental surprise for us.

CHAPTER 44
Sweet baby Jesus

SPERACEDES, *July 15, 2016*

Petrucci greeted us, like the day before yesterday, in front of his door. He gave Colombe a bouquet of flowers.

"So you'll forgive me, Miss," he said to her.

"For what, Mr. Petrucci?" asked Colombe, admiring the colorful bouquet of roses, violets, jasmine and tuberose.

"For not having told you everything. Please come in."

We all sat down in a darkish living room that betrayed his life as a sworn bachelor. Nonetheless, a tablecloth, vases with flowers and a sweater that he was knitting made us think that an old maid lived here. The former gendarme displayed a surprisingly feminine side.

He offered us some coffee and had set out a plate of cookies.

"Did you see what happened last night?" he asked us while pouring the coffee.

"We unfortunately had front row seats. A tragedy."

"It was terrible. The world is changing, I can feel it. We have to be prepared for dark days ahead. I'd like to still be working to contribute, modestly of course, to fighting against terrorism. But what can we do?"

"That's true, sometimes we feel like fictitious Don Quixotes who are somehow tilting after windmills."

"Anyway. I didn't ask you to come to talk about current events."

He took a deep breath before continuing.

"I didn't tell you everything about the Lacassagne file. But what happened last night was like an electroshock for me. I said to myself that I couldn't dirty Pierre-Hugues Lacassagne's memory. That I couldn't keep silent any longer. All lives stolen deserve the truth."

And for a long moment he remained silent.

"Tell us the truth then," I helped him continue.

He put his empty coffee cup down and closed his eyes.

"I used to have a big problem with alcohol."

∽

Théoule-sur-Mer, July 20, 1986

. . .

Lacassagne's sailboat had been detained for the past five days now by the authorities. The gendarmes didn't see anything that was abnormal about Pierre-Hugues Lacassagne's accident.

Sergeant Petrucci was sitting at his desk, holding the report he'd written. He reread it once again, analyzing what Edouard, Marie-Caroline and Charles Lacassagne had told him the night the accident took place. Something was bothering him. He couldn't put his finger on it. He read it once again, trying to find it.

An accident. Of course. What else could it be? But still, Pierre-Hugues was a great swimmer. Maybe someone helped him fall? Did they do everything possible to get him back onboard?

Petrucci closed the file wearily. Maybe he was overthinking this. Making a mountain from a molehill.

He quickly got up, left the gendarmerie and walked down to the Port de la Rague. He greeted the agent and walked to the sailboat.

He walked up and down the gangway and then onto the teak deck. For nearly an hour, he peered, bent over, looked up at the sails, overturned things on the deck and in the cabins. He operated the levers, ran his hand over the surfaces, touched the boom which allegedly hit Pierre-Hugues in his chest. He was looking for tiny clues that he thought must have been there.

Then he went down into the galley, opened all the cupboards. And there, he found an object he knew only too well, one he both desired and feared.

A bottle of whisky.

Full.

Eighteen years of age: a bottle of Octomore from the Isle of Islay, in Scotland. That whisky was worth a fortune!

Then he panicked.

He started to tremble.

He knew he shouldn't though he was attracted like a moth to a streetlight's lamp. The bottle seemed to shine more powerfully than Alexandria's lighthouse guiding lost sailors.

And Petrucci was also lost, realizing that a nectar like that was right in front of him, nearly mocking him.

What the hell! he thought, unscrewing the cap.

The cap had already been opened and closed and that was enough for him not to feel guilty. He said to himself that no one would miss a little sip. And who would check, anyway? It was his file.

The amber-colored beverage filled his mouth and throat.

Oh, sweet baby Jesus!

He could feel the liquid as it went down into his entrails and the alcohol revived him. It had a taste of "come back for more," so Petrucci did just that. Once. Twice. Three times.

It was so good, but he had to stop. He was wearing a uniform!

Now he had no choice. He had to take the bottle with him to see how the last drop tasted, later. He slid it under his uniform and went back to his office.

That night, at home, Petrucci contemplated the bottle of whisky that he'd put on the dining room table. Hard for him to resist another two or three sips. Then he stopped, as he wanted this exceptional pleasure to last another few days.

With a good buzz, he went to bed.

In the middle of the night however, he was awakened by terrible stomach cramps, quickly followed by vomiting. He threw up so many times that finally all that was left was yellowish bile and he had cramps in his lower abdomen. His head was heavy, as if his forehead was being squeezed between a vice. He took his temperature: nearly 104°!

In the morning he still wasn't feeling well, and he phoned his doctor, an old friend from his school days.

"So now what did you drink, Bernard?" asked the doctor after having examined him.

"Nothing, Denys, I swear."

"Listen. I wasn't born yesterday. You either ate some meat that was spoiled for at least a month, or you filled yourself with some adulterated wine. But I'd say it was the second hypothesis because you've got all the symptoms of alcoholic poisoning."

Petrucci felt trapped. He began to stutter.

"Okay, I found an old bottle of spirits in the basement, all dusty, it must have dated back to my grandpa Edmond's days."

"Well there you go. That old miser! All I can do for you is to prescribe a week of shots and some rest. And no more drinking, Bernard! You lucked out here!"

The following week, Petrucci went back to the office. On his way there, he stopped over at an old friend's laboratory, a friend who owed him a couple of favors. He'd often deleted his traffic tickets.

"Roger, can you analyze this for me? Discretely though?"

"That's easy, it's whisky," he replied jokingly. "Seriously, what are you looking for Bernard?"

"You see how much is gone? About a fifth. And that made me sicker than a dog. You know me, alcoholic beverages don't make me drunk. I think there's something that's not kosher in this bottle. It's not pure. Got it?"

"Got it."

"How long will this take?"

"Three days to get all the results. Is that okay?"

"Perfect. But mum's the word, okay? Thanks!"

Those three days seemed long to Petrucci. Finally, Roger called him back.

"Come and get your poison, Bernard!"

Petrucci rushed off to his friend's laboratory as soon as it had closed, and his employees had left.

"So I was right then? There was something in this bottle?"

"You sure were. And you got lucky there. Good thing you didn't finish it."

"What was it? Did you find out?"

"Arsenic. Luckily you didn't drink too much. Otherwise you could have died. What the hell were you doing with this, Bernard?"

But Petrucci couldn't give this information even to his old friend Roger.

~

Nice, July 15, 2016

"I NEVER PUT that in the file," Petrucci admitted to us.

Colombe and I didn't know what to think of that stupefying revelation. A piece of information that could have been official, had it not been dissimulated by Petrucci.

And changed the hypothesis of an unfortunate accident! That piece of evidence, without proving anything by itself, could have transformed the administrative file into a legal one! Poison means an assassination attempt.

"What did you do with the bottle, Mr. Petrucci?" I asked. "Why wasn't this in the file?"

"I couldn't or no longer could enter it. Not after I'd drunk some. Not after I'd illegally taken it. In spite of myself, I'd tampered with a piece of evidence. It's unworthy of my job and my title, that's why I've been so ashamed for years now."

"Did you throw it away? And only your laboratory friend knew about this?"

"No. One other person did."

"Who?" Colombe and I both said.
"Charles Lacassagne."

CHAPTER 45

If that's a joke, it's got poor taste!

NICE, *September 1, 1986*

PETRUCCI SPENT the whole month of August hemming and hawing and then decided to do something about it, as it was too serious. He called Charles Lacassagne and asked to see him as soon as possible. The businessman invited him to the holding, in his office, when his secretary Marie-Therese had already left.

The gendarme rang the bell and Lacassagne came down to meet him. The policeman was very impressed by the luxurious and modern furniture as well as by the size of the boss's desk. Not the same for us, he thought cursing public funding.

"Sergeant, what's so important that you have to meet me? asked Charles.

"I've got something to show you Sir, that concerns… you know… the accident."

"What?" asked the businessman, worried.

Petrucci reached inside his heavy jacket. For a fleeting moment Charles imagined that he was reaching for a gun.

But he put a bottle of whisky on his desk.

"Mr. Lacassagne, do you recognize this bottle?"

Charles, a seasoned businessman, looked the gendarme right in the eyes, unflappable. A while. He finally answered.

"It's an Octomore from the Isle of Islay, eighteen years old, a single malt, if I'm correct."

"You are. Would you say that this bottle came from your personal stock?"

"I do have a few dozen of them."

"You'll have to check, but one must be missing."

"What do you mean?"

"Mr. Lacassagne, I found this bottle a couple of weeks ago on your sailboat."

"That's impossible, I'm sorry."

"What are you so sure of yourself?"

"Because I've totally forbidden hard liquor on my boat. And I also reminded my children of that the day they went out alone."

"Yet it was there!"

"I have no idea how it got there."

"Maybe someone snuck it in. But that's not all. That would be too easy. I wouldn't have bothered you just for that."

"Will you please get to the point?" Charles asked impatiently. "And?"

"I had its content analyzed. The laboratory found poison in it."

Charles stared at him, his eyes wide open.

"But that's impossible! If that's a joke, it's got poor taste!"

"Unfortunately it's not a joke. And that means that someone was trying to kill someone else that night on your sailboat. Mr. Lacassagne, which of your children drinks whisky?"

"Only Pierre-Hugues," stammered Charles.

∼

Speracedes, *July 15, 2016*

"That's horrible," Colombe whispered. "Our suspicions of an assassination are not without substance."

"That's why I wanted to tell you this, even though I know that it's too late now."

"That's right, no one can go to jail now," I added. "Mr. Petrucci, what happened to this bottle?"

"Charles Lacassagne asked me to throw it away."

"Adieu to an eventual proof," said Colombe. "But why? Why would Charles want to hide a secret like that?"

"Fear of scandal. Just think of what could have

happened if people knew that bottle came from his estate. What that could mean."

Colombe and I looked at each other.

"Meaning that someone in the Lacassagne family wanted Pierre-Hugues dead."

"That's right. Charles Lacassagne had become aware that the attempt to poison his son came from a family member. A murderer in the family. Just imagine the negative impact on their name and business. This was why we both agreed to keep that discovery a secret."

"Both of you had sufficient motives," Colombe thought out loud.

"I don't know if there are motives that are strong enough to hide something like this. Anyway, he wanted to avoid a scandal, and I didn't want my superiors to know that I had a problem with alcohol. I could have had serious problems."

"Like what?" asked Colombe.

"Think it over: a gendarme who's working, who's the head of his squad, an alcoholic and who stole a piece of evidence! Not bad, huh? A double fault! At the minimum a disciplinary layoff, followed by a legal investigation by the IGGN."

"The IGGN?"

"The Inspector General of the National Gendarmerie. The people who investigate sleazy behavior of us gendarmes. Had they discovered this, I would have been fired. Finished!"

Despite his remorse, the gendarme's behavior shocked me. Shameful for his profession!

"How could you have lived with this for thirty years, and not have done anything?"

"Actually, there was a caveat. And this caveat made a huge difference and could justify the way I acted. If it can be justified. Remember what I said about that bottle when I stumbled upon it. I told you that the top had already been unscrewed, but that the content was intact. Not a drop was missing! That meant that no one, except for me was poisoned! The intention might have been there, but no action was taken. So, I had less scruples in hiding my discovery."

"Which still was incriminating evidence. Attempted murder is a crime, isn't it?" I asked.

"Of course. And that was the detail that Charles Lacassagne and I agreed on. We wouldn't say anything: his reputation was saved and my career too."

Colombe looked at him.

"And Lacassagne never wanted to understand who wanted his son dead? An official investigation could have allowed you to identify the guilty party."

"That's right. But maybe he preferred not to know. Or he knew and he didn't want anyone else to."

"You think he knew who did it?" I asked, astonished.

"Possible. We never talked about it. I personally always thought that it was settling scores in the family, disguised as an accident. A perfect crime. Out at sea, with no witnesses."

Petrucci was really affected by the memory of this story that he'd hidden for thirty years. Feeling that he was sincere, I also told him a few of my secrets.

"Mr. Petrucci, I personally feel and I've got good reasons to believe that your analysis is pretty close to the truth."

The gendarme was interested.

"Meaning?"

"I obviously don't have any proof, but we have reason to believe that both Edouard and Marie-Caroline had reasons to shut their older brother up for good."

"I'm all ears."

I told him what we'd just learned without giving my sources: the Blue Boy, the nude photos, dropping out of school, the fight Edouard and Pierre-Hugues had at the villa and death threats given in front of witnesses. Petrucci listened to me, regularly nodding his head.

"That confirms the suspicions I had. Now I better understand why Lacassagne insisted that hard not to reveal anything."

On this, our interview was finished.

The gendarme was undoubtedly relieved. As for us, it showed us even more how much the Lacassagne family was like a can of worms: each one was worse than the other it now seemed. Now I understood why the patriarch, at the ripe age of 80, was so adamant about writing his memoires. A smooth, clean, glorified story, one with no thorns. A story that didn't show the family's dark side.

Was I still ready to be a part of it? Could I continue to close my eyes and follow the words said by this father who, at the best, glossed over the fratricide committed by one of his children?

It now seemed impossible. Something was shifting inside: the ghostwriter for Charles Lacassagne was little by little being overtaken by the journalist who wanted to publish the truth.

We talked about this on the way back. Colombe supported me.

"Jerome, you have to follow your instincts. And whatever you decide, I'll be there for you."

"If I decide to put an end to my contract with Lacassagne to tell the truth, things could be pretty hairy."

"What do you mean?"

"Remember that anonymous letter I got at the hotel? And when I see what they're capable of, I don't think they'd hesitate to hush me up."

"Stop! You're scaring me Jerome. What are you planning on doing then?"

I was asking myself the same question while looking out at the countryside near Nice. Far down, you could make out the coastline and then the calm and blue Mediterranean Sea, sparkling in the sun. A sea that thirty years ago, day to day, caused the death of Pierre-Hugues.

I answered that question both to Colombe and myself.

"I'm going to tell the truth about the Lacassagne family."

PART Four

TROUBLED WATERS

Rewind...

Nice, 1986

Lying on the deck, Edouard, Marie-Caroline and I were working on our tans under the hot sun at the end of the afternoon. Dad's sailboat was gently swaying with the tiny waves licking its light wooden hull, we'd lowered the sails. Since Edouard had passed his sailing course at Glénans, we'd gone out together a few times. At this time of the year, we liked to get away from the beaches full of tourists and relax a few miles from the coast. Today was the first time that Caro was accompanying us.

She'd been asking to come with us for a couple of years now, but our dad always refused to have all three of us sail at the same time. And in the Lacassagne family, you do what your father says. Our mom doesn't really have much of a say.

So, this was a first for us. Following the events that had shaken our family up, we'd decided to make the most of this sailing trip to bury the hatchet between us and try to get closer together, like we were in the past.

Our father accompanied us to the front steps of Villa Gorbio.

"Be careful now!" he said. "Accidents happen all too quickly. And make sure you don't take any risks and if the weather gets bad, go back to the port. I'm counting on you, especially you Pierre-Hugues. You're the oldest one here and it's up to you to make sure your brother and sister aren't in any danger. Godspeed to you all!"

Then Dominique drove us in the limousine to Saint-Jean-Cap-Ferrat Port where our dad has a permanent slip. Lilie insisted on coming with us to the sea so she could see us weigh the anchor.

Caro had started sailing lessons. We're pretty good teachers. After we'd left the marina, I let her take the helm for a few minutes while I went downstairs to put my trunks on. We headed west and were sailing from port to port, with the coast starboard. Once we passed Cap d'Antibes, we headed south, out to sea. We lowered the sails after having passed Lérins Islands, put down the anchor and all dove in the warm clear waters.

After having swum around and played in the water, reminding us of when we were kids, we climbed back onboard. I asked:

"Caro, can you make us some lemonade?"

"Hey, I'm not your maid!" she answered immediately. "When at sea, the old saying 'no captain, only sailors!' goes."

"Gotcha," chuckled Edouard. "But now that I'm thinking of it, I think it's time for a drink, don't you?"

"Doudou," I added, "those are some very wise words! I'm going in once more and after that, let's crack out the drinks. Our old man isn't here to chaperone us!"

And I dove back in.

When I climbed back up the ladder, Doudou and Caro were preparing drinks.

Edouard is two years younger than I am. Intellectual kid, teacher's pet, thick glasses. He's been going out with Julie who he met at the university for the past two years. They haven't talked about getting married, they're making the most of their youth, but our dad likes Julie though she's not rich.

Caro is a beautiful redhead with cute freckles. All the guys are attracted to her, but if they insist too much, she just turns her back on them. Caro loves her freedom, her books and going to movies, especially films by Jacques Rivette, Francois Truffaut and Eric Rohmer. In spite of everything I learned about her, Caro is still a dreamer who'll marry Prince Charming, if of course our father will allow it!

"Where's that little whisky?" I asked when I was on the deck.

"Ready to be decanted, Your Highness," replied Edouard ironically with an exaggerated bow.

I ran up to him, still dripping wet, and rubbed his curly hair.

"Quit monkeying around, little bro."

We played, chasing each other around like when we

were little. The past months had been quite tense between us, but we all decided it was time to bury the hatchet. Leaving internal strife and sterile jealousy behind us. Together for the best or to avoid the worst?

"Hey, you two, you're going to make us capsize with your nonsense!" Caro joked.

I looked out at the sea with its tiny whitecaps starting to pick up. It was nearly sunset, and clouds were coming in. Perhaps the night would be a bit more agitated than planned.

Finally we all sat down around a little table with three glasses on it, ready to be filled. Edouard took the bottle of Bordeaux wine, poured himself and Caro a glass. Then he opened the bottle of whisky to serve me my favorite drink.

Right when the bottle touched my glass, I interrupted him.

"Wait! To celebrate our reconciliation and seal our secret pact, I'll have a glass of this good Bordeaux, just like you."

"Really?" Edouard said, astonished. "Because I know it's your delicious weakness, so why not, Pierrot?"

Why was he insisting like that? A little too nice.

"Yeah, I'm sure. Pour me a glass of Bordeaux then. It'll be like a symbol of our shared blood."

Edouard finally smiled, delighted at this conciliant and symbolic gesture. He closed the bottle of whisky and served me a glass of Saint-Emilion.

"This is the good life," *I said, looking at my glass of*

wine in the last rays of sunlight. "Don't you feel you're privileged?"

"Sure, like 'the world's your oyster,'" replied Edouard. "But don't forget that without our old man's fortune, we wouldn't have a sailboat, we wouldn't be spending the night here at sea."

"And just think, what about if we had to pay for our schooling?" continued Caro. "We'd have to work all summer and each weekend instead of lazing here at sea with drinks in our hands!"

"To Dad!" we said together, raising our glasses.

An hour later, the bottle was nearly empty, and the atmosphere had ratcheted up. During all this time we talked about the Lacassagne universe. Fueled by alcohol, we imagined our family's future once our father had decided to turn the company over to us, or when he would have passed away. But it seemed so long! When would this take place? And who would direct the company?

Suddenly, Caro, always practical, changed the subject.

"That's not all guys. We're drinking away here, but we have to eat something other than peanuts."

"Into the galley, lady!" I shouted, laughing. "Go cook us up a chicken, stat!"

She just sighed, disdainfully raised her shoulders, but did go down to get something that would soak up all that alcohol. She came up a few minutes later, with a tray with a nice loaf of bread, and a few tins of sardines and mackerels in tomato sauce.

I opened one of the sardine tins, cut myself a thick slice of bread and spread the oily fish on it. Delish!

Clouds were coming in above us and the wind was picking up. The sailboat had begun to rock gently in the waves.

I have no idea who poured it, but my glass of Saint-Emilion was full again. I emptied it.

Finally, it was nighttime, and the tins of sardines and mackerels were just as empty as the bottles. Only a few crumbs of bread were left, and the wind quickly blew them away into the sea.

We all dozed off.

An hour later, we were suddenly awakened by a gust of wind that must have been stronger than the others. The sailboat was pitching and dangerously leaning to the port side, pulling on the chain that anchored it to the bottom. The salt spray made the deck slippery and hard to get a grip on. Marie-Caroline and Edouard were the first ones awake, and I was finding it hard to emerge from my slumber. Two bottles of Bordeaux after a hot and sunny day must not have been the right recipe to fight off seasickness!

"What's going on?" I asked them.

"The weather surprised us," explained Edouard, going to the mast. "If we don't get out of here we're going to be shaken up something crazy pretty soon. Caro, go down into the cabin and make sure nothing will fall."

"Right away, captain!" she said.

"Pierrot, are you okay? You think you can help me

hoist the sails? We have to get back to dry land, tough luck for our project of spending the night at sea."

A flash of lightning lit up the sky, as if putting an end to our outing.

I felt like I was wearing a lead hat, and my head was on backwards. That Saint-Emilion was a bitch! I should have stayed with my whisky. Probably just more used to it.

"Come on, get the fuck moving! You take care of the windlass to raise the anchor while I unfasten the sails. Think you'll manage?" asked Edouard.

"Hey! Don't talk to me like that? Who the hell do you think you are? I'm not an idiot and I've been sailing for much longer than you."

"Oh Mr. Bragger is back! Mr. Better than you!" replied Edouard, rushing towards me like he wanted to pick a fight.

"Shut up, Doudou, we've got other things to do!"

But Doudou didn't want to shut up, as if his repressed bitterness had just surfaced. The alcohol must have disinhibited him.

"I can't stand your superiority, Pierrot! For years now everything has been about you and you only!" he shouted, violently pushing me.

"What are you talking about? You had too much to drink, Edouard."

"You're our dad's favorite child. The only one that counts for him. Don't tell me you never noticed? However, had he known!"

"What are you talking about? Quit making things up!"

At that very second a wave that was stronger than the others flowed over the sailboat's rail and hit me right in the face. I fell over and sprawled on the wet deck.

"Wow! That was a biggie! Caro, make sure the hatches are closed!"

A clicking sound confirmed that she had heard me.

"Come on, Edouard. We have to calm down and make sure this boat stays afloat. We'll settle everything else later."

"For sure," said my brother, glaring at me.

That salty wave woke me up and I was finally able to raise the anchor.

Now the boat was free to move around, but as we hadn't yet hoisted the sails, it only obeyed the wind. We'd only be able to control it when we'd done raised the anchor and hoisted the sails. That was what Edouard was trying to do. The rope holding the sail in had been unrolled and it quickly began to elevate. You could see the triangle of tissue, but we still had to control the boom.

The sailboat veered suddenly, and the boom flew out of Edouard's hands. It made a huge semi-circle, sort of like a baseball bat, and in its curved trajectory, brutally slammed into my chest as I was walking up to the helm.

The violence of the shock laid me flat once again. It took my breath away. The deck was wet and the sailboat leaning to port side. I found myself slipping towards the sea with nothing to hold onto. I could see Edouard, but it was as if he was paralyzed but he suddenly shouted out to me.

"Pierrot! Hold on!"

He rushed up to me while I was still sliding. My legs were hanging outside the boat, and I could feel the waves licking my thighs. Edouard was able to grab one of my hands while hanging on to one of the rails. I called out to him.

"Don't let me go, Doudou!"

Edouard didn't say a thing, I don't even know if he heard me with the wind. He looked straight into my eyes while our fingers locked together tensed up in the effort to hold on to me so I wouldn't fall into the sea.

The boat was drifting, its sails throbbing, its mast swaying. The noise of the elements joined those mechanical ones: waves breaking on the hull, the bow of the sailboat suddenly plunging into the troughs, the wind howling in the starless night.

Edouard called for help.
"Caro, help!"
I suddenly felt Edouard's fingers slip away.
There was nothing to hold me back now.
I slid into the unleashed waves.
My head was turning.
My chest was burning.
I was lost.

CHAPTER 46
Strong like Dijon mustard

NICE, *July 16, 2016*

In Negresco's breakfast room, Colombe and I were gazing at one another after having gobbled down the pastries and cold cuts on the huge buffet.

Last night, when we got back from Speracedes, she wanted to stay with me, showing me how much I meant to her. I was happy to be in a simple and tender relationship, quite the opposite of the one I had with Cynthia. Colombe didn't want to leave me alone to try to find an answer to the slew of questions running through my head and the difficult decisions I'd have to make.

The hardest one would be to abandon my mission with Charles and write the truth about this affair, after the 1986 attempt at poisoning his oldest son. His official autobiography had turned into a free-for-all and objective investigation for me.

Maybe I should play both sides? Officially continue my mission with the Lacassagne's and discreetly continue my personal investigations? That didn't seem ethical to me.

I had to resign. I doubted that the old man would be happy about this. I'd be losing a lot here: fifty thousand euros plus free room and board at the Negresco, I thought to myself, spearing a few more slices of smoked salmon to go with my coffee. Colombe was attracted by all the seasonal fruit: maybe it would be our last time enjoying a meal on the house here.

"You're not afraid of retaliation?" she asked, putting her glass of orange juice down.

"What would they do to me? Lacassagne isn't Don Corleone! This isn't Coppola's *Godfather*." I tried to reassure her.

Not that I was totally serene here though: the anonymous letter I'd received a couple of days ago was still trotting through my head.

"I agree with you though. You have to write the truth, even if it bothers some people. That's your responsibility as a journalist."

"Yeah, maybe being a ghostwriter isn't my vocation. The first thing I have to do is contact Gerard, see if he'll have my back on this."

As soon as I'd finished my breakfast, I called my boss at *New Business* and talked him through our latest discoveries.

"I'm totally there for you!" he said after I'd finished.

"Totally? What's in it for me?"

"I've got some editor friends who love tidbits like this. You just write, and I'll get it published, with thousands of books and loads of publicity. This is fantastic Jerome! You caught a whopper here! Almost like you were writing a book about the truth in JFK's assassination, of course in a smaller proportion. But what are you planning to do with Lacassagne?"

"Well, I was wondering the same thing and secretly hoping for some advice from you. I personally feel like resigning, giving him his money back, the money that links me to him and trying to find out the truth on my own then."

"Sounds totally like you Jerome. You're honest, straightforward, professional, ethical and all that. But you are also an idiot!"

"What?"

"You're naive, Jerome. A dreamer. Think about it! What would happen if you dropped everything now?"

"I'd lose fifty thousand euros?"

"Not just. But with your book you could earn them back later. In the meanwhile, you'll have lost contact with the Lacassagne family. You'll close every door and every possibility to advance in your personal investigation. Well, not that personal, incidentally. How are things going with your little intern?"

"Euh, not bad," I stammered. "Colombe will be an excellent journalist, very efficient."

"Ah. And by the tone of your voice, I suppose she's also good at making you feel good. I'm sure you already forgot your Parisian tigress."

"Shut up, Gerard," I joked.

"Okay, it's none of my business. So, as I was saying, if you tell the old Lacassagne what you're thinking of, he'll throw you out, right?"

"Right. But still, that's not really kosher."

"Jesus Christ, Jerome, you think everything is always kosher in journalism? And Lacassagne and company, they've always told you the truth and nothing but the truth?"

"Nope."

"So there you go. Got it? If you want to be efficient, you've got to be cunning, and strong like Dijon mustard. You keep on rubbing shoulders with the Lacassagne's, you write your book, you take advantage of the Negresco, and with the help of your little Colombe, you finetune your file on this case! Because if I understand correctly, you don't have any tangible proof yet? Just interesting testimonials, but no supporting evidence. Right?"

"I must admit that you're right once again, Gerard" I said after thinking it over.

"Okay, I gotta go now. I'm starting the morning brief. There are people who work in Paris you know, while others work on their tans in the Côte d'Azur! Keep me in the loop, I've got your back."

"Thanks. I'll give you a report as soon as possible."

I joined Colombe in the suite and it's true that I

was getting used to it. Comfort makes you sleepy, doesn't it? When I went into the living room, I heard the shower which woke me up. I couldn't resist joining Colombe.

It was an open, Italian style shower, with little pebbles on the floor, and easily big enough for two.

I slipped in maliciously and hugged Colombe's warm body. Standing against the hot wall tiles, we exhausted ourselves.

An hour later we left the palace, to go jogging on the Promenade. Neither of us were joggers, but we both felt we needed to do something to eliminate too many toxins. Colombe had borrowed a pair of tennis shoes her size, a privilege in luxury hotels where nearly all your dreams come true if you just ask.

We started off next to the beach and noted that life was coming back to normal already. Tourists were wandering next to the numerous bouquets of flowers, candles and commemorative signs. The show must go on! Same thing though for Pierre-Hugues Lacassagne, whose life had to be honored, I thought. As if Colombe was reading my mind, she asked, without slowing down:

"Let's sum this up then."

"Yeah," I answered. "A little oral exam for a master's degree in journalism. First question: facts and figures. What have we learned up to now?"

"That Pierre-Hugues was probably poisoned?"

"No! Someone had the intention of doing so, but

the bottle was full! Then: who would benefit from his death?"

"Edouard?"

"His motive?"

"Jealousy, the inheritance. Plus the shameful secret of his homosexuality?"

"Okay. Who else?"

"Marie-Caroline."

"How come?"

"Same thing: jealousy, inheritance, and her secret nude photos?"

"Okay. Who else?"

"Charles?"

"For what reason?"

"Um," Colombe hesitated. "Because he discovered he wasn't his biological father?"

"Possible. Who else?"

"Got me."

"Let me help you. Lucie?"

"No, I don't think so. But why?"

"And what if Pierre-Hugues had also learned that he wasn't Charles's legitimate son, but the son of his mother's former lover? Maybe she wanted no one to know so she eliminated him? To avoid the shame?"

"*Pff*. I don't think so. A mother wouldn't do that. Plus, anyway, Charles knew that, so she didn't have anything to hide."

"Unless she wanted to hide it from the rest of the family and friends, or even from the general public.

But I must admit that I don't really believe that either."

"Who do you think did it?"

"The brother and sister, of course. But we have to be sure."

"How though?"

I could feel that both Colombe and I were out of breath. For beginners, talking while jogging in the hot sun isn't the best thing to do. I headed for an empty bench.

"Ouf! Wanna sit down?"

"Sure do!" she said before sitting on the bench, her arms open and her head bent behind her. "We are crazy!"

Taking a deep breath, I continued.

"So how can we be sure? Easy - just by asking them."

"What? Just like that? Just say! 'Did you try to poison your brother in 1986?' or 'Did you push him overboard?'"

"So? Why not? Sometimes you have to be direct to advance your pawns."

"Radical."

"Sometimes you can't beat around the bush!"

"Ah. Ah. Now you're talking like Sharpers with old sayings."

"Yeah. He's a guy we have to see again pretty soon. I'm sure that he's got stuff he hasn't told us. We're still going to be surprised, in my opinion."

Colombe started to stretch.

"Remember, he talked about Dominique, the chauffeur? He thought he must have witnessed a lot of things."

"I think my boss in Paris is right. It's better to stay on good terms with the Lacassagne family and their employees, that way I won't close any doors. I'd like to meet Brigitte too."

"In a nutshell, everyone who knew Pierre-Hugues."

"Yup, but with what we now know about the accident, we'll be able to ask more targeted questions."

Sweating, huffing and puffing, we went back to Negresco, having exhausted our limited physical capacities. Colombe began to think out loud.

"We never thought that someone outside of the family or employees could have wanted to poison Pierre-Hugues. I mean, who says that it couldn't have been a friend, like this Sharpers guys, for example, he seems pretty sleazy to me, a huge porker."

"That's true. Or maybe someone we haven't met yet. Who hasn't been identified. Someone who wanted to attack the family or the holding indirectly. But didn't succeed."

"Right, he wasn't poisoned. But it had the same ending. Pierre-Hugues is dead."

And with those intelligent findings we arrived at the palace.

"I need another shower," said Colombe, with a wink.

"So do I."

Bis repetita, an offer I couldn't refuse.

CHAPTER 47
Maybe, maybe not

WHILE WE WERE HAVING a good time in our huge Italian shower, someone had left Colombe a voicemail.

"Hello, Colombe, I'm sorry to bother you, but you left me your phone number in case I thought of something else. So, I've got something else for you, if you can call me back, it'll be easier. Thanks."

The person hung up, then called right back, less than a minute later, with another message.

"Oh! I'm so absent-minded! This is Brigitte Garibaldi. Please call me back, it's really important."

Of course Colombe called Brigitte right back, putting it on speakerphone so I could listen to their conversation.

She asked us to come to her house as soon as possible. What she wanted to tell us was way too serious to be discussed on the phone.

We quickly got dressed and made our way to the

Mont Boron district where I also discovered, just like Colombe had told me, a very high-class neighborhood and a comfortable apartment.

Brigitte showed us into her living-room. There was a man sitting in one of the armchairs. He wasn't completely unknown, as we'd seen him two days ago at the Fenocchio ice-cream shop.

"This is my son, Simon."

What a surprise!

"Simon, this is Miss Colombe Deschamps and Mr..."

"Bastaro. Jerome Bastaro," I said, shaking Simon's hand, a Simon I couldn't stop thinking of as little Simon, but who today was a grown man who looked like an artist.

Brigitte then invited us to sit down and share a cup of coffee. While she was in the kitchen, I broke the ice with the young man who seemed intimidated.

"Really nice meeting you. I've heard so much about you in the past few days."

"Good stuff I hope!"

"Very good. Except everyone described the little Simon who was six years old and who played with little Lilie Lacassagne at Villa Gorbio."

"I have grown up a bit since then!"

"Yes, you did! Well? How is your life as an artist? You live in Paris, don't you?"

"Yes, in Montmartre, a place I love."

We talked about this, that, and the other until Brigitte came back with the coffee. She put the coffee cups down on the table, with Colombe, and thanked us for having come.

"Actually it's my son who has something to tell you. Go ahead, these people are here to help you, and they'll listen attentively."

Simon took a few sips of his delicious arabica before starting.

"I'm sure you know what happened here two days ago, on the Promenade?"

"We unfortunately had front row seats for that atrocity," I admitted.

"You can't imagine how my mother and I felt."

"Did someone you love lose their life in the terrorist attack?" asked Colombe.

"Thank God no," replied Brigitte. "But I think everyone is shattered by this. It was totally surrealistic. Simon and I had the impression to have escaped death, that rain drops fell around us, not on us. We'd come back earlier than expected, I wasn't feeling well, if not…"

Her voice broke as she was reliving the events of July 14, in Nice and the tragedy they had luckily missed. Simon put his hand on his mother's, who was beginning to tear up.

"Everything's fine, Mom."

Brigitte wiped her eyes with a handkerchief.

"Tell them, Simon."

"That terrible night was a turning point for us. My mother barely closed her eyes and yesterday she decided to tell me everything. Not to hide anything from me. After all these years!"

"I suddenly realized that life can brutally be ended," she said. "I decided that before I go I want my son to know, you never know what'll happen next... So I told him everything that I'd been keeping for myself for over thirty-five years."

She stopped speaking, and Colombe prompted her.

"What did you tell him, Mrs. Garibaldi?"

"The truth, Miss, the truth. Simon, tell them."

Simon closed his eyes and took a deep breath before starting.

"When my mother talked to me yesterday, the first thing I did was to go to the Lacassagne's head office, where I hoped the boss would be."

∽

SIMON GARIBALDI WENT into Charles Lacassagne's huge office. The old man was at first taken aback, as if he were glued to his seat: he didn't believe his eyes. No doubt about it, despite the years, the man standing in front of him with Marie-Therese right behind him had the same features as little Simon from the 80's. Maturity gave him an impression of... no doubts there either. It was evident!

"Well, little Simon!" said the millionaire using his cane to get up from his armchair. "I'm glad to see you again. You're lucky I was here this afternoon. What a nice surprise!"

"Hello, Mr. Charles," responded Simon, in an icy tone. "Or should I have said father?"

∽

COLOMBE and I were both stunned by what many would have qualified as a scoop.

"You mean that?" I awkwardly asked.

"Just like he said, Mr. Bastaro," answered Brigitte. "Yesterday morning I told Simon that he was the child of a very short liaison that I had with Charles Lacassagne, back in 1979. The first time I met him was in a café in Gorbio, where I had a summer job."

∽

GORBIO, summer of 1979

THERE WERE NEARLY no customers at Chez Félix at this time in the afternoon. There was a man, sitting alone, at one of the aluminum tables. Everyone in the village already knew and respected him. His name was Charles Lacassagne, and he wanted to refresh himself enjoying a cold beer, that he ordered from the new server. He'd never seen her there, though her face seemed familiar.

"Have we met before?" asked Charles when she brought him his beer. "You're from here, aren't you?"

Brigitte blushed.

"Yes, I am. And I know you too. You're Mr. Lacassagne? The villa, over there, is yours."

"'Tis!" said Charles, feeling that his position seemed to attract the young lady. "Would you like to visit my gardens?"

"Oh! Sir. I wouldn't dare. It wouldn't be correct, we barely know each other."

"It's up to us if we want to get to know each other better, Miss…"

"Brigitte, you can call me Brigitte."

She wondered what was behind all this. The man, who must have been in his forties, was appealing, no doubt about it. And rich. But she knew he was also married. And he had three kids, as far as she knew.

"Brigitte, when do you finish?"

∽

"AND THAT MARRIED MAN SEDUCED ME," admitted Brigitte Garibaldi in her apartment in Mont Boron, sitting next to her son, Simon. "That evening, when I left the Chez Félix Bar, he was waiting for me in his limousine with his chauffeur. I got in, greeted the chauffeur, Dominique, I imagine you already know him. He drove us to Nice and dropped us off in the old city where we spent a delightful evening. Charles showed me a Nice that was totally unknown to me: a rich and elite city, with districts I'd never even set foot in, too high-class for me. And then he drove me to an apartment that he had there, it must have been his bachelor pad where... you know."

"We understand," I assured her.

"I don't know why I did that. But today I don't regret a thing: I have a marvelous and talented son, one I raised alone."

"But you did spend a few years living with the Lacassagne family in Gorbio."

"That's true, it was sort of strange. But it was a necessity for me. Both a financial and a moral one, I'd say."

"Moral?" Colombe asked, wanted to understand.

"I mean, Charles was the father of the child we'd conceived that night in Nice. It was only fair for him to grow up in better conditions."

"That's unheard of," said Colombe. "You lived under the same roof as your lover and his own wife for all those years? How could you stand it?"

"Oh, it wasn't really like that. To tell you the truth, this was just a passing adventure. Not really a one-night-stand, but not far. A mistake, craziness. But once again, I don't regret a thing, you know Simon," said Brigitte, running her hand on her son's arm. "After that we hardly went out together again. There was that night, then nothing. Up until Lucie, two or three months later, got pregnant with Emilie. Quite unexpected, as she was nearing forty. And a tough pregnancy. Lucie had to stay in bed, she couldn't take care of her house and her other children, even though they were already grown. Marie-Caroline must have been fourteen or fifteen then."

"That's when you started working for them?" asked Colombe.

"That's right. When I learned that Lucie was pregnant and they were looking for a housekeeper, I went to see Charles and spilled the beans about myself."

"You both were pregnant at the same time," Colombe realized. "Did Charles know?"

"Not yet. Like I just said, after that night, we barely had any more contact with each other. I told him that I was pregnant then, calling him at his office. It was in December."

∼

Nice, December 1979

Marie-Therese picked up the phone. After having asked the usual questions, she agreed to talk to her boss.

"Mr. Lacassagne? There's a Brigitte Garibaldi who'd like to speak to you. She says it's urgent and important... Okay. Fine... I'll put her through."

"Thank you, Marie-Therese. Please don't disturb me under any circumstances now," said Charles to her.

"Hello? Charles? This is Brigitte, do you remember me?"

"Why are you calling? We'd agreed…"

"I know. It was a one-night stand, and we had to forget all that. I haven't told anyone. But today…"

"Today?" said Charles, cutting her off.

"Rumor has it that your wife is expecting?"

"News goes quickly in the village."

"And you're looking for a housekeeper?"

"That's true. And?"

"I'd like to apply for the job."

"What? You're completely out of your mind! Listen: just forget what happened. Stay away from my family. Do you imagine that situation? Living with us? After what happened to us? Brigitte, thank you for your proposal, but I'm really busy, I have to go. Bye."

"Wait! Don't hang up. You don't understand. I don't think you have a choice here."

"Excuse me? What are you talking about?"

"You're not the one dealing the cards here."

"Are you threatening me? What do you want? I don't owe you anything Brigitte. We spent a magnificent night together, but that's it. Hiring you to live with us, helping my wife. Impossible."

"You're saying you don't owe me anything? It's true that it was a magnificent night. But it left marks… permanent ones."

"What do you mean?"

"I'm pregnant, Charles. And you're the father."

"You really put the pressure on him," I said to Brigitte as I finished my coffee.

"I must say I wasn't proud of myself, I hated myself for forcing him to do that. But I needed that job. I was going to be a single mother, with no job, raising a child alone. I didn't consider it to be blackmail. Rather an exchange of services. They needed help and me too. We helped each other."

"Plus the secret that you and Charles shared," added Colombe.

"That's right, we made a deal, I didn't say anything about Simon's paternity in exchange for a stable job and a roof over my head."

"And you decided to keep your child."

"That's right. Best decision I ever made."

Brigitte looked happier when she said that. She touched Simon's hand, sitting on the right of her.

"It wasn't too hard, I mean physically, to take care of the villa while you were also pregnant?"

"Three months, yes. But I was young and strong. Dominique or the gardener took care of everything that was hard. Plus, right from the beginning I got on well with Lucie. As we were both pregnant, we had something in common. Without adding that both of us had the genes of the same man in us. I know it was strange. I don't really believe stuff like that, but who knows, maybe it has some subconscious influence? Or something chemical?"

"That could explain the complicity between Emilie and you Simon. You were really best friends?" I asked.

Simon pushed back a strand of hair before answering.

"Now I understand why I was so close to her. We shared the same blood. Do you believe in blood ties, Mr. Bastaro?"

This question, in the context of the Lacassagne family, suddenly seemed hard to answer. I concluded my thoughts by a vague "maybe, maybe not" answer.

"I suppose there are cases when blood ties make people closer and others where they generate tension and fratricide quarrels."

We were all silent. I tried to interrupt this moment.

"You worked for them for several years then."

"That's right. My initial contract was until the child was one year old. Little babies require a lot of energy and Lucie was tired."

"Why did they extend the contract?" asked Colombe.

"When Emilie was born, they saw that she had Down's syndrome and the Lacassagne's asked me to stay with them longer. Kids like that need more attention, care, and company. It was too much for Lucie to do everything alone, and with his job, Charles was hardly ever at home. So they decided I'd stay, or we'd stay, I should say, until Emilie could go to a specialized school. Which happened in 1986."

Ah! Once again, that year of 1986! Colombe and I had already heard of this, but I wanted to hear her version.

"You were laid off? What was that like? You lost

your room and board plus your job all at the same time."

"It was hard for us," Brigitte admitted. "But I was able to deal with it. I still had a good way to put the pressure on Charles."

"You blackmailed him? You got a heap of money as a settlement plan?"

"You're not far from the truth," she admitted. "I didn't ask for a lot of money, but a monthly pension."

"Meaning?"

"If I asked you to come, Mr. Bastaro, it's so I can rant and rave and tell you everything. When I was laid off, I insisted on having a private conversation with Charles."

∼

Gorbio, spring of 1986

BRIGITTE WAS STANDING across from Charles, in the villa's rose garden, where no one could hear them.

"I knew this would happen one day."

"There's an end to everything, Brigitte, you know."

"Don't think you can get rid of me like that, Charles. You can't dismiss us, Simon and I, and just throw us out."

"What do you want? You'll be paid what I owe you, don't worry, plus you'll get unemployment benefits for a while too. You'll find something else I'm sure."

"I'm not intending on living with unemployment, Charles. How could I buy an apartment, how could I raise Simon?"

"Like everyone else! You're not alone in that case. Find yourself a good husband. He'll help you raise Simon plus he'll be a father figure."

"Remember, Simon already has a father. A biological one. He grew up with him."

She began to cry.

"I understand. But it's not possible anymore. I have helped you out up till now, giving you a job and housing. But it's finished, you know."

"But you're morally obliged to keep on helping us. It's your duty, Charles. Otherwise…"

"Otherwise what?"

"Otherwise I'll have to tell the truth."

"You wouldn't do that. Can you imagine that scandal for my family and my business?"

"Ah, here we are! Your business! That's the only thing that counts for you! As for your family, it's more complex than it seems. Secret ramifications in your family tree. But I agree with you Charles, it would be a scandal."

"What do you want?" asked the businessman.

Both Colombe and I gaped when we heard Brigitte's story. Looking around this beautiful apartment in one of Nice's best neighborhoods, we weren't surprised when Brigitte continued.

"I got this magnificent apartment from Charles. Free of charge. For him, a real estate magnate, a millionaire, it was a mere drop of water. For us, it was incommensurable! We would never have been able to afford something like this!"

"The price of thirty years of silence?"

"Part of it," Simon said. "Up until yesterday, I didn't really know how my mom paid for this apartment, nor how she paid for me as a student at the Fine Arts School in Paris, and my apartment in Montmartre."

"You didn't have to pay rent?" Colombe said, cutting him off. "Another of Charles's presents to avoid a scandal?"

"That's right," sighed Brigitte. "Our silence is worth about half a million euros. All of it can be resold."

"But today that's not enough to get even with the Lacassagne's, is that right? That's why you went to see Charles yesterday, Simon?"

"Sort of. I wanted him to know that now I knew."

"That's all? Just for him to know? No other intentions?" I insisted. "I think I understand why you're telling us all this today. Why us. I can't wait to hear what you said to each other. I would assume that your meeting didn't go as well as you expected, is that right?"

"No, it didn't go well. Not at all."

CHAPTER 48

Bringing grist to our mill

NICE, *July 15, 2016*

"Hello, Mr. Charles," said Simon. "Or should I say 'Dad?'"

Charles stopped walking to the young man and plopped down in his armchair.

"What are you talking about, Simon? Did you have a sunstroke?"

"Don't bother, Charles, my mother told me everything this morning. How you met, her job at the villa, how well Lilie and I got along, when you fired her, the Mont Boron apartment and the one in Montmartre, my studies in Paris. I know everything! I had to wait thirty-six years for it, but now I know."

"There's nothing I can teach you then."

"Teach me, no. But catching up with all the lost time. All of the years where I didn't know anything."

"Simon, don't blame me. I couldn't do anything else, do you understand?"

"Oh! I don't actually blame you. I'm just sad that I didn't have a father. I don't blame my mother either. I just wonder why? You were ashamed of us? Because we were too low-class for you? Not rich enough? Because you would have lost too much had you told the truth? Because you had a child out of wedlock and that's not something that the Lacassagne's do? Why Charles? Why?"

The old man was slumped behind his desk, incapable of saying anything.

"See? I can't even call you dad, or father. It's sad. Yet I remember all the good times we had at Gorbio. Running around the lawn with Lilie. I remember sitting on your lap at mass, on Sunday morning. I remember the room I had, next to my mom's, in your house, protected by you. With a bit of love, I hope. Or at least true affection. But that wasn't fatherly love."

"Simon, you can be sure that it broke my heart."

"That's possible, who knows?"

"I did everything I could to help you and your mother."

"Because you were forced to! Wearing an iron ball of scandal attached to your ankle. In my opinion you bought our silence for all these years. Yet I came to say thank you. Thank you for having allowed us to have all this, even if it wasn't spontaneous."

"I would have liked to have done so much more."

Simon looked his father right in the eyes.

"Maybe it's not too late."

"Meaning what?"

"Well, I was told that you're planning on handing over your business to your children?"

"It's common knowledge. Even the Americans know about this. And? What are you getting at?"

"As I'm one of your biological children…"

Charles burst out laughing.

"Mr. Garibaldi has inherited his mother's greed!"

"Charles don't be cynical. You know perfectly well that I've got the right to…"

"The right to nothing, Simon! As far as I know, your last name isn't Lacassagne."

"I could have it changed. An official recognition of paternity can be done at any age."

"Sure. You make me laugh. You barge into my office, without calling for an appointment after thirty-five years and you want to have your cake and eat it too, right when I'm stepping down. It's a little bit too easy, isn't it? You think I'm a bank? I don't think I was stingy with you or your mother. Your real estate is worth half a million euros plus all the cash I gave you over the years. So, that's life! Anyway you still have to prove that I'm your father."

"A DNA analysis would do the trick."

"That's right. But I won't consent. Now Simon, you're a nice kid but I've got work to do. Please leave. Listen, if you want, we can go out to eat, all three of us, with your mother. How about that? How long will you be staying in Nice?"

Simon got up suddenly, a bitter mocking grin on his face and walked to the door. He turned around.

"I'll stay here as long as I need to get what's mine. See ya Dad!"

*

Gorbio, July 16, 2016, Mont Boron

Brigitte came back with new cups of coffee that she'd prepared while her son was telling us about his meeting the day before with Charles Lacassagne.

"What were you expecting?" I asked Simon. "That he'd welcome you with open arms? His hand on his wallet?"

"Of course not. I thought that maybe as he'd gotten older, he'd had given some lest to his positions. I sincerely thought that his fears of scandal were finished. And I certainly was also looking for a type of legitimacy."

"Give him some time," Colombe suggested. "He's got to digest all that, just like you. I mean, this is serious."

"Miss, time is against us," said Brigitte. "Charles is starting to get old, he's planning on handing over his assets to his children, and Simon deserves his share too, don't you think?"

I was surprised by her answer. It had a dose of venality that bothered me. In their eyes, was money more important than a father-son relationship? Also, it was evident that for all of these years the only link between Simon and Charles had been money, as Charles had paid for his schooling and apartment. His father had only been present through his bank account.

"I understand," I said politely. "What are you planning on doing?"

"Revealing what's true," said Simon. "That's why I need you, just as you needed my mother. I know that Charles hired you to write his memoires. I think that I've got the right to be in his souvenirs, but not just like the maid's son, do you understand?"

Without realizing it, Brigitte and Simon Garibaldi were bringing grist to our mill. Our interests overlapped. Working together would allow us to advance a few pawns in our quest for the truth.

"Do you think that publishing your story would force him to recognize Simon as his son? Do a DNA test?"

"We wouldn't lose anything by trying," concluded Brigitte. "Are you with us?"

Colombe looked at me quizzically.

"We're in."

CHAPTER 49
A German famous waltz god

WHEN WE LEFT Brigitte Garibaldi's, Colombe was stupefied.

"What a can of worms! Their son isn't their son, and the illegitimate son is trying to hop up on one of the branches of the family tree. I wonder what else we'll find out. That Marie-Caroline is actually Dominique's daughter? That Edouard was born a female and changed sex? Nothing can surprise me now!"

"And I'm sure we'll still have other surprises. On the other hand, I think that the farther we go, the more complicated things get. Each new revelation gives us some answers, but it also brings us more questions. Will one summer be enough to figure this all out?"

"Jerome, there are two of us!"

I stopped in the middle of the sidewalk to delicately kiss her on the neck.

"It's true, you're a big help, Colombe. You're my best summer revelation," I said, suddenly poetic.

"And I'm glad you came down south. My summer sure improved since you came! Both from an intellectual point of view, as well as having saved water by sharing showers!"

We wandered around the little roads in the old part of Nice, aimlessly, just for the pleasure of being together and relaxing a bit. The accumulation of days spent working, doing interviews, synthetic reports and hypotheses was quietly eating us up. We saw a billboard at a cinema.

"Oh! Ice Age: Collision Course! Wanna watch it?"

"I love animated films," said Colombe, dragging me in. We spent an hour and a half in the air-conditioned room, holding hands, laughing at what Peaches and Manny were doing.

That did us a world of good! For a while we were able to forget the atrocities of July 14th as well as the tangled Lacassagne family member's net. And Pierre-Hugues's death.

But that all came back to haunt us.

"Now what?" asked Colombe, when we got back to my suite in the Negresco.

We both flopped down on the king-sized bed, enjoying the air conditioning.

"We keep digging."

"In what direction? I'm confused. This story is going every which way."

"What intrigues you the most in everything we now know, and what don't we know yet?"

Colombe closed her eyes to concentrate.

"What I'd like to know right now is what Edouard and Marie-Caroline would think if we asked them about that poisoned bottle of whisky. What about you?"

"Totally! See if they'd pour us some too."

"For that, we can't let them get together. We have to lay this on them."

"Each of them, alone. Simultaneously. 'Coz I think they're both partners-in-crime, those two."

"Like they've got a shared secret? A pact that they signed on a sailboat, back in July 1986?"

"I'd sure pay a lot to know, my little Colombine," I joked. "Let's go have lunch and try to draw up an action plan!"

I took her to a little brasserie near Hotel Negresco and we both had delicious seafood salads while trying to draw up a strategy.

We decided to go see, separately and simultaneously, the two Lacassagne heirs. I'd take care of Edouard and Colombe would take care of Marie-Caroline. She didn't think she would be capable of doing it, but I convinced her saying that Marie-Caroline would probably be more at ease speaking to a woman. We prepared a list of key questions, and an ideal way to try to reach our goal without upsetting them.

Two hours later, we were back in my suite, phones in our hands though in different rooms.

Two minutes later we met back in the living room. I was able to reach Edouard, who was busy, but said I could meet him at the holding at six. Colombe was less lucky than I was, she only got Marie-Caroline's voicemail. She left a message saying she'd call back.

"Can't win 'em all," I said.

"Now what do you want to do?"

"I've got a couple of ideas," I whispered into her ear.

"Like?"

"Like, cooling off in the shower? Or a sweet siesta?"

"I'll take a sweet shower!"

Which is what we did.

Refreshed, calmed, we took advantage of some free time to do whatever needed doing. Contrary to what happens in novels or movies, in real life you often have empty moments, like that one. I was trying to outline Charles Lacassagne's biography. He was waiting for the first draft.

Colombe was lying on the bed, in her undies, doing crossword puzzles and other wordsearch games in a paper she'd picked up in the hotel.

"Do you like word games?" I asked, after I'd written two pages.

"I love them! Including spoonerisms, palindromes, and anagrams. You know there are some famous ones?"

"Really? Which ones? I stopped at 'This ear it hears.'"

"Not bad! No, I was thinking of things more

complicated than that. Listen to this one. 'Old west action'. You know its anagram?"

"Not the faintest idea," I confessed, too lazy to try to even find it.

"So, if you put all these letters in another order, that'll give you 'Clint Eastwood!'"

"Fantastic! You got others like that?"

"Sure do. 'A German famous waltz god.'"

"Which is?"

"Wolfgang Amadeus Mozart."

"Wow! My mouth is hanging open faced with all this useless culture!" I said, making fun of her.

"Idiot!" Colombe responded, maliciously sticking out her tongue at me.

She called Marie-Caroline back, and this time she picked up. They agreed to meet at six too in a cafe in town.

∽

WHEN IT WAS TIME, Colombe dropped me off in front of the holding and then turned around to go to the old city.

"Hello, Mr. Lacassagne."

"Hello, Mr. Bastaro, how can I help you this time?" asked Edouard. I don't have a lot of time but tell me."

"Thank you so much. I wanted to say that I'm making good progress in your father's memoires."

"That's good. Are you able to separate the Lacassagne clan's history from the business?"

"Yes, now I've got a pretty good overview of everything except for one episode that is still a bit obscure for me."

"Which one?"

"It's about 1986."

"This sailing accident is still obsessing you?" he sighed.

"Um. It's not an obsession, but I think it's still a critical turning point in your family's history, and yours…"

"What do you mean, mine?"

"Just that as you had front row seats then, I thought maybe you could shed some light on a couple of questions that have been bothering me."

∽

"Mrs. Micoud?" asked Colombe when she walked into the bar and recognized Marie-Caroline.

"Hello, Miss. How are you since yesterday? It was nice of you to have come, with Mr. Bastaro, to pay homage to my brother."

"Cemeteries aren't the best places to meet people. It's much nicer here. What can I get you?"

The two ladies ordered.

"So, how can I help you? You're assisting Mr. Bastaro in writing my father's biography, is that right?"

"That's it. It's my final internship and I'm learning a lot. Could I ask you two or three little questions?"

"About what?"

"About Pierre-Hugues's accident."

I could see the change in Marie-Caroline's face when she thought back on this.

"How could that be useful in my father's biography?"

"We believe that it's a major episode and one that impacted your family's history, and your father wants us to write about it. He visibly was affected by it."

"We all were affected by that unfortunate incident, Miss, and of course our lives were overturned, in one way or another. What exactly do you want to know?"

"Well, as you were on the sailboat during that outing, perhaps you remember some details that could help Mr. Bastaro tell the true story about this event."

"I'm listening."

∽

"What exactly do you want to know, Mr. Bastaro?"

"I just want to situate this event in its context. According to the police report, the weather was terrible that night?"

"Yes, it was. Severe weather conditions, like we say."

"Could that be why your brother slipped on the deck?"

"He slipped after having been hit by the boom, yes. I tried everything to hold onto him, but I couldn't."

Edouard looked very upset when he said this.

"I'm sorry that I'm talking about a difficult souvenir, you can believe me."

"I'll be okay, let's continue."

"There weren't other aggravating factors? Exhaustion, heat?"

"I suppose that could have contributed to it. We were alone at sea, far from home, and we took advantage of the situation to have a good time, all three of us."

"I understand. If I'm correct, both of you were going through difficult and tense moments and this outing at sea was to bring you closer together again."

"You're quite well informed, Mr. Bastaro, that's impressive. Even I had forgotten that."

"Mr. Lacassagne, did you bring alcoholic beverages onboard?"

An embarrassed silence followed.

"If you're asking me that, I suppose you already know the answer. So, yes, we had alcohol with us, and we all consumed."

"What kind of alcohol? Beer?"

"No, red wine, why this question?"

"I don't know, I just thought that young people usually drink beer. Didn't you also have a bottle of whisky?"

"Very well informed. We did have a bottle, but no one had any."

"Mr. Lacassagne, who prepared your picnic basket?"

"Oh! I really can't remember, all of that was so long ago. I'd say it must have been our mother, or Brigitte, who was our cook at that time. She generally was the one who took care of picnics."

∿

"It must have been Brigitte, our housekeeper and cook, who prepared the picnic basket with stuff to eat and drink. Our mother didn't do stuff like that," replied Marie-Caroline.

"What was in it? Do you remember?"

"That was long ago. I remember that there wasn't much: a nice loaf of bread, probably some cookies, some canned goods and some bottles."

"Bottles of what?"

"Milk, fruit juice, maybe some wine too."

"Do you remember a bottle of whisky?"

She was silent before answering.

"Now that you say it, you're right, Pierre-Hugues loved his whisky. But we didn't have any. We all only drank Bordeaux wine, I'm sure of that."

∿

"Mr. Lacassagne, what would you said if I told you that the bottle of whisky we're talking about contained poison?"

Edouard remained silent.

~

"Mrs. Micoud, what if I told you that there was poison in the bottle of whisky that fortunately no one had?"

Marie-Caroline didn't say a word.

~

"That is crazy, Mr. Bastaro!" Edouard burst out. What do you mean? You're delusional!"

"Not at all, Mr. Lacassagne. I was just as surprised as you when I found that out."

"And where did this crazy information come from?"

"From the gendarme who headed the investigation, Sergeant Petrucci."

"Ah! I remember that name. He's the one we talked to in Théoule. But how come no one knew anything about this?"

"I couldn't say," I replied so I wouldn't have to give any details.

"I don't understand. Who would have wanted to poison my brother?" asked Edouard in a shaky voice.

~

"Who could resent my brother so much that they tried to poison him?" gasped Marie-Caroline.

"That was what I was going to ask you," replied Colombe.

"I have no idea."

"Without offending you, I was led to understand that the relationship you and your brother Edouard had with him was quite tense."

"What are you insinuating? I'm afraid to understand. Are you suggesting that my brother or I could have wanted to kill our older brother? That's awful. We're not in a two-bit reality show. I loved Pierre-Hugues!"

"I'm sure you did, Mrs. Micoud, but we've still got this bottle full of... questions!"

"Let me tell you something. Of course, we had our ups and downs, of course we all had things to hide, we argued, we got mad at each other. Just like all brothers and sisters! But killing him, that is something I would never have been capable of doing."

∽

"Despite our quarrels, I never would have done anything to hurt my brother, never! This sailing trip was meant to bring us closer together."

"In this case and in your opinion, who would benefit from poisoning your brother and why? Who knew that all three of you were sailing that day?"

"That is an awful question!" said Marie-Caroline.

"Do you realize what you're saying? Who knew we were taking the boat out? I can count them on one hand."

∼

"Outside of my sister and I, all that's left is my father, my mother, my little sister Lilie and Brigitte, her son Simon and Dominique, our driver."

∼

"Maybe the gardener too," added Marie-Caroline, "but I'm not sure. That's horrible, it's beyond comprehension!"

∼

"All those people were devoted to our family. I can't believe that..."

∼

"Plus you have to exclude Simon and Lilie, who were only six then," added Marie-Caroline.

∼

"Mr. Bastaro, this interview is over," said

Edouard. "All this is behind us. No one drank any poison. The end!"

∽

"Miss Deschamps, there's no affair. Just an accident. Knowing who that hypothetical poisoner could be won't bring Pierre-Hugues back."

∽

I called Colombe when I left, and she picked me up.

"So?" I asked.

"I've got the feeling that it wasn't her, she seemed to be sincerely distraught when she learned about the bottle. And Edouard?"

"Same thing. He was shocked. I'd say that he had nothing to do with it. Jesus Christ, where did that bottle come from?"

"Yup. Who the hell prepared and supplied it?"

"How about calling Brigitte?" proposed Colombe, picking up her phone. "Maybe she can shed some light on this."

CHAPTER 50
Ragged and heavy breathing

NO ANSWER, despite two messages and five calls.

"Let's go to Mont Boron."

We took the Fiat Punto and went up the hills overlooking the Baie des Anges.

Same thing when we called her by interphone. We looked up, but the apartment's shutters were closed. Brigitte and her son seemed to be unreachable.

"Shoot," said Colombe.

"We'll try tomorrow."

When we returned to Nice, I felt like calling Angel Sharpers, as we hadn't spoken since the France-Portugal soccer final. I wanted to know what he thought about that poisoned bottle.

"Glad to hear from you, Mr. Bastaro!" he said when he picked up. "Well? Things going well for your official biography? Did you get to meet that gendarme I told you about?"

"Mr. Sharpers, you were spot on there: he had lots to tell us."

I brought him up to speed about what Petrucci told us about the bottle. On the other end of the line, there was complete silence. I could only make out the sound of his labored breathing: ragged and heavy notes of an obese man, sounds that seemed to have a hard time freeing themselves from his respiratory tract.

"Mr. Sharpers?" Are you okay? Talk to me."

Between two inhalations he was having trouble speaking.

"I never would have believed that people hated Pierre-Hugues Lacassagne so much that they wanted to poison him."

"It was premeditated, of course. You don't accidently poison people by arsenic."

"Who could have done that? Everyone says that only women use poison."

"We've been asking ourselves the same question. Maybe you can help us get to the bottom of this?"

"How?"

"Could you meet us at the Negresco?"

Sharpers' breathing was still labored. The intermittent sounds I was hearing on the phone worried me.

"I'll be there in an hour," the American said.

∽

Angel Sharpers put his cell phone down on his fat thigh. He put his head back and closed his eyes, trying to control his breathing. What Bastaro had said turned him upside down.

Poison.

All his theories were shot, everything that he'd mentally drawn up since 1986.

Those near certitudes that he'd had for thirty years, nourished with everything he'd learned since then crumbled, like a wall riddled with saltpeter.

He began to doubt once again. Jesus, what a story! What a story!

What if he didn't know everything?

What if they'd lied? Dissimulated important elements? Bent the truth?

What if he'd been manipulated?

But why?

What a strange family! thought Sharpers has he unbuttoned his shirt to free his panting chest. What other terrible secrets were left? He thought he knew them all.

What a family! Millions spark relentless lust.

Would some people kill to get their hands on those millions?

Money, fortune.

The empire, the holding.

The takeover bid.

Was it his turn to unveil things? Pick up speed? Find out the truth?

He needed help with that: he had to join the two journalists who would spread the word, form an alliance with them.

He hailed a taxi.

CHAPTER 51
Hard cash

NICE, *1980*

THE MAN WALKED into a café in the old part of town, where two pathetic looking men sitting at a table in the back were expecting him.

They greeted each other and the man sat down across from them.

"It's time."

"You sure?" one of them asked.

"Information from a close source! Do you trust me or not?"

"Of course! You're close to him."

"He's ready to sign with the Rodriguez group, but if you make him a better offer, he'll take it."

"How much did the Rodriguez's propose?"

"Five hundred francs per square meter, if he buys

the whole lot. Offer him four fifty for yours and you'll squeeze out the Rodriguez's."

"Okay. You're sure about this?"

"One hundred percent! I saw the file."

"How much do you want?"

"Two percent. Hard cash."

"When it's signed, that okay?"

"One percent now."

"You're a tough businessman."

"I was taught well. And you need me. I'm a good source."

"A done deal. What are you having?"

"Same thing as you."

CHAPTER 52
Covered in mud

WE WAITED in the Negresco's bar-lounge, sipping *mauresques*. From our table we could see the visitors to the hotel.

And the characteristic silhouette of the American could easily be seen in the lobby: an overhanging stomach, a bulging chest below a fat round head with swinging jowls, and all this under a Texan cowboy hat, no doubt about it, this was him.

I got up to greet him and walked him to the bar where he kissed Colombe's hand.

"Can I get you something to drink?" I asked.

"With pleasure, a whisky. I need something strong," he said, plopping his overweight body down in the leather club chair.

"You did seem pretty shocked on the phone."

"I guess this did surprise me. Sure not expecting something like that. Poison!"

"We were surprised too," said Colombe. "The premeditated aspect, I mean."

"Mr. Sharpers, can I ask you a question?"

"Go ahead."

"Why were you so shocked by that information? As if you and Pierre-Hugues Lacassagne were really close."

Sharpers nodded his head several times.

"We were like two brothers. Linked close together even beyond his death."

The American stopped talking, picked up his glass and emptied nearly half in one gulp.

"But who could have done something like that? Do you have any leads? From what I've learned, it's evident that only Edouard and Marie-Caroline had real motives to kill him. Do you think that one of them could have thought of poisoning him?"

"It's possible," I said. "Maybe they were hoping to stun him with the alcohol and poison and throw him in after?"

"Which would make it a murder and not just a simple accident," added Colombe.

"That would increase their chances of success" Sharpers said, thinking aloud. "Rather than hoping he'd fall into the sea by accident or by being pushed."

"You mean a fight?"

"It seems to me that in a fight Edouard and Marie-Caroline of course, would lose. Pierre-Hugues was much stronger than them, even both of them at the same time."

"Yeah but, no one touched the poison, so they didn't use it."

"Unless there was a second bottle?" I suddenly realized. "And that they threw it in after?"

We remained thoughtful faced with this new question.

"In that case, we're in an impasse: the proof is someplace in the Mediterranean Sea, covered with mud," Sharpers said. "Let's look elsewhere. Have you read Agatha Christie?"

"Sure have. Nearly all her books," said Colombe. "I've got about fifty of them at home. I'm a collector!"

"Congratulations Miss, you've got good taste. So of course, you've heard of Hercule Poirot?"

"Legendary."

"What does Poirot do to solve a mystery?"

"He sits down and lets his little brains cells do the work," said the young lady with a smile.

"I think we should do the same thing, with this question: who had the material possibility of putting poison into this bottle?"

"All depends on where it was. In the kitchen, in the wine cellar, in the living room," said Colombe.

"Or in the library?" I proposed. "I remember having heard that Pierre-Hugues and Charles regularly sat there on Sundays to enjoy a glass of whisky, just the two of them."

"I've heard that too. And that made his brother and sister jealous."

"That tells us where the whisky was stored and

consumed, but not necessarily where the poison could have been added."

"For that, you would have had to have been there back then. Which isn't the case."

"True," Sharpers nodded.

Our little brain cells were working, but not coming up with much. I tried something else.

"Mr. Sharpers, I've got a hypothesis for you, as you knew the family and their employees well."

"Not that well but go ahead."

"Here I go. Both Edouard and Marie-Caroline said that the picnic basket that they'd taken out to sea had been prepared by Brigitte Garibaldi, the housekeeper and cook who was working for them. Do you know her?"

"A bit."

Then I told him what she'd told us about her liaison with Charles and Simon's paternity. Sharpers listened to us, visibly flabbergasted by this.

"That is mind-boggling!" he stammered. "Simon is Charles Lacassagne's illegitimate son?"

"That's what he's trying to prove, anyway."

"How though?"

"A DNA analysis," responded Colombe.

"A good idea, unchallengeable! You can learn so much from genes."

We all took a couple of sips from our cocktails.

"So, knowing all this, would it be possible that Brigitte discreetly put the poison in the bottle, in the kitchen maybe?"

"I suppose that technically she could have," began the American. "It would have been quite easy because the bottles have twist off caps. Just twist it, pour in a couple of drops of poison, slip the bottle into the picnic basket, and the kids would take it out to see. Unnoticed," he concluded.

"But we still haven't answered the question: why would she have done that?" continued Colombe.

"Jealousy?" I proposed.

"Develop that idea," said Sharpers.

"Right. It's a type of syllogism. We all agree that Pierre-Hugues was the favorite son, and the successor Charles had earmarked to head the holding?"

"True," said Colombe and Sharpers in unison.

"But we know that Pierre-Hugues wasn't Charles's biological son and that he'd found out."

"Okay," said Sharpers with his Texan accent.

"On the other hand, Simon was Charles's biological son, even though he was the fruit of adultery. But no inheritance for him, as he'd never been acknowledged. Don't you think that a mother could be jealous because of this? To the point that she'd want to eliminate the favorite son?"

"It is logical," admitted the American, nodding. "But there's still that detail that Brigitte would have had to know that Pierre-Hugues wasn't Charles's biological son."

"Maybe Lucie told her? They were quite close," suggested Colombe. "Or even Charles, why not?"

"So, Brigitte had a motive plus the possibility to do

this. But did she have the intention and the courage? That's a whole other story."

A story I really wanted to know. I tried to call Brigitte once again, this time using my phone, as she wouldn't recognize the number. Would she pick up?

I only got through to her voicemail and didn't leave a message.

"No one there," I told the others.

We kept on examining all the different scenarios possible for the poisoning attempt, without finding any certitudes. Just assumptions, no proof.

Sharpers couldn't confirm nor invalidate our theory, and he left after an hour or so, still troubled by what he'd found out. He turned around when he was about to open the door.

"Sometimes truth is really close. All you have to do is put things in the right order and everything becomes evident!"

∼

A MAN and a woman were sitting on the patio of the Marco Polo *ristorante*, on Passeggiata Cavallotti de Vintimille. They were at the back of the building, right on the beach.

"This is heavenly, isn't it?" said the woman, putting her hand on the man's. "Just us two. What a good idea you had with this impromptu escapade."

"Yup, we're totally free here!" he replied, squeezing her hand.

They'd arrived by train last afternoon and had booked a small hotel right on the seaside. They'd just finished having a shellfish platter, followed by delicious *gelatti*, for dinner. The sun was quickly setting on the horizon and there was mist rising from the waves. Soon night would fall.

"Nothing to hide now!" said the woman enthusiastically.

"The hardest part is behind us: stepping across the red line, talking. Telling the truth."

"And reaping the fruits of it. Finally!"

The woman rummaged around in her purse for her credit card and picked up her phone at the same time.

"Oh! No network here. Too bad! That way we're all alone."

"Just the two of us, Mom!" said Simon. "Know what I want to do?"

"What?"

"Paint a picture of you here, with the sun setting over this Italian beach. It'll be magnificent!"

CHAPTER 53
Watch your language

NICE, *July 17, 2016*

Edouard Lacassagne had his hand around his sister's shoulders as they were walking down the Promenade des Anglais.

"That story of poison is crazy, Caro. I still can't believe what that Bastaro guy told me. What a muckraker, stirring up shit."

"Oh! Doudou, watch your language. But yeah, it was hard for me too. Who could have wanted to hurt Pierrot like that?"

"That's what I'd like to know."

"Doudou?"

"Yeah?"

You never hid anything from me, did you?"

"What do you mean? Of course I never did. You and me we're like two peas in a pod!"

"I'm serious here. I mean, if you did something awful like that, you would have told me? You wouldn't have kept the secret for yourself for thirty years?"

Edouard kept on walking silently. He looked out over the sea and sighed.

"How could you believe for one instant that I could have done something like that? Jesus Christ! Pierrot was our big brother. Yes, he was our father's favorite. Yes, he had everything going for him. Yes, sometimes we disagreed. Yes, I was jealous of him. But he was my brother, and I loved him like a brother."

"Me too, I loved him."

"That night, I did everything I could to catch him and keep him from falling in, but he slipped away. Fuck! He drowned right in front of me, and I couldn't do a thing about it, shit!"

He had tears in his eyes. He sniffed.

"I'm sure Doudou. I couldn't do anything either that horrible night, out there," she said, pointing at the sea with her chin.

"Let me tell you something, Caro. This Bastaro and his little intern irritate me by sticking their noses into everything, but if someone wanted to kill my brother thirty years ago and if they find out who it was, I want to help them!"

"You're right, it would be too bad not to take advantage of their help. What makes me sad about this poison is that the gendarme kept it for himself, that he dissimulated the proof. And if I understand correctly, so did our dad. Why?"

"I have no idea why! I wonder if he's hiding something. And what do you think about what they said about the picnic basket? Did Colombe say anything to you about it?"

"Of course. I told her that Brigitte usually took care of stuff like that. You don't think that…"

"I don't know what to think, anymore. Anyway, after thirty years, I'm sure she could never be tried in court. But I still would like to know."

"Even if that won't make Pierrot come back."

CHAPTER 54
Boosting my brain power

THE DAY BEFORE, Colombe had dropped me off at the Negresco and had gone to her parents' house, to get her washing done. I buckled down on writing Charles Lacassagne's biography.

Marie-Therese had emailed me from her professional address: secretariat@holding-lacassagne.com. She said that her employer would love to read the first draft of the biography, so he'd be able to release the second part of the sum we'd agreed on. She said she'd print it out so that Charles could read it as soon as he had time.

I spent the whole evening on this task, boring as it was. Before going to bed, I answered Marie-Therese and attached a PDF file of nearly a hundred pages, thinking that it would be enough for Charles for the moment.

I slept in until ten and saw that I had several text messages as well as voice messages on my phone.

The text messages were from Colombe. She said that she already missed me, and I must admit that it was a nice way to wake up. I wasn't surprised, our passion had grown during the past few days. What surprised me a bit more was the voicemail that Edouard Lacassagne had left.

"Mr. Bastaro, my sister and I would like you to know that we'd like to join forces with you in your quest for the truth. Or, to put it in other words, and even if this will hurt Marie-Caroline's delicate ears: just like you, we want to catch that son of a bitch who wanted to kill our brother in 1986! Please get back to me."

I suddenly laughed at Edouard Lacassagne's language, as he never had used words like this before. That man in his strict gray suit, his tie and Coke-bottle glasses was starting to relax. I immediately called him back.

We said that we'd share any eventual information between us. And I sincerely thanked him for his active assistance.

I met Colombe in a brasserie in the old city that we hadn't yet tested. Both of us loved trying new restaurants, new flavors, new things to eat. This restaurant was called Mama Délices, a Greek restaurant not far from Albert-Premier Gardens. She had a Metsovo smoked cheese salad, and I had Kassianis chicken with mashed potatoes and truffle oil: delicious!

"I called Brigitte several times this morning," I said to Colombe. "Unsuccessfully."

"And I swung by her house, the shutters are still closed."

"Too bad we don't have Simon's number."

"Strange that they disappeared just when they asked us to help them."

"Do you think that betrays some type of guilt?"

"It's too early to say, but it is unsettling. Or maybe we're just imagining things, who knows. We're focused on the family's quarrels, and we see evil wherever we look."

"You're right," I said, raising my glass of ouzo. "Let's relax. Cheers, health and happiness!"

"Happiness," replied Colombe, looking me right in the eyes.

"Are you satisfied with your internship?" I asked, smiling.

"Totally!" she said enthusiastically. "Talk about a first experience! I'm learning so much."

After our succulent lunch, we went back to the hotel to get changed. That afternoon we'd decided to laze around on the beach and go swimming in the Mediterranean, as we both needed a break. The water was perfect and opened its arms to our uncontrollable fits of laughter, kisses and underwater caresses.

Exhausted, we laid down on the pebbles on the beach. I'd brought a couple of San Antonio mystery novels with me, stuff that wouldn't boost my brain power but sure was funny! Colombe had brought a crossword puzzle magazine and was busy with anagrams and wordsearch games.

As strange as it may seem, that afternoon of completely trivial activities was a real eye-opener for us.

We'd already been surprised more than once since we started our investigations, but this new surprise exceeded by far everything we could have imagined!

Colombe was googling on her phone when she suddenly cried out, as Archimedes must have done in his bath, but she replaced the well-known *Eureka* with a more modern word.

"Oh! Fuck!"

I put my San Antonio down.

"What's wrong? Did you see a jellyfish?"

"Look at this."

She handed me her phone and I could see she was on Angel Sharpers' Wikipedia page, the same one that we'd consulted just a couple of days ago. I read through it, without finding anything that could justify her emotion.

"Yeah?" I asked.

"Read his full name."

"Angelicu Segeau Sharpers. And? The only thing I see is that his initials are ASS, which much not be evident for an American."

"That's not what you should be looking at."

"It's true that he has a strange name. It sounds like a Sardinian first name, and then a French middle name which must have been his mother's, and then his father's last name, an American one. An original mixture, but I still don't see what you're getting at."

Colombe rolled her eyes. "My poor Jerome, you couldn't find your nose in the middle of your face!

Count the letters.

I counted them twice.

"Twenty-two, more than sweet sixteen."

"How old-fashioned. You're right, there are twenty-two letters."

"It doesn't take much to amuse you," I said ironically. "Do you count everything you see like that?"

"I must admit I do have a few compulsive tics like that, especially for words."

"Sure. Okay! I think I've got it - is it a palindrome? If you read it backwards, it's..."

I tried, but that sure wasn't any words I knew.

"Almost. A little hint: think of an anagram."

"Hum, so what is it?" "Bloody English ham and egg? Something like that?"

"Congratulations! You didn't even realize it, but you had twenty-two letters in your phrase! Seriously, Jerome. Think of a person with a long name."

"I don't know, lots of people do. Franklin Delano Roosevelt? John Fitzgerald Kennedy?"

"Closer to us. Someone we've been talking about for the past few days, or even weeks. Someone we're obsessed with!"

I suddenly understood.

"Oh! Jesus Christ!" I exclaimed.

"Sure. You see it now? What did I tell you?"

CHAPTER 55
His breath was taken away

ANGELICU SEGEAU SHARPERS.

Twenty-two letters.

Pierre-Hugues Lacassagne.

Twenty-two letters.

Unsettling.

"A coincidence!" I suggested to Colombe.

She handed me her pen and her magazine.

"Here. Write the two names in capital letters, one under the other, and cross out the letters as soon as you find them in both."

I did what she said and the further I got, the crazier this was to me.

I crossed out the A in Angelicu, and in Lacassagne.

The N too.

The G in Hugues.

And twenty-two times in a row, up till the last S in Sharpers, which was also the last letter in Hugues.

"Jesus!" I shouted. "What the hell?"

I was getting pretty vulgar here, but this discovery was frankly mind-boggling.

"Yeah, either this is the craziest of coincidences or that Sharpers has been making fun of us since the beginning."

"But why? This isn't a game! That American must be a pathological liar. Of course, it's not his real name. What's he aiming for?"

"Trying to get ahold of the Lacassagne fortune? With his takeover bid?"

"But takeover bids are completely legal. I don't see why he has to hide his identity behind an anagram. And when you think of it, it's despicable."

"Yes, but at the same time, it wasn't evident. You're the only one who caught on. Had he wanted to be found out, he would have invented a name like Peter-Hugh Lawson, you see, PHL, something like that."

"Good Lord, who is this guy?" asked Colombe. "What does he want? Where's he from?"

"If Wikipedia's right, he's from around here, but is that really true? All we know if that he was close to the Lacassagne family. And especially Pierre-Hugues, his buddy, nearly his brother, he said. Oh! What if…"

"What? Another hidden brother? Gimme a break! Where would that one come from?"

"Got me," I sighed.

We put our things away and went to Hotel Negresco, while continuing to talk about Sharpers.

"I've got a crazy idea," said Colombe.

"Nothing can astonish me anymore. Go ahead."

"What if Sharpers was the poisoner who came back thirty years later to finish the job?"

"What job?"

"Taking over the Lacassagne empire. Or maybe he was on the boat, and he threw Pierre-Hugues in?"

"And then vanished since then? And the Lacassagne's forgot about this mysterious passenger? No, Colombe, you've read too many Agatha Christie's! Come back to earth."

"Yeah but still, he does know a lot about the family, doesn't he? Didn't you think it was strange how shocked and upset he was about the revelations on the poisoned bottle, and then about Simon's hidden paternity?"

"You're right, his breath was taken away," I said.

"Some ordinary guy wouldn't have been so affected, believe me. Those revelations opened deep and ancient wounds."

"There's one more possibility."

∽

Summer of 2014, southern France

Like every year at the same time, the same characters, the same joy of seeing each other again, the same fears too. And especially, the same hope that one day they'd be able to tell the truth.

This truth that's so incredible, so frightening too.

Right now, they're the only ones who know it, it's their secret world, their annual sentimental getaway: a hotel in the sun, cicadas chirping, time standing still as the poet Lamartine would say. And sometimes their hands, like a symbol of an indestructible link that has bound them together for nearly fifty years.

"So when's it for, mom?" asked the man.

"Soon, sweetie, soon. Your father is thinking of stepping down. I think that in a year or two, it'll be the right time. He's not ready yet. In 2016, he'll be eighty: he'll want to retire."

"I'll come back then for good."

CHAPTER 56
There is a code of honor

I DIALED ANGELICU SEGEAU SHARPERS' number, and he quickly picked up.

"Sharpers, you've been taking us for a ride ever since the beginning! What the hell are you playing? And who the hell are you? You used us to get closer to the Lacassagne family?"

A silence followed my tirade, then I heard the fat man's throaty breathing.

"It sure took you a long time! I'm on my way," replied the American. "Order me a double whisky, an Isle of Islay Octomore, my favorite. I'm sure they have that one at the Negresco."

And he hung up.

～

I HAD SHARPERS, as I still called him that, come up

to my suite and we all sat down at the coffee table. We needed some peace of mind.

When the groom brought the tray with our drinks, I took the glass of whisky and held it out to Sharpers.

"Your double Octomore, Mr. Lacassagne."

"How did you do that?" asked Colombe, astounded. "You were supposed to have died in 1986."

"That is the official version," replied Sharpers-Lacassagne.

"Could you please give us your version, in that case?" I asked ironically.

The American — but was he really one? — gulped his double whisky down and told us what he remembered about what happened thirty years ago.

"That night, Edouard, Marie-Caroline and I were on my father's sailboat and an unexpected storm blew up: the boat rocked, the sails rattled, it was thundering and slippery. We'd all had something to drink and were a bit tired. The boom blew right into my chest, making me fall. Edouard tried to catch me. But his fingers quickly slipped away. Edouard wasn't a strong kid. I fell overboard".

∽

The Mediterranean, July 15, 1986

Pierre-Hughes gasped. Though the water was far from freezing, it was a jolt to his system, and he was sinking. His head was spinning, the bottom was black. He was going down. But not without a fight, he was a champion swimmer after all. Kicking his legs, his head finally came up above the waves. He took a deep breath, and a sharp pain ran through his bronchial tubes.

The waves were high, the wind roaring, the rain beating down. Through a moist veil, he could make out the lights of the boat in the opposite direction. He looked around for a lifeline but doubted that his brother had thrown one out. Despite his beautiful talk of reconciliation, he was a *persona non grata*, someone who knew too much, he'd become embarrassing.

Pierre-Hugues decided to float, to calm down, to go with the flow. Trying to swim would accomplish nothing, except to exhaust himself up until he had no more strength left and all that he'd be able to do would be to sink, victim of a fatal cramp.

Calm down, weather the storm, wait until daybreak.

He floated, lost track of time, in a semi-comatose state, his mouth dried by the Bordeaux and saltwater. His ears were roaring, filling intermittently with water, making them ring. He thought he heard a different noise, something like a motor, and believed he recognized the sound of a light boat whose hull would hit flatly on the waves.

Then nothing. Up until the noise of the wind and rain hitting its surface.

Suddenly, in his semi-consciousness, he felt hands

gripping him beneath his armpits. Someone pulled him onto a rubber boat. Pushed him to the bottom of what seemed to be a Zodiac. Was that the noise he'd heard earlier? He relaxed and fell asleep, exhausted.

∼

"So you were rescued," stammered Colombe.

"Incredible luck, yes. One chance out of a million, I don't know. Probably my fairy godmother looking over me that night, who didn't want me to die so young, with a brilliant future in front of me."

"Was it a Zodiac from the Coast Guard?"

"No, not at all! Far from it. Rather a Zodiac who didn't want to be seen. And who wasn't really thrilled to happen upon someone like me floating in the storm. But in the sea, there's a code of honor, so that man saved my life."

"Who was it?"

"A drug smuggler."

∼

Pierre-Hugues emerged from his restless sleep when the Zodiac hit the sand in a little isolated creek. His savior dragged him up onto the beach, up to a little dip in the rocks that would shelter him from the wind and rain, a small cavity dug out by the elements at the foot of a cliff.

"Here you go," he thought he heard through his

mental fog. "We can wait out the storm here. Fuck! Only happens to me," that unknown person complained.

Pierre-Hugues fell back asleep.

A few hours later he was awoken by the sun in his face. It was shining, the storm was over. The sea was calm. He could hear gentle waves lapping the nearby beach. Turning his head, he discovered a man sleeping next to him. Pierre-Hugues awkwardly got up, shielded his eyes from the sun and walked towards the sea.

He remembered. Snippets of images came back to him: the sailboat, Edouard's hand when it slipped away, the water that submerged him and then some arms hauling him onto the rubber inflatable boat. Lastly this isolated creek. He stretched. Yawned.

Then went back to the unknown man who'd saved his life. Who was still sleeping. He went up to the Zodiac, attached to a rock by a rope so it wouldn't drift away. Not much to it, an extremely light boat, one that could speed along the waves. Ideal for adventurous men, those who smuggled drugs between Morocco, Spain and all the other countries on the Mediterranean. Including the French Riviera where both wholesalers and dealers shared a huge market of consumers from all walks of life, from humble hoodlums up until Russian billionaires.

He saw six leak-free containers with covers on them at the bottom of the boat. He opened one of them and not surprisingly found bags of cannabis resin. Just in this one their market value must have been hundreds of thousands of euros. Pierre-Hugues was frightened and put the cover back on the vat.

He walked back to the sleeping man and found he hadn't moved since he had woken up. He got closer and suddenly was worried. The man wasn't breathing. He put his hand on his wrist, looking for a pulse. Nothing. He turned the body over. The face was livid, hands already nearly rigid. There was a tourniquet around his left arm and a bluish mark in the fold of his elbow.

And a syringe in the sand next to the cadaver.

∼

"An overdose," gasped Colombe. "The man died next to you while you were sleeping. That's awful."

"Yes, it is," nodded Pierre-Hugues. "Collateral damage, risks of the trade, morbid temptation, call it whatever you want. He wasn't the first nor the last drug victim. From the producer to the consumer, the whole chain consumes at one day or another. Anyway, you can imagine how panicked I was, with a cadaver next to me and over a million euros worth of cannabis in the Zodiac."

"What did you do about it?"

"I thought of thousands of various scenarios in my head. And finally that unknown person who saved my life became the delivery system for my future. Everything that happened in my life since then stemmed from the decision I made that morning, on an isolated beach in the Mediterranean."

∽

Pierre-Hugues dropped the smuggler's wrist, as if it was burning. As if that cadaver would bring him bad luck, whereas the man, on the contrary, had saved his life. Should he thank him or blame him?

In conditions like those, why continue to live? When one after the other your family rejects you, when they want to disavow you, or even wish you were dead.

He felt useless, hated, dirty. You'd nearly say they were right, that suicide was a logical and even pleasant alternative.

Because your mother had discovered and hid your secrets, and she was so disappointed in you that she rejected you.

Because your brother was ready to kill you to prevent you from divulging the secrets of his sexuality.

Because your sister wanted to continue to hide from her family the fact that she'd exhibited her superb nude body to millions of people.

Because they'd decided to throw you into the sea, so they'd have a larger share of your father's fortune.

And because this father had discovered that he was not your biological father. Something that Pierre-Hugues also discovered just a few months ago, in the spring of 1986.

Gorbio, spring of 1986

Lilie pulled on Pierrot's, her favorite brother's, sleeve. She wanted him to play hide and go seek with her in the huge villa in Gorbio, with all its rooms and hiding places. Pierre-Hugues could never refuse anything to her. He went outside to count to one hundred. Lilie ran as fast as possible upstairs, right into her father's room, which she loved because it had a big fireplace and there were old books on its mantel. She loved looking at those leather-bound books with gold lettering. And totally forgot to hide. One large book was standing out a bit from the others. She grabbed it to rub the binding and cover page with the image of an old man with a beard and the back of the book decorated with curvy lines.

An object suddenly fell out of the book. Lilie picked it up. It was a key. She was sorely tempted to try to find the drawer that the key would open. Lilie ran up to her father's desk and tried out the key in the various drawers. Finally, one of them opened.

Inside it she recognized the photo that she'd seen in her mother's purse, the photo of her mom and Pehu.

"Found ya!" shouted Pierre-Hugues rushing up to his little sister.

Lilie was startled, the old photo fell out of her hands.

"Sorry sweetie, I scared you."

He picked it up.

He recognized his mother. Young and beautiful.

But he didn't recognize the man with his arm around her. It certainly wasn't his father.

An unknown face that stunned him.

An unknown person who was his spitting image.

╰╮

"That's how you understood that you weren't Charles's son then?" I asked Pierre-Hugues.

"Yeah, it was a bit harsh as a discovery, but at least I understood why Charles had changed the way he acted with me. For a couple of weeks he'd been begging off of our weekly whisky together on Sundays and our tennis match before going to mass, always finding something better to do."

"And you were persuaded that he really resented you? Because you were his wife's lover's son?"

"Spot on. That was starting to be a lot, everyone against me, everyone who resented me for this or that reason, who resented me so much that they wanted me dead. At least that was what I was saying to myself then, in that crick next to the drug smuggler's dead body. That's when I had an ingenious idea. And I decided to disappear. And organized my own death."

╰╮

Suddenly everything became clear in Pierre-Hugues' mind. He was no longer welcome in his family; they wanted him dead! But he was alive! On the other hand, the man next to him, the one he didn't even know his name, the one who didn't have an ID on him, was stone-cold, victim of an overdose of drugs. Like himself, this man was athletic and had dark Mediterranean skin and hair. Pierre-Hugues had an idea and drew up a plan.

He undressed the cadaver though it was already rigid and also got undressed. Then he exchanged clothing, dressing the unknown man with his shorts and his polo with the crocodile logo on it. Lastly, a very important detail. With regret he took off the expensive Longines watch that Charles had given him for his twentieth birthday, on which he'd had *P.H.L. 1980* engraved and put it on the cadaver's right wrist.

The panic and fear he'd had earlier in the morning had been replaced by determination. He'd decided to start over again, far from his family's can of worms. He already hated his name.

He dragged the rigid body to the Zodiac. He hoisted it in, untied the rope, pushed the inflatable boat into the water, got in and started up the motor. As soon as it started Pierre-Hugues accelerated, turned towards the port side so the boat would be heading out, where he was going as fast as possible towards new horizons, to his new life.

CHAPTER 57
Like a Trojan horse

"WHERE DID YOU GO, MR. SHARPERS?" I wanted to know. "Or should I say Mr. Lacassagne? Which one do you prefer? This is getting complicated!"

"I understand," replied Pierre-Hugues. "I also had problems working out my new identity! I headed out towards North Africa, with short stopovers in Spain to refuel. Not too far from the French coast, I turned off the motor and threw the cadaver overboard, after having said a little prayer for his soul. I knew that he'd eventually come back up, but I hoped that he'd float enough so that he wouldn't be recognizable, before washing up on the coast someplace. And that people would believe he was me, so that I'd cease to be my father's son."

"Looks like everything turned out for you then," said Colombe, "as the body was only found three months later and that your father in person identified it."

"My fairy godmother!"

"Maybe the Longines watch too," I added. "What did you do with the cannabis?"

"Those drugs. I was uneasy with all of these vats in the boat. I wasn't a smuggler or a dealer. So I opened up five of them and dumped them into the sea."

"And the sixth?" asked Colombe.

"I knew I'd be needing some cash to organize my disappearance and new life, far from France. So I kept that one. And was able to sell it easily in Tangier for a good price in dollars, more useful than dirhams. Then I boarded a cargo heading to Portugal, then another merchant ship that took me to Brazil, in Salvador de Bahia. I stayed there for a couple of months and that's where I bought my new identity."

"When you decided to become Angel Sharpers, right?"

"Spot on! I like playing with letters too, Miss Deschamps. That's where I got the idea of an anagram. Maybe I was afraid of completely losing my original identity. Those twenty-two letters unconsciously linked me to my past in Nice. So I moved to the United States, in San Francisco at first, then in San Jose, and I became an American citizen."

"Why those cities?"

"Because California had always attracted me, the beauty of the Golden Gate, the sloping streets of

Frisco. Plus San Jose was right in the middle of Silicon Valley, a dynamic and ambitious region. That's where I made all my money. I founded several companies, start-ups in IT technology and quickly made quite a bit of money."

"Partly because of dirty drug money?" I dared.

"You're right. I must admit my seed money wasn't very clean, but I didn't steal a dime. I happened upon that money and saw it as a sign of fate, and made it grow. I created jobs, and entire families depended on me. So I don't blame myself for anything, I could even see I'm quite proud, see what I mean? If you want to compare things, I prefer by far having succeeded with dirty money rather than living betrayals with so-called clean Lacassagne money."

"You succeeded in your second life," said Colombe, as if she admired the man. "Professionally, I mean. Can I ask you about your personal life?"

"You can. What you read on the Sharpers Wikipedia page was correct. I was married to a Venezuelan model, and we have two daughters. One's twenty and the other is twenty-three. Just as beautiful as their mother," replied Pierre-Hugues with a choked-up voice, looking at the wall across from him.

A silence followed this. I interrupted it, asking if they'd like me to call room service for a new round of drinks. A proposal unanimously received.

A groom came up with our drinks.

"If things were going so well for you, Mr. Lacassagne, a happy family, money, professional success, why show up suddenly today then? Why dive back into the troubled waters of your past, in the can of worms as you say, that was your first life?"

"Because I had to," Pierre-Hugues admitted. "Things didn't go as planned. You of course remember the huge financial crisis the States had beginning in July of 2007."

"The subprime economic crisis," Colombe said, cutting him off, proud of herself. "Were you a victim?"

"I'd made huge investments. Most of my companies were listed on the New York Stock Exchange and then the bottom fell out of the market. The shareholders withdrew their equity, jumped the boat, and I had to sell quickly and at a loss. I was nearly broke. I got depressed, started to drink, I became impossible to live with and my couple didn't resist. In just a couple of months, I lost my fortune as well as my daughters, as they went to Caracas with their mother. My ex-wife is really well known there, she hosts a talk show on nationwide TV. She bounced right back, I'm glad for her and my daughters."

"So moneywise, how are things for you today?" I asked.

"I spent every last dime I had."

"And the takeover bid then?" asked Colombe, astonished. "How were you going to pull that off?"

"The takeover bid! Anyone can file a takeover bid. Once it's filed, it has to be examined and validated by competent officials, or not depending on the financial soundness of the acquirer. And in my case, that would lead to a total invalidation."

"Why did you do it then?"

"To be able to get closer to the holding, with a Trojan horse-like action. That way the coconut tree got shaken up, everyone who was curious or journalists like you, got interested in the Lacassagne's."

"Like a financial electroshock."

"Exactly. I'll be withdrawing my offer tomorrow. There's no use for it now."

Talk about an incredible story! Everything that Pierre-Hugues had just told us was milling around in my mind. Then something came back to me, something I wanted to get to the bottom of.

"There's something in what I just heard that astonishes me. You told us the other day about a party, back in 1986, the Music Festival Day in June. Remember?"

"Yeah. What is so astonishing?"

"In that story you told us, there are times when both Angel Sharpers and Pierre-Hugues are there at the same time. Like when they had a race in the pool, for example. Admit that's pretty paradoxical!"

"That it is! But you know when you've played dead and then invented a new identity for yourself for three decades, your mind does get a bit confused."

"Totally schizophrenic!" added Colombe.

"I tried so hard to match my new identity that I must have started to believe myself that Pierre-Hugues Lacassagne was really dead and buried. I'd convinced myself I was a new man. So it seemed totally natural to me to tell this story with both of the characters there: the true one and the fake one. It's not a crime to believe in my own story, is it?"

No, it wasn't. That wasn't where the crime was, I thought.

CHAPTER 58
Crazier and crazier

MARIE-CAROLINE AND EDOUARD when into their father's huge office, astonishing him.

"To what do I owe this pleasure?"

"Father, we have to talk, this is serious."

"What's wrong? There's a problem with a client?"

"No, nothing professional," replied Marie-Caroline. "A thirty-year-old problem."

Charles sighed and put his head between his hands.

"I knew this would come up one day or another," he finally said. "Sit down."

He pressed a button on his interphone.

"Marie-Therese, could you please bring us three cups of expresso? And after that, please don't disturb us for any reason. Thank you."

He released the button on his interphone and looked at his children.

"I'm listening."

They both looked at each other and after nodding, Marie-Caroline started.

"Father, we've just been informed of something terrible."

"Of what?" Charles asked, the color leaving his face.

"I'm going to get right to the point. We know that someone tried to poison Pierre-Hugues in 1986. There was arsenic in a bottle of whisky, Octomore, to be precise. And we also know that you knew this, right from the very beginning. Jesus Christ! How could you hide something like that from us?"

Charles's mouth dropped open. Another terrible day, he thought, thinking of the day before yesterday when Simon had sat across from him. Kids... He finally opened his mouth.

"My dear children, I did that to protect you."

"Protect us?" asked Edouard. "But from what? I don't understand."

Their father sighed.

"When Sergeant Petrucci told me about what he'd discovered, I racked my brains to try to understand. And I must say that my thoughts led me to believe that either one of you or both of you were guilty of trying to eliminate Pierre-Hugues."

"What?" shouted Marie-Caroline. "You are crazy! You've believed for thirty years that we were capable of killing our brother and you didn't say anything? How could you live with suspicions like that?"

"Like I said, it was to protect you. Protect our family, protect our company."

"Afraid of a scandal, was that it? Always what people think, illusions! That's abject!" Edouard said sadly.

"So, it wasn't you? Either of you?"

Marie-Caroline and Edouard looked at each other, stupefied.

"Of course not! It was an accident! A tragic and unfortunate sailing accident," added Marie-Caroline, still shocked.

"But the bottle? Who brought it?" asked Charles.

"All I know is that when I opened the picnic basket in the galley to prepare our drinks and then dinner, the bottle of whisky was already there, on top of the peanuts, the loaf of bread, and tins of sardines. Everything had already been prepared."

"By who though?" Charles wanted to know.

"By Brigitte, as usual, what do you think? That's what she was there for."

Charles seemed to shrivel away in his chair when he heard that. He put his hands down on his desk, trying to get his breath back.

"Are you okay?" asked his daughter, running up to him. "What's wrong?"

Right then his secretary came in with the coffee.

"Marie-Therese, could you please bring me a glass of water?" asked Edouard, opening the window.

She came back with a tall glass of water and went back out, closing the door.

"Father, what's wrong?"

"The picnic basket... Brigitte," he stammered softly.

"What about her?" asked Edouard, impatiently.

∼

BRIGITTE WAS SITTING on Vintimille Beach. Her son Simon was seated outside the Marco Polo Restaurant, with a crayon in his hand. He had a large sheet of Canson drawing paper in his hand and was making a sketch for his upcoming painting. His mother was coming to life on paper, as an ancient goddess, wearing silk clothing that the wind was blowing. He saw her as a pure vestal, a free woman. Simon knew that his picture would be his masterpiece, the one that would surpass all the others, the one that would make him rich and famous.

In the background he'd paint the Mediterranean Sea and a tormented and avenging secondary character.

He'd add a sailboat.

∼

CHARLES RAISED his head after drinking the glass of water.

"Children, now it's my turn to tell you something. I've got serious reasons to think that Brigitte could have wanted to eliminate Pierre-Hugues."

"What reasons?"

"Jealousy."

And Charles told them the whole story, starting off from when he first met Brigitte up until Simon's recent visit to his office.

Both Marie-Caroline and Edouard were dumbfounded by what he told them.

"But that's impossible!" moaned Edouard. "How many secrets do you have, Father? All these years without saying a word. And committing adultery with the maid! How could you? Living with that woman and that child under our roof? That's disgusting."

"When I think back on little Simon playing in the yard, you holding him at church," added Marie-Caroline. "You knew it Father and you didn't say a word."

"It was finished," Charles said, trying to defend himself. "Just one crazy night, that was all, nothing ever came of it."

"What do you mean, nothing ever came of it? She lived under our roof. With your illegitimate child."

"Edouard, that's enough. I demand some respect!"

"Like you respected us for all these years of lies? You should be ashamed."

"All of this is water under the bridge now. We can't do anything. You have to accept it."

"Water under the bridge?" shouted Edouard. "Didn't you just say that that bastard came here two days ago to demand what was his? It's the past? Didn't you say that you thought Brigitte might have been the author of the attempted poisoning? A past a little too present in my opinion."

"If I understand correctly," Marie-Caroline said, "Simon will have the right to his share of the inheritance?"

Charles bit his lips.

"If I officially recognize him, yes. But I'm not going to. Especially if his mother tried to kill my eldest son. Recognizing him as my son would be like pardoning their sins."

That declaration seemed to quell their apprehension.

"What about our mother here? How much does she know?" Marie-Caroline wanted to know.

"For my whole life I did everything I could so she'd never find out. She's fragile, just like your sister Emilie. Let's leave her out of all this."

CHAPTER 59
A beautiful Russian doll

"WHAT SURPRISES me with this story, Mr. Lacassagne, is that no one recognized you. Not even your father, though you went to his office to talk about acquiring his holding. How can a father now recognize his own child?"

Lacassagne-Sharpers laughed loudly.

"Mr. Bastaro, you know when you're thirty years older with at least a hundred pounds of blubber on you, let me tell you that your features and your silhouette are no longer the same! Just imagine for a couple of seconds a handsome young man, twenty-five years old, athletic, wavy brown hair and an angel face and look at me now with my silhouette of a beached whale, my jowls and my gray thinning hair. Even if you put both pictures side by side, I'm not sure you'd find many similar points. Plus I had to have my nose operated on. Back in the day, when I was still agile, I boxed in San Francisco."

I understood. Sharpers today in 2016 had nothing in common with Pierre-Hugues Lacassagne back in 1986. Water had flowed under the Golden Gate.

"What did you do from 2007 till today, Mr. Lacassagne?" Colombe asked. "If I understood correctly, both your fortune and your personal life exploded then, at the same time as the American financial bubble. Why didn't you come back earlier and tell everyone you were alive and claim your rights to your inheritance?"

Good question, Colombe, I thought.

Pierre-Hugues had another sip of whisky before answering.

"I didn't wait till today to come back to France. To tell you the truth, I've been coming back here since the summer of 2008."

∽

Summer of 2008, southern France

It must have been siesta time in that sunny little village in the south of France as nearly no one was walking around.

The young cashier tending the merry-go-round saw two silhouettes nearing each other.

She saw the elegantly dressed lady first.

Then a more ordinary looking man.

They were both gazing at each other, and neither of them moved.

From where she was, the cashier couldn't hear them. But as they didn't seem to be speaking, that wasn't a problem.

They just looked at one another.

Then they both smiled.

Both of them looked around, as to be sure that they were alone on the village square, far from any prying eyes.

They finally hugged each other, at first timidly, then passionately.

And kissed each other, forgetting everything else.

"Two tickets please," asked Pierre-Hugues, a few minutes later.

What a nice couple, thought the young lady from the booth in her little merry-go-round.

~

Charles was suddenly exhausted and asked his two children to leave. His eighty-year-old heart was finding it hard to deal with all the strong emotions he'd experienced in the past few days. Right after he'd been released from the hospital, he had had the anniversary of Pierre-Hugues' death and then all of the revelations that had poured down upon him for the past few days. He felt that the walls of the Lacassagne house were crumbling and was sure that it wouldn't be long before it collapsed, burying everything beneath the weight of rubble of memories. Charles had the feeling that he could be the next victim.

"Is everything alright, Sir?" asked Dominique when he was bringing him back to their villa in Gorbio.

"Oh! I'm just getting old Dominique, you know. Time for me to rest. I think maybe I've been doing too much and that it's time for my children to take over."

Dominique knew his boss well, having been with him since the very beginning.

"Sir? Could I ask you something?"

"Of course. "What would you like to know?"

"Well, you seem much tenser than usual. And I don't think it's just because you're getting old. It's like you have some problems."

Charles nodded and smiled.

"You do know me well, my dear Dominique. It's true that right now, fate seems to have it in for me. One by one the ghosts are coming out, as if they want to visit me once again before I kick the bucket."

"Would it be because of this biography that Mr. Bastaro is writing? That must bring back so many memories. You look at your life and analyze it like in a rear-view mirror, so of course you remember things, good things like bad ones."

"Unfortunately, the bad ones are the heaviest ones."

"The most painful ones, yes. I think I understand. Is it because of your son's accident?"

"If only it were just that. It's simple. I feel like I'm

living the summer of '86 a second time, thirty years later. Everything's coming back, just like a boomerang. 1986: *annus horribilis!*"

Dominique looked back at his boss in the rear-view mirror.

"Everything?"

"Everything! Plus, who knows what I'll discover next! It scares me."

"Me too! I mean that I'm worried about you, Sir."

"Thank you, Dominique."

"It's sincere."

Charles closed his eyes and leaned back on the car seat, sleeping till they got to Gorbio, with one hand on his jacket, at his chest, as if he wanted to better control this cardiac rhythm.

~

"THAT WAS my very first day of my second life in France, if you could call it that," Pierre-Hugues continued.

"And who was that lady that you saw that day then?" asked Colombe. "A French love?"

"You're right. Someone I've always loved. Someone I hadn't seen since 1986 and who I missed horribly."

I strangely that of that Russian girl that Sharpers had told us about, what was her name again?

"Vanya?" I asked.

Pierre-Hugues burst out laughing.

"Funny. Vanya. No, unfortunately I never saw her

again either. And believe me, I would have liked to. But then again, you have to remember that Pierre-Hugues was dead, replaced by Angel Sharpers. No, to tell you the truth, that woman I saw starting back in 2008 each year at the same time was older than me."

"And it was?"

"Lucie, my mother."

∼

LUCIE LACASSAGNE WAS SURPRISED to hear the limousine pulling up. This was exceptionally early for Charles. Unless something happened? She ran out.

At the same time Dominique opened the back door of the car. Charles's white head came out, then his chauffeur helped him put his feet out and gave him his cane. Lucie had the terrible impression that her husband had aged ten years since this morning. She went up to meet him.

"Charles, is something wrong?"

"I'm just really tired, Lucie. I'd like to lie down a while. Can you come with me to my room?"

Dominique helped them up the steps leading to his bedroom.

"Thank you, Dominique, you can go now".

Lucie escorted her husband to the bed and helped him lie down.

"I'll go make you some soup, it'll do you good."

"Maybe I could eat some, even though I'm not hungry."

Lucie started to walk away, but Charles stopped her.

"Wait! Come back, please. Hold my hand."

Lucie was astonished by her husband's request; this certainly was something she wasn't used to.

"Lucie, I'd like to tell you how important you've been for me, for my whole life."

"Charles, your life isn't finished."

"Maybe. Who knows when it could end. Remember Pierre-Hugues!"

Something Lucie had of course never forgotten.

Charles continued.

"Despite our money, despite our children, life hasn't always been a bed of roses for us. I made mistakes and I regret them, especially those that hurt you."

Lucie sat down on her husband's bed, still holding his hand.

"Yes, sometimes you did hurt me," she started. "And probably I also hurt you sometimes too. Who can boast that they're perfect? Life is made from mistakes, good and bad decisions, successes and failures, loyalties and betrayals. That's what makes it worth living, right?"

"Undoubtedly, Lucie, undoubtedly. I'm suddenly really tired and I'm afraid."

"Afraid of what?"

"Afraid of what's coming in our lives. Afraid of finding out terrible secrets."

"Charles, what are you talking about? Explain yourself."

"I don't know, but it feels like something awful is going to happen."

Lucie had shared her life with Charles for nearly sixty years and squeezed his hand even harder. She began to speak.

"Charles. You have to listen to me, and you have to be strong."

"You're scaring me. What have you got to say?"

"Our son... Pierre-Hugues... He's alive!"

∽

"You mean that Lucie, your mother, knew that you were alive since 2008? That's incredible!" said Colombe to Pierre-Hugues. "Why didn't she say something, news like that is sensational, unhoped for."

"I'm not sure I would have been welcomed with open arms back then. I was persuaded that nearly everyone in my family had wanted me dead and had organized my death. On the other hand, I needed to see my mother and Lilie, my little sister who I also missed so much. And without knowing it, she's the one who allowed me to come back then."

∽

San Francisco, spring of 2008

. . .

Pierre-Hugues Lacassagne, alias Angel Sharpers, had returned to his favorite city in California. Since his bankruptcy and divorce, he was now alone in his little apartment on a sloping street just like the ones you see in Steve McQueen's movie *Bullit*, in a mythical car chase.

He'd officially disappeared for more than twenty years now. Declared dead in France. An unambiguous administrative death.

But he missed France and especially his little sister, Lilie, as he was her favorite, her idol, her reference. Little Lilie, who didn't understand the world like other kids did. Lilie who must have cried her eyes out since he disappeared, he was sure of that. Little innocent Lilie!

Tears were running down Pierre-Hugues' cheeks. Was their bitterness a resurgence of primitive times where men were mere marine animals? he asked himself strangely. A curious thought for him who was supposed to have drowned, his lungs filled with saltwater.

He got up. He had to do something, get back in the game, find solutions. He felt that his life was changing. There was Pierre-Hugues in Nice, then Angel Sharpers here. Maybe it was time for Pierre-Hugues Lacassagne's resurrection?

But how? Could he just show up and shout "Surprise! I'm not dead!" And then everyone would rush up and hug him? He didn't think so. Resurrection is a serious subject. It's more traumatic to see someone come back from the dead to see someone die.

Sitting in front of his computer, Pierre-Hugues understood that he'd have to do this carefully, without making any waves. But how? Where? With whom?

He couldn't imagine directly contacting Charles, Edouard, or Marie-Caroline. It would be child's play to contact them at the holding. Their emails and phone numbers were on the internet.

No, he had to find his mother. And through her, find little Lilie.

Emilie, disability, Down's syndrome.

Pierre-Hugues put in keywords. He had an idea, a line of thought he wanted to pursue. After trying several times, each time with more precise research, he finally found something interesting.

L'A<small>PETAM</small> : l'Association des parents d'enfants trisomiques des Alpes-Maritimes. (Apetam: Association of parents of children with Down's syndrome in the Alpes-Maritimes).

H<small>E SCROLLED</small> down through the pages, looking for photos, hoping to find his mother and sister. Nothing though.

He read through the minutes of the meetings, their activities, discussions on the forum.

Then he finally stumbled upon a name, then an email: lucie.lacassagne101@gmail.com

∽

Lucie was still holding her tired husband's hand. Sitting next to him on the bed, she listened to him. Lying down next to her, he heard her. Alone in their huge but empty villa in Gorbio, they told each other everything. Everything that remained unsaid for decades. Everything that they had guessed without asking for an explanation. All of those unsaid things that mark human lives, just like unaccomplished acts.

Charles's hand was trembling in his wife's hands, his little wife that he met one day back in 1958, when the traveling circus came to town. The wife he loved and who loved him, despite a few mistakes on both sides. As they kept talking, Charles was weakening. Soon, Lucie felt his hands she was holding cool down.

But his pulse began to accelerate. Then he couldn't breathe. He brought a knotty hand up to his chest.

"Lucie, I'm going. I'm going in peace."

Lucie rushed to the phone and called the rescue squad.

∽

"I was able to contact my mom using this email," Pierre-Hugues Lacassagne told us.

It was getting dark in my suite at the Negresco, but

no one wanted to leave, we wanted to understand what had gone on since 1986. I had room service bring up dinner for three and a bottle of Bordeaux. We didn't want to lose a single word of Pierre-Hughes' story and talking about it also seemed to unburden his soul, when he told us about his life as Angel Sharpers.

"Beginning in 2008, we saw each other once a year, in July, the anniversary month of my official death, for a couple of days, just the two of us. A pilgrimage, you could say. A way we could get to know each other again. Little by little. Each time I traveled from the States, and we met in the south of France. I missed it too. Its scrublands, its cicadas, the fragrances and the beautiful sun exploding on the waves of the blue Mediterranean."

"And it wasn't too complicated for Lucie to get away for several days at a time?" asked Colombe. "From what I understood, she was pretty much of a homebody."

"No. Ever since I died, my mother had been going to a convent in the mountains for a couple of days in July. A place off the beaten track, where you could meditate, decompress, and for a week, you made a vow of silence. That's how she got rid of the pain ever since I disappeared. So in 2008, we got together right near that convent. The following years, she shortened her stay there and the rest of the week we stayed together."

"A good camouflage then."

"Yeah. Religion has the advantage of being something intimate and secret, and no one would have dared to disturb her."

"What did you do then for those few days together?"

"We talked, we looked at the landscapes, we imagined my return. Each time my mother brought me photos of Lilie, videos too, that she had on her smartphone. I felt like I was with her."

"You never saw Emilie again?" I asked.

"Never."

"How come? You missed her so much."

"Because we thought that Lile was too fragile to understand and accept the unthinkable. People suffering from Down's syndrome are often hypersensitive. I was afraid for her mental health."

"And now, do you think you could see her again?"

"I do hope so."

Right then Pierre-Hugues' phone vibrated. He picked it up, and when he saw the name, his mouth dropped open.

∽

Brigitte admired the drawing Simon had just finished. Her son really was talented. She was proud of him and happy for him. He would become someone; she was sure of that.

They were counting on spending a few more days here, basking on the Vintimille Beach, far from the hustle and bustle of Nice. When they'd come back, they'd stand up to the Lacassagne family, forcing Charles to take that paternity test so that Simon would get his rightful share of the inheritance.

So that he could join the name Lacassagne to Garibaldi, as the blood of both ran through his veins.

The beginning of a new life, one where he'd be both rich and famous!

∽

Lucie was waiting, immobile on a plastic chair in a gloomy hall next to the ER ward. Charles had been admitted to the hospital in Nice, suffering from a heart attack.

A doctor walked up to her.

"Mrs. Lacassagne? I'm Doctor Recamier. Could you come to my office please?"

The old lady nodded and obediently followed the doctor. He invited her to sit down.

"How is he?" she managed to say.

Doctor Recamier sat down too, both elbows on his desk and his clasped hands under his chin.

"Your husband is not doing well at all. We were able to stabilize him for now, but his heart is extremely weak. We have to operate. We'll do it tomorrow early in the morning. I have to tell you that it will be an open-heart operation, one that is very risky."

"Dear Lord," Lucie sighed. "How risky?"

"Right now, not more than thirty percent of a

chance of survival. But we have to try. We need your consent though, Mrs. Lacassagne."

"You mean that it's up to me to decide whether or not you'll operate?"

"That's right. Spouses have this privilege or burden you could say. One chance out of three to save your husband. I'm sorry to have to tell you that, but we don't have any other choice."

Lucie began to tremble and cry, faced with that heavy choice.

"Do I have to answer now?" she stammered.

"You've got until tomorrow morning when the operating block opens, about six. Right now, like I said, your husband is in a stationary state. But the more we wait, the more risk there will be. Tomorrow morning, we need a decision."

Tears were running down Lucie's cheeks now. The doctor looked at her kindly.

"We're transferring your husband to a room in intensive care. You'll be able to join him there. Do you have any questions?"

"I'll think this over. Thank you for having been so frank with me, doctor."

He got up and showed Lucie out.

"I'll leave you with the nurses, they'll be there if you need anything."

"Thank you. I'll be fine."

Lucie went to the cafeteria in the lobby and took out her phone.

"Hello," replied Pierre-Hugues.
> He was silent.
> Listened.
> Closed his eyes.
> The color left his face."
> "I'm on my way."

CHAPTER 60
A familiar aria

LUCIE SCRUTINIZED the hospital's parking lot that night, hoping that Pierre-Hugues would soon arrive. Their time was now limited. Each time an ambulance or a taxi dropped someone off, she hoped he'd be coming out. There were three or four of them and then finally her son got out of one, his enormous body exiting it with difficulty.

She slowly walked up to meet him and then they hugged each other, as if each of them was supporting the other.

"Pierrot, we have to hurry."

"I hope we're not too late."

They went into the hospital.

Going to Charles's room, Lucie told her son what had happened during the last few hours. They decided on the best way to break this to the old man: whatever they'd say or do, it would be a terrible shock, but an inevitable one.

They stopped in front of his door.

"Wait here," she said. "I'll come and get you."

Lucie disappeared into the room with its subdued lighting.

She joined her husband whose body was hooked up to a slew of machines and IV drips, with their "beeps" and "tuts" playing a familiar aria for all the doctors and nurses there.

"Charles, I brought someone. I just want to warn you that you'll have to be strong and understanding."

He just listened to his wife, who tried to prepare him for the upcoming meeting. She finally came out.

Charles saw the door open once again. When Pierre-Hugues walked in, it was Angel Sharpers that he saw. Recognizing him, the old man jumped suddenly on his bed.

"What the hell are you doing here? You came to do me in? You want me dead?"

"Calm down, Charles," Lucie said. "Come here," she said to Pierre-Hugues.

"You know him?" Charles asked, astonished. "How?"

"*Shhh*! Let him explain."

Pierre-Hugues walked up to the old man.

"Don't you get near me!" he shouted, panicked. "Leave me alone! Lucie! Make him leave, now!"

Pierre-Hugues didn't pay attention to him and when he was next to the bed, he began to whisper to the patriarch.

"There has been a terrible mistake, father."

Charles squinted, and right after that, opened his eyes and looked straight at him.

"You are crazy. Leave my room immediately, you don't have any right to be here. You're making things up. Leave!"

"Charles," said Lucie calmly. "Please trust me here. I explained all that earlier. As crazy as it may seem, this man here is our son, he is Pierre-Hugues."

Only after she'd said that did the old man consent to listen to that person who said he was his son, who had come back from the dead. Like a ghost. A ghost of the past.

Pierre-Hugues outlined what he'd already told Jerome and Colombe.

The more he told him about what had happened in the past thirty years, the more he seemed to be disturbed. The cardiac monitor was picking up speed, his blood pressure was increasing.

"Mother," said Pierre-Hugues looking at his father. "Maybe we should just let him rest."

Lucie shook her head.

"Keep on talking, Pierrot. He's got the right but especially the obligation to hear the whole story."

So, Pierre-Hugues spoke and spoke, until an alarm went off in one of the machines his father was hooked up to and a nurse ran into the room.

"Let me through! He's relapsing!"

Accompanied by her other colleagues, she pushed

the bed through the halls up to the emergency ward, then to the operating suite.

The operation lasted three hours.

Until Charles Lacassagne was officially declared dead.

PART Five

BACK IN THE WATERS

CHAPTER 61
It's gonna be a bestseller!

NICE, *July 19, 2016*

WHEN PIERRE-HUGUES RUSHED AWAY from us last night to go to the hospital and see Charles, Colombe and I were both flabbergasted. Things were going faster and faster, as if the wheel of fate couldn't stop spinning.

We learned that Charles had passed away that night when we woke up, exacerbating our unease.

Things would get worse though. When we walked through the lobby to go to the breakfast room, the concierge called out to me and handed me an envelope.

"Mr. Bastaro, someone left this for you."

It was starting again. I didn't dare ask him if it was the same kid that had delivered it, but the same thing seemed to have happened again. I didn't want to open it, afraid to see what it contained. I couldn't ignore it though. I ripped it open.

"*Congratulations, Mr. Bastaro! With all your mud raking, you succeeded in killing Charles Lacassagne! Now it's time to stop. If not...*"

If not what? Jesus Christ. Who? Why?

"Someone who has a lot of information or someone who's really close to the family to know that he already died," noted Colombe.

Though for a while I'd thought that Edouard or Marie-Caroline wanted to shut me up, now I believed that something like that was impossible, or at least paradoxical: they were the ones who encouraged me to see the truth, weren't they?

Then I thought about Brigitte and Simon, whose sudden and lengthy absence was always in the back of my mind. But what would be in it for them if I hid the truth?

I tried once again to phone them. Once again unsuccessfully. They hadn't tried to contact me either. I started to build all sorts of scenarios in my head that could explain Brigitte's and Simon's disappearance.

I decided to call Gerard, my Parisian boss, and tell him everything, starting from the nearly miraculous resurrection of Pierre-Hugues up until Charles's sudden death. I mused that life sometimes plays strange tricks on families: taking one of the members right when another one appears.

Gerard didn't believe his ears. For him, all this was manna fallen straight from heaven: everything I'd told him would make sales of *The Truth About the Lacassagne Affair*, the preliminary title he wanted to give my book, take off like a rocket.

"All this is tangible, factual!" he said enthusiastically, flooding my ears with joyful shouting. "It's gonna be a bestseller, Jerome!"

I spotted his keen managerial eye, as well as someone who loved scoops.

"But," he continued, "your contract with Charles is now null and void, *de facto.*"

I hadn't even thought about that aspect of the problem! Indeed, without the main character, the one who was telling me about his life, I'd lost the source of the autobiography. What about the last third of the sum we'd agreed upon? I'd have to reread that contract carefully. That could wait. I didn't want to disturb the Lacassagne family's bereavement. They certainly had other things on their plates right now.

And Pierre-Hugues in all that? He'd just come back, and his father passed away. I hoped that they both had had enough time to see each other, at least for a few minutes. After thirty years of separation, the contrary would have been too bad.

I sent sympathy messages to Lucie, Pierre-Hugues,

Marie-Caroline and Edouard, ensuring them that they could count on my presence and my support, for anything they'd need.

I nonetheless wanted to leave them in their intimacy surrounded by their deceased father and their resurrected son. They'd be having strong and perhaps painful moments. Poignant ones.

In three or four days, Charles's body would be buried in the family's vault.

"Jesus Christ!" I shouted.

"What's wrong?" Colombe asked.

"The Lacassagne family's vault!"

"What about it? The one in the little cemetery here?"

"Right, the one where..."

"Pierre-Hugues Lacassagne is already buried," my dear intern completed my sentence.

"Or at least the person that everyone thought was Pierre-Hugues."

"But who in reality was a drug smuggler. That is crazy. If that is true, he's got nothing to do there. Charles won't want his final resting place to be above a stranger's. It would be indecent."

"In that case, they'll have to do an exhumation."

Colombe bit her lips.

"That would be terrible. I can't even imagine it. Something like that must require some type of authorization. Legal decisions, stuff like that."

"You're right. City Hall can order exhumations for example when they move or extend the cemetery, or when they recover a lapsed tomb. But that all takes lawyers. I'd imagine that Pierre-Hugues will have to prove that the man buried in his name in the Gorbio cemetery isn't him."

"But how?"

"He'll have to take a DNA test."

A meeting

Nice, 1985

Once again, the two men were waiting for their informer at a table in the back of the Chez Félix Bar: no good reason to change their habits.

"This time I'm taking extra risks," the man who was alone said. "I think that deserves a bit more, don't you?"

"Depends on what you've got for us. Let's see."

"Just a minute. Another one percent payable right now."

The two men looked at each other.

"Deal!"

"Deal!"

They shook hands on it.

Then the man pulled a bunch of papers out of his brief case and put them on the table, between two glasses of a *mauresque*.

"Here you go. These are photocopies of the market with the specifications."

"Nothing to write home about," muttered one of the men.

"Wait a sec, I've also got the list of candidates for the market with their detailed quotes. All you have to do is quote below them and you've got the market."

"Perfect. You're a pretty handy guy after all."

"Let's just say I've got contacts."

"Always a pleasure doing business with you."

They shook hands and finished up their drinks. When they were leaving, they didn't notice the man who was coming out of the restrooms and who had heard their entire conversation.

And whose name was Pierre-Hugues Lacassagne.

CHAPTER 62
When you're inspired

THE DEATH of the real estate magnate, Charles Lacassagne, was announced that night on the news. A well-known person in Nice. The journalist spoke lengthily about his most important projects as well as the tragedy that had struck his family in 1986. They also talked about the takeover bid that had just been withdrawn. Local politicians touted their friendship with the holding's boss, presented their sincere condolences and deepest sympathy to the family in this difficult time. The journalist added that only family members would be invited to the funeral. No one mentioned Gorbio.

The phone rang at the end of the afternoon. I quickly picked up.

"Mr. Bastaro? This is Brigitte Garibaldi. You wanted to talk to me? I just noticed that you called me several times. Simon and I went to Vintimille and I didn't have any phone reception there. We just got back to France."

And I did hear the sound of a train in the background.

"Have you turned on the news, Mrs. Garibaldi?"

"No, not yet, why?"

"Charles Lacassagne passed away. Last night."

There was silence on the other end of the line.

"That can't be true," moaned Brigitte. "It's too early."

I understood what she was getting at: Charles's death had put an end to their projects of paternity recognition.

"Could we meet up quickly?"

We decided to meet on the Promenade, at the foot of Mont Boron, as it was still nice outside.

I was surprised that she came alone, without her son.

"Simon stayed in the apartment. He started painting a picture and you know how it is, when you're inspired..."

"Yup," I nodded, "you have to seize the opportunity when it's there."

I told her how astonished I was about their getaway to neighboring Italy.

"You're right, it wasn't planned at all. We just wanted to get out of Nice after what happened on July 14th."

Understandable.

"Why did you want to talk to me?" she asked.

"Because we weren't sure of a couple of things that happened back in the summer of '86."

"Which ones? I think we went over everything the other day."

"We did. But in the meanwhile, we found a few other elements and I needed to speak with you about them. Mrs. Garibaldi, please think back to the day when Pierre-Hugues died, if that's possible."

"I never forgot that day, Mr. Bastaro," she said sadly and seemed sincere when she said it.

"Can you remember having prepared a picnic basket for the three sailors?"

Brigitte turned her eyes left, a sign that she was mentally going back into the past, dredging through her souvenirs.

"That was part of my job, yes. I did prepare their picnic basket."

"What did you put in it?"

"The same thing as usual when the guys went out sailing, I think."

"Meaning?"

"Some bread, milk, fruit juice, sardines, some cheese, a couple of apples and some peanuts."

I noticed that some of this was not in the previous testimonials. That made me think that if she was in charge of it, she was probably right.

"Did you also put a few bottles in?"

"No, because there was a reserve of drinking water on board."

"I was thinking of alcohol here."

"You're right, Edouard had asked me to add two bottles of Bordeaux."

"Nothing else?"

"No."

"Mrs. Garibaldi, what if I told you that a gendarme had found a bottle of whisky?"

"I'd say that it's possible, but I can assure you that I didn't put it in their picnic basket."

"You're sure of this?"

"Completely. There were just those two bottles of Bordeaux in the basket that I put in the car before they left. Charles himself chose them in his wine cellar. He had a lot of vintage wines that he gave his children."

Charles was the one who brought the bottles up, I thought to myself. Maybe a point to follow up on?

"Ma'am, I have to tell you something, as you're the one who prepared the picnic basket. There was poison in the whisky."

Brigitte's hand flew to her mouth. She looked as though she'd seen a ghost.

"Good Lord! That is awful! And you thought I'd be capable of doing something like that?"

"It was an eventuality, not a certitude, and I had to eliminate it. I'm sure you can understand how upset we were when we found this out."

"I do. And you'll also admit that I was horrified to find out that someone wanted to assassinate Pierre-Hugues, because I suppose that he was the one who was targeted?"

"Why are you asking that?"

"Because whisky was his favorite alcohol."

We already knew that, but it was interesting to hear her say that too.

"What terrible fates in this family," Brigitte said.

"A family that you and Simon are almost members of."

"At least in our opinion," sighed Brigitte.

CHAPTER 63
The family's orchestra conductor

CHARLES LACASSAGNE'S body was transferred from the hospital to the funeral parlor where his family could come to pay homage to him.

Lucie came as soon as possible, with her children: Marie-Caroline, Edouard and Emilie. Out of everyone, Lilie was the one who cried the most. She seemed aware that her father was no longer there and paradoxically still believed he was. A father she had always innocently loved, though he wasn't always there for her.

The day after that, Lucie went alone to be with her husband. She was with him for over an hour, her hand on his cold forehead, on the refrigerated table. It was as if she was touching a statue made of ice, a body that had been emptied of the warmth of its soul. She ran a hand over his features: his lips, his nose, his eyelids that had been closed. Then she ran them through Charles's white hair, as if making sure they looked nice for his last trip.

To prepare for the next day, she called Pierre-Hugues, then Brigitte and Simon.

It was time for a family reunion. With everyone!

∽

I RECEIVED a call from Lucie and once again said how sorry I was for her loss. She asked Colombe and I to attend Charles's funeral service. I replied that it would be an honor for us.

In the meanwhile, we decided we deserved to relax, evacuating some of the tension and pressure generated by this very strange job with the Lacassagne family. Had I known when I left Paris just a few weeks ago what I'd be going through, I perhaps might have turned it down. But then I wouldn't have known Colombe.

We rented a jet ski with the intention of having fun, inebriating ourselves with its speed. I was the first one in the driver's seat. Colombe, wearing a two-piece swimsuit, was behind me, holding me very, very tightly, something I was loving. I could feel her arms around my side and her hands caressing my abs and pecs... okay, let's be honest here: my stomach and my chest!

We raced through the waves along the Théoule coast, then headed out to sea, towards Lérins Islands. I thought that we must have been close to the spot where Pierre-Hugues had fallen in thirty years ago, but also pretty close to quite a few vats full of cannabis resin. Millions of euros at the bottom of the sea, beneath the hull of our jet ski.

Colombe took us back to the coast after being out nearly two hours, with a few breaks where we swam around though we remained close to our little boat! After that, we worked on our tans on the beach. Suddenly Colombe jumped up.

"Hey, so if Brigitte is innocent..."

"She is! She was sincere. Unless she's the greatest actress in the whole world, and in that case, she deserves an Oscar!"

"I agree. So, if Brigitte's innocent, who the heck is guilty? This is crazy, isn't it? Like an Agatha Christie novel. And I thought that stuff like this only happened in books."

"The whodunit specialist has spoken," I joked. "You know what? We're going to put that aside, give them time to bury Charles and think of ourselves now, especially as I'm now out of a job. Anyway, it's a crime without a victim. Pierre-Hugues is alive, in flesh and bones. Plus no one can be tried now."

"But still, you don't want to know what really happened?"

"Of course I do. Plus, I haven't forgotten that threatening letter, whether its author was serious or not. But I need some rest, and you do too. Sometimes truth comes all by itself when you're no longer looking for it!"

Lucie took care of all the formalities linked to organizing her husband's funeral with a formidable cold-blood and efficiency. She also took care of what it would take to reintegrate Pierre-Hugues back into the family. She had to contact the Grand Instance Court in Nice, so that they would order the exhumation of the body buried in 1986. As that man wasn't her son, she didn't want him in the family vault. And he had to leave before Charles was placed there. But for the French administration, Pierre-Hugues Lacassagne was dead and buried! You could even read it on his marble tombstone!

Pierre-Hugues discreetly went to the cemetery in Gorbio. It was really strange when he discovered his name and dates, even if they were merely letters engraved on a tombstone. Words though are always so powerful that it was hard for him not to shiver. Plus, the man who was buried in his casket was someone he'd known, albeit just one night. He'd slept next to him, died next to him too. That brought them close together you could say. And just to think that the man who was buried there, six feet under, was the one he'd thrown into the sea thirty years ago. Plus, and above all, the one who had saved his life!

Life goes on. An endless wheel.

Of course, the law wouldn't just believe him and that wasn't enough to authorize the exhumation of the body. The Grand Instance Court ordered him to carry out DNA tests, both for Pierre-Hugues and Lucie as well as the body that had been buried. For those who were alive, it was a mere sample of their saliva that was taken directly in a Court accredited laboratory. On the other hand, for that thirty-year-old cadaver, it was a bit more difficult. Just like paleontologists, they had to use his bones and teeth to get their DNA samples.

None of the Lacassagne family members wanted to be there. The funeral home employees thus worked alone, supervised by a bailiff that the Court had mandated.

The mechanical shovel dug through the earth, and when it hit the coffin, the employees finished the job with shovels. They put cinches around the dirty coffin and hoisted it out of the grave, and still under the surveillance of that bailiff, drove it back to the morgue where it was opened.

Inside all that was left of the anonymous smuggler was his skeleton and shreds of clothing including a bit of red shorts with a crocodile embroidered on them. Around his radius and cubitus, a Longines watch whose needles had stopped.

Their tests confirmed what was foreseeable: Pierre-Hugues's DNA matched Lucie's whereas the DNA that had been taken from the femur of the skeleton had nothing in common with theirs.

Officially, in the eyes of French justice, Pierre-Hugues Lacassagne's identity was confirmed and the note "died on July 15, 1986" was deleted in his papers.

All of those important legal procedures postponed Charles's funeral by a week, and he remained in the morgue.

During that time, Lucie Lacassagne, who had become the family's orchestra conductor, wanted to reunite the entire family, in the best possible conditions.

The first people she went to see were Brigitte and Simon Garibaldi.

∾

When Lucie walked into Brigitte's apartment, neither of them knew what to say. The two ladies remained immobile and silent for a minute before Lucie began to speak.

"Brigitte, it's a real pleasure to see you again. It's been such a long time!"

"Oh! Mrs. Lacassagne."

They kissed each other delicately on their cheeks.

"Come in, please," said Brigitte, showing her into the living room. "Simon, look who's here!"

The young man ran up to Lucie, a huge smile on his face.

"I'm so happy to see you again Madame Lucie!" he said, as if he were still a six-year-old kid running around the yard in Gorbio Villa with Emilie. "In spite of the circumstances. My deepest sympathy... Charles, it's awful."

Simon turned his head away, masking his eyes behind a strand of hair.

Lucie took his hand.

"Simon, I could also address my condolences to you."

"Madame..." the young man stammered.

"Come over here," said Brigitte, bringing in a box of cookies and a steaming pot of tea.

Lucie sat down in one of the armchairs and looked around the apartment.

"It's very nice here. And I see that you live in one of the nicest parts of town."

Brigitte smiled shyly.

"I must say I can't complain."

"Brigitte? Don't bother. I know everything."

"Everything?"

"Everything! Starting from your adventure with Charles and so I know about you too Simon, including your Parisian apartment."

Brigitte looked down.

"I'm so sorry, so terribly sorry."

"Don't be. All that is water under the bridge. We can't change things and at our age, it's better to look on the bright side of everything."

"What do you mean?" asked Brigitte, trying to compose herself by pouring the tea.

"I mean I didn't come here today to try to get even. Had I wanted to, I would have done it ages ago. But I preferred to close my eyes on it and forget. After all, you didn't steal my husband. And I can say that I'm actually sad for both of you," she added, looking at them. "Simon, you really didn't get to know your father. And you, Brigitte, you lived your whole life with this secret buried deep inside. But I must add, I know what you're going through. I'm not above reproach, far from it. So, let's focus on the future now."

Lucie took a sip of her tea. Then she looked at the easel, where Simon's painting was nearly finished.

"You did that? What a talented young man you are! The courses at the Fine Arts Institute really were good ones then."

"Thank you, Madame Lucie," replied Simon timidly. And thank you too for the art courses, for Montmartre… Without you, I never would have been able to afford all that."

"You're quite welcome, Simon. When I see a painting like this, I realize that it was a good investment," joked Lucie. "I'm delighted that you're an artist. That makes me think of when I was young, when I was an artist in the traveling circus. Did I already tell you about that?"

"Yes, you did," replied Simon, his face lighting up. "You had a Bohemian lifestyle too."

Lucie put her cup of tea down.

"Right. Enough about the past. Brigitte, Simon, I know your intentions and I respect them. I'm even going to help you. I weighed the pros and cons of it during the night that Charles passed away. And arrived at the conclusion that Simon has a right to be recognized as one of my husband's sons."

"Oh! Mrs. Lacassagne, thank you!" said Brigitte submerged by emotions and surprise: the widow of her lover, the wife he'd cheated on, was going to help the illegitimate child.

"Don't say thanks. It's normal. Simon grew up at our house, like a son, with Lilie next to him. Let me tell you what I did and what we'll do now together."

Simon and Brigitte were hanging onto every word Lucie said. She went through her purse and took out a wad of papers. She looked at them.

"The other day, before Charles was admitted to the hospital, we spent the whole night in his bedroom, where he was resting. We talked lengthily about everything. We both talked about our lives and we both made some difficult decisions. And that's why I'm here."

She handed the papers over to Brigitte, who began reading them. Lucie helped her out.

"Go right to the last page and read the last paragraph."

Brigitte did as she was told and read with a murmur that made Simon shiver.

"Mrs. Lacassagne," she said, holding the sheets of paper to her chest. "I don't know what to think, or what to say."

"Just reread them out loud for Simon then."

"*This is a codicil to my will, written by myself, with full awareness and as is my own will, on July 18, 2016, in the presence of my wife, Lucie Lacassagne, née Lucia Sganarelli. With this present document, I want to add to my beneficiaries Mr. Simon Garibaldi, born on March 23, 1980, whom I hereby recognize as my legiti-*

mate son, born from Mrs. Brigitte Garibaldi and myself. For all due intents and purposes, I, Charles Lacassagne, undersigned."

Brigitte finished reading, her eyes full of tears, her voice scratchy with emotion. Simon, sitting across from her, also had red eyes caused by the cold but emotionally meaningful words Charles had written, designating him as one of his heirs.

"How did you do that?" Brigitte wanted to know.

"When I understood that Charles probably wouldn't make it through the night, I insisted that he write this paragraph for Simon."

"But why? I mean like... like you're his wife."

"Because Simon shares Charles's genes, making him a Lacassagne. So that means he has the right to his share of the inheritance."

"Thank you so very much. May I kiss you?" asked Simon, standing up.

Lucie stopped him.

"Wait! There's one last thing. Before I contact your notary public, I have to make sure that Charles really is your father. Because right now, I've only got two confessions: yours and my husband's."

"What kind of proof do you need?" asked the young man.

"A proof that can't be questioned by anyone: a paternity test."

Once again Lucie put her hand into her purse to get a small bag, that she took a type of swab out.

"What's that?" asked Simon.

Lucie explained that it was an applicator to get a sample of his saliva for a DNA analysis. She handed it to him. He looked dubitative, almost fearful. Lucie's approach was surprising, audacious, but undoubtedly legitimate. He had nothing to lose. Despite that, he looked at his mother silently questioning her, and she encouraged him by nodding. He did as he was told, and Lucie put the swab back in the little sachet.

"And for Charles's DNA?" Brigitte asked.

Lucie went back into her purse where she took out an identical sachet.

"These are a couple of Charles's hairs that I cut yesterday in the morgue. I'll give both sachets to a private lab for a genetic comparison. It only takes three or four days. But this is just a formality: I don't have any doubts about your sincerity. You just have to look at Simon to see that he's Charles's son. Now young man, come and give me a kiss!"

And he rushed to the lady he'd always called Madame Lucie but who he'd always sort of considered as his second mother.

∽

THERE WERE STILL a few days separating us from Charles's funeral which was planned for July 28th, and we took advantage of them. Colombe and I took the typical tourist routes, visiting Tourrettes-sur-Loup, Saint-Paul-de-Vence, and Grasse without having to look at our watches or go see the Lacassagne family. A real vacation down south!

During that magical interlude I even forgot my contract. Anyway my employer's death must have put an end to our agreements about his biography. That was something I'd have to talk about with Lucie.

She had called me to tell me about her visit with Brigitte and Simon. And she was soon going to have a family reunion, one that everyone would attend.

∼

Gorbio, July 25, 2016

However it would end, this would be a day no one could forget. Lucie had organized everything so it would take place in the best conditions possible. She feared Lilie's reaction, as she was her most fragile child. The other were adults, it would be easier for them.

She wanted Marie-Caroline and Edouard to meet up with Pierre-Hugues in advance. Which they did.

∼

The day before, Marie-Caroline and Edouard were waiting at the Saint-Jean-Cap-Ferrat Port, in front of the sailboat.

Pierre-Hugues, still seen as but another fat American, showed up a few minutes later. He stopped a few yards from his brother and sister. His heart was racing, there was a tear welling up in an eye. Then he walked up to them.

"Is it really you?" asked Marie-Caroline, surprised when she saw that deformed and horribly obese person, so very different from the Pierre-Hugues that she remembered.

"It is," he replied hesitantly.

Then as if to prove it, he began chanting.

"Humpty Dumpty sat on a wall..."

Humpty Dumpty had a great fall..." continued Edouard.

"All the king's horses and all the king's men..." Marie-Caroline said, a half-smile on her lips.

"Couldn't put Humpty together again!!!" they all shouted out in unison, like they did when they were kids.

They all then hugged each other warmly, the three of them finally together, trying to make up for thirty years of emotional drought, thirty years of misunderstandings, thirty years of useless bitterness.

"Why didn't you come back earlier, Pierrot?" asked Edouard.

"I always believed that you wanted to..."

"Jesus Christ, shut the hell up! How could you believe something like that? We fucking love you, bro!" shouted Edouard, pushing his shoulder.

"Watch your language, Doudou," Marie-Caroline joked.

"We have to get back on, one of these days," said

Pierre-Hugues, pointing at the sailboat with his chin. "All three of us."

"Totally," confirmed Edouard. "To ward off the ghosts."

"How about hopping on right now?" proposed Marie-Caroline.

They all looked at each other, smiled, and went up to the gangway.

"You go first," Edouard said to his brother.

Pierre-Hugues put his foot on the metallic gangway that creaked loudly under his weight.

"Wow, I guess I gotta start that diet now," he joked.

When he set foot on the deck, it was like an electroshock for Pierre-Hugues. He had a flashback, seeing himself falling in, but chased it away.

He turned around to take his sister's hand, inviting her on with ridiculous bows. They were suddenly kids again, happy to be with each other, and any bitterness or betrayal was forgotten.

They spent a few minutes walking around the deck and the galley, touching the sails and precious wood. The sailboat seemed to breathe again underneath their palms, as if it were impatient to go out to sea again finally.

They decided to make a date for the outing on the first weekend after their father's funeral.

In the meanwhile, they'd meet again at the villa in Gorbio, where Lucie had decided to invite everyone.

∽

Marie-Caroline and Edouard were already there, in the library with Emilie.

The limousine driven by Dominique pulled into the driveway. Pierre-Hugues, in the back seat, was holding Lucie's little hand. They'd picked him up on the Promenade des Anglais where he was waiting for him, his Texan Stetson on his head, sticking out amongst the crowd of tourists.

Dominique had gotten out of the car to open the door and help him in, and then went back to the front seat.

"Dominique, I'm going to say something that will startle you," began Lucie. "Don't start driving yet. Do you recognize the man next to me?"

The chauffeur looking in the rear-view mirror at the Texan cowboy.

"I think I saw him a couple of weeks ago, coming out of the holding. Would you be that Mr. Sharpers we've heard about?"

"Yes, he was known as him," replied Lucie. "But in reality, it's an alias. Could you tell our chauffeur your real name?"

Pierre-Hugues knew his mother was just teasing him, that she was joking to surprise the chauffeur, that she was convinced he would be happy to see him.

"I was born a Lacassagne," the pseudo-American replied.

Dominique squinted, intrigued.

"Another hidden child?" he briefly thought to himself.

"And my first name is Pierre-Hugues."

This time Dominique's eyes popped wide open. From surprise? From fear?

"M... Mr. Pierre-Hugues," he stammered. "How is this possible?"

"You look like you saw a ghost!" Lucie joked.

"But, I thought..."

"Dominique, it's a long story," replied Pierre-Hugues, putting a hand on his shoulder. "One day I'll tell you it all."

"Are you happy, Dominique?" asked Lucie.

"Uh... yes, of course... it's just that it's..."

"Get yourself back together then and drive us to Gorbio. I'm sure Lilie can't wait to see her Pierrot again."

Lilie was playing a game of *Chutes and Ladders* with Edouard and Marie-Caroline in the library when she heard the limousine pull up.

That morning Lucie had spoken to her, preparing her for Pierre-Hugues's arrival. Little by little she had led her to accept the crazy idea that in reality, her brother didn't die when she was little. That he wasn't buried in the little cemetery in the village. That he'd had to travel far, far away and that he wasn't able to come back earlier. And that he was now a fifty-six-year-old man with gray hair who'd gained a bit of weight. And that she probably wouldn't recognize him right away. But that she could trust her mommy, that she was telling the truth and that she was happy to have all four of her children with her.

So, when the limousine arrived, Lilie jumped up, flipping the board game over and ran outside. She saw a big cowboy hat and then a fat man with a huge smile on his face. A man walking up to her, holding his hands in front of him.

They were just a couple of feet from each other.

You could tell just by looking into Emilie's eyes that a myriad of questions was colliding in her mind.

Lilie stared at that puffed-up face, that gray hair and the twisted nose, trying to conjure up something that would help her see things clearly. But when she saw the man's eyes twinkling, she immediately understood that it was her big brother who had come back for her and ran into his arms.

"My Pehu!"

The whole day was filled with joy, laughter, questions, answers, as well as some tears. They played, had lunch, walked in the park, went to the tennis court now full of weeds. They also prayed for Charles.

That afternoon, another surprise was awaiting Lilie.

"Look who's here!" said Lucie to her, pointing to the lady who was walking into the rose garden.

"Oh! Brigitte!" shouted Lilie happily, recognizing her former babysitter.

Right behind her the was a man with long blond hair that fell on his forehead.

"Who dat?" Lilie asked Brigitte.

"You don't have a little idea?"

"Umm..."

"It's Simon, honey. Just like you, he's grown up now."

At first Lilie was shy, something she rarely was. Then Simon came up and gave her a big kiss.

"It's been so long, you're a real little lady now!"

Lilie blushed.

Lilie smiled.

Lilie laughed.

CHAPTER 64
No embellishments, no lies

GORBIO, *July 28, 2016*

THE ENTIRE LACASSAGNE family was there for Charles's funeral.

One by one, they threw a handful of dirt onto the patriarch's coffin. There was Lucie, Emilie, Edouard, Pierre-Hugues, then Marie-Caroline with Philippe and their twins, Lauriane and Leana. As well as Brigitte and Simon, and then standing back a bit, Dominique and Marie-Therese, their loyal employees.

Colombe and I were the last ones to throw our handfuls of dirt in.

Lucie had organized a buffet prepared by one of the best caterers in Nice and we enjoyed it while talking about Charles, his successes, his passions, his mistakes, and then the biography, as well as my book on what really happened, something that could annoy them. Lucie walked up to me.

"Speaking of which Mr. Bastaro, what about that contract you had with my husband?"

"I would imagine that it's now null and void."

"Technically speaking, yes. I imagine that he was going to pay you the last installment when the book was finished?"

"That's right. But there won't be any more book."

"Jerome. I'd like you to finish your own version of our family's history. No embellishments, no lies, just the truth. I'll honor the contract you and Charles signed. You'll be paid what you two agreed upon, and if you want, you can remain at the Negresco as long as you need to finish writing the book."

Lucie surprised me with this proposal. I had been thinking that I'd never receive the last third, and now she was not just promising to pay me, she was also inviting me to continue writing the story in the best conditions possible.

"I don't know what to say here. You're sure of this?"

"My family deserves this book, and you deserve to be the author. So just say yes now, before I regret it," she joked.

I thanked her warmly and assured her I would only tell the truth.

I was able to speak with everyone. You could tell they were relieved and happy to be reunited, thinking of the patriarch. The Lacassagne clan would enjoy a new era: they had thirty years of catching up to do!

We left Gorbio to go to Nice at the end of the afternoon. Several vehicles were following each other. The brothers and sisters were going to go out, all five of them, including Simon, to a nice restaurant in Nice. Marie-Caroline's husband would go back home with their twins. Edouard was driving Marie-Caroline, Simon, and myself. As for Lilie, she didn't want to leave either Colombe or Pierre-Hugues, so all three of them sat in the back seat of the limousine Dominique was driving. We had all planned to leave each other at the Negresco.

Lilie was overjoyed sitting between Colombe and Pierre-Hugues. Happy to have found her big brother again, though she maliciously blamed him for taking up too much room. Everyone was joking as Dominique was carefully driving in the shoestring streets leading back down to Nice.

The day could have calmly drawn to an end had Colombe not told me about something weird she observed in the limousine.

It was like a thunderclap.

CHAPTER 65
A fantastic collective investigation

COLOMBE and I were lying naked on my king-sized bed, exhausted from love. I could tell Colombe was thinking of something.

"What's up? You didn't like it?"

"No, idiot!" she laughed, elbowing me in my ribs. "I was just thinking about what happened earlier in the limousine. Maybe it's nothing, but still, I can't get it out of my mind."

"Shoot."

"As we were nearing Nice, Lilie asked for something to drink. It had been a hot day, and despite the air-conditioning, I think we were all thirsty. She asked Dominique if there was anything to drink in the car. He opened the glove compartment; I would imagine that it was a refrigerated one. When he grabbed a bottle, some sort of orange soda, anyway it was yellowish and orangish, Emilie began to shout.

"*Oh! Dominique, the orange bottle!*

That one!" "What about the orange bottle?" he asked.

"Not good for me!" replied Lilie.
"But it's just a Fanta, Miss Emilie."
"No, not Fanta, whisky! Not good!"

You could tell she was a bit panicked. And I also noticed that the chauffeur seemed annoyed when he heard the word "whisky." I took Lilie's hand to calm her down and said that I'd try the bottle of Fanta too. Which I did. Pierre-Hugues, who was sitting next to Lilie, didn't say anything, though he also squinted, as if trying to recall something."

"Yeah, pretty strange what Lilie said about the whisky," I confirmed. "What do you think?"

"Like she had a *déjà-vu*."

"Some old memory that made her remember something similar, even years after?"

"Something like that, yes. Anyway she visibly was quite upset and refused to touch the bottle. But she calmed down after that."

"You think she knew something about the whisky? We never thought of asking her."

"Maybe she'll have something interesting to tell us."

"We're just going to have to ask her then."

∼

THE NEXT DAY Colombe went to Gorbio and asked Lilie to walk to the rose gardens with her.

"Hey Lilie, what were you talking about yesterday with that story about the whisky?" she asked."

" Sailboat day."

What do you mean, 'sailboat day'? When you were a little girl?"

" Pehu dead."

"But he's not dead, now you know that, right Lilie?"

"Not dead, too good."

"But you saw a bottle of whisky that day in the glove compartment?"

"Yes, kiki no good," the young lady answered, just like when she was a child.

"Did you see Dominique take an orangish bottle out, like he did yesterday?"

"Um hmm. Same thing. Remember!"

"And what did he do with the bottle on the sailboat day, Lilie?"

"Picnic basket!"

"He put it in the picnic basket for your brothers and your sister on the sailboat?"

"Sailboat picnic basket."

∽

"Jesus Christ!" I said when Colombe finished telling me this. "So Dominique was the one who put the poisoned bottle in the picnic basket right before they went onboard."

I was dumbfounded. How was Dominique

involved with all the problems in the Lacassagne family? Why did he want to assassinate Pierre-Hugues? Or what was he hiding that Pierre-Hugues could have discovered?

"I'm gonna call Pierre-Hugues right now to try to get to the bottom of this!"

∽

"Yesterday you were there when there was some funny stuff going on between your little sister and the chauffeur," I said to Pierre-Hugues on the phone. "Didn't anything seem strange to you?"

"Actually, yes," he confirmed. "When it happened I thought that maybe Lilie had been out in the sun too much and that got her confused or she was being capricious like when she was little. But now that you pointed it out to me, you're right, it was unsettling."

Then I told him about the discussion between Colombe and Emilie a few hours earlier.

"It's mind-boggling!"

"Do you think it's plausible that Dominique wanted to poison you?"

There was silence on the other end of the line.

"I can only see one explanation".

∽

The explanation that Pierre-Hugues gave me and

told the other family members resulted in Dominique being fired on the spot.

The chauffeur, confronted with the evidence, admitted that he was the one who had tried to poison him. He also admitted that he was the one who had been writing me the letters I'd received at the Negresco. He said he was just trying to frighten me so I'd abandon the research that might lead me to him.

Thirty years later, he legally was no longer in danger. There was a statute of limitations. Plus, the "dead" person was alive, victim of a simple accident.

∽

"I'd discovered that Dominique was hanging out with some of his old friends from Corsica. Today we'd call that insider's information. He'd taken advantage of the position he had with my father to look in his files, overhear confidential conversations and sell good tips to his partners-in-crime."

"How'd you find out?"

"One day, in a bar, I was in the restrooms and when I was coming back out, I surprised a voice I knew well, talking to two other men. It was Dominique of course, but he didn't see me."

"And then you went to see him to tell him what you saw and heard, I imagine."

"Exactly. I was planning on smoothing things out without alerting my father. He had other fish to fry. Plus, he trusted him so much that he would have been deeply disappointed. And, as Dominique told me that day after having denied the evidence, my father never lost any money in his deals because of him."

～

"Mr. Pierre-Hugues, believe me, I'm sorry, so sorry. I never should have done anything like that, I don't deserve Mr. Charles's trust, but they pulled me into this. It was so easy, and there were hardly any risks involved."

"Ah, there you go! Easy money."

"Let's just say it was a little extra."

"Because you're not paid enough maybe?" Pierre-Hugues said angrily. "That's disgusting, Dominique. You're probably the highest paid driver on the whole French Riviera! So why betray my father like this?"

"He didn't lose any money because of me," he said, trying to defend himself. "All I did was to discreetly facilitate deals for some of my friends who gave me a tiny percentage for that information. Mr. Charles never lost a cent. On the contrary, he gained better and cheaper contracts because of my friends."

"Sure! Soon you're gonna tell me that you do volunteer work for your boss! Lobbying for the holding! You're dreaming. You know you can go to jail for giving out insider's information, Dominique?"

Dominique looked down, ashamed.

"I'm sorry, sir."

"You should be! I should tell my father and get you

fired. But I appreciate you, that's the problem. I've known you ever since I was little, and I don't think you're really a bad person. I'm not going to say anything on the *sine qua non* condition that you swear you'll immediately stop all this crap."

"I will. I promise. It was a mistake, one that I sincerely regret."

"Make sure you behave now! If I ever get wind of something else like this, I'll tell my dad everything and you'll lose your job. As well as the source of your unlawful profits. Think things over. Unless you want to go back to raising goats back in Corsica."

∽

"When did this explanation with Dominique take place?" I asked Pierre-Hugues.

"I'd say end of 1985, beginning of '86."

"You think he continued his trafficking despite your warning?"

"I always thought he'd stopped. But now that I know he's the author of the attempted poisoning, he must have continued. Or else he was under the control of the mafia in Corsica, and they were putting pressure on him. Financial delinquency is just as tough as drugs trafficking: I'd imagine it's hard to get out of the system."

"Meaning you'd become a liability for him and his friends. So if you were dead, he'd be able to continue his activities while hanging on to his job and its many advantages."

"Exactly. That secret sunk with me to the bottom of the Mediterranean Sea."

"As he noticed that everyone in the family seemed to be holding a grudge against you at that time, he must have thought that if the poison worked, members of the family would be blamed for it. And it worked!"

Pierre-Hugues sighed.

"And that was the hypothesis I'd always believed. Thanks to you, Mr. Bastaro, now it's much clearer."

"You also helped us find out the truth, Mr. Lacassagne. As did those close to you, including Brigitte and Simon."

"Without forgetting Sergeant Petrucci!" added Pierre-Hugues.

"That's true, and it was a fantastic collective investigation!" I concluded.

"Mr. Bastaro? Are you going to publish the whole story?"

"Of course, your mother really wants me to."

"Perfect," Pierre-Hugues said, validating the idea. "The book will let people be the judges and jury members. And I thank you for it."

"And I thank you. And I wish you many marvelous moments of happiness with your family."

"This time we'll try to stick together."

Epilogue

SAINT-JEAN-CAP-FERRAT, *July 28, 2016*

Brigitte took Lucie's arm. They were standing on a pier in the Saint-Jean-Cap-Ferrat Port, where the Lacassagne family sailboat had just set out to sea, for the first time in years. It had undergone a complete revision, from the hold up to the mast, and passed its annual technical check-up: it was now ready to sail again and sported a whole new range of cutting-edge navigation instruments.

The two women waved at their children who were reunited. There was Edouard, Marie-Caroline, Pierre-Hugues, Emilie and Simon, the five heirs to Charles Lacassagne's fortune. The three oldest ones would continue to manage the holding, as agreed before 1986. It had taken thirty years to hand over the reins, but now it was finally finished.

"It's so sad that Charles isn't here to see this," said Lucie sadly.

"He would have been so happy," Brigitte confirmed.

The sailboat turned when it reached Saint-Hospice, disappearing from the eyes of the two mothers. They got into the taxi which had been waiting for them for half an hour.

Pierre-Hugues was at the helm, as his siblings had all promoted him to the rank of captain, probably because he was the oldest. Despite all the years he'd spent on the ground, he hadn't forgotten how to sail. Edouard, on his right, was manning the instruments. Marie-Caroline, wearing a straw hat with her still beautiful red hair dangling down on her bare shoulders, was holding on to her older brother's arm.

Emile was playing figurehead at the front of the boat, her arms wide open and enjoying the sun.

Simon, sitting at the stern with an easel in front of him, had just begun to draw his blood and heart brothers and sisters on a canvas which would become a magnificent family portrait. A painting to immortalize their newly found union.

One bothersome brother had turned into one more brother.

It was nice outside, not a cloud in the sky. Blue skies, a slight breeze gently feeding the sails, iodine filled air. In a nutshell, ideal and idyllic sailing conditions.

Brigitte said she'd prepare the picnic basket. There

was to be no alcohol onboard, neither officially nor unofficially.

They had dinner on the deck with a background of orangish sun shining over the waves with thousands of shimmering reflections.

They talked, laughed, admired the tranquility of the sea then admired all the twinkling stars in the sky, as there was no light pollution to interfere with the great show going on in the sky.

Their cruise was perfect, except for a minor incident.

As the night was falling, Pierre-Hugues tripped on a rope on the deck when coming up from the galley. Unbalanced by his enormous gut, he slid on the slippery deck, sliding towards the rails. Incapable of getting back up alone, he once again found himself dangerously close to the edges of the boat, with dark waves licking the hull.

Hands suddenly grabbed him. Edouard was holding him, nearly laughing this time.

"Hey bro, you turned into a landlubber or what?"

He helped Pierre-Hugues get back up.

"Thank you Doudou, luckily you were there. I really have to go on a serious diet. And hit the gym!"

"You could start by swimming," added Marie-Caroline. "It's a complete and easy sport when you start out."

The five brothers and sisters all hugged Pierre-Hugues, who was already like a cornerstone for them.

"How about some music?" proposed Simon.

Everyone approved the idea and he took his phone out of his pocket and opened a musical app with offline access. He clicked on one of his favorites, that they all sang together, and whose words meant something to all of them, for different reasons.

Jean-Jacques Goldman's unique voice resonated on the sailboat's deck.

« *À tous mes loupés, mes ratés, mes vrais soleils,* (To all my mistakes, my failures, my true suns,)

Tous les chemins qui me sont passés à côté, (To all the paths I never took)

À tous mes bateaux manqués, mes mauvais sommeils, (To all the boats I missed, all my sleepless nights)

À tous ceux que je n'ai pas été. (To everyone I wasn't).

Aux malentendus, aux mensonges, à nos silences, (To misunderstandings, to

lies, to our silences)

À tous ces moments que j'avais cru partager, (To all those moments I believed I'd shared)

Aux phrases qu'on dit trop vite et sans qu'on les pense, (To the sentences said too quickly without realizing what was said)

À celles que je n'ai pas osées, (To all those I never dared to say)

À nos actes manqués. (To everything we didn't do).

À tout ce qui nous arrive enfin, mais trop tard, (To everything that finally happenes to us, but too late),

À tous les masques qu'il aura fallu porter, (To all the masks we were forced to wear)

À nos faiblesses, à nos oublis, nos désespoirs, (To our weaknesses, our forgetfulness, our dispair)

Aux peurs impossibles à échanger. (To our fears that are impossible to share).

À nos actes manqués. (To everything we didn't do)."*

THE WIND PICKED UP, the bow cut through the waves.

The Lacassagne family was once again afloat.

---

* *À nos actes manqués*, Fredericks/Goldman/Jones, Columbia, 1991.

CHAPTER 66
Addenda

PARIS, *December 2016*

I saw Colombe coming out of the train at the Gare du Lyon. Her TGV was on time, and I saw that as a good omen for the rest of her stay here in Paris. The station was crawling with people as Christmas was getting close, some of them wearing heavy coats and wool caps and other hauling suitcases or carrying their skis on their shoulders.

Since July, we had been seeing each other regularly, either in Nice or in Paris, or sometimes in between, like when we met up in Lyon for their annual Light Festival at the beginning of the month. Each time it was the same joy to hug again, the same pleasure of being together, but the same sadness when we were forced to leave.

Of course, and I'm sure you thought this would be

the case, I broke up with Cynthia as soon as I got back to the capital.

I'd finished writing "The Truth about the Lacassagne Affair", and the book was at the publishers with a proofreader and editor going through it, looking for any lingering typos, incoherencies or layout mistakes. It would be coming out in the middle of February, with a lot of publicity.

Colombe was now in her last year of school, and she'd be defending her final thesis in just a couple of months. And of course, all her professors were impressed by her internship report.

She snuggled against me, trying to get warm. The wind was blowing in through the train station's lead-glass roof.

She suddenly held a daily paper out to me.

"Look what I found."

She handed me a *Nice-Matin* that she'd bought in the station before getting on the train.

In the "Regional" section, she'd circled a small article that could have been inconspicuous, but not with her eagle eyes.

"*The body of a sixty-year-old man that the coastguard fished out last week has just been identified. It was the body of Dominique Bastelica who was Charles Lacassagne's private chauffeur. Mr. Lacassagne passed away last July.*

Will this put an end, after so many twists and

surprises in the Lacassagne affair, which, as a reminder, began exactly thirty years ago when Pierre-Hugues, his oldest son, lost his life in the same body of water?"

AFTER THAT THE journalist waxed for a long time and I just ran through the article.

"Shit!" I said, giving the paper back to Colombe.

"I guess you could say the circle has been closed."

"Yup. It's a sad ending though for Dominique, even if justice was finally served here."

I called my publisher right then and told him I wanted to put an addendum to my novel telling the true story.

As for the story of my love for Colombe, it just begun.

Discography

Vivaldi, les Quatre Saisons
    Jean-Jacques Goldman, À nos actes manqués
    Johnny Hallyday, *L'Envie*
    Sex Pistols, God Save The Queen
    Trust, Antisocial
    The Beatles, Lucy in the Sky with Diamonds
    The Ramones, Blietzkrieg Bop
    Stéphanie de Monaco, *Comme un ouragan*
    Samantha Fox, *Touch Me*
    Bananarama, *Venus*
    As well as:
    Niagara
    Queen
    Elton John
    Cock Robin
    Gold.

Acknowledgments

I want to start by thanking my wife, Natacha. Without her, this novel would never have been the same. Or maybe it would never have been written. Without her crazy ideas, without her attentive and thorough proofreading and her unending support in this project, including when I had doubts, the idea I had upon beginning this novel could have simply remained in a drawer. That would have been too bad, don't you agree?

I'd also like to thank my advanced readers, who were able to read and comment on the successive versions of this novel. And I hope I'm not forgetting anyone: many many thanks to Gérard M., Sandrine L., Amélie L., Laurie P., Magali H., Nadine H., Cindy T., and Séverine L. Many thanks also to Jacquie Bridonneau who translated this novel from French to English.

And my warmest thanks to my readers, without whom an author is nothing. Without knowing it, you all contributed to giving me the courage and strength to finish this book. And even before it was finished, you were already asking me for the next one! Talk about motivation!! See you for the upcoming adventures of Colombe Deschamps and Jerome Bastaro!

Available Now

A COLOMBE BASTARO MYSTERY - BOOK II

Biscarosse, March 2020

"I'll get it!" shouted out my girlfriend when she saw the mailman opening our mailbox at the end of the driveway.

I'd met Colombe nearly four years ago, while I was working in the historical center of Nice and she'd become my intern.

Since that time I've been spellbound by her, and our love story grew until we found it normal and natural to live together. We started out with me still in Paris and Colombe in Nice, where she was finishing up her university degree while I was making sure my career was taking off. Then thanks to what I'd been able to save from the money Lucie Lacassagne had given me when her husband Charles passed away, I had a serious down payment allowing me to purchase that little house in the pine forest, not far from Lake Biscarosse, which was where we'd fallen in love when we'd gone there on vacation.

Colombe went back into the living room, holding up the package she'd been expecting.

"It's here!" she said triumphantly, joining me on the couch

where I was finishing up an article for *New Business in France*, the magazine that I remotely worked for.

"Let's go! Unwrap it, I can't wait!"

She ripped the envelope open, and we admired the much-awaited grail, full of shiny and brilliant colors: the photo book of the week we'd spent in Guadeloupe end of February, beginning of March 2020, right before the beginning of the lockdown here in France. We were so lucky to have been able to spend a week on the island right before France rolled up its carpet and shut its doors because of Covid 19, and nearly got stuck in the Caribbean, something that we really wouldn't have complained about though.

A fantastic vacation, in a bungalow in the little town of Deshaies, and we'd come back to France with great memories, having met friendly people, having enjoyed memorable cocktails and all we wanted to do was to return there as soon as possible.

Our souvenirs though would fade as time flew by, becoming just a few images, fragrances or emotions. That's why Colombe had spent so many hours sorting hundreds of photos, putting them in chronological order, comparing them with the pages of notes she'd taken so she wouldn't forget the names of the places or sites so we wouldn't get mixed up later on when thinking back on our stay. That mass of images had been transformed into a hundred-page book of photos that we avidly were going through, sitting on the sofa in our living room.

Page after page, we relived *Gwada*, as they called it there.

A thousand and one memories, a thousand and one colors. Images, words, laughter, questions.

She had chosen dozens of photos of our group when we climbed to the top of the Soufriere Hills volcano at the end of that glossy papered book. Especially one where we were proudly posing in front of the volcano with its green cone topped with sulfurous smelling fumaroles expulsed by the craters.

And Colombe finally stopped on a curious photo, frowning, a sign that she was thinking something over, an internal question as boiling hot as was the mouth of the Soufriere volcano. And an enigmatic sentence, that she said, almost to herself, lost in her thoughts.

"Jerome... I think we were close to dying there..."

"What are you talking about?" I replied, surprised.

Colombe was now white as a sheet, trembling. She put the photo album back down, got up suddenly and walked into the office. She came back with her laptop, its browser opened to her inbox.

"You remember the email that I got back in response to one of mine, a couple of days ago?"

"Of course I do."

"Have a look at this."

She logged into her Facebook account, searched for two friends in the profiles, clicked on the results and turned the screen towards me.

"Well? What do you think of that?"

Reading through the latest posts on those profiles, my face crumbled. After the last word, I could only stammer.

"That's completely crazy... How could that be possible?"

"It's too exceptional to be a mere coincidence. Just think. All those people dying in such a short time, like statistically speaking, it's impossible!"

"The law of series, maybe?" I tried.

"Like, 'tough luck, losers?' I don't think so. But still, that story is terrifying me. Especially when you discover who died, it makes me shiver. Honey, I'm scared."

"What are you scared of?"

"Um, I don't know... afraid that we'll be the next ones on the list..."

"But come on, what list are you talking about? You're not making any sense."

"I sure would prefer this to just be a delusion of my overactive imagination, but once again, all those coincidences... We were there too, at the same time they were!"

"So what? We don't even know them, except that we were on vacation with them in the same place during the same week. It's a fluke. Just as if you told me: *Mr. so-and-so died, and another guy too who was on the same plane that we took...* You really think the five hundred other passengers on that plane are in danger of dying? That's crazy, just fiction, that's what I'm saying!"

Colombe thought that over, tense.

"But still, I need to understand that crazy story. I'm going to investigate it. For my own peace of mind."

"Or not!" I replied ironically.

But I knew that now that Colombe had that idea in her cute

little head, she would hold on to it until she'd clarified that case. I was far from imagining where that crazy story would be taking us.

"Let's look at the photos again," she proposed. "That'll help us remember everything, you know when we see the images we'll reminisce back on what happened, little things that maybe we weren't even paying attention to while we were there. The common denominator of these deaths seems evident to me: our week in Guadeloupe! We must have missed something."

"Sweetie, you're getting worried about nothing."

"Jerome, please. You know about my notorious intuition."

"That I do. Okay! What do you want to do?" I abdicated.

"We're going to go through the photo album and my notebook, examine the photos, reread what I wrote. Like we're reliving our week of vacation. I'm sure that we'll discover a tiny detail that we missed. To understand the origin of those deaths, the why, when, who, and above all, the how…"

I had no other choice than to defer to Colombe's determination.

We sat back down in the sofa, with the photo album and notebook on our knees. On the first page of the album, she'd put the title:

"Welcome to Gwada!"

Who am I?

Nino S. Theveny is one of France's leading indie authors. He's married and has two children. In 2019 he was laid off from a multinational company and decided to make the most of his newly found liberty, turning to writing, his passion, which is now his day job.

With 15 books published to date, Nino S. Theveny has over 250,000 readers. Translated into English, Spanish, Italian, and German, his thrillers are appreciated throughout the entire world.

With his fourteen-year-old son, he has also co-authored a thriller for young adults which was published in March, 2024.

Bibliography of books translated into English

THE KAREN BLACKSTONE SERIES
Into Thin Air (2022) *(Winner of the Cuxac d'Aude Favorite Novel, 2023 / Finalist in the Loiret Crime Award, 2023)*
I Want Mommy (2023) *(N°1 in Amazon Storyteller France sales 2023)*
The Lost Son (2023)
Alone (2024)
Volume 5 to be published in 2025

THE BASTERO SERIES
French Riviera (2017) *(Winner of the Indie Ilestbiencelivre Award 2017)*
Perfect crime (2020)
Bloody Bonds (2022)

OTHER NOVELS

BIBLIOGRAPHY OF BOOKS TRANSLATED INTO ENGLISH

True Blood Never Lies (2022)
Thirty Seconds Before Dying (2021)
Eight more Minutes of Sunshine (2020)